# The One You Don't See

by

Brenda Huber

**The One You Don't See**

Cover Art by *Rae Monet Inc.*

The Wild Rose Press, Inc.
PO Box 708
Adams Basin, NY 14410-0708
Visit us at www.thewildrosepress.com

Publishing History
First Edition, 2021
Trade Paperback ISBN 978-1-5092-3700-5
Digital ISBN 978-1-5092-3701-2

Published in the United States of America

"You kissed me."

"Yep," he said easily, sliding a melting square of aromatic apple crisp onto her plate. "I believe I'll be doing it again too, every chance I get."

Harper stood there, mouth agape, staring at him like a halfwit. With way more relish than warranted, Aiden ran his finger along the edge of her plate where some of the apple crisp had dripped. Then he licked the golden, spiced sauce from the pad of his finger with a low hum of appreciation. His grin, complete with arched eyebrow, was nothing short of wicked.

Nonplused, all Harper could do was stare…and frown, first at her plate, and then at him. Aiden loaded a double-sized helping of apple crisp onto his own plate and moved on down the table.

Spurred by his nonchalance, she stomped after him, determined to set the record straight. She'd thought she'd been all tangled up before? Now her emotions churned and seethed.

But a sweet flutter winged low in her belly now too. His words…stunned her. She couldn't believe the sheer nerve of this man.

"Why—" She was so floored, she couldn't even finish her own sentence.

He leaned close, till their heads were mere inches apart. Her eyes widened when she realized he was staring at her mouth, intently. And then his warm, deep brown eyes met hers, and the intriguing flutter low in her belly became a violent trembling.

"Because you kissed me back, sweetheart." Aiden smiled then, wholly unrepentant. "And I liked it. An awful lot."

## Praise for Brenda Huber

"Brenda Huber is an author to watch. The way she paints a scene is fantastic."

*~ Catherine Bybee, New York Times and USA Today Bestselling Author*

"Ms. Huber has the ability to draw you into the story and keep you thoroughly entertained."

*~ The Romance Reviews*

"TEMPTATION by Brenda Huber is imaginative, vibrant and completely addictive. Another amazing tale from this compelling series!"

*~ Fresh Fiction Reviews*

"(Brenda Huber's)ability to infuse romance, action and humor will certainly keep me coming back for more. Reading Chronicles of the Fallen Series is a must for any PNR fan."

*~ The Jeep Diva*

"Thrilling, Dangerous and seductive. Brenda Huber has done it again with her continuation of a fantastic plot, amazing characters and sizzling passion."

*~ Fresh Fiction Reviews*

Chapter One

"What did you do?" Scooter whispered. He stood in the doorway, just barely across the threshold, staring wide-eyed and slack-jawed at Danny's reflection in the tarnished mirror.

He tried to keep his focus on the image of his brother's face, afraid to look down, scared to death of what he might see. But it wasn't working. He'd already caught a glimpse of garish red and, like a shocked bystander at the scene of a fatal crash, horrified by what he was witnessing, he couldn't look away.

The stark light bulb dangling overhead lent garish shadows to the hollows of Danny's cheeks, made his eyes appear sunken at this angle. Violent crimson splatters arced across Danny's white T-shirt, drawing his unwilling attention down, down. Right where he didn't want to look. Danny worked fluffy pinkened lather between his fingers and around his wrists, across the backs of his hands and up his forearms.

"Oh God, Danny!" He wanted to push farther in, but there was so little room for him as it was. "What did you do?"

Eyes the color of pea soup met his in the mirror, just for a moment. Eyes so like his own, and yet different…unsettling. One corner of Danny's mouth edged up in that familiar, cocky way of his.

"I took care of the problem, Scooter." Danny thrust

his hands beneath the feeble, spitting flow of water. The bloody foam slid from his skin to drip into the small, chipped porcelain bowl, where it circled the rust-stained drain before disappearing. Danny scooped up the white sliver of soap and set to work once more.

If only Scooter could scour the image from his mind so easily.

"Took care of—" Frowning, he shook his head. His thoughts raced until he circled back to the confrontation he'd had with his supervisor just that morning. Dread swamped him. Mr. Decker had been so mad, yelling at him, berating him, threatening to fire him because he'd messed up. Again.

And, weakling that he was, he'd never been able to keep such shameful secrets from his brother.

*Please. Please. Oh God,* please*, no.*

"Oh, don't look at me that way," Danny chided, shooting him a disappointed frown. A hank of shaggy, dark hair wafted down to tease the eyelashes of his left eye. Danny shot a quick puff of air from the corner of his mouth, absently dislodging the strands while he used a scrub brush to remove crusty red stains from around and beneath his nails. "That bastard had it coming. You think I don't know the mean things he called you? The way he treated you? He was an asshole. And I made you a promise a long time ago. Nobody picks on my kid brother."

"Is he—" Scooter swallowed, forcing the bile back down his throat. God, he didn't want to ask. But wasn't it better to know? Better to be prepared? He closed his eyes for a second as the narrow room went wobbly. "D-did you…" His voice trailed away, ending on a strangled note.

"Finish your sentences, Scooter." Through the spotty mirror, Danny flashed him a teasing grin before he turned his attention back to the faucet. He shook the extra droplets from his hands and cut the flow of water from the faucet with a deft flick of his wrist before reaching for a towel.

Scooter's mouth was dry as sawdust. His stomach churned. That sick feeling climbed the back of his throat. He didn't want to have to move again. He liked it here, liked his job, liked the people he worked with. Well, everyone but Mr. Decker. But that didn't matter. Mr. Decker didn't matter. There were so many other nice people here. He *really* didn't want to have to move again.

He closed his eyes again and swallowed the sour taste in the back of his throat, willing his stomach to settle. No, he didn't want to ask.

But he needed to know.

As steady as he could, he met Danny's stare. "D-did you kill him?"

*Please, say no. Please…just this once, say no.*

Danny's lazy grin slid away, replaced by an offended scowl. He straightened and cocked his head to the side. "Now why would you even have to ask me that?"

Not the answer he was looking for. Not really an answer at all. Unless you took into account Danny-speak. Danny had a way of talking circles around Scooter, especially if he didn't want to answer a question.

"B-but you p-promised me, after Denver, you p-promised you wouldn't—"

"You worry too much. I told you I took care of the problem," Danny scoffed. In fact, he looked downright proud of himself. "I even cleaned up after myself.

Nothing for you to do this time. Besides, you have more important things to think about today."

"I do?"

Danny's green eyes danced, the dimple in his left cheek deepened, and even white teeth flashed. "You sure do. There'll be lots of work for you now. Play your cards right, you might even get yourself a promotion." Then, with an ominous wink, he added, "I have it on good authority there's been a recent opening."

Scooter's eyes widened and his lips parted, but he was quick to mask his reaction. He hoped. He blinked, glanced down to the towel he was twisting in his hands. When had he picked that up?

Reaching around, he carefully arranged the towel on the towel bar, and then smoothed out the damp material so it would dry.

He drew a deep breath to steady himself. And then another. But that sickening coppery scent lingered in the air, and the smell made him want to gag.

He wanted to be sick, wanted to puke his guts out. Wanted to curl up in a ball and cry his eyes raw. But he couldn't do either. To do so would hurt Danny's feelings. And he couldn't let that happen. Danny was the tougher of the two of them. Rock solid through and through. Protective. Scooter's hero. His brother didn't let anyone walk all over him.

Only Danny had soft feelings about some things.

So, it was his job to protect Danny, the only way he could.

Because the last time Danny's feelings had been hurt, Danny had gone away, left him all alone. For a long, long time. He'd been so lost, missed his brother so much. He didn't want Danny to leave him, not ever again.

He'd do anything to make Danny happy.

Even if, deep down, he knew it was wrong.

Besides, Danny always took care of him, looked out for him. Had ever since they were little kids. The way big brothers do.

Sometimes he might not agree with Danny, or like how Danny handled things. But Scooter had learned to accept Danny the way he was.

Because that's what little brothers were supposed to do.

So he forced another swallow, pasted on a smile, and held out a steady hand. "Let me wash your shirt for you."

Chapter Two

Alexander's assistant was already waiting for Harper the moment she stormed through the still opening elevator doors. The statuesque blonde shook her head and folded her hands at her waist, a bright, fake-as-her-man-made-boobs smile firmly in place.

"I'm sorry, Miss Colby, Mr. Grant is in a very important meeting right now and cannot be disturbed."

Harper didn't spare her fiancé's assistant even the meanest semblance of a greeting, and not so much as a second glance. She marched straight through Alexander's posh waiting area and kept right on going, a woman on a mission. By all that was holy she'd be getting some answers.

The latest voluptuous specimen in the seemingly endless supply of Alexander's executive assistants gave a small squeak of distress at Harper's lack of cooperation. Balanced precariously on ice pick heels, the assistant—whatever this one's name was—trotted out from behind her desk and scampered after Harper.

Harper was a tolerant woman. Usually. But just now, as upset as she was, Alexander's string of gorgeous assistants was yet another irritant that rubbed her the wrong way. Well, the blinders were off. The rose-colored glasses had been snapped in two. And she was calling bullshit.

"Mr. Grant left specific instructions that he did not

want to be disturbed for any reason. Miss Colby, *please*!"

Alexander could have been in a meeting with the President of the United States and it wouldn't have made an iota of difference to Harper. She stomped right up to the big mahogany double doors and shoved her way inside.

"How *dare* you," she hissed the moment she spotted her fiancé, her body nearly vibrating with fury.

Alexander, looking every bit the corporate executive in his tailored suit and expensive haircut, glanced up from his perch at the edge of the massive mahogany desk. He closed the leather-bound folder in his hands, cool as you please. The two gentlemen, seated in matching wingback leather chairs in front of him, swiveled to stare at her.

Alexander dropped his dangling foot to the floor, though he continued to lean casually against his desk. He turned to his clients and offered a polite smile, oozing pearly white confidence and gracious charm. "I apologize for the interruption, gentleman. As you can see, my fiancée is a bit…distraught. Would you please excuse us? My assistant will call you later this morning to reschedule this meeting."

Harper barely noticed the curious glances aimed her way as the two men gathered their things and exited the room in silence. Nor did she feel the slightest bit of sympathy for the blonde bombshell standing beside her, wringing her hands in obvious distress.

Harper had eyes—very angry eyes—for her fiancé only.

"I'm so sorry, Mr. Grant," his assistant all but groveled. "I tried to tell Miss—"

"That will be all," Alexander said, his tone arctic.

Even though he'd addressed his assistant, his cool stare never left Harper. That was just fine by her. She wanted his undivided attention for once, and a damned good explanation. A reasonable explanation. Something—*anything*—to prove her wrong for jumping to conclusions.

She'd always known he could be hardnosed when it came to business. But they'd discussed this. How could he go against her wishes like this? How could he resort to such dirty tactics to get his way?

Harper had fumed the entire drive over from the bank—the bank where she *used* to work—and it was all she could do to maintain even the thinnest veneer of composure.

"Yes, sir," the assistant whispered. From the corner of her eye, Harper caught the way Alexander's assistant lowered her head as she backed toward the door. Something about the action only added to Harper's ire. The soft click of the door's latch echoed in the tension-filled room. It may as well have been the crack of a gun.

Either way, it was like the first volley in a war she hadn't been expecting to have to fight. She'd been under the misconception that they'd come to a truce.

Apparently, she'd been wrong.

Harper's rare-to-make-an-appearance temper detonated the second they were alone. "How *dare* you! You *knew* how I felt about my career. I thought you, at the very least, would respect my wishes. And don't even try pretending you don't know what I'm talking about. I saw your thug Sloan slithering from Mr. Gunther's office this morning. Only minutes, in fact, before I got fired on some trumped up load of crap."

Alexander continued to rest against his desk in stony silence, his features perfectly schooled.

Which only made her angrier. She'd never been this upset before. Certainly, never with Alexander.

"Do you honestly expect me to believe it was just a coincidence when less than ten minutes later Mr. Gunther calls me into his office to tell me I'm being suspended pending an investigation into," she raised her hands and worked her fingers in a sarcastic mockery of air quotes, *"professional improprieties and customer complaints?"*

Her direct supervisor, a normally easygoing yet forthright man, had been sweating bullets, unnaturally pale and unable to look her in the eye all through the meeting. She couldn't even call it an inquisition. He hadn't asked her a single question, hadn't given her any chance whatsoever to defend herself. Just told her what was happening before pressing a button to summon bank security.

Harper had done nothing to warrant the disciplinary action, and she'd been utterly mortified to find herself in such a position. Humiliation flamed heat into her cheeks just remembering how everyone had stared.

"For the love of God, Alexander, say something. Tell me I'm wrong."

Without uttering a word of denial, Alexander straightened to his full six feet two inches. His flinty stare never left her as he reached to his side to drop the leather binder onto the gleaming desktop.

At his lack of denial, Harper took a step forward. "That was over the line, no matter how strongly you felt about me quitting my job. I told you I need more purpose in life than to be arm candy. I'm damned good at my job...or I *was*. I like working. And I won't be—"

He struck so fast she barely had time to register that he'd moved. The back of his hand seemed to come out of nowhere. Pain exploded through Harper's cheek and the coppery tang of blood flooded her mouth. One minute she stood on solid ground, squared off against the cultured, ever-calm man she loved. And the next moment she sprawled on the cold marble floor with her face on fire and the room spinning.

Harper pushed up on her smarting elbow and cupped her cheek. She blinked owlishly at the enraged figure looming over her. She couldn't form words, couldn't reconcile what had just happened, what she was seeing.

"How dare *you* barge in here like some screeching, hysterical, self-absorbed bitch." He'd carefully modulated his voice so it wouldn't carry beyond those heavy, closed doors, but he didn't extend any other effort to suppress the acid dripping from each and every syllable. His face had turned a mottled shade of red. Spittle flew from his sculpted lips. Steel grey eyes glared at her from a familiar face, but Harper didn't recognize them.

These were not the eyes of the man she'd fallen in love with, not the eyes of the man she was supposed to be marrying in just a few short months. These were the eyes of a...of a soulless, ruthless shark that had scented blood in the water and was, even now, circling, moving in for the kill.

"How dare *you* embarrass *me* like that?" he went on, towering over her. "How dare *you* question me or demand answers? What makes you think, even for one moment, you have the right?"

With her cheek throbbing and her lip rapidly

swelling, Harper shook her head, unable to speak.

The wrath in Alexander's eyes, the tone of his voice...

Her soul cowered in the face of the hatred he spewed. Her heart shriveled.

Without warning, he bent down and clamped his hands around her upper arms, startling a gasp from her. Alexander dug his fingertips deep into her flesh, unmindful—seemingly uncaring—of the pain he deliberately inflicted, and he hauled her to her feet so quickly the room spun once more. She sucked in a sharp breath as she struggled to gain solid footing on the slippery marble.

The thought crossed her mind, fleetingly, that if she could just demand that he release her, he would realize what he was doing and calm down. But before she could speak, Alexander gave her a rough shake. A whimper formed deep in her throat, working its way up to a shrill cry. He shook her harder, and her cry died before it could break free. Her head snapped back, the vertebrae in her neck cracked and popped and her teeth clacked together, catching the tip of her tongue.

More blood. More pain.

"How stupid are you?" he snarled. "Do you know who those men were? Do you have *any* idea how you've affected my position in these negotiations?"

"Alexan—"

He rammed a fist into her side, knocking every last ounce of breath from her lungs. And then he shoved her away. She lost her balance and went down hard. Her palm stung as it slapped marble. Pain shot from her wrist to her shoulder. Agony exploded in her hip.

Harper instinctively curled into a ball, cradled her

arms around her middle as she wheezed around the pain and shock.

Alexander reached across his desk and pressed a button on his phone. Harper could only lay there, her battered cheek pressed to the cold floor, stunned. She gasped for air, gagged in agony as she followed his movements with tear-blurred eyes.

*This isn't happening. This isn't real.*

"Get in here," Alexander barked before jamming his finger down on another button. He glared at her as he dabbed blood, her blood, from his knuckles with a white as snow kerchief. He refolded the kerchief and replaced it in his pocket, then readjusted a cufflink. And all the while he peered dispassionately down his nose at her.

A moment later the door behind her opened and closed with another quiet click. She hurt too much to even try to see who it was, hurt too much to care if anyone saw her in this humiliating position. Tears rolled down her cheeks as she gasped for air like a landed fish.

*How could he do this to me?*

A man's leather Oxfords came into view. Malcolm Sloan, Alexander's personal assistant. Alexander's hired thug. Harper died inside, just a little more.

"Clean that blood off the floor and get her out of my sight. Take her down the back way and put her in her car," Alexander snapped. And then he turned that steely-eyed gaze and a damning finger in Harper's direction. "I'll deal with *you* when I get back to the penthouse."

As if nothing out of the ordinary had happened, despite the fact that Harper's world had just turned inside-out, Alexander took a seat behind his desk and reached for the leather portfolio he'd dropped to the desk earlier. He didn't look at her again.

Chapter Three

Harper brought her car to a stop at the rural highway intersection and readjusted her sun visor. She squinted down the deserted roads, forward, left, right, and then to her rearview mirror. Not a soul as far as the eye could see.

Taking a moment longer, she angled the mirror toward her face to survey the damage. She probed the angry discoloration on her cheek, poked at the mark on her lip, pulled her sunglasses down to the tip of her nose and peered once more at her black eye. She winced. The swelling was beginning to lessen…somewhat, but the livid purple discoloration was an ugly reminder of her own naïveté. It didn't hurt so much anymore. Not physically.

But her pride sure did sting.

Sliding her sunglasses back into place, turning her gaze back to the road, she cursed Alexander for the bastard that he was all over again. Why on earth she'd ever thought she might be able to calmly discuss what had happened with him, or request that they seek counseling, let alone try to convince him that her moving out was the best thing for everyone, she'd never know.

Yes. She did know. She'd been a naïve fool.

Her face would heal. She wasn't so sure about the ache in her chest. And she wasn't talking about her bruised ribs. She'd been so wrong about him. A complete and utter idiot.

She blamed him.

But she blamed herself too.

She blamed herself for not packing her bags and leaving right away, like her instincts had urged her to do, the very minute she'd left his office complex and arrived back at their penthouse. Maybe somewhere in the back of her subconscious, she'd thought all he needed was a second chance, that it would never happen again. That he'd feel horrible about hurting her and beg her forgiveness as soon as he walked in the door.

Talk about getting your eyes opened the hard way. The moment she'd suggested she move out, just to give both of them some time and space, the shit had really hit the fan…in the form of a fist to the face.

When she'd come to, once again sprawled on cold hard marble, this time alone and with her left eye all but swollen closed, she'd finally gotten a clue. And so, with the sound of Alexander moving around in the shower as her countdown timer, Harper had quietly rushed to the bedroom.

There she'd shoved the bare basics into an overnight bag…a couple changes of clothing, her running shoes, some panties and bras, her wallet and purse, and her jewelry box.

Did she end up taking some of the jewelry he'd given her? Yes, albeit unintentionally. But she hadn't exactly had time to stand there sorting rings and necklaces, watches and whatnot. And there was no way in hell she was leaving the few reminders she had left of her mother behind.

Besides, he'd cost her a good career, a solid income. She wasn't loaded financially. At best, she had a modest savings, conservative investments. But that wouldn't last long if she were forced to dip into it too often. Who was to say she might not need to hock something later on? She might have been naïve, but she was practical too.

Practical, and pissed off.

So, in the end, she'd snuck out like a thief in the night. Looking back, it had probably been a wise decision. Who knows what he might have done had he caught her with an actual bag in her hand on the way out the door?

Even so, Harper still had a hard time believing things had come to this. How had her life fallen apart so quickly? She dragged in a deep breath and readjusted the rearview mirror for a better view of the empty road behind her…and she readjusted her attitude.

*No more looking back. No more feeling sorry for myself. I've done enough of that already.*

She was starting over with a clean slate. She had nothing to keep her in Philadelphia. No job. No home. And no fiancé. She'd left the worst of her baggage in Philly, and things could only get better from here on out.

And she was going to choose to look on the bright side of things. She didn't have her fiancé's hired thug to deal anymore, either.

Harper spread the map she'd picked up at a gas station just this side of the Montana border on the seat beside her. Using the tip of her finger, she traced her travels. She'd turned off I90 just passed Missoula and angled north on 93. Speaking softly to herself, she recited Emmie's directions to the Bar L. According to the map and the road signs, she was nearly there.

Harper hadn't seen Emmaline Landry in years. They'd kept in touch, sort of. A Christmas or Birthday card here or there. Though, admittedly, Emmie was much better at remembering those kinds of things than Harper ever had been. There'd been social media, of course. And random, occasional phone calls.

And two funerals.

A double funeral for Harper's own parents who'd been killed when the biplane her father had been piloting had suffered mechanical failure and crashed. Harper had just turned twenty. The other funeral had been for Emmaline's husband Mark, a soldier killed in Afghanistan by an IED.

Coming to Montana hadn't been Harper's original plan. Besides, it wasn't like Harper to tuck tail and run. But it had fast become obvious she didn't have much choice. Not when the morning after she'd left Alexander, she'd opened the door of her hotel room to find Sloan in the hallway waiting for her. That sick smile on his ugly face.

Dizzy with fear, she'd slammed the door and instinctively bolted it. Harper had called security, her heart lodged in her throat. While Sloan had been otherwise occupied, she'd once again grabbed her bags and snuck out.

She was damned sick of having to sneak out of places.

After driving aimlessly, she'd done the only thing she could think of. She'd called Emmie.

Thank God for Emmie's generous offer.

Normally Harper never would have dreamed of imposing, particularly since the two hadn't been especially close for such a long time. But Emmaline had plenty of room, she'd reassured Harper, for as long as Harper needed it. And Harper needed, more than anything, to get away from the city. Away from Alexander. Away from his hired thug. She needed some downtime to regroup and decide what next to do with her life.

So she'd drained one of her accounts, made sure the remaining account would be secure—thank heaven she'd held her ground when Alexander had tried to talk her into giving up her own accounts to share his, and she'd driven off without telling anyone where she was headed. Not that there was anyone left to tell, she'd let Alexander drive a wedge between her and every last one of her friends. Everyone except Emmie. Now here she was, halfway across the country. And she was bone-tired of driving.

Mile after mile flew by as her little MINI Cooper climbed higher and higher up the side of the mountain. Harper's ears popped. She worked her jaw to alleviate the pressure. The road wound round and round, up and down. Trees crowded the highway. Hairpin turns put her nerves on edge. Sheer drops nip and tuck with the edge of the road in some places nearly stopped her heart from beating more than once.

Just as she was about to give up all hope of ever finding the Bar L, when she was absolutely certain she was well and truly lost, she rounded the next bend in the road and a big green sign came into view. Devil's Canyon, eight miles ahead.

The quaint town nestled in the heart of a picturesque valley proved to be a pleasant surprise. A very good thing since, according to Emmaline, Devil's Canyon was the only city close to the Bar L for over thirty miles in either direction.

Harper followed the highway, slowing accordingly

as the pavement marched through narrow streets. The buildings all up and down the business district appeared to have been, for the most part, refurbished. Stripped awnings shaded windows filled with pretty displays. Cheery hanging baskets dripping seasonal colors were suspended from old fashioned streetlamps. The sidewalks were broken up here and there by inlaid patterns of brightly colored pavers.

The residential areas appeared to be much the same. Manicured and maintained. Cozy. With the mountains forming a breathtaking backdrop worthy of glossy magazine covers.

Harper smiled and waved back at an older woman on her knees tending one of the bountiful late-season flowerbeds in her front yard. Catching sight of the highway marker, Harper steered onto fresh asphalt and continued her journey, more optimistic than she'd been in days.

*This move might be just what the doctor ordered after all.*

A spare handful of miles later, Harper took in the breathtaking view as she drove slowly up the long, gravel lane leading to the Bar L. Harper was happy for her friend. Emmie had herself a pretty nice setup.

Gorgeous scenery as far as the eye could see. A massive log structure was nestled at the end of the lane. Along the way, she passed a sprawling, busy stable complete with exercise ring. Two separate paddocks took up a sizable strip of land behind the stables. An ancient looking tractor and an old wooden hay wagonwere parked along the opposite side of the lane, decorated with bales of hay and an assorted collection of pumpkins and gourds.

Harper downshifted as she maneuvered passed whitewashed stables. She caught a glimpse through massive double doors flung wide open to the day. A small handful of people worked industriously inside, mucking out stalls, carrying galvanized pails, or brushing down steaming horses in the cool late morning air.

The activity spilled over outside as well. In a slightly smaller exercise ring, a tall, broad-shouldered man was putting a pretty horse the color of caramel toffee through its paces. The cowboy wore faded jeans, a blue plaid shirt with the sleeves rolled up to his elbows and dusty boots. Shaggy dark hair beneath a ragged baseball cap nearly reached his shoulders.

Worn, tan, work gloves held the reins in a confident grip. The man didn't just sit in that saddle. He owned it. Riding with a fluid grace Harper couldn't help but admire.

She couldn't resist. Harper pulled to a stop and rolled her window down. She twisted in her seat, propped her forearms along the open window, bracing her chin on the palm of one hand and watched for a few moments. The air, crisp with the first days of autumn, smelled faintly of wood smoke, fresh hay, horses and sunshine.

She caught her attention straying to the man again, and she dragged her focus back to the horse. She had neither the time, nor the inclination to open *that* can of worms. Not anytime soon, that was for sure.

But she found herself sneaking another peek all the same.

He certainly was a looker, what she could see of him…all long dark hair, strong jaw line with the shadow of thick stubble, and lanky build. But the hat, a pair of reflective sunglasses and the angle of his head made it impossible see his face very well, not much more than a strong, intriguing profile really. He appeared engrossed with his chore. He didn't turn his attention away from the horse once, not even to glance at her idling car.

Harper felt a stirring of interest despite herself. Imagine being the center of that kind of absolute focus. Frowning, shaking her head at her own foolishness, she deliberately focused on the horse again, and only the horse. What a beauty. She'd always wanted to learn to ride but had never had the opportunity. She allowed herself a few minutes more to follow the horse's graceful motions before Harper straightened in her seat and shifted her car into gear. A quick scan of the area had her aiming for the small gravel parking lot in front of the lodge.

Harper pulled in between a huge, mud-splattered black truck and a boxy SUV. As she climbed from her car, she shielded her face against the bright morning sunlight with the flat of her hand.

Upon closer inspection, the rough-hewn timber structure itself was a work of art. Enormous, but inviting all the same, with an added layer of rustic charm. A wide-open porch ran the length of the structure, peppered here and there with wooden rockers, whiskey barrels filled with flowers, and wicker furniture groupings. And, sprinkled throughout, were the obligatory fall cornstalk bundles and small bales of straw forming charming backdrops for clusters of pumpkins and gourds.

Harper shoved her keys into the hip pocket of her jeans and made her way up the wide porch steps. The heavy front door opened easily, setting off the light tinkle of a bell. She stepped inside an enormous two-story room filled with timber beams, antler chandeliers, and a charming mixture of authentic-looking Native American décor and genuine hunting lodge furnishings.

She paused for a long moment, just taking it all in, before she recalled herself and closed the door softly behind her. Drawing a bracing breath, Harper approached the long high counter to her left.

It didn't take but a single glance at the two women standing behind that counter, their expressions tense, to figure out she'd just walked in on something.

The older of the two, probably in her late fifties, turned a wide, if somewhat strained smile on Harper. Vague recognition tugged at Harper as the woman greeted her. "Good morning. Welcome to the Bar L."

"But I told you *last* week I wanted this weekend off." The younger of the two women crossed her arms and glared at her counterpart, ignoring Harper completely.

The older woman's smile turned brittle. "Excuse me a moment." She swiveled to face the shorter blonde, propped her fists on her generous hips and hissed through gritted teeth. "And *I* told *you* last week, *and* the week before, *and* the week before that…it's not going to happen. We're booked full this season, and I can't spare you. You knew that when we hired you. You said it was no problem."

"We're *always* booked full." By the blonde's indignant tone, Harper was surprised there wasn't a stomped foot or a petulant lip involved.

"Shelby," the older woman warned, holding up a hand to fend off any further argument. She turned back to Harper, but before she could speak, Shelby interrupted once more.

"Damn it, Kathryn, that's not fair. You let Sue take two whole months off this time last year."

Recognition hit Harper like a balloon popping, and for a moment gray hair, wrinkles and fifty pounds or so melted away. Before her stood a curvaceous woman with deep brown hair pulled up in a habitual ponytail, clear blue eyes, and just the hint of the laugh lines that would come.

This formidable woman was Kathryn Morris, Emmaline's mother. And with that popping balloon came the whisper of memories, of warm cookies after school, of kind smiles and gentle motherly-type scolding, and countless sleepovers filled with pizza and scary movies and laughs.

"For the love of...she was on maternity leave!" Kathryn dropped her chin to her chest for a split second and expelled a long, measured breath. It was clear she was struggling to scrape together what little was left of her patience. When Kathryn glanced back up, barely restrained temper crackled in her stormy eyes.

Lightning looking for a good place to land.

"I'm sorry, sweetie, I'll be with you in just a moment," she told Harper with a carefully controlled smile. Then she turned back to Shelby, and this time her tone held a note of steel. "Once again, Shelby, you knew weekends were a requirement when I hired you."

"Yeah, well...well, either I get the weekend off or...or I quit." Shelby lifted her chin and angled her head, flipping her hair over one shoulder with a healthy helping of smug sass.

Kathryn's nostrils flared. A tiny muscle bunched along her jaw, her back stiffened, and her eyes narrowed.

Harper experienced the brief impulse to warn the younger woman she was treading on dangerous ground. That, or she considered taking a step back in the interest of self-preservation.

Before Harper could do either, Kathryn snapped, "I'll mail your final paycheck to your mama's house. Collect your things, Shelby Ann. I want you outta that cabin in two hours."

Shelby's eyes widened and her mouth fell open. Apparently, she hadn't expected to have her bluff called so spectacularly. Harper could have warned her. Mrs. Morris was fair, fiercely so, but she had a notoriously low tolerance for bullshit. From anyone.

"B-but…"

"Two hours, Shelby. Times a wastin'. Better get a move on. And if that cabin is anything other than spotless when you close the door, I'll be deducting clean-up cost from your pay." With that, Kathryn dismissed the girl completely and turned to face Harper. "I'm so sorry you had to see that. And I'm sorry to keep you waiting. Now, how can I help you?"

Shelby stood for a moment longer, sputtering. Kathryn kept her unwavering stare and unflinching smile fixed on Harper. Shelby spun on her heel and stormed through a door behind the counter, giving it one last good slam.

Harper, caught up in the dramatic byplay, took a moment to remember why she was there. Slowly, mindful of the shape her face was in, she eased her sunglasses off. "Oh, um, yes. You probably don't remember me, Mrs. Morris, but I'm—"

"Harper Colby! My lord, child! I didn't even recognize you, you're so grown up now." Kathryn tsked as she bustled out from behind the counter. Before Harper could think to respond, Mrs. Morris enveloped her in a big hug, stirring up more bittersweet memories. "Last time I saw you, your hair was down to your backside and golden blonde, bright as a ray of sun. Why'd you go and chop off all that glorious hair, and dye it brown of all colors? Oh, never mind that. Emmie told me you were comin'. It's so good to see you."

"It's good to see you too, Mrs. Morris," Harper said, returning the hug with all her heart.

Tears pricked the backs of her eyes. Mrs. Morris reminded her of her own mother. The tight hug, the way the older woman patted her hair, caused a lump to form in the back of Harper's throat. So she tried to focus on something that wouldn't unleash the emotional storm she'd been dodging semi-successfully until now.

Harper decided to roll the dice. "Sounds like maybe a job just opened up?"

"Well, now, first things first. You're old enough, there'll be no more of that '*Mrs. Morris*' nonsense. You call me Kathryn, just like everybody else." The woman stepped back and captured Harper's face in her hands as she looked Harper over with a thorough, speculative gleam in her eye. "A job, huh? Well, well, it so happens there just might be. You lookin'?"

"Might be." Harper bit the inside of her cheek, praying Kathryn wouldn't ask about the bruises. Harper wasn't sure how much Emmie had told her mother about Harper's situation. And Harper wasn't sure how she would react to Kathryn's questions. Tears or swearing. Six of one, half a dozen of the other. Clearing her throat, she said, "Depends on what the job is."

Kathryn eyed her shrewdly for a long moment.

"Housekeeping mainly, though apparently the boss is a real witch," she remarked, but then she softened that proclamation with a rueful smile. "Full time. The position, not the witch part," she shot a meaningful glance toward the door behind the counter and added, "depending on who you ask."

Kathryn grinned and Harper chuckled, recalling now that Emmie's mother also had a wicked sense of humor.

"There are additional responsibilities on occasion as well. Generally, everybody around here helps everybody else out whenever the need arises. Front desk, cooking and waitressing in the cafe, stables, errands, whatever's needed."

Harper could have kissed Kathryn then and there for not addressing the questions that lingered in her kind blue eyes.

"Housekeeping I can do. Front desk, errands, and waitressing are no problem. I can even help with bookwork if you'd like. I'm proficient with computers, and most any office equipment. I've never worked with horses, but I'd be more than willing to learn." She paused, drew a deep breath. "Cooking's another story. Trust me, you don't want me anywhere near your kitchen. Not unless you keep the local fire department on speed dial."

"Some things haven't changed, huh?" Kathryn gave her a conspiratorial smile. She squeezed Harper's shoulder reassuringly as she stepped away. "Don't you worry. We can work with that. Cooking isn't for everybody. Hang on a second."

She darted around the counter, ducked her head through the doorway and spoke quietly to someone beyond Harper's line of sight. Harper caught a murmured response, and then Kathryn was motioning Harper toward a grouping of gnarled, wooden-framed furniture nestled around a behemoth fireplace.

White and tan faux leather designed to resemble cowhide covered deep cushions that invited a body to sit and sink in. Flanked by a massive bank of sparkling glass, the colossal fieldstone fireplace occupied a position of prominence on the back wall of the Lodge. And the view through those floor to ceiling windows and the enormous deck beyond? Well, breathtaking didn't even begin to describe it.

"Emmie went into town, by the way. Had a few last-minute things pop up. She's gonna be so disappointed she wasn't here to greet you, but she ought to be back around suppertime or so. Have a seat and let's catch up a bit."

"I didn't know you'd moved to Montana," Harper said, settling back against the cushions.

Kathryn braced her elbow on the arm of the chair, clasped her hands, crossed her legs, and leaned in Harper's direction. Her brow wrinkled. "I should have asked, can I get you anything, sweetie? Coffee? Soda?"

"Oh, no thanks. I've had enough caffeine the past few days to last a month, at the very least."

Nodding, Kathryn leaned back and went on, "Well, we'd been talking it over, ever since my Harvey passed, but I didn't want to impose on Emmie and Mark, being newlyweds and all. Things just sort of snowballed after that. Tim got married and moved to Alabama, and then Tina took that job out in Vegas. There really wasn't much left in Philly to keep me.

"Then Mark's dad passed, God rest his soul, and

Mark inherited the Bar L. It was so much for the two of them to take on. They started pushing for me to come out here again. And you know how my Emmie is when that girl gets something in her head. Then Mark got deployed, and Emmie really had her hands full keeping on top of things. They finally had me wafflin' about moving." Kathryn paused, drawing a deep breath. "Then Mark was killed. I couldn't hold out any longer. My baby needed me."

An IED had taken out the armored vehicle Mark had been driving, killing him and wounding two others. He'd just celebrated his twenty-eighth birthday. Harper had flown out for the funeral. But she hadn't been certain Emmie had even known she was there. The poor girl had been all but catatonic. Harper ached for her friend. Some losses you never got over.

"I thought maybe she might sell the Bar L then, move back home to Philadelphia," Kathryn said. "But she wouldn't even consider it. It'd been in Mark's family for three generations. There was no one left in his family to take it off her hands, and she couldn't sell it outside the family, said she'd be letting her husband down. So, here we are."

Harper could do little more than murmur sympathy, the lump in her throat was so big. It broke her heart just to think about Emmie being widowed so young.

Mark had been the love of Emmie's life. They'd met in college, a real love-at-first-sight-whirlwind-romance kind of thing. Mark had taken one look at Emmie, a city-girl through and through, and decided she was the one for him. From that very moment, Mark devoted himself to charming Emmie senseless and sweeping her off her feet. And, having swept her off her feet, he'd cherished her like a precious jewel. Not with money and fancy dinners, but with his time and consideration.

If only Alexander had been the same.

"Emmie filled me in on your situation," Kathryn said, interrupting her thoughts. "Sweetie, I can't tell you how sorry I am. First your momma and daddy passin' when you were so young, God rest their souls, and now this—"

Before Kathryn could say anything else, and blessedly before Harper was forced to respond, the bell over the front door tinkled. Both women turned their attention to the newcomer.

Chapter Four

The cowboy in blue plaid, the one from the training ring, stepped inside the Lodge. He plucked his baseball cap from his head, curled the bill and shoved it deep in his back pocket as the door closed behind him. He removed his reflective sunglasses and hooked them in the pocket on his chest. After glancing around, he spotted Kathryn and strode across the big room, confident as if he owned the place, each fall of his big boots thudding softly on the polished hardwood floor. Harper couldn't stop staring as he approached the seating area.

From a distance, mounted on that beautiful horse like a modern-day cowboy, he'd captivated her.

Up close, he stole her breath and made her forget her own name.

He was tall. The closer he got, the more she had to crane her neck to watch his gorgeous face. She'd thought him lanky atop that proud horse, but with this proximity his shoulders were much wider than she'd expected. And that lean frame was packed with hard muscle, the kind you couldn't buy from any high-priced gym.

His skin held a naturally deep golden tan. His features were sleek and somewhat sharp, with high cheekbones, a strong jaw, and a narrow, straight nose. His eyes were a deep, deep brown, his dark hair wild and just a bit too long for convention. All combined, he presented a package that made her more than a little flustered.

When Harper realized he was watching her just as intently as she'd been watching him, studying her face with a growing frown, she recalled herself. Turning abruptly away, she snatched up her sunglasses and thrust them back on her face.

*Lot of good that does now. He's already seen the damage.*

And now she looked stupid and self-conscious to boot.

Stealing a glance from the corner of her eye, she caught the infinitesimal headshake Kathryn directed toward the newcomer. Harper couldn't decide whether to be grateful, or humiliated.

She cursed Alexander all over again for putting her in this position.

"Harper," Kathryn addressed her. "This is Aiden Whitebear, foreman of the Bar L."

Plucking up what meager shreds of dignity she had left, Harper lifted her chin, pasted on her best customer service smile, and turned to face the cowboy once more.

"Aiden, this is Harper Colby, a good friend of Emmaline's. She'll be staying with us for the duration. In fact, as of today she'll be joining our staff. She'll be taking over Shelby's position."

Aiden cast a curious glance Kathryn's way before he dipped his head to Harper in acknowledgment. And even though he offered her a friendly smile, she could feel those dark, dark eyes probing beneath the tinted lenses of her only shield. Harper forced herself to hold her smile in place, even though she wanted nothing more than to shy away from the scrutiny…or find a hole and crawl right on in.

"Nice to meet you, Ms. Colby." His voice was deep and husky, resonating through her system. Despite her self-consciousness. Despite her resolve to not get involved with another man for the next eighty or so years.

Determined to keep things businesslike, she called upon years of professionalism and quality customer service. Harper rose with grace and decorum, faced him and offered her hand.

"Mr. Whitebear. It's a pleasure to meet you."

He blinked at her for a split second, like he wasn't sure what to make of her. Then he stepped forward and took her hand in his. His fingers were long and strong, his skin calloused and warm, and his grip was...just right. Not too tight, but not too gentle either. No, his grip didn't give her pause. It was the odd tingle that shot up her arm and caused a shower of sparks to cascade in the pit of her stomach that made her suddenly wary.

Her chin lifted, just a fraction of an inch more, when she caught him inspecting the bruising on her cheek, and the mark on her lip again. Something inside her went frosty, and she pulled back. Mentally and physically. She didn't deserve or want pity. She'd left the bastard that had done this to her, hadn't she?

However, mindful that this man was—as foreman of the ranch—probably something akin to a boss to her, she kept her smile firmly affixed, even if it felt forced. She faced Kathryn and took her seat again, clearly handing the conversation back over to Emmaline's mother.

Kathryn's gaze bobbed from Harper to the foreman and back for a minute, her brow creased ever so slightly.

"I'm looking for Em," Mr. Whitebear said, breaking the awkward silence. "She up here?"

Something in the way his tone softened, in the way he used the shortened, affectionate version of Emmaline's name pricked Harper's awareness.

So *that's* the way the wind blew. Okay then. A few years had passed since Mark's death. Emmie was young and beautiful. It was only natural she move on eventually. If Emmie was happy, then Harper was happy for her. Even as the thought crossed her mind, Harper felt her shoulders relaxing. That was one line she'd never crossed before, and never would. It was as if Mr. Whitebear had suddenly been placed in a nice, neat little box. One she could safely put on a shelf and ignore. The one marked 'taken'. Which, in her mind, equated to 'safe'.

"She went down to Devil's Canyon," Kathryn said. "Had several errands to run. She should be back around supper."

"If you see her before I do, can you tell her I'm looking for her? I'd like to add Blossom and Shadow to the roster for trail rides next week, and the vet cleared Sundance. But I'd like Em's opinion on Jezebel. She's been a little prickly with riders lately."

"Sure thing. Say, you have a minute or two?"

"Got a good two hours or so before the next group of riders is due in."

"Good, good," Kathryn said as she pushed to her feet. "Could you give Harper a quick tour of the spread? Give her a brief rundown so she knows what she got herself into. Show her where she'll be working for the most part and then take her up to Eagle's Nest so she can get settled in. Shelby should be packed up and cleared out by then."

"Oh no!" Harper rushed to object, standing up as

well. Nervous for reasons she couldn't fathom, she thrust her hands into her pockets. "I'm sure Mr. Whitebear has more important things to do."

The foreman cocked his head and regarded her in silence long enough to make her want to squirm. So did Kathryn. And Harper was left wishing she'd kept her mouth shut.

"Nope. Nothin' better to do," he drawled at last. "We'll take my truck."

"But I have my own car—"

"Trails are getting pretty muddy in some places higher up. And Otter Creek ran over its banks last night. That little car of yours'll be stuck before you make it to Badger Sett, let alone Eagle's Nest." He turned his attention to Kathryn. "If she's working here now, and staying way up at Eagle's Nest, she's gonna need a better set of wheels. I'll have one of the guys gas up an ATV and bring it round for her. I think number six is available if you want to assign that one to her."

Harper had no idea what he was talking about. And how did he know what her car looked like? He hadn't glanced up once while she'd been watching him work with that horse. For all he knew she could be driving any one of the trucks parked in the parking lot, maybe even that big SUV.

"Will do," Kathryn assured him. She gave Harper another hug. Then, all but pushing the two of them out the door, Kathryn called, "Come on back down for supper at six, Harper. Emmie'll be back by then, and she's going to be so excited to see you."

Not ten minutes later, Harper was bumping along beside Mr. Whitebear in that big mud splattered truck she'd parked beside while he gave her the grand tour...or most of one. Emmaline's spread was huge, Mr. Whitebear had explained, and he just didn't have time to show her the entire ranch. They'd have to do that another time.

Not that she planned on it.

It was an odd position she found herself in. Uncomfortable. Agitated. And yes, whether she willingly admitted it or not, attracted. Not that it should matter. Finding a handsome man attractive was perfectly normal. But she'd firmly locked her emotions away for the time being. She wasn't the kind of girl to bounce from one bed to the next. And she'd just broken up with her fiancé, after all. Not that he deserved any consideration. But emotions couldn't be turned on and off like a faucet, nor should they be. She'd loved Alexander. But there was a fine line between love and hate, she'd come to learn the hard way. And now she…well, she didn't need to deal with the confused reactions Aiden Whitebear elicited. Harper turned her face to the side window to escape the sidelong glances he kept sending her way.

Just being this close, snug, and cozy in the cab of this truck, whether he belonged to her friend or not, was turning out to be a special kind of torture.

Harper had been nervous when she'd spoken to Emmaline on the phone a few days back, unsure of how much information was enough and how much would get her a polite rejection, old friend or not. Generally, the moment someone heard you'd been let go from a bank pending an investigation, they couldn't get rid of you fast enough. But Harper had been determined to be honest. Besides, sooner or later, the truth always had a way of coming out.

Likewise, she felt it best to be upfront about her situation with Alexander as well. It wasn't an easy thing for her to talk about, but Emmaline had offered a sympathetic ear. They'd spent the better part of three hours on the phone catching up.

Now Harper couldn't help but wonder exactly how much of her story Emmie had shared with her boyfriend.

Regardless, here she was, accepted on the spot, with a job and a place to stay all squared away. It had been more than she could have hoped for. She owed Emmie so much for this chance. And Kathryn too. So, Harper forced herself to listen carefully as Mr. Whitebear outlined the job in between pointing out landmarks and roadways, such as they were.

The pay wasn't stellar, but the benefits, as far as Harper was concerned, rocked. Since she didn't already live in the nearby community, she would get a cabin all to herself at a drastically reduced rate as a perk of the job. Meals were included as well while she was on the clock if she so chose to partake. And use of the facilities on her down time was an added bonus, including the indoor pool and exercise room. She was also free to use the stables, provided she took lessons first…and the Bar L stable manager—Mr. Whitebear himself—cleared her for riding.

It took the better part of forty-five minutes to visit the locations of all the cabins around the spread that Harper would be responsible for cleaning. Thank God the trail for each cabin was well-marked, and a map had been provided for her, or Harper would have been screwed trying to figure out which one was which.

And she now understood his statement about the ATV. There was no way her little car would negotiate the deep ruts and muddy trails she'd be required to navigate. In fact, she didn't think her car would even make the trip from the parking lot of the Lodge to her own cabin way up here in the middle of nowhere.

"Sounds like Kathryn's planning on letting you get settled in today, but I'm guessing she's going to want you at the lodge by eight in the morning. Housekeeping generally isn't needed till a little later on, not as early as some of the other positions around here, but you're still gonna need an early start. Especially until you get your routine down, get familiar with the layout of the trails to the cabins and such. That gonna be a problem?"

"Nope. Always been an early riser."

"Good. Getting Shelby out of bed in the morning was like pulling teeth."

Harper didn't know how to take that, given what she assumed was his relationship with Emmaline. Then again, for all she knew, he could be sleeping with half the female staff at the Bar L. Wasn't her place to judge. And she sure as certain wasn't interested in being added to any notches he may or may not have accumulated on his bedpost, no matter how sexy that intense stare of his was or how the sound of his voice made her muscles want to go liquid.

She turned to watch the foliage whip by the truck windows. The lanes were so narrow in some places that leaves and tree branches actually scraped along the sides of the truck.

"Jim ought to have your ATV up to the lodge by now. He can show you how to run it, if necessary, and show you where to gas up. If you have any trouble with it, be sure to let one of us know. As long as you work here, it's yours."

"Is that standard for all employees? Their own ATV?"

"Nope, only the ones who live farther out on the spread. Especially the ones who'll be going cabin to cabin on a daily basis. These trails can be a bitch in the rainy seasons. And a real nightmare in the winter."

"Thank you for showing me around, Mr. Whitebear—"

"Aiden," he corrected her, shooting a half smile over the extended arm he was using to control the bucking truck.

"Aiden," Harper grudgingly allowed, careful to keep her tone polite and respectful. Whether he was Emmie's boyfriend, or just Harper's boss, either way he could make life difficult for her. Best to stay on his good side if she could help it. "I appreciate your taking time out of your busy day to show me around."

He shot her another one of those odd, studying looks.

"Here we are," Aiden finally said as he turned off a particularly narrow stretch of lane. Harper caught a glimpse of a small wooden sign proclaiming this Eagle's Nest. She couldn't even see a cabin until they'd driven another hundred yards or so and rounded a hairpin curve. "This'll be your place."

Aiden pulled the truck to a stop in front of a miniscule log cabin tucked right up against the steep incline of the mountainside. It wasn't much to look at from the outside. Brown logs. Green shutters. Weathered, moss-covered shingles. Not much at all.

But it suited her right down to her toes.

Trees closed in tight on two sides and dotted the sharp slope a few meters behind the small building.

There was just enough room for a single vehicle out front. As it was, Aiden's truck was a damned tight squeeze. Harper climbed down from the vehicle and followed the foreman across the narrow porch.

"Not much to look at on the inside either," he said as if he'd been reading her thoughts. With one arm, he reached out and held the door open for her.

Ducking her head, she quietly thanked him and hurried past. Even so, she couldn't help but catch the warm scent of cedar and spice and man. Her reaction was visceral. A fluttering sensation swarmed through her chest, and she had to resist the urge to turn her nose into his chest and breathe deeper.

*Emmie's guy*, she reminded herself and put as much space between them as she could. Besides, men were as dangerous as the plague to her right now. She obviously couldn't trust her own judgment when it came to her hormones. If she needed proof, all she needed to do was look in the mirror.

She glanced around. He was right. Eagle's Nest was basically a one room hunting cabin with a small corner walled off as a nod to a bathroom. And a stingy one at that. She could pretty much rest her elbows on the sink while she made use of the toilet. And one peek at the narrow shower let Harper know she'd better have a good grip on the soap because there wouldn't be enough room to bend over to pick it back up.

A full-sized bed took up most of the opposite corner of the main room. A nightstand, a small dresser, and a cabinet-style closet clustered nearby. A petite kitchenette with an apartment sized stove and fridge filled the skinny space to her right. A two-person dining room set nestled in between the kitchenette and the living area where a sturdy looking couch and a coffee table faced a TV that was probably older than Harper.

Miracle of miracles, a stackable washer and dryer butted up against the narrow refrigerator. No more Laundromats for her. Yay!

"Thermostat's here, fire extinguisher is over there. Sorry, there's no air conditioning." Aiden pointed the keys at each in turn. He hooked the thumb of his free hand in his back pocket. "Extra bedding's in the closet. Anything goes wrong, furnace breaks down, hot water heater dies, faucet leaks, roof drips, let me know. I'll see it's taken care of directly, same as when you're cleaning the other cabins. Notice anything's wrong, just give me a call. There aren't any phone lines running to any of the cabins, and cell service can be spotty. So we'll get you a two-way radio when you come down for supper."

Harper nodded, still checking out the cabin. Still carefully avoiding making eye contact.

"Mostly you'll find me round the stables if you need me; I've got an office there. Otherwise, I live a quarter mile or so farther on up the trail from here in Cougar's Den. I didn't show you that one as it's not on your cleaning list. Stables, maintenance and repairs, transportation, trail guide, I pretty much oversee it all. Well, everything but the lodge, the cafe, housekeeping, and office work. That falls to Emmie and Kathryn. So...you got any questions, or you seen enough?"

Unable to avoid looking at him any longer, not without being flat out rude, she finally turned to him. "No questions."

"All right. We'll head back to the lodge." Aiden jingled the keys. "You need help with your stuff? I've got a little time left before the next guided ride goes out."

"Oh, no. I can handle it," she hurried to assure him.

He gave her another of those inscrutable looks. "Well then, I'll take you back so you can get your things, load up the ATV, come back and settle in.

She nodded, not knowing what else to say. But it didn't seem like he was in any great rush.

"Think you can find your way back?"

"You bet." She smiled widely to cover the lie. She'd rather get lost in the woods and have to shack up with a grizzly than tell him the truth and risk spending any more time with him than she had to.

Aiden headed for the exit, stepped to the side and held the door for her once more. Harper gritted her teeth. Holding her breath so as not to be tempted to bury her nose in his shirt to steal a deeper whiff of his distinctly masculine scent, she squared her shoulders and strode forward. But as she stepped through the narrow opening, her shoulder and the side of her arm brushed his abs.

Very hard, very warm abs.

Startled, she glanced up and sucked in a sharp breath to excuse herself before she realized what she was doing. His appealing scent swamped her senses. His heat warmed her clear to her toes despite the chill in the air.

Dark eyes glittered down at her, intense. Enthralling. His gaze skimmed her face once more, searching, lingering on her mouth, and this time she didn't think his interest had anything to do with the bruises.

*The bruises!*

Harper ducked her head and double-timed it back to the truck.

She climbed inside and slammed the door behind her. Harper carefully studied the knees of her jeans as he settled himself behind the steering wheel and closed his door. A long moment passed in silence, but she refused to look up, refused to meet his stare.

"You'll need to go to town to pick up some food if you want to keep any out here," he said calmly, as if nothing had just passed between them. Maybe it hadn't. Maybe she'd just imagined the whole thing. Yeah. That was safer. She was just going to go with that. She'd imagined it all.

"Actually," he went on, "heading into late fall and winter, it might be good to have food on hand anyway. Though you want to make sure you store it securely. You know, bears and all." He offered an offhanded shrug. "Once the snow starts falling travel can get tricky some days. Some days you might not make it out of your cabin for a day or two. Though we do a pretty good job of keeping those instances at a minimum. We have snowmobiles for later in the season. You ever drive a sled?"

"Nope."

"Well, stick around long enough and I'll show you how. We try to do a good job of keeping the lanes clear, but guest cabins come first, so you might not get blown out before breakfast. You should be able to buy whatever you need in Devil's Canyon."

Aiden handed Harper the keys to the cabin. She accepted them, careful to pull her hand away before his fingers could brush her skin. All the same, she found herself glancing up to see why he was suddenly so quiet.

He considered her for a long moment before saying, "You sure are a quiet one."

Harper gave him a small smile and a careful shrug. She pocketed the keys, buckled up, and waited for him to start the truck.

But Aiden took a moment longer, still studying her face—scrutinizing the bruises once again, she just knew that's what he was doing—in silence before he reached for the key in the ignition.

"Welcome to the Bar L, Harper."

His voice startled her. She hadn't been expecting him to say anything else. Turning her head, she glanced over once more. But he'd already slid his sunglasses back on and begun to back from the lane, and all she could see was his profile.

This time she let her gaze linger. And as she studied him, she really started to worry. Aiden Whitebear had been nothing but a gentleman. Hadn't made a single wrong move, hadn't stepped out of line, not once.

And that scared the living hell out of her. Because she found him very, very appealing. And he *had* been a perfect gentleman.

And a perfect gentleman had fooled her once before.

Chapter Five

Scooter rolled his conversation with Danny round and round in his head as he tossed the last bale of straw onto the stack in the corner. Dust tickled his throat as he brushed off his shirt and jeans. After swiping the back of his arm across his forehead, he tugged his gloves off, pushed them into his back pocket and then glanced around the stables. Everyone else had cleared out for the night. Everyone else but Aiden, of course. Aiden was always the last to leave.

Aiden was moving around in his office. The soft squeak of the chair behind Aiden's desk, the swish and click of desk drawers opening and closing blended with the snuffling and shuffling of the horses. The sounds, the smells of the stables—even Aiden's presence—soothed him, took the edge off his nerves. Aiden was a good guy. Aiden looked out for him like Danny did.

A troubled frown tightened his forehead.

Well, not *exactly* like Danny did. Danny was…especially energetic in looking out for him. But Aiden looked out for him too. Aiden made him feel safe, so he could breathe easy…at least for a little while.

He'd been nervous all day, walking on eggshells. Surely somebody would say something. Somebody must have noticed already.

But nobody had.

The stables had been quiet today, relaxed. It usually

was when Mr. Decker wasn't around. But it was Mr. Decker's scheduled weekend off though, so it was to be expected.

How would things go when Mr. Decker didn't come back tomorrow morning?

He felt bad for Aiden because Aiden would have to shoulder extra work, at least until Mr. Decker was replaced. He really didn't like that Danny had, however inadvertently, inconvenienced Aiden that way. Aiden was nice.

He glanced toward the small room at the back of the stables where the employees kept their things, and he hesitated.

He really should get his coat and go try to find out what Danny had done with Mr. Decker. Just in case Danny hadn't cleaned up after himself as well as he thought he had.

Scooter had fretted and worried about it all day. But he couldn't come up with any good ideas, other than that Danny had hidden Mr. Decker away somewhere here on the Bar L.

But guilt and a heavy sense of responsibility steered his feet toward the door to Aiden's office instead. He paused, just at the threshold, lifted his hand and knocked lightly on the door frame.

"Excuse me, Aiden," he said, careful to keep his voice soft so he wouldn't startle his foreman. "Sorry to interrupt."

Aiden glanced up from the papers and logbooks spread out across the surface of his desk, his smile sincere and friendly. He put his pen down and folded his hands, all ears. "Oh, hey. I thought you'd left for the day."

That was one of the great things about Aiden. He was never too busy for anyone, not even a stupid stable boy.

He shuffled his feet. "I checked on Susanna one more time and put some fresh ointment on that cut. She finished off her grain, and I replaced her water. I looked and looked, Aiden, and I finally found the nail in her stall where I think she hurt herself. I pounded it down with a hammer so there aren't any more rough edges. And I checked the rest of the walls. I don't see anything else sharp in there."

"Thanks for that. I was wondering where she could have gotten that cut. You have good eyes. I looked around in there and didn't see a thing."

He smiled and his chest puffed up beneath the praise. "I hope you don't mind, but I gave her an apple."

"I don't mind at all. I'm sure you made her night. Did you happen to check Jezebel?"

"I tried, Aiden. But when I got close, she charged her stall again."

"That's Ok. Don't worry about it. I called Doc Tisdahl. He's coming out first thing in the morning to take a look at her." Aiden glanced at the clock on the wall. "You're here awfully late."

"I wanted to get the last of that straw moved so no one had to worry about it tomorrow. It's all stacked up now."

Aiden tilted his head and rocked back. The chair squeaked. "Thanks. I appreciate that. But you didn't have to stay so late. Somebody would have gotten to it in the morning."

"I know." He shoved his hands deep in his pockets, rocked back on his heels and shrugged. "I don't mind.

Don't really have anything to rush home for."

He shouldn't have said that. He sounded ungrateful. Danny would be waiting for him. Probably.

But that thought made him just a bit nervous too. Danny had been angry lately. Really angry. And restless. Which made him worry even more. He didn't like it when Danny got angry. Or restless. Bad things happened. Yesterday wasn't the first time he'd found blood on Danny's hands.

Now that Mr. Decker wasn't going to be around to yell at him, maybe Danny might not be so mad anymore.

"I just wanted to say thank you for the bonus this month."

Aiden folded his arms, his grin stretching wide. "No need to thank me. You've more than earned it. I really do appreciate how hard you've been working around the stables. And Em mentioned you've been making a point of helping up at the lodge too, taking the trash out and such. She's grateful as well. So I'd like to thank you for that too, for helping me look out for Em like that."

He ducked his head as heat flooded his checks. Ms. Emmaline was kind to him too.

Kind and pretty.

Giving it more thought, especially the way Aiden had phrased it, his chest swelled with pride even more, until he was darn near floating with it. And with new purpose. He *had* been looking out for Ms. Emmaline, hadn't he? In his own way.

"Well, if you don't need me for anything else, I suppose I'll head on home." He couldn't wait to tell Danny what Aiden had said, about how he'd been doing a good job looking after Ms. Emmaline. Danny would be proud of him.

"You've done enough for the day. Be sure to stop on up at the lodge and grab some supper before you go."

He hesitated for a moment. Should he confide in Aiden, tell him what he knew, or *thought* he knew, about Mr. Decker? Give Aiden warning that he'd be short-handed? But then he let out the breath he'd been holding. His first loyalty was to Danny. Always had been, always would be. No matter how much he liked Aiden.

"I will," he settled on saying. "Good night, Aiden."

"Night," Aiden said as he went back to pouring over his papers and logs.

As Scooter made his way to retrieve his coat and Aiden's praise came back to him, there was an undeniable spring in his step. Pride lifted his chin. It had turned out to be a good day after all.

Chapter Six

A glance at the clock on the far wall, and his growling stomach, told Aiden it was about time to wash up and head over to the lodge for supper before it was all gone. He dropped his stack of mail on the desk, powered his computer down for the night and rubbed at the ache in his thigh.

It was a bone deep ache that brought back unwanted memories he tried his best to push through, push aside. As if the nightmares he occasionally suffered weren't reminder enough. His thigh, where he'd taken the brunt of his injures, usually bothered him after an especially long day. And this one had been one for the books, though not necessarily in a bad way. In fact, he couldn't remember the last time he'd had a truly awful day. Not since he'd arrived at the Bar L almost three years ago.

There was just something about this place—whether it was the land itself, being out in the fresh air a majority of his day, or working with the horses, he couldn't say— but *something* here worked as a talisman of sorts for him. Staving off the insomnia and that itchy sensation that someone was watching him. He wasn't flinching at unexpected, loud sounds.

He had purpose. People depended on him once more. Life was good. Really good.

He'd spent the morning with the horses, more a treat for him than a chore really, followed by a brief tour of the ranch with Em's friend. Then he'd taken out a small group on the Fledgling Guided Trail Ride, a basic course for beginning riders on the lower, easier-to-navigate trails. The rest of his day had been split between maintenance calls, mechanical work…and trying to get that odd, quiet woman out of his head.

Yet again, he found his thoughts circling back to Harper Colby. That one was a puzzle, all right. He'd found her drifting through his thoughts when he least expected it. Which was pretty much all day long.

Quiet as a church mouse. Pretty as a spring morning, despite the vicious bruises on her face. He'd bet dollars to donuts her ribs were tender too, given how she seemed to be favoring her side just a bit. Somebody had worked her over pretty bad. Maybe that's where she'd gotten the wariness in her cornflower blue eyes.

Maybe that's why she looked as if she'd rather chew broken glass than spend more than five minutes alone in his company.

She had a story, all right. And he was damned curious about it. And that was unusual for him. For a guy like Aiden, there was a line you just didn't cross when it came to nosing into somebody else's business. If they didn't volunteer information—and they weren't hurting anybody—then you left them the hell alone. Same as he'd expect to be treated.

But that woman had layers upon layers he was dying to peel back. God above, she could make his blood rush with just a look, just a half-smile. She intrigued him as he hadn't been intrigued in longer than he cared to admit. And she was closed up tighter then Scrooge's vault.

Lord knew Emmie hadn't helped one bit. A few days ago, she'd mentioned an old friend from way back was coming for a visit. The length of that visit was undetermined. Emmie hadn't given any other details, and Aiden hadn't pried.

Now he wished he had. Not that Emmie would have caved. Emmie, an open book about herself, was Fort Knox when it came to keeping other people's secrets.

Try as he might, Aiden couldn't quite figure out what to make of Harper. He'd caught her watching him with those big fathomless eyes of hers. Studying him. Observing every move he made. A wary glint in her eye and a grim cast to her beautiful mouth. Just when he thought he'd spotted a glimpse of vulnerability, quick as a flash, she'd close herself off, tucked all her emotions away nice and neat. Before he could pin down how she was feeling, or what she might be thinking, she'd be giving off this cool, sophisticated, touch-me-not, confident, all-business vibe again.

Frustrating as all-hell was what it was.

He was usually pretty good at reading body language. That ability had gotten him and his unit out of some pretty sticky situations. More than once he'd sworn her body language had screamed "stay away" loud and clear.

All except for that split second at Eagle's Nest when she'd brushed up against him going through the doorway. It had been purely accidental on both their parts, of that he was certain. But he'd bet his next paycheck, in that hair's breadth of time, she'd been thinking awful hard about kissing him.

And, if he were being honest, he'd admit he'd been thinking awful hard about kissing her right back.

Yes, sir. She was a damned sexy puzzle, bruises and all.

He heaved a deep sigh. Those bruises of hers were another thing altogether.

He never could stand violence against women or children. Just the reminder of Harper's black eye made him clench his fists, protective anger burning like acid in his gut.

Shaking his head, he tried to push the thought of those bruises, and the feelings they evoked, aside. Tried, being the operative word. It wasn't his business, he reminded himself.

It didn't help.

She'd made that abundantly clear in every speaking glance she sent his way that she didn't want anything to do with him.

That didn't change things either.

Because he was thinking awful hard about making it his business. Making *her* his business, despite his previous determination to butt out of other people's business. Whether she liked it or not.

Whoever had knocked her around better have enough sense not to follow her to the Bar L. Aiden would be more than happy to teach that bastard the error of his ways. Besides, Harper was Em's friend. And if something threatened Harper, then there was a very good chance that threat might spill over onto Em.

And that *was* his business.

He'd promised Mark years ago, way before the day their envoy had been ambushed, that Aiden would look after Mark's young bride and the ranch should something happen to him. And that gut wrenching day as he'd stood helpless and hollowed-out, trapped in the moment of Mark's death as he'd watched his best friend be lowered into that raw, gaping hole in the ground, he'd sworn that solemn vow one last time.

Aiden had crawled through the searing flames, shards of glass and shrapnel and the sharp, twisted wreckage of their transport to Mark's side, dragging his ravaged leg in his wake. One glance at Mark's body—what was left of it—convinced Aiden he didn't have much time. So, when Mark gasped Emmie's name as he'd gripped Aiden's bloody gloved hand tight in his own, Aiden hadn't hesitated to reassure Mark. Aiden was a man of his word and would do whatever it took to keep his promise.

Aiden had sworn a solemn promise that would end up changing his own life. More than he'd ever dreamed possible.

Now here they were, three years later. Mark cold in the ground; Emmie a young widow with a huge operation to run all on her own. And Aiden doing everything in his power to make sure his friend's widow not only survived but thrived.

Man, he missed Mark. Every day.

Anxiety began to settle in, as it did whenever Aiden thought of Mark. That tight itchy feeling in his chest, making him want to crawl right out of his own skin. The tunnel vision. The inability to breathe. He realized he was rubbing fresh bruises into the extensive scarring that covered his thigh all over again. Drawing one deep, measured breath after another, he fought free of the memories and focused on what came next.

Shuffling papers, he found his checklist. He crossed off from his to-do list the furnace in Crow's Lookout, the toilet in Coyote's Den, and loose shingles on the roof of Deer Meadow. All the cabins were, once again, up and running and ready for business.

His thoughts strayed to tomorrow, and the coming confrontation he couldn't see any way to avoid. How that confrontation would go was anyone's guess. He wasn't altogether happy with the way the meeting with Jeb Decker had gone day before yesterday. For the most part, Aiden got along with the stable master, even if he didn't particularly like the man.

Decker was decent with the clients, better with the horses. But his skills as a supervisor sucked. Morale in the stables was on a serious decline. Not something Aiden could let slide considering a big chunk of Bar L business hinged on the stables.

So, bottom line, either Decker changed his tune in how he managed his staff—which meant he enforced the rules where they needed to be enforced and stopped playing favorites—or Aiden would be looking for a new stable master. One man, whether he was upper management or not, was easier to replace than a stable full of workers. And that's exactly what he'd be looking at if things didn't change and change damned soon. Outright mutiny.

Well, the guy had been duly warned, and he'd had the weekend off to consider his position. He better come back to work tomorrow with a brand new attitude.

Or he'd be looking for a brand-new job.

Emmie backed Aiden one hundred percent on the matter. She told him yesterday that she'd already started working on an ad for the position, just in case.

Satisfied, he shuffled Decker into a tidy little mental compartment, closed the door, and moved on to the next thing on his list. He'd scheduled guided trail rides for this week, and the next, and booked another guided camping trip two weeks out. Wouldn't be many more of those this season. Winter would be here before they knew it. And Em had been talking to the school about hosting a Halloween event here at the ranch for the younger classes. Flipping a page, he penciled that into his calendar.

The cold and snow came earlier to these elevations than even down in the valley only a few miles below. He just prayed the warmer weather would hold out a little longer. Then again, sometimes the snow was easier to deal with than the rains. Any more storms like the last one, and they'd be lucky if they weren't looking at mudslides in addition to overflowing riverbanks.

*I need to get the plow blades and the snow blowers out and ready to go. And we're gonna need to put the canoes in storage soon.*

After penciling *snow blowers/plow blades* and *canoes* to the bottom of his list, he tucked the scratch piece of paper away in his top drawer. Aiden yawned and stretched. Another day had gotten away from him…and he wouldn't have it any other way.

After rising, Aiden took his hat from the hook by the door, grabbed his jacket, and tugged them both on as he strode back through the stables for one last visual check. The big doors had already been closed against the chill of the evening air. His crew was dependable, but he stopped to make sure everything was locked up tight for the night all the same. Crime was all but nonexistent up here, but better safe than sorry.

Aiden walked along the lane on his way to the lodge, gravel rolling and crunching beneath his boots. Headlights speared the darkness, and he moved over to the side of the lane to allow the car to pass.

A moment later, a shiny red MINI Cooper whipped

by, the same one he'd noticed that morning as he'd been working with Jezebel. Harper's car. She must have gone to town for supplies after all. The car nipped neatly into one of the open parking spaces in front of the lodge, and he watched as her door opened.

He knew he wasn't being very professional. All the same, he couldn't help but let out a long low whistle as the woman who'd been haunting him all day climbed from her little car. Pretty as a picture didn't cover it. She was beautiful. Delicate. Fragile.

Dangerous.

The kind of woman a man either put a ring on or spent the rest of his life regretting.

That sudden and unexpected thought put him back on his heels. But only for a minute.

She'd gone around to the passenger side and was struggling to pull out a large cardboard box.

"Need some help with that?" he asked as he came up alongside her.

She let out a screech shrill enough to make his ears bleed as she dropped the box on the seat. Before he could blink, she whirled around, fist flying.

Thankfully, he had the reflexes of a cat. In one easy motion, he leaned back at the waist, neatly avoiding a punch to the throat, and he caught her fist in his hand.

Unfortunately, he hadn't been anticipating the kick to the shin. Could only thank his lucky stars she hadn't aimed higher. And that he wore cowboy boots.

In the brief tussle that ensued, Harper lost her balance. He'd only intended to keep her from falling when he'd snaked his arm around her waist. Apparently, she hadn't understood his intentions though, because she turned into a hissing, spitting wildcat in his arms. Curled fingers came clawing for his eyeballs about the same time her knee aimed for his ball sack.

And so, Aiden did the only thing he could. He pinned her up against the big SUV beside them, trapping her small squirming body with his much bigger one. Somehow, he managed to capture her face between his hands even as he tightened his abs against the sharp jabs she plowed into them.

"Harper," he all but shouted in her face. "Harper, calm down, for God's sake. It's me. It's Aiden." He finally got her attention.

She went absolutely still. Even seemed to stop breathing for a moment. And then she was shaking like a leaf. She sucked in one ragged breath, then another and another. Suddenly he was half afraid she was going to hyperventilate on him. Or start crying, God help him.

"I'm sorry," she whispered. "I'm sorry. I'm so sorry."

"Shh, it's okay," he rushed to assure her as he strained to search her pale face in the shadows. Dear lord, please don't let her cry. "I didn't mean to frighten you. Are you okay?"

"I'm fine. I'm okay," she kept repeating. But the full body shakes hadn't stopped yet, so he kind of doubted it.

He eased his hands to her shoulders, slowly slid them up and down her arms in smooth, soothing strokes. She wore a long-sleeved T-shirt, but her skin was icy even through the cotton.

"Where's your coat?"

"I don't have one," she said, her eyes were closed, and she was visibly struggling to regulate her breathing.

"What? It's freezing up here, especially at night. Winter is just right around the corner."

"No, really?"

The hint of sarcastic defiance sent relief surging through his veins. Relief and admiration. She was a fighter all right, in more ways than one. If he hadn't been trained, had been any other man, her attack probably would have left him writhing in the mud in excruciating pain.

Without giving it a second thought, Aiden stepped back and slipped off his fleece-lined denim jacket. He quickly moved closer to whip the coat around her, gathering it snugly beneath her chin. She shuddered, and he hoped it was because of the lingering body heat trapped inside the lining, and not because he'd frightened her again.

"Oh, no, I can't—"

"Keep it on," he ordered. "You're a block of ice."

He watched while she wiggled around until she managed to thrust her arms into sleeves that ended way past her fingertips. The waistband, which normally hit him around the belt line, reached below her hips. An unexpected pang of lust arrowed through his system at the sight of her wrapped up in his coat. Stupid, but true. He wanted her. She was utterly adorable standing there in the faintest glow of moonlight, swimming in his jacket. He knew, without a doubt, he was well and truly screwed.

As if somehow sensing his train of thought, she self-consciously overlapped the front of the coat across her chest, wrapped her arms around herself and hugged tight. A gust of wind whipped through the parking lot, pushing hair across her face. Before she could react, Aiden reached up, unable—unwilling—to stop himself. He captured the wayward strands and smoothed them back behind her ear, taking his own sweet time, savoring the silky texture.

Her pretty blue eyes, ringed by thick lashes, were enormous as they blinked owlishly up at him.

He couldn't resist. Didn't even try.

Aiden slid his fingers down that silky hair, slipped his hand around the back of her neck. Applying only the smallest amount of pressure, Aiden drew her relentlessly closer, until her palms, still covered in his long sleeves, rested against his chest.

Keeping his movements slow and easy, as one would for a skittish horse, Aiden lowered his head until only a whisper of air separated their lips. He let an eternity spin out as he lost himself in her mesmerizing eyes. In the scent of her, something crisp and clean and feminine swirled straight to his gut. As the heat of her breath whispered tantalizingly over his lips.

And then he kissed her.

He didn't know what possessed him do it. No, that was a lie. He'd been able to think of little else since that moment at her cabin, the second when she'd brushed against him and looked up at him with desire brimming in her beautiful eyes.

Maybe even since the second he walked into the lodge looking for Emmie and found Harper sitting there on the sofa visiting with Kathryn instead.

He moved his lips over hers, lightly at first. Testing. The softest of whispers. A fleeting brush. A lingering touch. A gentle nip. Nice and easy. Until her lips, cold from the night, tight from her fright, began to warm and soften, began to blossom, until they sought his in protest each time he drew back just a tiny bit.

Encouraged, he eased forward a step, eased into her

space. When she didn't object, he angled his head a bit more and smoothed his lips over hers again. Adding a little more pressure. A little more demand. Once. Twice. Then he held back, hovering his parted lips there, close, so close, but not quite touching. Waiting. Breaths mingling. Tiny, warm, shallow puffs of air. An unhurried, gentle seduction of the senses.

God knew, she was seducing him with every response. Every little catch in her breath thrilled him. Every time her chin rose whenever he pulled back, as if to prolong each second of contact between his mouth and hers drove him crazy. The way her fingers dug into him through layers of cotton and denim urged him closer.

His chest was suddenly so tight it was hard to breathe. His blood rushed in his ears, his heart raced. If he didn't know better, he'd swear he was about to have another anxiety attack. But this was pure pleasure, raw and unsullied by bad memories. And he gave himself over to it completely. Surely, he'd die if she pushed him away right now. He didn't mean to, but he found himself clutching her a little tighter, holding her steady. Pressing her closer to his body.

He daubed the tip of his tongue to her lower lip. A deliberate glide. A test. A question.

Her breath shuddered from her. Her lips parted wider, her jaw dropped a bit, and she angled her head, pressing against the side of his hand. Accepting.

It was all the invitation he needed. Aiden delved inside her mouth, stroking, tangling his tongue with hers over and over. Honey and spice. At the same moment, he eased closer still, stepping into her again, until her back pressed up hard against the SUV behind her. She slid her hands up to clasp his shoulders, went up on tiptoes.

Aiden pressed against her, savoring full body contact, cursing the thickness of the coat between them.

She slipped her arms up around his neck, speared her fingers into his hair, moaned into his mouth, and set his body aflame. Somehow his jacket parted, and her breasts crushed against his chest, nothing but a few thin layers of cotton separating them now. Better, but not quite good enough. Man, what he wouldn't give to lose those layers of clothing right now. Feel skin on skin. To really touch her. To taste her skin.

Harper melted into him. There was no other way to describe it. Acceptance and trust, desire and need. It was the most exquisite, erotic sensation he'd ever experienced.

He drifted his hand to the curve of her hip, glided it around behind her and angled it lower as he nudged a knee between her legs. Aiden, bending both knees now, pressed his throbbing erection against the cradle of her thighs. He dragged the rigid bulge in his jeans languidly, sensuously, carefully up over her pelvis, pressed it insistently against her abdomen as he straightened, letting her know exactly what she was doing to him.

Her response nearly brought him to his knees right there. She moaned again and trembled in his arms. Lifting her knee to hook around his leg, she clutched him to her even tighter and rocked her hips into him.

Aiden groaned and angled his head, took the kiss to a deeper, darker place. He dragged her beneath the waves of desire he couldn't hold at bay any longer, until he was pretty sure she was drowning right along with him. Still clutching her amazing ass with one hand, holding her in place as he tilted his hips and rubbed his erection against her abdomen, he slid his other hand down the side of her neck, slipping it beneath the lapel of his jacket. He skimmed her delicate collar bone, slowly angling down, the need to feel the weight of her breast in his hand burned a hole clean through him. The frantic, solid thud of her heart pounded against his palm, reassuring him she was lost in the moment every bit as deeply as he was. The top button on her shirt was smooth and warm beneath his fingertips.

The approaching crunch of tires on gravel nearby barely registered. Even then it was a moment longer before the blinding flash of headlights sweeping over them jolted him to his senses. It took every bit of his control, and some he hadn't realized he even possessed, to not ignore that light, to not say the hell with it all and dive right back into her.

Regardless of the interruption, he loathed releasing her, despised the very thought of ending what had turned out to be the best full-body kiss of his life. But someone was coming, and he didn't want her to be any more embarrassed than he suspected she would be already, just as soon as she had time to think about what had passed between them.

Aiden slowly brought the kiss back to the surface, until he was once again nipping and nibbling, skating shallow brushes of his lips over hers until he could force himself to stop tasting her. His hand settled on the curve of her waist, deprived of the feel of heaven that had been so close. Even so, having ended the kiss, he still couldn't quite bring himself to let go and step away.

And so he savored the moment, lapped up the dazed, aroused softness of her expression like a cat at a bowl of cream. Reveled in the swollen, definitely-been-kissed-senseless puffiness of her lips. Right up until the second she opened her eyes wider and looked up at him. Really looked.

There was an instant of confusion, like she couldn't understand why he'd stopped kissing her. Or maybe wondering why he was holding her and watching her closely. Then a glimmer of self-awareness, of what she'd just let him do, what they'd just done together, flickered. Followed by flashes of shock, and yes the embarrassment he'd anticipated.

And suddenly, as expected, she was shoving at him, sputtering and inarticulately demanding release.

He let her go, albeit with a great deal of reluctance, and stepped back at last.

Harper pressed a sleeve covered hand to her mouth, her blue eyes enormous. Until he reached up and tucked her hair back one last time.

The motion seemed to jumpstart her faculties. She jerked back, stopping only because her back was, once again, pressed like a second skin against the SUV.

"Aiden," she breathed. The sound of his name on her lips was candy to his ears. She shook her head. "Why?"

"Because you needed it."

Her mouth fell open, and temper snapped in her eyes. Before she could blast him, however, he pressed one fingertip to her warm, slightly swollen lips and admitted ruefully, "I needed it too."

It pleased him more than words could say when her lips went slack beneath his finger, and her eyes widened. She sucked in a ragged breath around his finger. Her pale cheeks flooded with color.

God, she suited him. Right down to his toes. Stifling a smile, he turned away and easily took the box she'd been struggling with from her car. He turned back to her.

"Where are we going with this?"

She stared at him, long and hard. Started to speak. Stopped. Stared again, only to press her lips together tight. Harper huffed out an aggrieved breath and clutched his coat closer to her chest. "The ATV."

"Need help getting this into your cabin later?"

"No!" Her reply was very firm. Very deliberate.

And it made him grin from ear to ear.

## Chapter Seven

Harper followed Aiden up the steps, across the porch and inside the Lodge like a wooden puppet tugged along by strings she couldn't see. Her mind was too tangled up trying to make sense of what had just happened to come up with idle conversation, her emotions a jumbled mess. She almost bumped into him when he paused inside the door. She knew she was staring at him…again…with what surely must be a dumbfounded expression. And she wished to high heaven she could stop. But she just couldn't seem to help herself.

And she sure as hell wished he'd stop looking at her like that. Like he was enjoying the hell out of himself. Like he was amused by her flustered behavior.

Like he was giving serious thought to kissing her again.

He paused long enough to help her take his coat off and hang it on a massive elk horn coat rack in the corner of the deserted Great Room. Then, without asking permission, he took her by the hand and led her down a long hallway. Harper self-consciously tried tugging her hand from his. To no avail.

That amused grin of his only seemed to get bigger.

Anyone who came upon them right now—with the two of them holding hands, his grin cocky and her face on fire—would immediately know they'd been kissing.

And she didn't want anyone to know. She didn't even want the two of them thinking overly hard on the subject.

But how could she *not* think about it. She was still tingling.

"The crew—whoever happens to be working that day—just grabs a bite at the café for breakfast, lunch and supper." The sound of Aiden's voice made her jump a little, she'd been so lost in thought, so busy stewing. "As I said before, perk of the job. Emmie's very generous that way. Having a solid head for business, Kathryn objected of course. But Em held out. She's the heart of this place."

So, if Kathryn was the level head of the business, and Emmie was the heart, what did that make Aiden?

The backbone?

Hearing Aiden speak of Emmie with such obvious affection shoved the razor sharp blade of guilt a little deeper. What had she been thinking? How could she have forgotten? Had she betrayed Emmie already? The very first day she'd set foot on the ranch? Didn't matter that she'd never intended to, she'd still allowed Aiden to kiss her. She felt suddenly like she should be wearing a big, scarlet A on her chest.

And what about Aiden? He sure didn't seem to be suffering the burden of the guilty. Was this an everyday occurrence for him? Kissing random women whenever the mood struck? Protective anger kindled to life. How dare he treat Emmie this way? She tugged harder but still he refused to release her hand.

"Anyway, every Sunday evening, Em caters supper for the crew. Kind of a tradition around here. Sunday dinner with the family kind of thing."

*Twist the knife a little more, why don't ya?*

That was it. She was stronger than this. She didn't

need to be led around by the hand like a little kid. And she sure as certain wasn't about to let anyone—Aiden included—get the wrong idea about their relationship.

With perhaps more vehemence than she'd intended, Harper finally succeeded in jerking her hand from his. Then she braced herself for his displeasure.

Aiden blinked down at her, as though she'd taken him off guard. But instead of getting angry, or reaching for her hand again, he only slanted her an amused grin. Shrugging nonchalantly, he pushed open one of the double doors in front of them labeled Banquet Hall.

The minute they walked through the door, a flurry of flowing, curly black hair and bony arms filled her vision. The impact knocked Harper back a step, the wind all but squashed from her lungs. She let out a soft *umpf* beneath the force of the enthusiastic hug.

"Oh, my goodness, Harper! I'm so happy to see you. I'm sorry I wasn't here when you came in this afternoon. How are you? Let me see you!" Emmie pulled back to tug Harper's arms out at her sides for a good once over.

Emmie hadn't changed the teensiest little bit in all these years. She still topped Harper by a solid four inches. Emmie's hair was a little longer maybe, reaching nearly to her waist now, but her eyes were still that startling, vibrant green. She was still thin as a reed and overflowing with that seize-the-day, effervescent energy that had always been her defining feature.

Overwhelmed, Harper ducked her head. Talk about an emotional rollercoaster. Her head still wasn't screwed on straight after that mind boggling kiss. Hell, she'd barely been able to form a coherent thought as she'd tromped beside Aiden, torn between bemusement, anger, guilt and reluctant arousal, her hand all but swallowed up in his.

Now Emmaline was gushing all over her. And there were all these strangers standing around staring at her. She glanced up to find Aiden, tall and stalwart, standing just a few feet away, watching the two of them with unfathomable, dark eyes and an inscrutable expression.

*Why on earth did he kiss me?*
*Why did I let him?*
*How will Emmie ever forgive me?*

Unnerved, she turned her face away only to catch Kathryn watching her too. Only Kathryn had this odd little smile on her face.

Emmie carefully cupped Harper's face in her hands as she surveyed the damage, turning Harper's face from side to side, unmindful of the people behind her that were openly staring at them.

Emmie hissed, "I hope that bastard burns in hell," beneath her breath before tugging Harper back into a bone-grinding embrace. "Don't you worry about a thing, sweetie. He won't get anywhere near you ever again. We'll see to it, won't we, Aiden?"

All thoughts of earth-shattering kisses and who belonged to whom flew out of her head the moment Emmaline slipped her arms around Harper's middle and squeezed. Harper wheezed out a sharp breath and winced, though she managed to keep the grunt of pain from slipping past her lips. Just barely.

"She's turning blue, Emmie," Aiden said abruptly, a hint of unmistakable concern coloring his voice. "Best ease back so she can catch her breath."

"Oh! Oh, Harper, I'm sorry. I'm just so excited you're here." Emmie immediately released her and stepped back. But she wasn't done. Not by a long shot.

She captured Harper's hand and dragged her farther into the room. Harper plastered a smile on her face, even as she let out a long, controlled breath around the throbbing ache in her side.

She could almost feel the weight of Aiden's dark scrutiny following every step she took.

*Damn him.*

"It's okay, really. I'm happy to see you too, Emmie."

"I can't wait to catch up. But first, let me introduce you around to everybody."

Though she was vigilant to keep a smile plastered to her face, inside Harper cringed. She'd really been hoping to put this off, at least until her face was back to normal. But Emmie was a force of nature and would not be denied.

"Everybody, this is my good friend Harper Colby. Harper…well, this is everybody," Emmie declared, a kindergartener with a new toy on Show-and-Tell day. She pulled Harper over to the closest person, a woman with wispy blonde hair pulled back in a loose bun, snowy white skin, and round, rosy cheeks. "This is Berta Connelly, Kitchen Manager of The Ranch Café. She makes the best desserts this side of the Mississippi."

Berta carefully placed the huge, covered pan she was carrying on a nearby banquet table already groaning beneath a mountain of food. She flushed and smiled shyly beneath Emmie's praise. After she smoothed her palms down the long white apron wrapped around her thick middle, Berta held out a hand. "Pleasure to meet you."

Harper murmured what she hoped was a gracious reply as she shook hands with the friendly, obviously curious, older woman. Next Emmie tugged her over to meet a nondescript man of medium height and build who appeared to be in his early to mid-twenties, and another man, thirtyish, who was built like a bull. They were sitting at the end of one of the emptier tables, already digging into loaded plates.

"And these guys are Todd Sweeney and Bruce Grafton," Emmie labeled them respectively.

Todd immediately put his silverware aside and rose to shake her hand, offering her a shy smile. Bruce the bull was a little slower to rise. He grunted his greeting, dipped his head in a terse nod, and then fell back on his plate like a teenage boy replenishing calories after football practice. Harper didn't envy anyone stupid enough to get between that man and his food.

Both worked in the stables, Emmie had explained, as did three of the other men at the end of another long table, including Jim Potts, the man who'd brought her the ATV. Harper had already lost track of names as Emmie squired her on down the line. By the time she'd finished introducing all fifteen or so people present, Harper's head was spinning. She couldn't remember a single name anymore. And she wanted nothing more than to go back to her cabin, bury her aching head beneath a mountain of pillows, and pass out.

"Emmie, let that girl grab a plate and a seat," Kathryn instructed from the next table over. "She looks ready to drop."

"Goodness, I didn't even stop to think—"

Just then, the woman wearing the apron—Berta was her name, Harper thought—called to Emmie.

Emmaline turned and spoke over Harper's head. "Aiden, would you make sure—"

"I've got her," Aiden replied, his voice much too close for Harper's comfort. "You go on."

Harper blinked and peered over her shoulder. Sure enough, Aiden had been trailing them like a watch dog.

Emmie shot Harper an apologetic, if bolstering smile, gave her arm a little squeeze, and scurried away. Harper turned to Aiden, apprehensive as she recalled the unrestrained passion that had passed between them out in the parking lot only a short time ago. As if he were reading her thoughts, Aiden let a wicked grin spread slowly, meaningfully across his face, and he let his gaze dip to her mouth.

Heat flooded her cheeks, and Harper caught her lower lip between her teeth. She darted a quick peek at the exit. Before she could make an excuse, before she could slip away, he claimed her elbow and gently, if insistently, ushered her toward the banquet table along the far wall.

"I'm really not that hungry," she said, maintaining a polite, if cool tone, all too aware of the inquisitive stares following them.

Aiden sent her a knowing look. "You probably haven't eaten all day, have you?"

"I'm a grown woman. Whether I eat or not really isn't your problem." Pressing her lips together, Harper tried, unobtrusively, to pull her arm away.

Though he was careful not to hurt her, Aiden clung like a burr.

"You need to eat." Then he caught her completely by surprise. He dipped his head closer and asked softly, "Are your ribs okay?"

Harper jerked back slightly. Her lips parted, and she blinked up at him.

*How could he possibly—*

"I've had bruised ribs myself, more'n once," he drawled. "Recognized the wince."

Harper snapped her mouth closed and turned her head so he could only catch her profile.

"Though you did an admirable job of covering," he whispered in a subdued, intimate aside.

"I don't know what you're talking about. I'm fine."

"Uh-huh." Hearing the disbelief in his tone, she couldn't help but glower at him. Aiden went on as if she weren't skewering him with her eyes, "If the pain gets stronger than the pride, June keeps a bottle of ibuprofen in the top left drawer of her desk in the office. That's through that door behind the long counter in the Lodge's great room."

"My pride and my pain are none of your business," she hissed.

"Uh-huh." Same skeptical tone. Like he didn't agree but was being too polite to argue. Damn him.

She hadn't wanted to even bring up the incident in the parking lot. Wanted nothing more than to just pretend that kiss had never happened. Apparently, she wasn't going to have that luxury. She needed to clear the air, was worried he might have gotten the wrong idea after all. That kiss hadn't meant anything. Hadn't changed anything. Should never have happened.

And it sure as hell hadn't made her, or anything to do with her, any of his concern.

She narrowed her eyes at him and, though no one was in close proximity, Harper lowered her voice. "Look, we need to talk."

"Yeah?" His elevated eyebrow and the laughter in his voice said he found her furious order amusing. A fact she did not appreciate. By now they'd reached the buffet table. He finally released her and reached for a plate, handed it to her.

Either she took it, or she'd appear rude in front of all these people. Shooting him a furious glower, she grudgingly accepted his offering. He laughed out loud; the sound rumbled up from deep in his belly to spill over her as he grabbed another plate for himself.

Harper seethed.

He ladled up a hearty helping of chicken gravy and biscuits and—without asking—plopped it onto her plate. "What would you like to talk about?"

Her mouth fell open at his audacity.

He thunked an even bigger serving of the main course onto his own plate and turned to survey the rest of the food being offered. Not a care in the world.

Harper sputtered as he next dumped a big, slotted spoon full of mixed veggies—way more than was considered a healthy serving size—onto her plate. When she finally looked up at him, the first words that popped out of her mouth surprised her. "You kissed me."

*Damn it! He's got me so rattled I can't even think straight.*

"Yep," he said easily, sliding a melting square of aromatic apple crisp onto her plate. "I believe I'll be doing it again too, every chance I get. So what's there to talk about?"

Harper stood there, mouth agape, staring at him like a halfwit. With way more relish than warranted, Aiden ran his finger along the edge of her plate where some of the apple crisp had dripped. Then he licked the golden, spiced sauce from the pad of his finger with a low hum of appreciation.

His grin, complete with arched eyebrow, was nothing short of wicked.

Nonplused, all Harper could do was stare…and frown, first at her plate, and then at him. Aiden loaded a double-sized helping of apple crisp onto his own plate and moved on down the table.

Spurred by his nonchalance, she stomped after him, determined to set the record straight. She'd thought she'd been all tangled up before? Now her emotions churned and seethed.

But a sweet flutter winged low in her belly now too. His words…stunned her. She couldn't believe the sheer nerve of this man.

*"I believe I'll be doing it again too, every chance I get."*

*Yeah? Well…well, not if* I *have anything to say about it.*

What made him think he could kiss her like that? That she wouldn't object? Why say these things to her? Why deliberately try to drive a wedge between her and Emmie? Why toy with Harper this way?

"Why—" She was so floored, she couldn't even finish her own sentence.

He leaned close, till their heads were mere inches apart. Her eyes widened when she realized he was staring at her mouth, *intently*. As though imagining sampling it the way he had her apple crisp. And then his warm, deep brown eyes met hers, and the intriguing flutter low in her belly became a violent trembling.

"Because you kissed me back, sweetheart." Aiden smiled then, wholly unrepentant. "And I liked it. An awful lot." He winked at her, actually winked, took a quick nip from the extra biscuit in his hand, spun on his heel and strolled away.

Because she'd…

Because she'd kissed him back?

And he'd liked it?

*What the hell kind of answer is that?*

Outraged, she took a step to follow, ready, willing and able to blast into him. That's when she remembered all those watchful eyes. She glanced around. Yep. They were still staring, albeit unobtrusively. At least, she was sure they *thought* they were being furtive.

She paused, much like the new kid at school, looking for a sympathetic face. She found one in Kathryn, who patted the table beside her. Unfortunately, it placed her squarely across from Aiden. Her flagging appetite suddenly soured.

Dragging her feet, trying not to *look* like she was dragging her feet, she made her way to Kathryn's side, offering the older woman a limp smile. As soon as she put her plate down and took a seat, she realized she'd forgotten to get something to drink. She made to rise, but Aiden was already pushing to his feet.

"I'll get it," he said.

She glanced over. "Thanks, but I can—"

"I'm going that way anyway. Iced tea? Coffee? Pop?"

She glared daggers at him, smiled with icy sweetness, and spoke through clenched teeth. "Iced tea, please."

"Sweetened or unsweetened?"

"Unsweetened."

"Coming right up." She scowled at his back as he walked away, wanting with every part of her being to throw her plate at his retreating head.

A gentle touch on her forearm nearly sent her through the roof. Embarrassed, she turned to her forgotten companion. Emmie's mother had that same odd little smile on her face that she'd been wearing earlier. Harper didn't know quite what to make of it.

"Our Aiden's a good man, Harper."

Harper did her best to mask the cringe.

*"Our Aiden…"*

Would Kathryn still think that if she knew how he'd been sneaking around behind her daughter's back? Would she still be so gracious to Harper when she found out Harper hadn't exactly been the one to put on the brakes?

It was a damned good thing the fork in her hand was metal and not cheap plastic, or she would have snapped it clean in two.

She was spared from having to reply by Aiden's return.

"Thank you," she said woodenly when he placed a tall glass of ice and amber liquid beside her plate.

"Welcome." His lips twitched. He was laughing at her. The big jerk.

Fuming, she shoveled up a big forkful of gravy covered biscuits and filled her mouth. Chewed slowly as she glowered his way. After a few minutes, and some rather loud throat clearing on Kathryn's part, Harper turned her focus on the older woman.

"Are you all settled in up at the cabin?"

"Yes. I drove back to Devil's Canyon and grabbed a few supplies." She turned a smile that didn't quite reach her eyes on the silent man across the table. "Aiden was nice enough to help me load them onto the ATV."

He didn't even have the good sense to look worried

she might spill the beans about that kiss. He just sat there, cool as a cucumber, working his way around the mountain of food on his plate.

Almost against her will, she followed his movements as he carried a large bite of apple crisp to his lips. She scanned his face as he savored the flavor of tart apples and cinnamony sweetness. A dribble of golden sauce had been left behind on the fork. She struggled to control her breathing as he slowly, carefully licked the utensil clean, his eyes never leaving hers. And she recalled how he'd done the same to the finger he'd dragged through her own dessert. The same finger he'd pressed to her own lips earlier.

The way his lips curled up, just at the edges, was her first clue that she'd been staring.

Her second was the way Kathryn repeated her name.

Mortified, she turned to Kathryn. "I want to thank you again for having me here. And for the job."

"Nonsense. You're family, same as Aiden here. We're happy to have you with us." Kathryn patted her shoulder. "As I was saying, you come on down to the lodge by eight in the morning. We'll get the paperwork squared away. I'm sure Emmie wants some time with you. Then I'll have Melanie show you the ropes."

Melanie…Melanie…oh yes. Tall, skinny redhead, Harper recalled. Freckles. Nice smile.

"I'll have you follow her around for a few days till you get the hang of things, then we'll work you into the schedule."

"Sounds good." She was anxious to get into a routine and feel useful again. Harper took a bite of apple crisp. Flavor exploded in her mouth. Sweet. Tart. Heaven. The chicken and biscuits had been delicious.

But the apple crisp was to die for. Comforting as summer sunshine and a hug from grandma. Harper nearly groaned aloud.

"I know one of the boys showed you how to use the ATV earlier and gave you one of the walkies. I just wanted to make sure you're comfortable before you go off on your own up the mountain."

"I think so. I've got the map Aiden gave me earlier, and the ATV has a compass. I should be able to find my way back with no problem."

"Good, good. But you be careful up there. Those trails can get a might confusing, especially in the dark. Don't be shy about calling for help if you need it. Aiden or one of the boys will be happy to come out and get you back on the right track. Won't you, Aiden?"

"You bet."

He'd been silent for so long, that the sound of his voice made her glance over at him despite her earlier determination not to. A dark-eyed gaze roamed her face. Her cheeks heated as he continued to stare. She ducked her head and used eating as an excuse to break eye contact.

"We got an extra coat around here that might be her size?" Aiden asked Kathryn.

Harper's head popped up. "I don't need—"

"Sure you don't. Right up until your teeth are chattering and you fall over from hypothermia while you're driving back up to Eagle's Nest later tonight."

She pressed her lips together. She could bite her tongue to keep the words from rolling out, but there was very little she could do to curb the fire that must surely be shooting from her eyes.

Just then, Emmie joined them, plopping down on the

seat to Aiden's left. She leaned slightly to the side, linked her hands around his bicep and rested her head against his shoulder.

*Knife. Twisting.*

"So what are we all talking about?"

"Harper needs a coat," Aiden informed her. "Probably gloves and a hat too. Do you have any extras around here?"

"Oh, no, I don't think so. Well, maybe gloves and a hat, but not a coat. I'd give her one of mine, but I think it'd be too small." Emmie turned a worried frown Harper's way. "I can ask around and see if somebody can lend you one for the night. Maybe tomorrow we can go back to town. Schaller's opens around nine, I think. We should be able to find you something there."

"Don't worry about it tonight," Aiden said, chasing the last bite of gravy and biscuit with his fork. He finished the last of his milk, set the glass aside, then rested his hand over Emmie's. "She can keep using mine for now."

"I can't possibly—"

"Yes. You will." His tone didn't leave any room for argument. "Stop being stubborn."

Harper glanced helplessly to Emmie, then to Kathryn. They both smiled as if the subject were already closed. There would be no help coming from either of them.

It was becoming abundantly clear, at least as far as these two were concerned, that this man walked on water.

Well, she wasn't prepared to drink *that* Kool-Aid...not ever again.

"And talking of stubborn," Aiden went on, turning

his focus on Emmie now, "I forgot to ask you about Jezebel earlier. She's been touchy lately. Charges the stall every time certain stable boys go near her. And she nearly tossed a guy into the bushes from one of the guided groups on Friday. Only thing kept him from a nasty fall was the fact he's already had a lot of miles in the saddle."

Emmie's brow creased and she nibbled her lip. "Maybe he was rough with her?"

"I thought maybe so too, at first. But then she tried biting Todd later that same evening, and then Jim on Saturday morning. And she kicked her stall a couple times when Bruce walked by."

"What do you think we should do?"

"Well, we can't have her throwing clients or biting stable boys. I pulled her from the trail roster for now, till we figure out what's going on with her. Up until lately, she's been pretty reliable for guided tours and she used to follow Todd like a love struck puppy dog." He paused for a moment, as if giving it some thought. "I called Doc Tisdahl. He'll be up in the morning to take a look at her. Could be she just needs a break. But it's best to know if there's something else at play."

"Do whatever you need to. I don't like to think she might be feeling poorly. Besides," she nudged him good-naturedly with her shoulder, "I don't know why you bother asking my opinion anyway. I may technically be the owner, but the stables and the horses are your babies. You'll do what you see fit to make sure everything runs smoothly no matter what anyone else has to say about it."

At that pronouncement, little bells and whistles started going off in Harper's head. Could Aiden possibly be exerting some kind of control over Emmie, the way Alexander had controlled her? Goosebumps ran down her arms.

Or was she being overly paranoid?

She hated that she couldn't trust her own judgment anymore.

The sound of moving chairs and tables being cleared drew Harper's focus. She looked down at her plate. Her empty plate. And she gave a tiny little harrumph. She hadn't even realized she'd been that hungry.

Rising, she joined the others in cleaning up, then hugged Emmie and Kathryn goodnight, promising Emmie that the two would spend time the next day having a nice long visit. Emmie and Kathryn turned one way down the hall to go to their own suites. Harper followed the crowd to the door. But before she could slip outside with everyone else, Aiden stepped into her path. He held his jacket up with both hands by the edges of the collar, clearly expecting her to turn around so he could help her put it on.

"It's too big."

"It's better than nothing," he countered. "And it's warm."

"What are you going to use?"

"I have another up at my cabin. And my truck has a heater."

They stared at each other a moment longer, locked in a silent battle of wills. Harper was all too aware they were the only ones left in the Great Room.

Finally, he said, "It's either this, or I give you a ride back to your cabin in my heated truck instead of just following you there. And then I'll only have to come back to get you in the morning since you won't have a ride."

Her eyes narrowed. "Why do you have to follow me anywhere?"

Why did it seem she was always asking him "why" all the time?

"Well, number one, you're new here, and you're not familiar with the trails. Two, you've never driven an ATV. Three, it's getting dark and those trails can be tough to negotiate even in daylight. Four, it's on the way to my place." Just when he'd started winning her over with common sense, something even she couldn't argue against, he went and pushed his limits. "And I need to make sure you make it home safely."

She narrowed her eyes at him. "Why?"

*Lord, there I go again.*

A muscle bunched in his jaw. Harper suddenly experienced an unwelcome urge to squirm beneath his all-too-discerning gaze.

"I don't think you're ready to hear the answer to that yet," he finally said.

She huffed out a puff of breath, pressed her lips together and scowled. He lifted the jacket an inch or two and gave it an impatient shake.

"Fine," she muttered before spinning around to thrust her arms into the sleeves. As she turned to face him once more, she growled, "Happy?"

"Almost." His lips twitched. Without a word, he reached down and captured the end of one sleeve. Slowly, his gaze locked on hers, he rolled first one cuff, then the other. She couldn't seem to force herself to break the connection. And then he was buttoning the coat up. And brushing her hair back from her face. And leaning closer. His focus clearly on her lips.

At the last second, she jerked her arm up between them and caught his face in her splayed hand. His eyes, wide-open and clearly surprised, peered between her fingers as she flattened his nose with her palm.

"I'm not falling for that again," she snapped. "Save it for Emmie." Then she darted around him and sprinted out the door.

## Chapter Eight

She was there one moment, staring up at him with those big blue eyes, giving him hell. And then, having caught him by surprise, she was off like a shot, out the door and down the porch steps. He couldn't say what had startled him more. The fact that she'd just caught his face in her hand, or that she'd run off like the hounds of Hell were chasing after her.

He'd moved too fast, Aiden could see that now, trying to kiss her again. He should have waited, given her time to adjust to the idea. He just hadn't been able to resist. Now he was staring at a swinging door. Obviously, she'd been hurt, abused. Who'd done the abusing, he didn't know. How badly, or how long the abuse had gone on, he didn't know either. And he cursed, because he was going into this blind.

Blind, yes. Willing to give up? No.

*Hell no.*

There was some kind of connection between them. Visceral. He didn't know what it was, or why it had happened. Knew only that he was drawn to her. Felt like...like he was meant to be there for her, be *with* her.

With a low groan, and an eye roll at his own stupidity, Aiden followed.

She was already vaulting inside the maroon-colored Mule by the time he'd gathered his wits and burst outside. As he hurried across the gravel, Harper jabbed at the dash, cursing loud enough for him to hear her as she frantically attempted to start the ATV.

He reached her side just as she managed to get the thing to roar to life. Aiden jumped onto the passenger seat and gave the key a swift twist, shutting the machine down.

Harper's eyes went wide, and she slammed back against the seat, cringing away from him. Seeing her reaction sent ice through his veins.

He didn't know what to do. Only knew that he couldn't stand to see her looking at him like that. Like she expected him to lash out at her. Or take a swing at her. The only time she wasn't watching him with that wary glint in her eye…was when those beautiful eyes had been filled with passion.

Operating on instinct alone, he snaked his arm up and cupped the back of her neck in a gentle but unbreakable hold. Without a word, he dragged her across the seat and fused his lips to hers.

Not as gentle as he probably should have been.

For a moment, Harper flailed against him, her fisted hands thumped and pushed at his chest as she reared back in his grip. But Aiden held firm, moving his lips against hers, brushing, nipping and nibbling until she began to respond. Gradually the fight went out of her. Her hands stopped pushing, started clutching instead. Her lips, previously stiff and clamped tight, softened and became deliciously pliant. He didn't wait a second more. He pushed inside, sweeping his tongue against hers, tangling, dueling, dragging her into the same haze of need that swamped him. She tasted of apples and cinnamon. Of moonlight pleasures and promises of tomorrow.

He didn't pull back until they were both breathless.

"What the hell was that all about back there in the lodge?" Aiden demanded, hoping he'd given her something else to focus on aside from the fear he'd seen in her eyes a few minutes ago.

She peered up at him, dazed, clearly confused, and she shook her head. Not an ounce of fear in her beguiling eyes. Well, at least he'd gotten that right.

"You kissed me again."

"I warned you I would." He leaned back, released her neck, though he left his arm stretched along the seat behind her. "I'll ask again, what the hell was that all about? Running out of there that way? What was your plan? To go tearing off into the night up unfamiliar mountain trails on an ATV you've operated a total of one time? If you won't give a second's thought to your own safety, then at least damned well think of how Emmie would feel if you got yourself killed because you were being reckless and stupid."

Her back went ramrod straight, and she glared holes in his hide. "Oh, you're a fine one to be worrying about Emmie's feelings now, after you kissed me. Twice."

"What?" Ok, he was lost. What did Emmie have to do with his kissing her?

"Look, Aiden. I don't know what kind of lothario you think you are, or what you've been getting away with behind Emmie's back, but you're barking up the wrong tree, buddy."

"Lothario?" He frowned, tilting his head. *What the hell?*

"Do I really have to spell this out for you?" she ground out, as if speaking to a simpleton. "I won't mess around with you behind Emmie's back. So cut the crap."

"So that's what this is about? You think Emmie and I are together?" He shifted his weight on the seat, his anger cooling. "Are you're jealous?"

"Don't be ridiculous," Harper snapped. "I don't even know you. I just wish Emmie had chosen someone who could have been faithful to her. And besides, I'm not interested."

"Bullshit."

Her mouth fell open. He leaned closer, crowding into her space.

"Bull. Shit," he enunciated. Before she could rally her wits, he went on, "I kiss you and you melt in my arms. Oh, you're interested all right. You're interested, whether you like it or not. And as far as Emmie goes, she's a friend, nothing more, nothing less. Hell, she's damned near a kid sister to me. I made her husband a promise. I swore to him as he was…I swore to him I'd look after her. Help her in any way I could. Always be there for her. But let me be very clear on this, I did *not* swear to take his place in her bed. I haven't. And I won't."

Harper leaned back, her eyes widening with unmistakable unease.

"You're right about something else though," he continued. "You don't know me yet. So I'll give you a pass. This time. But I'm gonna clue you in so pay attention. When I give my word, I keep it. No matter what. I'm a fair man, but if I make up my mind about something I want, I stick with it. I'm not afraid to go after it, and I'll fight dirty if I have to.

"And one more thing you better get through your head?" He reached up and brushed his finger over the purple and yellow bruise on her cheek, traced his fingers down to feather over the mark on her lip. His gentle touch so at odds with the fierce determination in his expression. "I'm not him, Harper. I'm not the bastard that gave you all those bruises."

His hand fell to gently cradle her side right where, he'd lay odds, she had bruised ribs. She stiffened even more but didn't pull away. Progress? Or did she just not have anywhere else to retreat to? He didn't particularly care. As long as she was listening. "I'm not him. I won't hurt you like that. Not ever. I'd rather cut off my own arm than raise a hand against you, or any woman. Sooner or later, you'll figure that out, Harper. I pray to God it's sooner, for both our sakes. But either way, I'm sticking."

"Sticking?" She blinked up at him, an adorable mixture of lost little waif and indignant siren. While she was still off balance, Aiden took shameless advantage. Ducking in, he stole one last brief kiss, one she didn't even bother trying to fight, he was pleased to note, and then he slipped from the ATV.

"Sticking." Without another word, he stalked away, climbed inside his truck. Aiden turned the key over, and he sat in the idling truck, waiting.

Watching.

Thinking and wondering. Had he played his cards right? Or had he just screwed up? Damaged his chances beyond all hope?

He didn't really know when he'd made the decision. Or even if it had been a conscious choice. All he knew was Harper Colby belonged in his future. He wanted her. Wanted her in his bed, and in his life. Wanted to get the chance to really get to know her. To take care of her and protect her. For today, and for tomorrow too. And maybe for all the tomorrows that came after.

The certainty, the unexpected surprise of his epiphany left him rattled.

Rattled, but resolute.

He'd left his Native American heritage behind when he'd enlisted, the only way he could think of to get off the reservation at the time. Then he'd gone off to war, and life had spun out of control, pushing the old ways farther and farther away. Maybe the old ones would have said the Great Spirit had sent Harper to him to heal his crippled spirit. Maybe they'd say it was the warrior buried deep within calling to him, urging him to take what he knew to be his.

Then again, maybe he was just looking for a convenient excuse for his impulsive decision.

Aiden was usually the type of guy to carefully consider things before he took action. To weigh his options before he committed. The trait had saved his ass more than once.

Except for his promise to Matt. Hadn't had much time to consider that one. But he didn't regret his decision. Coming to the Bar L had been the best thing he'd ever done.

And now there was this attraction to Harper, this determination to shelter her, protect her, keep her a part of his life.

No, attraction wasn't a strong enough word. Because this went deeper than physical chemistry. Though the chemistry between them was there in spades. Her spirit, her passion, her loyalty called to him. Her pride. Her prickly, feisty, self-righteous anger rubbed at his soul.

No, not attraction. Affinity, maybe?

Whatever the hell it was, he couldn't shake it.

Hunger for her boiling in his blood. The desperate need to protect her, to keep her safe. The unquenchable desire to see her smile, to make her laugh, or the urge to tease her and make her forget her troubles. An undeniable drive to make her…happy.

He intended to stick all right. He wasn't going anywhere. And neither was she, if he had any say in the matter.

After an interminable time, obviously refusing to so much as glance his way, the stubborn woman started the ATV and pulled from the parking space. Heaving a sigh, shifting his truck into gear, Aiden followed.

He had an unsettling feeling he'd be doing a lot of chasing after Harper Colby in the days and weeks to come.

****

Harper rolled over and blinked blearily at the alarm clock beside her bed. Six a.m. flashed back at her in blinding neon green. She was still tired. Even after nearly ten hours of sleep. Guess all that nearly nonstop driving had finally caught up with her. She considered rolling back over, going back to sleep for another hour, but she knew it would only make her even more tired.

With a groan, she whipped the tangled blankets off and pushed herself up. The wooden floor was cold beneath her bare feet, and she shivered. She'd have to buy a rug of some kind the next time she went into town.

Moving like a zombie, Harper crossed to the kitchenette and pushed the button on the most important machine in the cabin. The temperature in the cabin was several degrees cooler than the warm bundle of blankets she'd huddled beneath last night. Harper shivered in the T-shirt and shorts she'd slept in as she waited for that precious, fragrant, life-reviving brew.

Wrapping both hands around the sturdy steaming mug, Harper wandered over to stand at the window. She let the strong, hot coffee warm her insides and the crisp morning air cool her skin, shocking her awake. Sort of like jumping out of a hot tub and straight into a cold swimming pool.

As far as the view went, it wasn't the worst one she'd had in her life.

Trees, trees, and more trees. Nothing but wilderness for miles and miles around.

All in all, she was pretty happy where she was. Except for that one pesky fly in her ointment.

Aiden Whitebear.

What was she to do about him?

How could she be attracted to him? How could she have let him kiss her? Twice, for the love of God. She'd just ended a relationship. She'd been committed, regardless of how it had ended. She'd been faithful. She'd thought her relationship with Alexander had been solid...right up until it had ended.

Good grief, regardless of the fact that Alexander had turned out to be an abusive, controlling bastard, what did it say about *her*? About her character? About her morals, or her decision making skills right now? How she could jump so easily from one relationship straight into...well, whatever it was that was happening between her and Aiden.

She had no business even thinking about the man, let alone kissing him.

Shaking her head, she took another long sip, and weighed her feelings. How could she feel guilty about kissing Aiden after what Alexander had done to her? But, on the other hand, how could she not?

And then there was the fact that Aiden claimed there was nothing going on between him and Emmie. It was as if a roadblock had been removed. One she didn't *want* removed. Because that meant Aiden was available after all. Not safely tucked away in that "*taken*" compartment she'd stuffed him into.

*Ugh. I can't think about him anymore. I just can't.*

She'd made up her mind. No more men. She needed to…to level herself out first. And she sure as hell couldn't trust her gut anymore.

*Put that man out of your head. You're here for a fresh start, remember?*

She took her time savoring what she decided would be her new morning routine. Coffee and a view. And when her second cup of bliss was gone, she still had plenty of time to shower. Though she didn't stay under the spray as long as she would have liked. Turned out the water heater was tailor-made for the cabin.

Economy-sized.

After drying off and dressing, Harper took on the monumental task of dealing with her face. Gingerly, Harper probed at her eye. The swelling was completely gone now. She angled her head this way and that, trying to catch the light. Was the coloring getting better?

Or was it just wishful thinking on her part?

Either way, she was determined not to let it get her down. Not today.

So she applied make-up strategically, let her hair air dry. She's chosen what she hoped would be comfortable work clothes but made a mental note to see what Devil's Canyon had in the way of clothing stores. Harper glanced around one last time before locking the cabin behind her.

She was still getting used to operating the ATV, thought she was doing a damned fine job in fact, but she navigated the trail to the lodge carefully, nonetheless. As she pulled up by the back service door, the one Jim had shown her last night, she glanced around nervously. But there was no sign of Aiden. She let out a long, relieved breath.

So far so good.

Chapter Nine

As Harper made her way around the counter of the Great Room to punch in at the office, she overheard voices through the cracked door.

"Has Aiden checked in yet?" Emmie asked.

Harper hesitated, holding her breath.

"Almost an hour ago," a female voice Harper didn't recognize replied. "Said he was taking an Advanced Guided Group up the mountain. Sounded like an all-day ride so he probably won't be back till late."

Just like that, any lingering tension in Harper's shoulders melted away. One less thing to worry about. She really hadn't wanted to deal with him today, or with the whirlpool of churning emotions he seemed to stir up so easily.

Now she just had to get her talk with Emmie out of the way—a talk she was very much dreading. She needed to clear the air. She didn't want anything hanging over her head, particularly where Aiden was concerned. And, despite what Aiden might have claimed last night, that he and Emmie were nothing more than friends, Harper had seen the way Emmie had leaned on his shoulder.

One way or another, Emmie had feelings for Aiden. It was more than obvious the two were close. Harper didn't want there to be any miscommunications or misunderstandings getting in the way. She was here for a job, a roof over her head, and to spend time with her friend. Not for an autumn fling with some cowboy Casanova wannabe.

"Good morning," she chirped as she pushed the door open and stepped inside a brightly lit room.

Emmie stood behind and slightly to the right of the older woman seated behind a behemoth desk flooded with papers and files, folders and office doodads. A matching set of tall filing cabinets stood sentinel on one side of the far wall, on the opposite side was a huge box lined with small cubbies, presumably—by the plethora of assorted folded papers and envelopes—some kind of onsite mail delivery system. And on the wall between the two, an old-fashioned punch time clock. Both women looked up and smiled.

"Harper! You're early. I wasn't expecting you for another half an hour." Emmie bustled around the desk to engulf Harper in hug. This time Harper was careful to keep her arms low, inconspicuously protecting her tender ribs. She gave Emmie's waist a squeeze.

Emmie stepped back. "June, this is my good friend Harper Colby. Harper, June LaMott, the woman who keeps me organized and this place running like a well-oiled machine."

June laughed at Emmie's effervescent introduction as she rose from her seat and stretched her arm across the desk. Shaking Harper's hand with a nice firm grip, she said, "The girl exaggerates something terrible. It's nice to meet you, Harper. I'm so sorry I didn't get to stay last night for the Sunday supper, or I would have met you then."

After a few moments of small talk, Harper caught Emmie's eye. Best to get this out of the way. "Say, Emmie, if you don't mind, I was hoping I could have a word with you."

"Oh, sure." She turned to June. "If you wouldn't mind, could you call Walt at the dealership and let him know we'll take the truck and the plow blade Aiden picked out. Oh, and check in with Stanley, let him know we're still waiting on quotes for those generators that we requested."

"You bet." June was already pressing buttons on the phone as Harper followed Emmie from the room.

Feeling slightly sick to her stomach, Harper waited until they were seated by the big fireplace. She dreaded having to broach the subject. She'd been thinking about it all morning and still hadn't come up with a good way to break the news.

"Before we get started," Emmie said, smoothing her ponytail over her shoulder as she sank down on the oversized armchair, "I wanted to make sure you're settled in all right. Do you have everything you need up at the cabin?"

"I do, thanks."

"It's not too isolated for you, is it? Because if it is, we can do some reorganizing—"

"No, no. It's just fine, I promise. The fresh air and solitude will do me good right now."

Emmie tucked her feet up underneath her. "So what's up?"

Harper bit her lip, shifting uncomfortably on the butter-soft faux-leather. "I…I'm not sure how to say this."

Emmie frowned, tilting her head slightly.

"I don't want you to think I came here with the intention of…that is to say, I never invited anything to happen. I would never, never hurt you. I hope you know that. And I'm so grateful to you for everything you've done for me. The last thing I'm interested in right now is getting involved with—" Dear God, how was she supposed to say this. Emmie had trusted her. Opened her home to Harper, given her a job. She couldn't let Emmie think, even one moment, that Harper had ever set out to betray her.

Now Emmie's frown deepened. "What are you trying so hard *not* to say, Harper?"

Harper drew in a bracing breath, then she just spit it out. "Aiden kissed me last night…twice."

And then she waited for the other shoe to drop.

Emmie sat there, her brow wrinkled in confusion, silent for the longest time. She blinked and angled her head forward slightly.

"Aiden kissed you?"

Filled with remorse, Harper nodded miserably. "Twice. Once before supper…and then again after."

Slowly, a smile spread across Emmie's face, until she was all but beaming with it. "Aiden kissed you!"

Now Harper was the one frowning. She gripped her hands in her lap. Why wasn't Emmie upset?

Quite to the contrary, Emmie was as far from upset as a girl could get. She clapped her hands, her eyes twinkling merrily. "So what did you think? Did you like it? Was he good?"

Harper's lips parted and her eyes widened. This was not how she expected this conversation to go at all. "Why aren't you angry?"

"Why would I be?" Emmie shook her head. "Oh, this is great!"

"No, no it's not." Harper came to the edge of her seat. "I don't think you heard me right. Or you don't understand. He kissed me. Like *really* kissed me."

"Oh, I understand alright. I bet he did," Emmie chuckled. "And I have to say, it's about damned time!"

"What?" Harper asked incredulously.

"Oh, not about you. Though, I mean, seriously, that's great too. But I was talking about Aiden. He's been here three years now, and all this time he hasn't shown even the slightest interest in anybody, romantically that is. And let me tell you, he's been presented with more opportunities than a man could shake a stick at. I'd just about given up hope of him finding someone." Emmie folded her arms over her middle and snuggled back in her seat, the very picture of satisfied. "Well how about that."

"But…but aren't you and he…"

"Aiden and me?" Emmie burst out laughing. Laughed until tears welled. When she finally wound down and caught her breath, she said, "Oh, heavens, no. Aiden is…well, he's Aiden. He's like Tim," she said, referring to her older brother. "Me and Aiden. That's funny." She started laughing again.

Harper shifted in her seat, crossed her own arms, disgruntled now.

"So, you and Aiden," Emmie said on a speculative note.

"No, not me and Aiden either. There is *no* me and Aiden."

"Why ever not?"

"Two weeks ago, I was happily engaged. I thought I was marrying Prince Charming. How can I go from that to…to *kissing* another man, feeling *anything* for another man, so fast? Not that I'm feeling anything. Because I'm not."

"Honey, you're most definitely are feeling something. If you weren't, this wouldn't bother you so much." Emmie put her feet on the floor and stretched to grasp Harper's hand. "I want to tell you something, as an old friend, one I hope you trust."

At Harper's nod, Emmie went on. "From the very few times I spoke to him on the phone, and from things I've picked up here and there from you over this last year, Alexander...well, Alexander was a coldhearted, self-centered, conceited, controlling, abusive asshole. You have every right to go out and find happiness. I would urge you not to wait another day out of deference to that bastard. Trust me, no one here will judge you. So stop judging yourself. And if that happiness happens to be in Aiden Whitebear's arms, then all the more power to you."

"But after what happened with Alexander, I just...I just don't..." She sat up straighter and squared her shoulders. "I have no interest in getting involved with any man, ever again. Not for a long, *long* time."

Emmie's expression softened, sympathy radiated from her. "Oh, Harper. Not every man is Alexander Grant."

"I know that," Harper insisted, bruised pride lifting her chin a notch. "I do."

"Do you?"

"Yes, I do. But that doesn't mean *I'm* ready."

"Sweetie, sometimes it's the one you don't see coming that changes your perspective. The heart doesn't always wait for you to get ready. Sometimes you just have to get back on that horse, whether you're afraid of getting bucked off or not."

Harper didn't know what to say to that, so she

remained quiet.

"Aiden's a good man. Honorable. Dependable. Straightforward." When Harper continued to maintain her silence, Emmie leaned over to give her a nudge and a limber eyebrow wiggle. "Sexy as all get out too, huh? Come on, I bet he's a good kisser."

*Good kisser doesn't even begin to cover it. The man melted inhibitions with his kisses. Melted panties with—*

As soon as the thought crossed her mind, she slapped it back down.

*Not interested, remember?*

Changing the subject, Harper said, "I'm sorry I wasn't here earlier this morning to visit. I got a little turned around on the trails."

"Oh, no worries. It's happened to me a time or two as well. We can get together another night this week. Then you can tell me about those kisses."

She rolled her eyes at Emmie, stood up, and glanced at her watch. "I better get going. I'm supposed to meet Melanie in five minutes to stock up on supplies before we head out to make rounds."

Emmie rose with her, gave her a quick hug. But as Harper began walking away, Emmie called after her, "Don't think this conversation is over, Harper. I'll be expecting details."

Harper closed her eyes, shook her head, and groaned to herself. She should have kept her mouth shut and put Aiden Whitebear as far from her thoughts as she could. So much for trying to do the right thing.

Nearly four hours later, armed with cleaning supplies, a checklist, and her map, Harper pulled her ATV up in front of the cabin dubbed Deer Meadow.

"According to the list, this cabin isn't booked out

until late tomorrow afternoon." Beside her, Melanie angled the clipboard toward the dappled sunlight filtering down through the canopy of red and golden leaves overhead. "But we'll clean it up this morning, on the off chance that the client shows up early. It doesn't happen often, but there's always that exception to the rule, and Emmie likes to be prepared ahead of time, just in case."

Both women climbed out of the ATV, went around to the back of the Mule and began unloading cleaning caddies and fresh supplies.

Once inside, they set to work, falling into the routine they'd established early on in the day. Harper liked Melanie. She was down to earth, friendly, helpful without being bossy.

"How long have you worked at the Bar L?"

Melanie glanced up from the fitted sheet she was tucking in. "Almost two years. Best thing I ever did, coming here."

"I've heard a lot of people say that," Harper remarked as she emptied the trash cans.

"Well, it's true."

"Preaching to the choir, sister," Harper said with a smile.

Just then the two-way radio on Melanie's hip buzzed. "Melanie?" Kathryn's voice crackled over the airwaves.

Melanie unhooked the radio and thumbed the button, "Yep?"

"Harper still with you?"

"She is."

"You girls be careful. Aiden just radioed down that he's spotted signs of bear in the area. So everyone at the higher up elevations, from Rooster's Roost on up to Bear's Den need to be on the lookout."

Harper pulled the folded map from her back pocket and traced her finger from Rooster's Roost north. Dear Meadow sat right smack in the middle of the danger zone. Eyes wide, she glanced back up to Melanie.

"Will do," Melanie told Kathryn, and then she hooked the radio back on her belt. Turning, visibly nervous, she addressed Harper, "I wanna wrap this up as soon as possible. Nothing spooks me more'n bears. I haven't ever run into one, but, oh, lord, the stories I've heard down in town."

Nodding, Harper grabbed a caddy. "I'll clean the bathroom if you want to do the kitchenette?"

"Deal."

Harper made her way into the bathroom. It was slightly larger than her own. But it smelled musty, damp. Deciding a little fresh air was in order, especially since she'd been sniffing toilet bowl cleaner all day, she went to the window and, after flipping the latches, gave it a push up.

The aroma that hit her almost put her on her ass. She slapped a hand over her mouth and nose and instinctively quelled the urge to gag.

"What the hell?" Grimacing, she hurried to shut the window. And as she did so, the curtain moved just enough that she caught a glimpse of something dark in her peripheral vision. Something dark and hairy...and really, really big.

Harper bolted from the bathroom. Melanie glanced around in surprise, a sponge dangling from her fingertips. "What's—"

Harper raced to the front of the cabin. She latched

the screen door, then jumped back to close the inside door and bolt it. Frantic, she backed away, her gaze rapidly sweeping the room.

"Help me, quick," she urged as she rushed to the dresser in the corner.

"What are you—"

"Not now! I'll explain in a second. Just, for God's sake, help me!"

Frowning, Melanie dropped the sponge and hurried over to give Harper a hand. Once the dresser was firmly wedged against the door, Harper crossed to the small window above the kitchen sink and drew the curtain back. She motioned Melanie to join her.

Side by side, the two women peered out the window in horrified silence. There, not ten feet from the rear of the cabin was the biggest, ugliest, most terrifying bear Harper had ever seen.

Chapter Ten

"Oh God, oh God, oh God," Melanie whispered.

Harper glanced over. Melanie was white as a sheet. Her hands clutched at the ledge of the sink, her knuckles bleached of all color. The poor girl looked as though she might drop at any moment.

Letting the curtain fall back into place, Harper slipped an arm around Melanie's shoulder and steered her toward the sofa. "You better sit down before you fall down," she instructed. "Melanie? Sweetie, come with me, okay?"

The girl was pliant but unresponsive, her stare filled with terror.

"Shit," Harper muttered beneath her breath.

She glanced around the room, her mind racing. Not a weapon in sight. What were they to do if that bear decided to play a reverse game of Goldilocks, decided to come in and give the bed a try? Maybe look for a snack?

She drew an afghan from the back of the sofa and draped it around Melanie's shoulders before she took the radio from her belt.

Thumbing the button as she'd been taught, Harper mentally crossed her fingers, and she prayed. "Kathryn? Kathryn can you hear me?"

"I'm here."

"Kathryn, it's Harper. Ah, we have a problem. That bear you warned us about? Yeah, it's right out back of the cabin we were cleaning. Please advise."

"Holy God," Kathryn breathed through the radio. When her voice came through the airwaves once more, it held a definite note of urgency. "Are you outside now? Can you get inside somewhere safe? Where are you?"

"We're at Dear Meadow. We're inside, and the door is closed. We pushed a dresser in front of it, but I don't think it will stop that bear if it decides it wants in. Kathryn, that thing is huge. What do we do?"

Harper felt her control slipping, felt the slippery slope of panic creeping closer. Okay, deep breath. Good air in, panic out. It wouldn't do either herself or Melanie any good if she hyperventilated and passed out.

"Okay, stay calm, honey. I have help on the way."

"I think Melanie is in shock," Harper thought to add, her worried gaze scanning Melanie's unnaturally pale face, her bloodless lips and hollow eyes. A fresh coating of perspiration dotted Melanie's forehead and upper lip. Crouching before the girl, Harper patted Melanie's hands where they were clutched tight in her lap. Her skin was clammy, her hands trembling.

"Christ Almighty," Kathryn intoned. "Okay. Stay inside the cabin, stay quiet. Whatever you do, don't make any noise. Don't draw its attention, and for God's sake, don't startle it."

What kind of advise was that supposed to be? Of course, she was going to be quiet. And she sure as hell wasn't going to do anything to draw its attention.

It wasn't as if she'd intended to go out, tap it on its shoulder and try to take a selfie with it.

"Sit tight. Aiden is on his way."

Aiden?

Her heart dropped to her shoes. Wasn't he on a

damned horse? What the hell was *he* going to do? Hadn't she read somewhere once that bears were faster than horses?

*Oh, God! He could be killed.*

Before she could object, Kathryn's voice burst from the radio once more. "Can you still see it? Can you tell where it is?"

Loud. The radio was too loud. Didn't bears have really good hearing? Could it hear the radio through the log wall? Scrambling, fumbling with the tiny buttons and knobs, Harper hurried to turn the volume down.

She crept closer to the window and cautiously eased one of the curtains to the side just a bit, half expecting to see a big hairy face and razor-sharp fangs peering back at her.

For a moment, she couldn't see anything. The small clearing appeared to be empty. But if she strained really hard, she could just barely make out the soft, muffled sounds of leaves shuffling, of an animal snorting, and…a crack, like something hard had broken. Bracing one hand on the counter, she went up on her tiptoes and craned her neck.

Immediately, she cowered back down. The bear was still out there. Only it had moved closer to the cabin. Tilting her head forward, she scrunched her eyes closed and battled the urge to cry like a baby. Or throw up.

Harper dragged in a shaky breath. She clenched her fists at her side, unclenched, clenched.

*Keep it together.*

She glanced over at Melanie. She had to do something. She couldn't just wait for that thing to come inside and think, "Oh, look! Picnic!"

Harper hurried to Melanie's side. She urged the

nearly comatose girl to her feet and shoved her toward the bathroom, figuring the more walls and doors, the more barriers between them and the bear, the better. Harper closed the lid on the toilet and pushed Melanie down to sit once more. Once she was certain Melanie wasn't going to fall over, she turned and closed the bathroom door with a soft click. Then cursed.

It didn't even have a lock.

Well, there wasn't much she could do about that right now. Maybe the barrier would at least provide them some extra time, maybe it wouldn't.

She tiptoed to the bathroom window, pulled the curtain aside just a bit and peeped out. From this angle, she had a better view of the bear.

The animal was on all fours, hunched over something, its backside to her. It pawed at a big lump of something on the ground, jerking at it with its head. The beast reared up a little and then came crashing back down on its front paws. Once. Twice. Crack. Crack. Then the bears head whipped violently from side to side, like a dog with a tug rope, its furry hide quivering with its efforts.

She couldn't quite see what the animal was playing with…or was it eating? Didn't matter. Either way it was occupied. And if it was occupied, it wasn't trying to break into the cabin. Wasn't trying to eat *them*.

"Kathryn?" she spoke quietly into the radio, her wide-eyed gaze riveted on the animal.

"I'm here, honey. Just hold tight. Aiden's almost there."

"No! He can't come here, not alone. That thing is massive. It's too dangerous."

"He's not alone," was Kathryn's reply, which didn't

help Harper's frame of mind any. He would still be here. Still be in harm's way.

"Kathryn, he could be—"

She did even know what she'd been about to say. For in that moment, the bear lifted its head, its ears perked and alert, and it turned slightly. Just enough for Harper to see the limp human hand dangling from its bloody maw.

A limp *human* hand.

Her vision blurred for a split second, and she let her mouth fell open on a stunned, horrified gasp. But then, just as quickly, she recalled her precarious circumstances and slapped her hand over her mouth. She blinked, shaking her head in mute denial. But the evidence was right there.

Bile rose in the back of her throat, but she forced it down. Breathe in. Breathe out.

It wasn't helping.

That…that bear out there was…was eating…*someone*.

She gagged. Pressing a shaking palm to the wall, she doubled over and gasped for air. When she was steady once more, she forced herself to look again. But the bear was crouched over its prey again, and she couldn't see anything but a hulking mountain of quivering deep brown fur.

"Kathryn! Kathryn, it's eating—"

Her words strangled off when she heard the blare of a horn. Her gaze flew to the door as the honking intensified. The rev of a muscled engine, the spray of gravel seemed awfully loud, even through the layers of wood and glass. She shot one last glance out the window.

The bear reared up on its hind legs, alert and ready

to fight, ready to defend its meal. Certain Aiden would rush around the corner of the cabin at any second, positive she was about to witness his brutal death, Harper's stomach dropped to her shoes. She couldn't move, couldn't look away.

But then the animal dropped back to all fours, the motion enough to break through her terror. She had to warn Aiden. The bear chomped down on the...on the body and began dragging it across the blood-smeared grass. Viscera and ragged flesh. Torn, gory fabric. Harper hunched over the sink and gagged. Somehow, just by the skin of her teeth, she managed to not throw up.

But the sight would be forever etched in her memory. The shredded, blood-soaked flannel and denim. Mud, bits of leaves, twigs and grass clinging to the tattered material. And flashes of ragged, ravaged hunks of...of meat and...

After one last, reluctant glimpse out the window—the bear was gone now, nothing but a bloody trail left behind to mark its direction—she wrenched open the door and ran toward the front of the cabin. Throwing a shoulder against the dresser, she pushed and strained until the dresser had moved enough for the door to open part way.

And then she burst from the cabin like a bullet shot from a gun.

\*\*\*\*

Aiden had barely cleared the front of his truck, a gun in one hand, before his arms were filled with a violently shaking Harper. She wrapped her arms around his neck in a death grip, buried her nose in the crook of his neck and plastered herself against him. She'd hit him so hard, he'd staggered backward a full two steps.

"Is she okay?" Jim asked from nearby.

Handicapped by the gun he wasn't willing to put down until he knew where the bear was, Aiden patted her down with his free hand. "I think so." He wrapped his arm tight around her shoulders, relieved beyond words to see her in one piece, safe and unharmed. "Harper, angel, are you ok? Where's Melanie?"

She nodded her head, her breath coming and going in sharp, jerky sobs. "Gone. It's gone. It was eating— Oh, God, Aiden, it was eating—"

"The bear is gone?"

She nodded again, her head bumping his chin.

"And Melanie?"

"She's in here," Jim shouted from somewhere inside the cabin.

Some of the tension drained from Aiden. Reaching to the side, he set his gun on the hood of his truck. Out of his hands, but still close enough should he need it. Free of the weapon, he urged her head up so he could see her face. She was so pale, which only made the bruises stand out all the more.

He peered into her eyes, one arm around her waist, and he brushed her hair back. His fear had all but consumed him as he'd pushed his truck beyond speed limits that were safe on the trails all the way here from the lodge. Would he make it in time? Would Harper be hurt before he got to her? Would she already be—

He hadn't even been able to finish the thought.

The sheer relief he'd experienced upon seeing her bolting from the safety of the cabin, unharmed and alive, had nearly brought him to his knees.

Before he could speak, she went up on tiptoes and

pressed her lips to his. His eyes widened, then slowly slid shut as her icy lips moved against his, gradually warming. For a split second, he stole control of the kiss from her, savoring the feel of her in his arms, the taste of her upon his tongue and lips. Glorying in the raw heat that rushed through his veins.

But now was not the time, or the place, much as he might wish otherwise. And, he had a strong feeling, if she weren't so frightened, she'd never have acted like that whether, deep down, she wanted to or not. He wouldn't take advantage of the situation.

"Are you all right?" he asked as soon as he broke the kiss, searching her face.

She nodded, clearly struggling to find her voice. Her eyes were glassy. "Okay. I'm okay. Melanie. Melanie's in shock."

*Melanie isn't the only one.*

"Can we go inside?" He'd feel a lot better without the woods closing in all around them…good cover for a predator who lived and hunted in just such foliage. Good cover for a predator who was known for its curiosity and might well double back to investigate. He had the gun, but he wasn't sure it would be enough to stop a determined bear.

She nodded, but he still had to take hold of her wrists and pry her arms from his neck. She was shaking so badly he worried she wouldn't be able to stay on her feet. So he tucked her under one arm, picked the gun up again, and guided her toward the cabin, his alert gaze sweeping the foliage around them. Once inside, he shut the door, noted the dresser's odd placement. Wouldn't have stopped the bear, but he gave her an A for effort.

Melanie huddled beneath a blanket on the sofa,

staring at nothing at all. Concern spiked, and Aiden guided Harper over to sit beside the girl. He'd intended to drop down to eye level to assess Melanie for himself, until Jim waved him over.

"Aiden, you're gonna wanna see this," Jim said, his voice strained. He stood at the counter in the kitchenette, peering out the window, his back to the room.

But when Aiden tried to cross to his side, Harper latched on to his wrist, and she wouldn't let go. His blood ran cold. She'd seen whatever it was that was out there, whatever it was that made Jim sound as if his lunch were trying to make its way back up his throat.

"It's okay. Stay here, all right. I'm not leaving. I'm just going over there by Jim." Gently prying her hands from him, he stole a peek at Melanie. A closer glance at the girl confirmed Harper had been right. She was, indeed, in shock. They needed to get her help as soon as possible.

"Stay here, just for a minute, okay? Can you do that for me?" He smoothed her hair back, worried by the hollow look in her eyes. "Can you…can you look after Melanie for me, sweetheart?"

She turned to look at Melanie, gave a barely imperceptible nod, and slipped a protective arm around her shoulders. Aiden dragged in a steadying breath, tenderness and pride sweeping through him, before he hurried to the window.

The first thing he saw was the bloody trail. He traced the path from the edge of the woods where it had disappeared back, back, back to a huge puddle of glistening, nearly black viscous liquid. Deep red slashes and smears marred the ground all around.

"Jesus," he whispered, covering the lower half of his

face with one hand. But when he glanced to Jim, Jim wasn't looking at the bloody puddle…or the trail. He was staring off to the right. Looking at—

Aiden turned to follow his gaze.

"Holy shit!" He jumped back a step, his stomach lurched.

A massive branch had splintered from one of the big oaks. It hung at an odd angle, splintered, but partly still attached. All along the wide base of the trunk, deep furrows and angry gouges marred the tree.

That bear had been determined, desperate, and damned aggressive in getting to whatever it was that had been hanging from that tree.

And somewhere in the middle of that cockeyed, broken branch was a frayed and bloody yellow rope tied to a…a severed *human* leg.

Slamming his eyes closed, Aiden whipped his head to the side. The first thing he saw when he opened his eyes was Harper staring right back at him, her haunted eyes filled with the grim knowledge of what he'd just seen. As if the pool of blood and the crimson smears all over the back yard hadn't been bad enough.

Jesus, she should never have had to witness anything like that. The urge to protect her was strong, undeniable…and frustrating. Because it was too late. She'd already gotten more than an eyeful. He couldn't shield her from this, much as he might wish otherwise.

Dragging his radio from his belt, he thumbed it on. "Kathryn?"

"Go ahead, Aiden."

"You need to call Jonah Pedersen," he said, referring to the county sheriff. "Tell him he needs to bring an ambulance…and the M.E."

"Oh, lord…the girls…"

"No! No, sorry. Harper and Melanie are okay. They're both all right. Well, Melanie's in shock. Harper, too, I think. Just…just make the call, Kathryn. I'll explain it all later."

Chapter Eleven

Aiden sat beside Harper on the sofa, holding her hand, their entwined fingers locked tight, wishing to heaven and back that there was something more he could do for her. She was so pale. Pale and silent, her eyes huge and glazed.

She was in shock.

That she allowed him to hold her like this in front of Jim and Jonah and a cramped cabin swarming with strangers was a pretty strong indicator. Without even a token of resistance. Proof enough of how traumatized she was by what she'd seen. He had her tucked snug against his side, his arm curled protectively around her, his free hand chafing up and down her arm. Their joined hands rested on his thigh. He ran his thumb back and forth across her knuckles, his heart twisting over how tightly she gripped his hand. As if she feared what might happen to her if she let go.

Seated in the worn green armchair across from them, Jonah Pedersen, Kramer County Sheriff, took notes in a tiny notepad. He ignored the medics fussing over Melanie, the small clusters of men standing around muttering to each other, his focus solely on the woman at Aiden's side.

"Did you see anything else, Miss Colby," Jonah asked, his voice gentle and low, his alert green eyes studying her intently.

Beside Aiden, Harper licked her lips and shook her head in jerky motions. She inhaled deeply, her breath hitching. Aiden tightened his arm around her reflexively. He hadn't left her side since he'd arrived, not even to go with the others when they'd trekked into the woods to follow the garish blood trail. Nor had he left her when they'd come back, some pale-faced, some of them green around the gills. Every last one of them with haunted eyes.

"You're sure you didn't see anyone else around the cabin when you and Melanie first got here? Nothing seemed out of place? Nobody driving away?"

"Jonah, let it go. She's told you all she can." Aiden respected the hell out of the sheriff. But enough was enough. Couldn't Jonah see she's had about all she could handle just now?

About the same age as Aiden, Jonah had taken the job of sheriff only a few short months before Aiden had arrived in Montana, just about the time they'd laid Mark to rest. In fact, Jonah had been present when Emmie had received the official visit to notify her of Mark's death.

The man took his job seriously. Maybe a little too seriously at times. He was friendly but no-nonsense, outgoing and kind. A real dog with a bone when he was on the clock. And direct as hell whether he offended anyone or not. A real shoot-it-straight-from-the-hip kind of guy…except when it came to Emmie.

With Emmie, the sheriff was reserved, unfailingly polite. In short, he treated her with kid gloves. He'd put the young widow on a pedestal as soon as he'd learned about Mark and left her there despite the fact that it was long past time for Emmie to move on.

The sheriff had been carrying a torch for Emmie all

this time, Aiden had figured that out right away. Hell, anyone who wasn't blind, deaf, or dumb as a box of rocks could see it. Anyone, it seemed, but Emmie.

Emmie, as far as Aiden could see, didn't give two extra thoughts to the tall, golden-haired sheriff. The day would come—sooner rather than later, Aiden hoped—that Jonah got tired of holding back and dancing around his feelings for Emmie.

Aiden was Mark's friend and seeing Mark's wife with another man might be difficult. But through the years, he'd become Emmie's friend too. And Emmie deserved a good life, a full life, one with a *living* husband and a house full of rowdy kids and laughter, not a life spent mourning the past and pining for a dead man. Watching the doggedly determined sheriff and the stubborn widow tangle might be damned entertaining.

Jonah shot an impossible-to-misinterpret glance of annoyance Aiden's way. Turning his attention back to Harper, he said, "Okay, Miss Colby, I think I have what I need. If you remember of anything else, anything at all, please give me a call." He dipped his hand into an inside pocket on his coat, and then held out a small business card to Emmie.

Seeming to be running on auto pilot, she accepted the card with a soft, "Thank you."

Watching her hand tremble as it took the card, Aiden swore. He rose, dragging her up with him. "You need anything else, Jonah, you know where to find us." Without waiting for acknowledgment or permission, overwhelmed by the need to get her someplace safe, someplace quiet and away from this horror, he began steering her toward the door and his truck beyond.

He'd think about the blood trail, worry and wonder

over who it might be, what they'd found out there in the woods, and the ramifications for the ranch later. Here and now, Harper was all that mattered.

Once at the truck, Aiden spanned his hands across her hips and helped her up into the truck. It worried him to no end how compliant she was being, letting him put his hands on her like this, letting him lead her around. He snapped her seatbelt into place and reached across her to start the truck. After flipping the heater on high, he paused to look at her. He'd give just about anything to take that eerie, shell-shocked expression from her face. Unable to resist, he reached up and carefully feathered his fingers down the side of her face. The eyes she turned his way were glassy, and blank.

He opened his mouth, but he didn't know what to say, didn't know how to make this better for her, and it was killing him. Swearing to himself all over again, he backed out of the passenger-side doorway.

Jonah call to him from the cabin, "Hey, Aiden, wait up a sec."

Aiden ran one more worried gaze over Harper's chalky complexion. Gritting his teeth, he stepped back and gently closed the truck door, hopefully blocking out whatever it was that Jonah was about to say.

Jonah glanced briefly at Harper through the windshield before turning to Aiden. "You need to put everyone on high alert. That bear out there, it's a man-eater. I've never—" He broke off, passed a hand over his face and shook his head. "I've never seen anything like that in my life."

Aiden frowned, impatiently waiting for him to go on.

"I don't know how much you know about bears."

"Enough," Aiden replied. "I know they normally avoid contact with people. Most attacks result from a bear that's been surprised at very close range, especially if it has a supply of food nearby, or if it's a female protecting her cubs."

"Well, from the leg—what's left of it—still attached to the tree by that rope, I'd say the bear wasn't surprised, not this time."

"You think it was foraging? Wandered close enough to catch scent of whoever it was strung up in that tree? Saw it as another opportunity to prepare for hibernation?"

"I think maybe that's exactly what happened. Which leads us to the question of *how* that body got up in the tree in the first place. And who it was. And was the guy dead or alive when the bear got to him."

All of which, Aiden had no answers. To be honest, once he'd heard that Harper was within mauling distance of the beast, nothing else had penetrated his mind, nothing but getting to her in time, praying that she was safe. And then, once he'd realized she wasn't hurt physically, he'd been too worried about her emotional state. Which was completely unlike him. Worrying over one person enough that other crucial facts fell by the wayside, facts like a severed leg dangling from a tree. Or a half devoured human body.

Aiden crossed his arms. "Did you find anything on the trail? Any ID? A backpack or anything? Any clue as to who it might be?"

Jonah's expression changed, the lines around his mouth and eyes turning grim. "Yeah. We found something all right. Not any ID though. Not yet. Bear's trail went into the woods just behind the cabin. Headed west a hundred yards or so then turned, angling up the mountain."

Aiden frowned. "It took what was left of…of whoever that was up to its den? Wait, don't they usually hibernate in elevations farther up? Beyond five and a half thousand feet? And on the north-facing slopes? We can't be over three and a half, maybe four thousand feet, and we're on the east side of the mountain."

"They do, usually. But we didn't get that far. We found what was left of the remains stashed up under a pile of ripped up bushes and vegetation, buried, for lack of a better term. Looks like the bear planned on coming back later to finish it off."

"Jesus," Aiden whispered, rocking back on his heels.

"Vince Abernathy has some experience tracking bears. Said he figured this one to be a full-grown male, five hundred and fifty, maybe six hundred by the prints and such."

Big enough to do some major damage if it wanted to.

And it had been within striking distance of Harper.

Aiden's stomach flopped over, and he fought a wave of nausea.

"We're gonna need to cordon off the area. It's officially a crime scene now."

Aiden nodded.

"Who rented this cabin last?" Jonah pressed. "How long ago did they leave?"

"Why? Far as I know everyone was accounted for at checkout. Emmie never mentioned otherwise."

The sheriff crossed his arms, mirroring Aiden. "Well, somebody isn't accounted for."

"Emmie would have all the records down at the Lodge. But no one was reported missing or I would have heard about it."

"Could be a hiker, or someone trespassing. All we know is, we have a severed man's leg from the knee down, a pitifully small bundle of what's left of a chewed up man, and a worn hiking boot, size eleven. No ID. I need to start somewhere. Is all your staff accounted for?"

"Kathryn said everyone checked in." Then Aiden frowned, considering.

"What?" Jonah asked, zeroing in on Aiden's expression.

"Could be nothing, but you might want to check on Jeb Decker. He didn't show up for work today."

"That normal for him?"

"No…but we've had some problems with Decker. In fact, I had a bit of a confrontation with him Friday."

"Oh?" Jonah tilted his head. "What sort of confrontation?"

Aiden shot a glance over his shoulder to the woman in his truck. "Look, can this wait? I really need to get her down to the lodge, away from here."

Jonah looked as if he might argue, but then he too glanced to the truck. Harper had tilted her head back against the seat and closed her eyes, but she was visibly shaking.

Jonah drew a deep breath. "Yeah, go on. I'll stop by the stables when I'm done here to finish this conversation."

Aiden dipped his chin on an abbreviated nod before rounding the front of the truck. He climbed into the sweltering cab and slammed the door behind him.

"Harper?"

She was staring out the window now, her unwavering gaze riveted on the tree line. As if she half expected that bear to come charging out at them. At the sound of her name, she didn't flinch, didn't even glance his way.

"Honey, are you okay?" he tried again.

Nothing.

Unsure of what else to do, he shifted the truck into gear. After carefully maneuvering around the myriad other vehicles now littering the narrow trail, he steered them down the mountain. When they were less than a quarter mile from the lodge, Aiden let out a heated expletive and jerked the truck to the side of the gravel trail. He slammed the truck into park and then turned to the silent woman beside him.

"Harper, look at me."

She didn't turn. Just kept right on staring, unblinking, at the trees around them.

"Damn it, you're killing me, angel." He floundered, desperate to get through to her, frantic to connect somehow.

Operating on instinct alone, he pushed the middle arm rest up, unsnapped her seatbelt and reached across taking hold of her waist. Finally, she focused on him. But it wasn't enough, not anymore. He lifted Harper from her seat, turned her and settled her across his lap so they were chest to chest, hip to hip.

"Aiden," she whispered, barely a breath of sound.

With one arm cradling her, he pushed her hair back and then cupped her cheek. His hard stare captured her, held her focus. And then, unplanned, he was kissing her.

At first, she was stiff, cold and unresponsive. But then, by degrees, her lips softened. Her hand crept up his chest, slid around the back of his neck. Her soft breasts pressed tighter against his chest as she melted into his arms.

For a moment, driven by his fear for her, desperate to break through to her any way he could, he gave himself over to the power of the kiss, to the unmitigated strength of the attraction he felt for her. And she responded in kind, kissing him right back, meeting him stroke for stroke. A tiny little whimper left her.

He tore his mouth from hers to trail kisses along her jaw, over her cheek. But when he came back to the corner of her mouth, that's when he tasted it…the salt of her tears.

Pulling back, he searched her face. She was crying now, silently sobbing, damp tracks marching down her face. Relief swept through him. Not that he was happy she was crying. The sight of her tears tore him apart. But crying was a damned sight better than being locked up tight and unresponsive, he figured.

He cradled the back of her head and gently pressed her forehead to his throat, her cheek to his chest. And he murmured encouragement, crooned comfort against her hair as she wept, soaking his shirt.

And as she wept, she rambled on, nearly incoherent, about blood and bears, horses not being fast enough, and doors with no locks. On and on she sobbed, the dam finally having broken. He held her until she wept herself out, until she quieted, until she sniffled and pulled back a bit and looked up at him.

"I was so afraid, Aiden."

"You and Melanie were probably safe inside the cabin. And I'm so sorry you had to see that."

"I thought you were on a horse! When Kathryn told

me you were on your way, I thought— I was so afraid that bear would—"

She'd been afraid for herself and Melanie, but she'd been afraid for him too. As soon as the realization registered, he was left stunned. He blinked down at her, unable to speak. The woman was mystery to him. And, Lord love her, he felt himself falling a little more under her spell.

He captured her chin between his thumb and forefinger, tilting her head until their eyes met. "I'm okay."

"I know," she sobbed, and then, once more, she dissolved into tears.

His heart melted. His shoulders drooped in defeat. He pulled her close once more and let her work her way through this latest round of hysterics. Finally, she quieted. By now his shirt was thoroughly soaked. He handed her a handful of tissues and waited while she dabbed at her face and then blew her nose.

When she was done, she rested her head in the crook of his shoulder and toyed with one of the buttons on his shirt.

"I'm sorry," she said, her nose still stuffy and her voice husky from crying.

Stroking his hand up and down the length of her back, Aiden leaned his head down and kissed the top of her head. "Shh. It's okay. You had every right to be frightened. Every right to cry. Honest to God, I'm glad you did. You were starting to scare me."

"You kissed me. Again," she accused. She leaned back slightly and pinned him with a look, one designed to put him in his place. But it lacked effectiveness considering her eyes were puffy and bloodshot, and her nose was bright pink from crying. She had to be the sweetest, most adorable thing he'd ever seen.

"Uh-huh."

"You can't do that anymore, Aiden."

"Uh-huh." He couldn't help it. The grin got away from him.

Just as she opened her mouth to lambast him, no doubt, he captured her lips once more. This time the kiss started out tender, but it didn't stay that way. Before he realized it, they were both breathing hard, straining to get closer, and his hand was up under her T-shirt. Explosive. That's all he could think. Every time he kissed her. Every time he got her in his arms. Explosive.

Somehow her bra had come undone, and he held her breast in his hand. Her nipple pebbled against his palm as he savored the weight of it, the shape of it, and texture of her skin. He caressed it, molded it. Releasing her breast, he dragged the rough pad of his thumb down over the pearled bud, wringing a soft moan from her, causing her to arch her back. The sound, the movement brought an answering ache to his shaft, and he rocked his hips up against her side.

Harper sank her fingers into his hair, and she curled her knees up tight against his ribs. The moment she released his hair and angled for his shirt, when his buttons popped free and her hot little hand was exploring his bare chest, he lost touch with reality. Aiden started tugging her T-shirt up. His only thought in that moment was getting her naked and getting inside her.

But as she leaned back to accommodate him, her shoulder hit the horn on the steering wheel, shocking them both into awareness. Harper jolted and peered up at him, eyes wide, kiss-swollen lips slightly parted, hair wantonly mussed. She was a siren, luring him in a way he'd never been tempted before.

Dear God, how he wanted to give in.

But it was broad daylight, and they were parked in the middle of a trail that was about to see some very heavy traffic sooner rather than later. In fact, it was surprising they hadn't been interrupted already.

Besides, when he finally got Harper naked, there was no way in hell he was going to be in a rush.

With a tortured groan, he helped her crawl back to her seat and snapped the seatbelt into place; her fumbling hands shook too badly to see to the task herself. The only consolation he had was the fact that this time it wasn't fear that was making her hands tremble.

Chapter Twelve

After seeing Harper safely into the Lodge and Emmie's waiting arms, Aiden made his way to his office in the stables. His body was still strung out on that kiss like a junkie going through withdrawals. Lord, that woman was under his skin.

He nodded to a couple of the stable hands but didn't stop to talk like he usually would. Instead, he closeted himself up in his office, pulled out a stack of spreadsheets, and prayed the work would take his mind off the woman currently turning his life inside out.

A knock at his door caught his attention. He glanced to the clock on the far wall. Nearly half an hour had passed, to his utter chagrin, and he was still staring at the same spreadsheet he'd been looking at since he'd started.

What was worse? He didn't even know what he'd been reading.

Rolling his eyes, rubbing the back of his neck, he tossed the papers to the corner of his desk and groaned aloud. His mind had been spinning circles over Harper. What she'd witnessed today. Her stubborn pride. How she melted every time he got her in his arms. How good she felt once he got her there. And the mystery of what had brought her to the ranch, and to him, in the first place.

"Come in," he called.

The door opened, and the sheriff stepped inside. He

closed the door behind him.

"Everything squared away up at the cabin?" Aiden asked, motioning the man to the chair on the other side of the desk.

"Almost. Gonna need you to keep that cabin and the immediate area closed down."

Aiden crossed his arms and frowned. "How long?" A closed cabin was a loss in revenue. The ranch was doing well, but bottom line, it was still a business. And no business could prosper when its source of income was stunted.

"A few days maybe. Depends on what we find for forensic evidence. Weather's supposed to hold for a bit. I'll probably want to go back up later on today, maybe tomorrow to do another walk through."

"Shouldn't you be up there now?"

"Jeff and Clayton are processing the scene. Randy's assisting." Jeff Darby and Clayton Jensen, two of Jonah's best deputies. And Randy Bartlet, a part-timer on the local police force with a level head. Aiden relaxed a little in his seat. At least the job was in competent hands.

Jonah settled back in his seat, propped his ankle on his knee, laced his fingers over his lean middle. "So, tell me about this confrontation you had with Jeb Decker."

Aiden leaned back in his seat, crossed his arms. "What about it?"

Jonah arched a brow, and he waited.

Aiden heaved a sigh. "The guy's been a real asshole. Takin' advantage of his position, intimidating the staff. Someone worked up the courage to come to me to complain and that, combined with what I was seeing…well, I confronted him Friday toward the end of the day. I basically put it to him that he had a choice. He could change his attitude, and his behavior, or he didn't need to show up Monday. When he didn't punch in for his shift this morning, I assumed it was his way of flipping me the bird, if you get my drift."

"Did things get physical between the two of you?"

Aiden's eyes narrowed. "No."

"Any witnesses to this confrontation?"

"No."

Jonah grunted.

A noncommittal sound if ever Aiden had heard one. And it just plain rubbed him the wrong way.

"If I need to address an employee's behavior, I make it a point to pull that person aside and speak with them privately. People tend to be slightly less defensive, a little more open to constructive criticism if they don't have to maintain a reputation in front of an audience."

"Where did this confrontation take place?"

"Right here in my office."

Aiden watched as Jonah glanced around, his expression considering.

*What the hell's he looking for? Blood splatter?*

"You got a reason for questioning me like I'm the prime suspect?"

"Now, you know I have to ask these kinds of questions, Aiden. I'm just trying to get a handle on things," Jonah drawled, his expression bland, his body language laid back.

Aiden knew that could change in the blink of an eye. He'd seen Jonah in action down at the Keg and Kettle. Soon as Jonah got involved in a bar fight, the fight was over. And not just because he wore a badge and a gun. The man might be lean, but he was tough. He had a mean right hook on him and a jaw of pure steel…and he wasn't afraid to use either of them when the occasion called for it.

"Have you sent someone to check on Decker yet?"

"Yep. Grover should be headed over now."

Aiden nodded. "You sure that's a good idea?"

"In case you hadn't noticed, I'm getting a little stretched thin right about now. Besides, Grover's been Chief of Police for Devil's Canyon since you and I were in diapers."

"That's what I'm afraid of. Decker's got a hell of a temper on him, and Grover isn't exactly in the prime of his life anymore."

"Grover can handle it."

Aiden grunted. Jonah was probably right.

"Any theories about what happened up there?"

Aiden raised his eyebrows. "Why are you asking me? Isn't that what all that fancy forensic equipment and Vince Abernathy are for?"

Jonah shifted in his seat, settling in. While the two were genial acquaintances, they hadn't really hung out much, different circles and all that. There was no active dislike between them, but neither had they gone out of their way to be friendly. Still, Aiden was pretty good at reading people, at least he thought he was. And what he was reading from the sheriff told him the man wasn't so much testing the waters as feeling his way through a difficult situation and doing a damned thorough job of getting all the facts.

"Somebody strung that guy up like a deer carcass waiting to be field dressed," Aiden finally commented. "Why, or how, and what happened before that point, I couldn't even begin to guess. But it's pretty safe to say he didn't string himself up there."

"So that makes it a crime scene," Jonah finished for him. "And what happened after he got strung up, well, it's pretty obvious what happened after that point. Bear drags him down, chews on him for a spell, drags what's left of him off and stashes him for another day. Not typical of a bear, but not unheard of either."

"Aside from Decker, you got any idea who it might be?"

"Not as of yet," Jonah admitted. "Got a deputy checking missing persons data bases in a fifty-mile radius. So far zip. Maybe once we get the remains— what's left of them—back to the morgue…" He shrugged.

Then Jonah stretched his arms above his head, yawned and stood. "In the meantime, keep your eyes and ears open and report anything you think seems strange or anyone that's behaving out of the ordinary."

"What are you gonna do about the bear? Now that he's gotten a taste of human, he might decide to stick around."

Jonah paused by the door. "You might want to keep your crew and clients to the lower elevations if at all possible, at least for a little while. I put in a call to Montana Fish and Wildlife. They'll be sending somebody over in the morning."

Aiden watched Jonah leave. Keeping everyone to the lower elevations would seriously cripple the ranch. Not to mention several of the staff lived in cabins at the higher altitudes. Including himself.

Including Harper.

He wasn't overly fond of the idea of her up there all alone with a man-eating bear on the loose. Granted his own cabin wasn't all that far from hers. A half mile maybe. Give or take. But a half mile could mean the difference between life or death. All things considered, maybe he could talk her into staying with Emmie till the bear wasn't an issue anymore.

But what about the other predator that had invaded their little corner of the mountain? Like he'd told Jonah, that guy hadn't strung himself up in that tree.

Aiden toyed with the pen on his desk, spinning it in circles as he considered that last. A troubled frown pinched his brow. He glanced once more to the clock. Barely five o'clock. Heaving a disgusted sigh, he tossed the pen and pushed to his feet.

Talk about useless. He wasn't getting anything accomplished like this. Not with the memory of Harper's pale face and enormous, vulnerable eyes haunting him.

Not with the need to see her again. The need to touch her and feel for himself that she was okay.

His long legs ate up the distance between the stables and the lodge. He stepped inside the main room, and straight into a heated argument.

"I'll be fine," Harper insisted.

His gaze swung to the long counter to his left. Harper stood on one side, Emmie on the other, the counter between them like drawn battle lines.

"Oh, for the love of God, will you stop being so pigheaded? Just stay here! I'll make up the sofa in my apartment."

"Really, Emmie, it's okay. You've done enough as it is. I just want to go back to my cabin and go to sleep and forget this whole afternoon even happened."

"Harper, I would feel a lot better if you'd—" Emmie broke off, turning to him as he approached. "Thank God,

Aiden, will you please try talking some sense into her? I'm getting nowhere."

Aiden took one look at Harper, took in the way her hands were planted on her hips. The stubborn angle of her chin. The glint in her eyes. And he knew it was pointless.

But he'd try anyway. For Emmie. And for his own piece of mind.

"Harper, Emmie's right. Even the sheriff said it'd probably be best to keep to the lower elevations for a while, at least until we know that bear is gone."

"How can you be sure it will ever go away? Maybe it's decided it likes it here." She pinned him with a narrow-eyed stare. "And what about you? Are *you* going to stay at the lodge too?"

"No, of course not."

"Of course not," she mimicked, crossing her arms. Then she turned to Emmie and, in effect, turned the tables on him. "If he can go back to his cabin, why can't I go to mine? Isn't he in just as much danger as I would be?"

That snapped Emmie's mouth closed. Then she turned to him and braced her hands on the counter. "She makes a point, Aiden. You should probably—"

"Nope," he said, holding up a hand to head her off at the pass. "Not gonna happen. Besides, the lodge is already booked full what with relocating the clients in Coyote's Den, Badger's Sett and Crow's Nest."

"Well, if he doesn't have to stay, then neither do I." Harper shot Emmie a pointed look. "I've done enough running for one lifetime, Emmie. This time I'm staying put."

Aiden's eyes narrowed, his interest peaked. Now

what had she meant by that? He'd lay odds ten to one that it had something to do with those bruises that were finally beginning to turn a sickly shade of yellow.

Jonah wasn't the only one that could be a dog with a bone. Emmie's lips thinned and her brow knitted. "But, Harper, this is different—"

"No, it's not. Not really."

"You aren't running, you're just…relocating till the threat has passed. It's perfectly reasonable."

"Dress it up in all the fancy words you want, Emmaline, it's still the same. My answer is no."

Whatever had her nose out of joint, Harper wasn't about to back down. It troubled him to see her so hell bent on taking a course that could potentially be dangerous. And yet he could read between the lines. The two women were discussing something far deeper than temporarily moving in with Emmie now. Something he was woefully out of the loop on.

A fact he'd soon be correcting.

"I'll make sure she's safe," Aiden said, going with his gut, stepping up to Harper's side. Closer than she was probably comfortable with, judging by the way she shifted her weight to the foot farthest from him, trying to move away, trying to put space between them without *looking* like she was trying to put space between them.

He shifted closer, deliberately slipped his arm around her waist. She stiffened, slanted a warning look his way, but she didn't pull back.

"I'll take you up to your cabin." When she opened her mouth to argue, he rushed to insert. "I don't want anyone out on ATV's up there, not until we know where that bear is."

"How am I going to get to work in the morning?"

His grin widened. "I'll bring you back down. Just think of me as your own personal chauffer for the time being."

She snapped her teeth together. It was little wonder steam wasn't rolling from her ears. The knowledge that she was effectively caught between a rock and a hard place glowed in her eyes. Or maybe it was the light of battle. Either way, she was sexy as hell.

"Fine," she said through gritted teeth.

Aiden turned to Emmie, already preparing to argue on Harper's behalf. But he was brought up short at the sight of Emmie's radiant smile. His eyes narrowed. She grinned at the two of them like a loon.

*What is she up to?*

"All right then," Emmie echoed as if the matter had been settled exactly to her liking. She skirted the long counter and headed toward the door. "Let's go grab a bite to eat at the café, and then you two can head out, call it day."

"But it's barely past five. I've still got—"

"Nothing at all to do today," Emmie blithely informed him.

"Like hell I don't. With Decker gone, I need to—"

"Oh, for Heaven's sake! The ranch won't fall to pieces if you take an evening off. You work too hard, Aiden. In fact, I'm ordering you to take the rest of the day off."

He gawked at her. "What the hell do you think—"

"Ah-ah," Emmie interrupted, shaking her finger in his direction, a smug grin plastered to her impish face. "Boss's orders."

Frowning, Aiden glanced to Harper. She, in turn, shot him a questioning look, her expression puzzled. He was sure he probably looked much the same. At a loss over Emmie's sudden one eighty, they both turned back to Emmie and watched her saunter away with a spring in her step.

Despite Emmie's suspicious edict, she was on her best behavior all through supper, making small talk, jotting down on a napkin some changes Aiden wanted to begin implementing as far as their guided camping trips. And she didn't utter a word of complaint as Harper and Aiden prepared to depart.

"Don't forget your jacket," Emmie reminded Harper.

Harper headed to the pegs beside the door...and to Aiden's coat, the one she'd been using.

Grinning, Aiden beat her to the coat. He lifted it and took great relish in helping her put it on, knowing perfectly well she was probably cussing him a blue streak beneath her breath.

"I intend to go into town first chance I get and find a coat," she hissed over her shoulder, "then you can have this one back, just so you know."

He couldn't resist. As she pushed her arms into the sleeves and adjusted the cuffs, Aiden reached up and gathered her hair in his hand. He pulled the silken tresses from the collar of the coat, and draped them over her right shoulder, letting the warm strands slide through his fingers. Then he leaned in, his chest almost but not quite brushing against her back and placed his lips perilously close to her left ear. Aiden let his breath whisper along her skin in a long, deliberate, sensuous caress.

"Don't rush on my account, angel. I like knowing it's *my* coat keeping you warm."

Her lips parted slightly, and her breathing hitched.

He turned her around to face him with every intention of buttoning the jacket for her. He couldn't help it if he was thinking about the last time he got his hands this close to her breasts. But the moment he released her shoulders, she bolted for the door.

Chuckling, Aiden shot Emmie a brief salute, and then he followed after Harper. Again.

She was already clamoring into his truck by the time he crossed to the parking lot. The woman was fast, he'd give her that. He climbed into the truck, his gaze sliding to her. She even had her seat belt buckled; her hands folded primly in her lap. Wasn't leaving anything to chance, apparently.

He barely stifled the urge to laugh. The woman might claim an aversion to running from confrontation, but she'd been doing a damned lot of it where he was concerned.

What she wasn't taking into account was Aiden himself. He could be a patient man. And a determined one at that. Sooner or later, either she'd stop running, or he'd catch her.

Chapter Thirteen

Aiden flipped on the headlights, turned the heater down but not off, and began navigating out of the parking lot and up the trails leading to the cabins.

The first few moments were spent in silence. Tree branches scraped along the sides of his truck in a few places, reminding him that he needed to send someone up to trim them back a bit. The sun had set while they were still eating, and now the darkness pressed in, giving the warm glow of dash lights an air of intimacy to the cab of the truck.

Surprisingly, Harper was the first to break the stillness. "So how will this bear affect the ranch?"

He thought about it for a moment, considering how best to answer. That she had completely glossed over the severed leg tied to a tree branch was telling.

"Revenue will go down some, I imagine, as the cabins higher up are off limits for the time being. And it's hard telling how long Jonah will want to keep Dear Meadow cordoned off. But we won't be able to keep those cabins closed up indefinitely. And the Advanced Trail Ride will also be impacted too. The last two scheduled guided camping trips will have to be cancelled. It's not ideal, but under the circumstances, there isn't much else we can do. We can't put clients at risk, or the staff."

Silence while she mulled that over.

"Look, I know you said you don't want to stay at the lodge," he pressed, "but I'd feel better if you weren't up here all alone. You could come stay with me tonight."

She hesitated. For a moment, he thought she might agree. But then she shook her head. "That's not a good idea."

"You sure about that?" He shot a wicked grin her way. "It could be a really good idea, if you ask me."

"Is this standard protocol? Closing off part of the Ranch when a bear is sighted." She'd pointedly changed the subject, so he let it go. For now.

"Couldn't say before I got here, but not as long as I've been around."

She finally tore her gaze from the road ahead and glanced over at him. "Is this the first time a bear has wandered onto the ranch?"

"No. But it is the first time one of them decided to make a picnic out of somebody on the premises."

Compressing her lips together, Harper faced the road and fell silent once more. He could have kicked himself for the crude remark. Then again, maybe she needed the reminder of what she could be facing, considering she was determined to stay up here in her cabin all alone.

With a barely stifled sigh, guilt and worry creeping in around the edges, he tried one last time. "Look, Harper, maybe Emmie was right. Maybe you'd be better off if you—"

"No. Trust me, I wouldn't."

He hesitated, debating. *What the hell?* "What were you running from that that has you so determined to stick this out now whether it's crazy or not? Or should I ask *who* were you running from?"

At his direct question, Harper's attention shot to his face. Her eyes were rounded, lips parted. She sucked in a sharp breath as she snapped her focus back to the narrow dirt road ahead.

She was quiet for a long time, and Aiden began to think she didn't intend to speak to him again. He didn't know whether to be irritated with her for her prolonged silence, for keeping everything bottled up inside, or with himself for pushing her too hard too soon.

Then her fingertips crept up to brush over her bruised cheek. From the corner of his eye, he caught the way she licked her lips, the way her fingers trembled. And he held his breath. And then her arm dropped, and she clutched her hands together on her lap till her knuckles turned white.

Remorse stabbed at him. He had pushed too hard, too fast. He should have eased her into it. Waited until she was ready. But, damn it. How was he to know how far to push, or when she'd be ready? Or if she ever would be? Nobody had told him a damned thing about her past. He was floundering here.

He should say something to her, let her know—

Let her know what? That he'd be here when she was ready to talk? How trite was that? Especially when what he really wanted to say was that he'd happily break the son of a bitch who'd knocked her around in half for her—

"His name is Alexander. Alexander Grant."

At the sound of her voice, Aiden turned his head to stare at her face, and damned near crashed them into a tree. She jolted, throwing her hand toward the dash to brace for the expected impact. Aiden whipped his head forward, jerked the truck back onto the road, and muttered, "Sorry."

Slowing down a bit, he kept his eyes on the trail, but all his attention was glued to the woman beside him. His peripheral vision caught her working the fingers of her right hand nervously over her left ring finger, and something inside him seized up, locking down like a drum. Married. She was married. Damn it all to hell.

Somehow sensing she wouldn't want him to stop the truck for an in-depth conversation, he kept driving, strung tight and on the edge of his seat. And he waited.

A few moments later, his patience paid off.

"He is—*was*, he *was* my fiancé."

His pent-up breath slithered from him on a long, relieved sigh. She wasn't married. That was good. A husband would be harder to deal with. Not that it would matter all that much to him one way or another, not if the bastard had been knocking her around and she wanted out. Which she obviously did, considering she was here in Montana and not back in Philadelphia with this Alexander Grant.

But the way she kept twisting the phantom of an engagement ring on her finger told him this situation was bound to be more complicated than he'd imagined.

Yeah, well, when had he ever done things the easy way?

He had a feeling he'd walk through fire for this woman. Which was totally bat-shit crazy, considering he'd only known her such a short time. But sometimes— some *things*—you just knew. And that's what he knew. Absolutely.

For this woman, he would walk through fire.

"I was a stupid, naïve fool," she whispered. "And I lost everything."

That brought his gaze back to her face, albeit briefly.

He was relieved to see the turnoff to Eagle's Nest. He wanted to be able to face her, give her a hundred percent of his undivided attention.

But the turnoff was a double-edged sword as well. Would she stop talking once she realized she had someplace safe to hide?

"How?" he dared to ask, then caught his breath, hoping she wouldn't clam up on him.

She huffed out a breath, tilted her head back and closed her eyes. "I had a job—a damned good job—made a comfortable living. I had a nice apartment, good friends. A great life. And then Alexander Grant happened. Before I knew it...hell, maybe I just had my head in the sand the entire time." She dragged both hands down over her face, heaved a sigh.

"Alexander came from money. He's the youngest powerhouse CEO ever of Tideplex. It's a multimillion dollar acquisitions corporation based in Philadelphia. After just a few months together, he pushed for me to move in with him. It didn't matter to me one way or the other, I just wanted him to be happy, so I did. Pretty soon, his friends and business associates were the only people I hung out with. My friends were just...gone. And then he decided my career was getting in the way, so he managed...somehow, he managed to get me fired, though I'd done nothing wrong."

By now Aiden had angled up the drive to her cabin. He crossed his fingers as he shifted the truck into park, and prayed she'd keep talking.

"I was so angry. Madder than I've ever been in my life. I went to his office to confront him. When I did," she waved a hand randomly toward her lip, "this happened. I guess I was in shock maybe. I couldn't believe he'd hit me. My first reaction was to pack and leave. But that's not how I was raised. I was brought up to believe that when you make a commitment, you honored it. You stuck it out, you know? You didn't just walk away when things got tough.

"So, I gave him another chance. I waited at the penthouse, thinking he'd calm down and we could discuss the situation. Maybe we could get counseling or something. I don't know what I was thinking. Long story short, I learned the hard way that he didn't feel any remorse for hitting me. And he didn't hesitate to do it again. So I snuck off like a thief in the night. And I don't even know why I'm telling you all this."

While she'd been talking, Aiden had turned in his seat. Now he tilted his head, regarding her with a solemn expression. "Because you need to talk about it with someone. And you trust me."

"I don't trust you. I barely know you," she scoffed, but there was no heat in her voice. To the contrary, she sounded drained. Utterly exhausted.

Which she probably was, considering all she'd been through today. Her defenses were low. And he should feel like a total shit for taking advantage of it, but this was the first time she'd really opened up and let him in. He wasn't about to stop her now

Taking a chance, he reached out and smoothed his hand down her hair. "You do trust me, angel. You just don't know it yet."

She opened her mouth to argue, but he pressed a finger to her lips before she could speak. "I won't let you down like he did. But it's early. You need more than the words. So I'll prove it to you. Every day until you believe me. And then every day after that. I just need you to give me the chance, Harper."

She searched his face for what seemed like forever. Then a bittersweet smile twisted her lips, and she shook her head sadly. "I don't think I can, Aiden."

"You can. And you will…because I don't give up so easy."

Without warning, he slipped his hand around to grasp the back of her neck, and he pulled her closer for a moment. His lips found hers, gentle but determined. He wouldn't accept defeat. And his kiss told her so.

She didn't even try to resist. Harper's hand came up and she cupped his cheek. Her touch warmed him to the tips of his toes.

When she finally pulled back, breaking the kiss, a tsunami of emotion swirled over her features. Desire, doubt, confusion, and yes, unless he was mistaken, guilt. Pieced together with the nervous way she was twisting at her ring finger again, it didn't take a genius to figure out what was going through her mind.

"He didn't deserve you, Harper." Aiden reached up and ran the pad of his thumb carefully over the bruise on her cheek, just below her eye. "When he hit you, he gave up any rights he had on you, on your loyalty."

Her brow creased. Aiden took her chin between his thumb and forefinger, squeezed to get her attention. For a moment, her eyes searched his. Hopeful.

But then she clasped his wrist and dragged his hand down and away. She shook her head again. "I'm sorry, Aiden. I just can't do this."

With that, she climbed down from the truck and hurried to her cabin. He thought about going after her. But he knew it wouldn't do any good. Not yet. In fact, it might drive her to run yet again. And that was the last thing he wanted.

Heaving a soul deep sigh, he waited until she closed the door behind her and flipped on a light in the cabin, and then he shifted his truck into reverse.

He could wait. He'd meant what he'd said. He would prove it to her. He just needed time to do it.

****

Harper woke up much as she had the morning before. With her stocking-covered feet on the cold wood floor and a steaming mug of coffee clasped between her hands. She leaned against the window frame, her shoulder pinning back one side of the curtains, as she watched a squirrel dart across her driveway, the stem of an acorn clamped in his little mouth.

Where yesterday the woods all around had rejuvenated her, today they pressed in on her, made her wary. Was that bear still out there somewhere nearby? Would it be safe to venture out? How would anyone even know?

Then again, maybe her nerves were a product of a poor night's sleep. A night spent tossing and turning, reopening not-so-old wounds and recalling the look on Aiden's face, the words he's spoken to her...the way he'd touched and kissed her. She rolled her head on her shoulders, trying to work out some of the kinks. And then she took another long sip of the bracing brew.

He'd had it wrong when he'd implied she might feel guilty or disloyal about kissing him.

And, even as the thought crossed her mind, she called herself a liar.

She *had* felt guilty. Like she was betraying Alexander. But that was just crap. Because Aiden *had* gotten something right. Alexander didn't deserve her loyalty. He didn't deserve *her*.

But it wasn't that easy to flip a switch on and off on your emotions, was it? She didn't love Alexander anymore, couldn't after what he'd done to her. But how could she develop feelings for someone else so quickly? Not that she had feelings for Aiden.

Or did she?

She was certainly attracted to him. Admired him for what he'd done for Emmie. But the way he made her feel when she was with him, the way he looked at her sometimes…

Good grief, what was she to do with him?

She'd known the man less than a week, and he turned her inside out. He'd just stepped right into the middle of her life like he had every right to be there. Seemed to view himself as her caretaker of sorts, giving her his coat, chauffeuring her around, dishing up plates for her, rushing to her rescue. Taken over her every waking thought.

Just like Alexander had done.

But then she backtracked. Not *exactly* like Alexander, if she were being honest.

Aiden was…different. A whole other kettle of fish. And she didn't even know where to begin sorting him out or sorting out her feelings where he was concerned.

Giving a disgusted groan, she downed the rest of her coffee and turned from the window. If she didn't hurry up, he'd be here to pick her up before she was even out of her shower. And there was no way in hell she was greeting him in a towel. The frustrating man would probably take it as an invitation.

A slight thrill shot through her at the thought.

She rolled her eyes and shoved the thought, and the

thrill, away. No. She wasn't going there. Not even in her imagination.

*Think ten foot pole, Harper.*

She washed and rinsed her mug, turned it upside down in the strainer to dry. And then she rushed through the rest of her morning routine.

She'd just applied the last coat of mascara, blinked at her reflection, when the throaty rumble of his truck approached the front of her cabin. She slid the tube of makeup into the small padded pouch, dropped the bag on the back of the sink, and then hurried to grab her coat. Aiden's coat. She picked the heavy jacket up and, unable to resist, pressed the thick material to her nose to steal a quick sniff.

Lingering wisps of his cologne, woodsy musk and fresh air and man, loosed wild flutters low in her belly.

Shaking herself free of those dangerous flutters, and what they meant, she tugged the coat on. Stupid. Weakening her defenses when she was about to face the man himself.

*Not smart, girl. Not smart at all.*

Squaring her shoulders, she opened the door just as he was lifting his hand to knock. His smile stretched wide as he let his gaze travel down over her and back up.

"Mornin', beautiful," he drawled, his voice a little husky with the early hour, and a whole lot sexy. And then, before she could step back, indeed, before she even anticipated that he might do something like that, he leaned down and dropped a kiss on her surprise-parted lips. A brief press, chaste almost…if not for the heat in his eyes. "You look good enough to eat."

"Don't. Just don't." She reared her head back, pressed her lips together and scowled up at him.

"Not a morning person, are we?" The corner of his mouth edged upward.

She jabbed a finger at the middle of his chest, pushing him back a step, and she narrowed her eyes at him. "So help me, if you make some lame wisecrack about morning sex improving my mood, I will not be held responsible for my actions."

Now his grin was full on, heart-stopping wicked. "You said it, angel, not me."

She huffed and shook her head, elbowing past him. But he was quick. He strode around her and opened her door, held his hand out for her, the perfect gentleman. She gritted her teeth, glared at the hand, and climbed inside the truck. But he, apparently, wasn't done assisting her. So she did her damnedest to ignore the warmth, the size and strength of the hand he slid beneath the bottom edge of her coat—his coat—as he clasped it against her hip to help her up and in.

She glowered at him and quickly snapped her seatbelt in place before he could reach to help her.

He attempted to make small talk on the way down the mountain. She maintained a stony, stubborn silence. As they pulled into the parking lot beside the lodge, and Harper reached for her seatbelt buckle, his warm hand closed over hers, stilling her movement. She glanced up, questioning.

Aiden reached around the steering wheel with his left hand and shifted the truck into park. Then, without warning, he leaned across the seat and kissed her again. A real whopper of a kiss.

Damn the man.

But her chagrin didn't last long. It melted away beneath the intensity, the sheer lust he submersed her in.

Mid-kiss, he cupped her cheek, tilting her head as he deepened the contact, dragging her straight into a maelstrom of unquenchable desire.

She grasped his wrist, not to pull his hand from her face, but to anchor it in place. And she met him stroke for stroke, actively participating. When she was seconds from climbing over the seat to crawl into his lap, he broke contact for a split second. Long enough for her to blink up at him in confusion. Then he dropped one more brief peck on her lips, one she willingly, if absently met part way.

He leaned back in his seat, a self-satisfied smirk on his face. "Have a great day, gorgeous."

Her lips parted, and she tilted her head, frowned. Lost. What had just happened?

The moment he touched her…she was lost. Her body. Her thoughts. Her resolve.

Before she could blast him for kissing her again, he turned away and jumped from the truck, slamming the door behind him. Her breath left her in a rush, deflated.

"Damn it," she muttered, flinging her seatbelt off.

He'd already rounded the hood of the truck by the time she'd gathered her ire around her like a shield. Aiden opened the door for her, then held a hand up to assist her down.

Feeling petty, she pushed his hand away and hopped down under her own steam. And steaming she was. How dare he keep doing this? Kissing her without permission, without warning, getting her motor revved up and then pulling back. Like he wasn't as worked up as she was. When she damned well knew better. His breath had been every bit as choppy as hers. And she'd seen the way he'd readjusted the bulge in his pants before he'd slammed the door closed behind him.

Wait, that wasn't why she was mad. She was mad because he'd kissed her. Again. When she didn't want him to. Yeah, that was why. Nothing more.

His hand settled on the small of her back as he came up beside her. She glanced sideways at him, ready to lay into him, but they'd already reached the base of the wide stairs, and the radio at his side went off.

"Aiden," a masculine voice said.

He paused midstride and pulled the radio from his belt. "Go ahead, Jim."

"You need to get to the lodge as soon as possible."

Aiden's brow pulled tight as he picked up his pace, propelling Harper along beside him with his free hand. "I'm here. What's going on?"

"It's—" The radio cut off for a moment, then, when Jim's voice came back, it was strained. "Jesus, you better get in here quick."

Chapter Fourteen

Aiden took in the scene in a glance, and nearly rocked back on his heels, utterly floored. Nearly.

Instead, he gave Harper a firm nudge back toward the door, wanting her out of the room and away from what looked to be an impending, nasty brawl. Then, cursing when she only sidestepped toward the far wall, he rushed into the fray.

The normally quiet, good-natured Todd Sweeney stood toe-to-toe with a guy that easily outweighed him by at least fifty pounds and was wearing seasonal hunting camouflage. Veins bulged at the side of Todd's neck and forehead. His face was florid. His expression one Aiden had never seen the mild-mannered stable boy wear before.

The hunter bristled right back. His companion, similar enough in features to pass for a younger brother maybe, gripped the hunter's elbow, tugging him back to no avail.

"Apologize, now," Todd roared.

Emmie stood just to the side and slightly behind Todd, her hand on his sleeve, frantically tugging. "It's all right, Todd."

"I ain't got nothing to apologize for," the hunter shouted right back. "I got reservations. I paid in advance."

"Calm down, Gavin," his buddy interjected. "I'm

150

sure we can—"

"The hell I'll calm down." He gave his elbow a vicious jerk, but his friend wouldn't be dislodged.

Aiden inserted himself between Todd and the two straining men, put a hand on Todd's chest, and pushed a little space between them.

"What the hell's going on?" he barked. Looking between them.

"I understand you're upset, Mr. Thompson, but as I explained," Emmie rushed to address the hunter, "we just can't allow guests to stay in the cabins at the higher altitudes while the bear is still in the area. I'd be happy to give you a full refund or find other accommodations for you. But I just can't offer you a room here in the lodge as we are booked full."

"Apologize," Todd barked over Aiden's shoulder.

"Who's gonna make me, you?" Thompson taunted, completely ignoring Em.

"Fuck you, asshole," Todd snarled, pressing forward once more, bumping into Aiden's back. "You'll eat your words, and your fucking teeth."

At the shocking outburst, Aiden's alarmed gaze swerved around until he peered over his shoulder at Todd. The brief moment of inattentiveness on Aiden's part afforded the hunter the opportunity to move closer. Jim rushed forward and grabbed the hunter's shoulder.

"Emmie, damn it, get back," Aiden ordered as he wrestled with the two straining men. The last thing he wanted to have to worry about was her getting hit if fists started flying. Which looked like a damned good possibility just then.

Harper leaped forward, and Aiden drew a ragged breath to warn her away as well but stopped when he realized she was only pulling Emmie out of the line of fire. Turning his focus back to the mess at hand, he gave Todd a shove back, bracing both his hands on the slightly smaller man's chest. He was surprised by the resistance he felt. Behind him, Jim waded into the middle of the scuffle as he dealt with the hunter.

"Todd! Todd!" Aiden yelled until he finally got the man to look at him. And the moment their eyes connected, Aiden jerked back a little. If he didn't know better, he'd swear he didn't know this man. Pure rage emanated from Todd. His eyes were cold and flat, merciless. Hungry for violence.

But then Todd blinked. Seemed to come into himself again. "Aiden?" He glanced around with a frown, caught sight of Emmie and Harper standing a little off to the side, looked to the red-faced hunter, and his expression darkened all over again.

"Todd," Aiden said sharply, pulling Todd's gaze back to him. "Go to the stables, now."

Todd hesitated, and Aiden feared he might disobey, or argue. Or take a swing at the hunter. But then, his shoulders drooped, and Todd did an about-face. He left through door behind the counter.

Aiden watched the closed door Todd had just gone through for a moment longer, unsettled.

"I don't know what kind of bullshit operation this is, but ain't no way in hell you people are gonna get off insulting me like that." Thompson finally succeeded in jerking his arm from his buddy's grip.

Aiden turned to the irate hunter. "Okay. I think we all just need to calm down so I can figure out what's going on here."

"I'll tell you what's going on. I plan this vacation for

three fucking months, pay my reservations well in advance," the hunter snapped, stepping aggressively up into Aiden's space. His arm swung out to the side, and he pointed at Emmie. "And when I show up, that bitch tells me I ain't got a place to stay, that I can't hunt on this mountain." He gave Aiden's chest a hearty shove. "And some punk-ass creep gets up in my face telling me I need to fucking apologize. Now I got you," another shove, "gettin' up in my business."

"First, you need to keep your hands to yourself," Aiden warned, his tone going quiet and dangerous.

"Gavin—" his friend warned.

Ignoring his friend completely, Thompson pushed farther into Aiden's space.

"Yeah?" Another shove. "What the fuck are you gonna—"

Instinct and training took over. In the blink of an eye, Aiden had the hunter bent over the counter, his cheek slammed down and held in place on the cold hardwood by Aiden's elbow. Aiden had the hunter's arm bent up at an uncomfortable angle, twisted high on his back. He hooked an ankle around the hunter's calf, ready to drop him to the floor if need be. The hunter howled, the sound filled with shock and pain.

"Now, let's try this again," Aiden said, just as quiet, just as dangerous as before. "Only this time, we're going to start with that apology."

"I'm sorry, man. I'm sorry," Thompson wheezed.

"Not to me." Aiden twisted a bit, maneuvering around so Thompson had somewhat of a view of Emmie. The motion wrung another painful grunt from him.

"I'm sorry, ma'am," he groaned.

"Now, I'll tell you what's going to happen. Your

card will receive a full refund. You're gonna collect your bag from the floor over there, and you're going to get in your car and clear out. I don't care where you go, but you're gonna get off this mountain, you feel me?"

The hunter moved his head, as much as he could with Aiden pinning it this way, a nod of acknowledgement. Still, Aiden waited a moment longer, keeping a wary eye on the hunter's companion all the while, just to be sure.

"Yes, yes," the hunter wheezed once more.

Aiden released him and stepped back, alert, and ready to tangle again if need be.

But the hunter had had enough. Thompson hurried over, snatched up his bag, and then he and his companion all but ran for the door. As soon as they were gone, Aiden moved toward the women. His concerned gaze skimmed over Harper before coming to rest on Emmie.

"You okay?"

Emmie, her arms wrapped around herself, nodded, turning her gaze from the doorway. Not the door the hunter had left through, but the door Todd had exited. Todd's behavior must have taken her by surprise as well. "Yeah. I'm fine."

"What happened?" Aiden was vaguely aware of Jim coming back from the front door where he'd gone to make sure the hunter had followed through with Aiden's instructions.

"He's gone," Jim murmured.

Aiden nodded; his focus still pinned on Emmie's pale face.

"I tried all day yesterday, ever since the," she flicked a glance to Harper, "the incident up at Dear Meadow, to get Thompson on the phone. But I couldn't get through to him, kept getting a full voicemail box. Then he showed up a little bit ago. I tried to explain to him about…well, everything. But he was irate that his cabin was in the off-limits area. I would have given him a room here in the lodge but we're booked full, so I offered to make arrangements for him elsewhere. He became belligerent, started swearing at me. That's when Todd came in."

"He was helping in the office, emptying trash cans, that sort of thing," Jim chimed in. "I was in the office clocking in. When we heard Thompson yelling at Emmie, Todd damn near knocked me over rushing out here to help her. He got up in Thompson's face, demanding he apologize to Emmie. I thought they'd come to blows, Aiden, I swear to God! I don't know what got into Todd. I've never seen him that stirred up before."

Aiden reached out and ran a hand up and down Emmie's arm, squeezed her shoulder lightly. "You sure you're okay?"

"Yeah, he never got anywhere near me, thanks to Todd I guess."

"Okay." He turned to Jim. "You go on down to the stables, check in on Todd. Let me know if there are any problems. Then you can get after trimming those trees back like we discussed on the radio this morning. Take Bruce up with you. I don't want him in the stables right now pushing any of Todd buttons. You two be on high alert. Take a gun with you."

"Will do, boss." Jim spun around and trotted from the room.

Turning back to the women, Aiden caught the way Harper was staring at him, wide-eyed. Damn. Hopefully he hadn't frightened her. But just as he made to go to her—he didn't even know what to say to her—she turned to Emmie and grabbed her up in a quick squeeze, stalling Aiden.

"I'm going to get to work, unless you need anything?"

"No, I'm fine. Go on, I'll see you later. Be alert out there, okay?"

"I will."

Without another glance his way, Harper bolted for the door. Aiden watched her go, frustrated beyond belief. That old saying, one step forward, two steps back, ran through his head.

Heaving a sigh, he faced Emmie. "Let's go to your office."

Nodding, she set off down the long hallway toward the wing opposite the conference rooms, stopped at the door at the end of the hall. Once inside, she took her seat behind the tidy desk. Aiden dropped onto one of the thickly padded seats facing her. He propped his ankle on his knee, braced his elbows on the armrests.

"Did Jonah talk to you about what happened up on the ridge by Dear Meadow yesterday?"

"Some," she said, leaning back in her chair and crossing her blue jean clad legs. Exasperation was thick in her tone. She rolled her eyes. "But you know how he is. Sugarcoats everything. Like I might wilt away if I hear anything remotely unpleasant."

It was the first time she'd ever acknowledged the way Jonah tried, in his own ass-backward way, to protect her.

"I'm sorry. I should have stuck around last night so we could talk about it."

"No, Aiden," she countered, holding up a hand to interrupt. "You were right where you needed to be. The last thing Harper needed was to hear us rehashing all that. Thank you, by the way, for looking after her like you have been. I've been doing a damn poor job of it, and she's been through too much as it is."

He waved that aside. "You're busy, Emmie, running this place. She understands that. Though, I wish to God someone would have filled me in about her ex."

He wasn't doing Emmie a favor by looking after her friend. He was simply…watching out for the woman he was interested in, the woman he was attracted to beyond reason. A woman that baffled him and irritated him, ticked him off sometimes and made him question his own sanity.

His instinct urged him to follow her around today, make sure she didn't get into any more trouble. Indeed, danger seemed to tail her like a stray puppy. But he knew she wouldn't appreciate it. And besides, he had his own job to do. Which brought him back to the matter at hand.

He quickly and concisely…and admittedly with as little attention to gory detail as he could manage, all things considered…filled Em in on what had gone down at Dear Meadow yesterday. They discussed options for the reservations for the cabins presently off limits. Then they hashed out details of day-to-day operations, deciding to go ahead with the plans they'd already set in motion over the purchase of two new mares despite the temporary crimp on revenue.

"Before you go, Aiden, there's one last thing. I had one other guest come in this morning." She seemed indecisive, troubled. Like she was second-guessing herself. And that wasn't like Emmie.

"Okay?"

"Well, I rented him Badger Sett."

"Single or family?"

"Single. He was insistent—polite," she rushed to explain, given, he imagined, the experience with Thompson, "polite and charming, but determined that he stay with us. He paid double the going rate for the cabin."

Aiden frowned. "Double?"

"Yeah."

"For how long?"

"Two weeks, with a possible extension."

"Double, huh?"

Emmie crossed her arms. "Yeah. But he flashed a lot of cash. Had expensive new gear, and a Rolex. Didn't look like our typical hunter type. But who can say? Maybe he's one of those weekend warrior types. Maybe he's from big money, used to getting what he wants, and right now he just wants a quiet couple weeks away. I put him in Badger's Sett, figured it was close enough to Cougar's Den if he had problems."

Close to Eagle's Nest too, he reflected, not liking that so much. His eyes narrowed. "Where's he from?"

"Back east. Pennsylvania driver's license."

All the hair on the back of Aiden's neck stood on end. He narrowed his eyes. "Alexander Grant?"

Emmie's brow creased. "Of course not. I'd never let him stay here, not after what he did to Harper," she scolded.

He should have known better than to even suggest it and felt bad as he soon as he had. Still, the whole thing didn't sit right. Men who knocked their spouses or girlfriends around tended to be possessive. Wouldn't have just let her walk away without a fuss. "Have you ever seen Grant? Would you know if it was him with a fake ID?"

"I've seen pictures of him with Harper. Believe me, it's not the same guy. Wait a second," her brows arched, "she told you about Alexander?"

"Some. Last night."

"*Well.*"

"Don't '*well*' me like that," he said, shaking his head. "She was messed up over the bear incident, exhausted. And regretting it this morning. Did you tell the guy about the bear?"

"Of course." She scowled at him.

"What about the leg tied to the tree and what that meant? That there's a killer up here?"

Emmie shifted in her seat. "No, that part I left out. That's what I'm second guessing. At first, I figured, let Jonah do his job. And it was bad enough that we had to close half the ranch down. Then the guy offered double and…well, honestly, I thought the bear would be deterrent enough."

"And we don't want to spook the rest of our guests."

"Not if we don't have to," Emmie confirmed. "Could be it was a onetime deal, a crime of passion thing."

Aiden didn't say anything for a moment. Dropping his foot to the floor, he ran his hands along the top of his legs, mid-thigh to knee, and stood up.

"Don't worry about it. I'm sure it'll be fine. In fact, if it would make you feel better, I'll stop and check on him off and on." And in the process, give himself a chance to scope out the situation and get a handle on the man for himself.

"Thanks, Aiden." Emmie smiled up at him. She

reached for a stack of papers, shuffled them until she found the one she wanted. As she scanned, she absently said, "He went into town for supplies and to look around a little bit ago, but he should be back this evening, or he said. He also said he wouldn't be eating at the lodge at all when I mentioned the café. Likes his privacy, I guess."

"Ok. I'll keep the check-ins brief." Aiden reached for the doorknob.

"Ah, here it is," Emmie said, glancing up from the registration ledger. "His name's Smith. John Smith."

Aiden tipped his head in acknowledgment and closed the door behind him.

Chapter Fifteen

Todd paced the length of the stables, ran agitated hands through is hair. Nearby horses snickered and moved nervously in their stalls, shuffling and thumping the walls.

"It's my fault. I shouldn't have gotten in that hunter's face like that. I should have just gone for help like I normally do."

"No," Danny said, a little calmer now. "Stop beating yourself up, Scooter. You tried to do the right thing for once. I'm proud of you for trying…but you see what happened, don't you? This is exactly why you need me. This is what I'm supposed to do. I'm the one that looks out for you. You need to let me handle these kinds of situations."

Cold fear swept through Todd. "But—"

"No, Scooter. Now you listen to me. This wasn't your fault." Danny's voice dropped, filled with venom. "It's all that hunter's fault, pickin' on our pretty little Emmaline."

Todd trembled. He was sick to his stomach. He'd been so vigilant never to talk to Danny about Ms. Emmaline, prayed she'd pass below Danny's radar. He'd always been extra careful, never to let Danny near Ms. Emmaline, or Aiden. Tried not to ever let Danny come with him to the ranch at all. But that was stupid, wasn't it? He'd never been able to control Danny. And look how well he'd managed to keep Danny from going after Mr. Decker.

"I was just trying to look after Ms. Emmaline, stand up for her."

"Well, you screwed that up, that's for sure," Danny snapped. "Damned near got your ass handed to you too."

"Aiden wouldn't have let that happen," Todd rushed to placate Danny. But all he did, it seemed, was make Danny angrier.

"Making sure you don't get your ass handed to you is *not* Whitebear's job. It's mine."

"Aiden was only trying to help. He's a good man. He's always nice to me. He—"

"Nobody can take care of you like I can," Danny snarled. Todd had only meant to point out how Aiden wasn't a threat to them, but in defending Aiden, he'd stirred up Danny's temper.

And when Danny was angry, bad things happened. Really bad.

"I know. I know, I'm sorry. You're right." He was just messing everything up today. He wanted to curl up in a ball and cry. Maybe he'd even frightened Ms. Emmaline. Maybe she wouldn't want him around anymore. "I was only—"

"Trying to help. You help in the stables, where you're good at helping, Scooter. You let me worry about the rest."

"But Aiden said—"

"I don't give a damned what Whitebear said. You listen to me, little brother. I know what's best for you, don't I?"

"Yes, Danny." He ducked his head.

"That's right. I know what's best." Placated, Danny

fell silent for a moment. Then, his tone turned speculative. "Boy, oh boy, how about that friend of Emmaline's though, huh?"

While it was comforting to hear the anger leave Danny's voice, his interest in Ms. Harper made Todd uneasy.

He twisted his hands together and tried his best not to let how he was feeling show on his face. Or in his voice. "What do you mean?"

He never knew how Danny might react to someone or something, so he'd always gone out of his way to keep Danny separate from the ranch. He loved it here, loved his job. He didn't want Danny to do something to cost him his job.

And Ms. Harper had been very nice the few times they'd spoken. Considerate and kind. She'd treated him like an equal. Not somebody stupid to talk down too. Though she'd tried awful hard with makeup and sunglasses, she hadn't been able to hide the bruises on her face. He felt bad that somebody had hurt her.

He didn't want to see her hurt again. And it might not be safe for her if Danny decided she was for him.

And even as the thought crossed his mind, he felt guilty. He owed Danny a lot. He shouldn't doubt his brother, shouldn't fear him. Shouldn't begrudge him any happiness.

"Oh, come on, Scooter, even you had to notice all those sweet curves. Now, Emmaline's a looker. Easy on the eyes and all that. But that Harper," he let out a lecherous whistle. "She's a sweet piece of work. A man could take a nice long, slow ride on all those curves and still—"

"No!"

"What was that?" Danny's voice dropped warningly.

Panicked, Todd swung around, his frantic gaze flying to the door at the far end of the stables. What if someone came in? Found Danny here? Or, God forbid, heard him talking about Ms. Harper that way.

She was Aiden's woman. Or would be soon. It was pretty obvious, the way Aiden acted around her. And that Danny was currently put out with Aiden wouldn't help the situation.

Oh, could things get any worse today?

"Ms. Harper is off limits, Danny. Please don't—"

"Off limits?" Danny stopped pacing. "Because you think Whitebear is staking a claim?"

Todd swallowed the bile rising in the back of his throat. How could he fix this? He loved his brother, loved him desperately. But he felt a great deal of loyalty to Aiden too. Torn, Todd started pacing, ran his suddenly sweaty palms across the flannel of his shirt, down the denim on his jeans.

"Well now," Danny crooned in that way of his that made Todd's skin crawl. "We'll just have to see about that, won't we?"

Filled with anxiety, Todd scrambled for something to say, anything to divert Danny's attention from Ms. Harper and Ms. Emmaline.

But he was saved by none other than Danny himself.

An eerie smile crept over Danny's features, and Todd went bone still. Danny rubbed his hands together. "So tell me, Scooter, what are we gonna do about that hunter?"

****

Harper cursed her luck. She'd been cleaning one of

the cabins closer to the Lodge, Coyote Den, when she'd realized there was a pipe leaking in the bathroom. She'd tried her best to fix it, but with a limited supply of tools, and even less knowledge, she'd finally admitted defeat.

And so, in spite of fervently wishing she had another alternative, she'd gone in search of Aiden. After being redirected several times, she finally located him in a midsized shed set off and behind the stables.

As she cleared the door, her eyes adjusting to the change in light, she came up short. All she could see of him was a grease rag hanging from the back pocket of a faded pair of jeans, and long legs as the rest of him was currently lost somewhere beneath the hood of a rusty old Ford pickup truck.

She paused there, just inside the doorway, and she admired the view. She was a healthy, red-blooded woman, wasn't she? The man, frustrating as he might be, had a gorgeous rear end.

Just then, he leaned back, and his dark head came into view. He shook his hair back, ran a grease-smeared forearm along his hairline. He'd shed his button-down flannel, and his baseball cap. His broad shoulders and defined muscles stretched his faded red T-shirt to mouthwatering perfection. The random smears of dirt and grease on his clothing and his deeply tanned skin only served to enhance his sex appeal.

"Try her again."

Only then did she realize there was someone else in the shed with them. A young kid, barely sixteen if he was a day, sat behind the steering wheel. Richie, she recalled, though she couldn't remember a last name. He was a part-timer, worked in the stables if she recalled correctly.

Drawing a deep breath, she glanced around, taking

in the rest of her surroundings. Inside, the structure looked like a well-used, two-stall garage. A massive toolbox took up most of the right side of the back wall, and a battered bench seat from some kind of truck took up the rest. The floor was old, pock-marked concrete. Car ramps, a huge fifty-gallon drum with a pump on top, an odd tire, and various other mechanic paraphernalia littered the outer spaces.

Aiden cocked a hip and watched the motor, appearing to listen intently as Richie turned the engine over. The ignition caught, and the ancient beast roared to life. Aiden stood for a moment more, wiping his hands on the rag that had formerly hung in his back pocket as he listened.

At length, he nodded to himself, gathered up the array of tools that littered a dirty towel on the top of the corner panel. He dropped the hood on the truck and gave the young man a thumbs up. "You're good to go, Richie."

"Thanks, Aiden. I owe you, huge! I'll see you tomorrow after school." With that, Richie backed from the shed. Aiden pushed a button on a remote on the end of a thick cord that hung from the ceiling, and the huge overhead door began rumbling closed. Then he turned to the ginormous toolbox behind him and began putting tools away.

"You comin' in, or you just gonna stand in the doorway all afternoon?" he called over his shoulder.

She jolted, hadn't even realized he'd known she was there.

"Hey," she said, suddenly, unaccountably jittery. To mask her nerves, she strode purposefully inside the shed, stopping just a few feet away. "I just needed to let you know there are some pipes leaking over at Coyote's Den."

"You could have radioed," he commented, glancing her way with a half smile as he arranged tools.

"I would have, but my battery wasn't holding a charge." So there, her tone implied.

Frowning, he turned her way, held out a hand. "Let me take a look—"

"Already fixed," she took great pleasure in saying. She was perfectly capable of taking care of some things all by her little self. "When I stopped by the stables a few minutes ago looking for you, Todd found a new battery in your office. The old one's on your desk. By then, I figured I was already this far, might as well take the few extra steps."

"Hmm," he grunted. Aiden turned back to drop the last of the wrenches into a drawer. "Just let me finish cleaning up here, and we can head over now."

"It's the bathroom pipes, just a slow drip under the sink. You don't need me to go along, do you?"

"You in a hurry to get somewhere?" he asked, closing the last drawer. He tossed the towel he'd used to clean his hands into a medium sized metal can in the corner as he walked toward her. "Hot date?"

"Actually, yes."

At his sharp glance, she fidgeted. Damn it.

"Supper with Emmie and Kathryn. Then Em and I plan on spending the evening catching up since we haven't had a lot of time yet. So, you don't need to worry about giving me a ride back up to my cabin."

And why was she pouring her guts out to him? She didn't owe him anything, certainly not an explanation.

He stopped just a few short feet away. A safe enough

distance. Safe enough…if the air between them wasn't already crackling with tension. "Oh? You staying with her tonight?"

"No, she said she'd give me a ride back herself."

"Like hell," he scowled.

Her spine stiffened. "Emmie is perfectly capable of driving me back."

"She doesn't have any more business up there on those trails alone after dark with that bear on the loose than you do. Not to mention a possible killer."

That brought her up short. She hadn't thought of that. Would never dream of knowingly putting Emmie in danger. "I'll just see if she has time this weekend instead."

"Don't bother. You have it set up for tonight. Stick with it. Just give me a call when you're done, and I'll come get you."

"It could be late," she objected.

"Doesn't matter. I've got stuff to do, always something around here that needs fixin'." He shrugged. "If I decide to go home, I can always come back down for you later."

She opened her mouth to argue, but he cut her off.

"End of discussion, Harper. I don't want either of you out by yourself especially after dark. Not until that bear is caught. And not until Jonah figures out who tied that guy to the tree up at Dear Meadow. Don't push me on this."

Reason fell by the wayside. It didn't matter that he had a valid point, only that he was, once again, telling her what to do. She dropped her fists to her hips, pressed her lips together. Sparks, she was sure, must be shooting from her eyes.

"God, you're sexy as hell when you're mad," he muttered.

And then he closed the space between them. She was already reaching for him when he swept her up into his arms. His mouth came down over hers, open and hot and hungry.

Three long strides had her back pressed against a rough wooden wall, held pinned there by his weight. Heat radiated from him, melting her along his length, nearly fusing them together. What was it about him that set her on fire so quickly?

He angled his head, deepening the kiss as he rocked his hips against her. The rock-hard ridge of his erection pressed against her, low on her abdomen, and a corresponding shiver worked its way through her system. With a muffled whimper, she lifted her legs and wrapped them around his waist. Strong hands gripped her bottom, hoisting her higher, squeezing, fingertips digging in. Her fingers got all tangled up in his hair. And then, somehow, one of his hands ended up under her shirt.

With a deft motion, he loosened her bra and slid his hand up to cup her breast. Her nipple hardened against his calloused palm, scorching heat seared her bare flesh, and her brain went haywire. He rocked against her again, and this time, cradled as he was between her thighs, his erection rode her cleft. Fireworks exploded behind her eyelids. She was drowning in desire, his for her, hers for him. Panting, unable to catch her breath. Suffocating.

His tongue explored her mouth, claimed it. Tangled with hers. Thrust and swept against and over hers. And then his mouth left hers. She whimpered her disappointment.

Gasped her pleasure aloud.

She'd thought she'd been on fire before.

Nothing held a candle to this. His mouth moved down along the column of her neck. Suckling. Nipping. Nibbling. Licking. And his hands were busy, unbuttoning, tugging, maneuvering flannel down and off her arms. Pulling at her T-shirt. Up, up and over her head. Gone. And her fingers were back in his hair, sinking deeper, gripping frantically, clutching as his mouth closed over her nipple.

Her mouth fell open on a gasp, her head fell back, her eyes slid closed. His hands clamped tight around her waist, bruising, as he gripped her, lifted her up and away from the wall. Harper tightened her legs around his waist.

They were moving. She didn't know where. Didn't care. Cared only that he kept working the magic he was working with his mouth and hands. And then they were sinking. Down, down.

She glanced behind him, briefly, and moved her legs to accommodate their new location on the battered, dusty bench seat. Her knees slid into place on either side of his hips. His hands, already gripping her bottom, tugged her closer, until the only way he could get closer to her was if they were naked and he was already embedded inside her.

Keeping one hand on her butt, holding her tight, he ghosted his free hand up the ridges of her spine. His mouth was back on her breasts, first one, then the other. Hot. Oh, so hot. Drawing her nipple deep into his mouth, flicking the taut bud with the tip of his tongue.

He released her after what felt like an eternity. Sweet torment. Brutal pleasure. And he tilted his head back.

She came down to him, sealing her mouth over his. Commanding the kiss for a moment. She was coming out of her skin, breaking apart. The more time she spent with him, the less control she seemed to have. But, in this moment, it didn't matter. In this moment, she controlled the kiss. She felt...empowered. Liberated. And, yes, sexy as hell.

He arched forward, stripped his shirt off, tossed it aside. His arms came around her, steel bands, strong and steady, and he crushed her to him. The feel of his chest against hers, skin on skin, hot and hard, was decadence. Sinful delight.

But not enough. Not nearly enough.

Her arms wrapped around his neck. And she gave control over to him. The hard bulge pushing up against the juncture of her thighs tempted her, teased her. Making her want. Desperately. Her world, in that moment, narrowed to the man who held her, and what he was making her feel. Nothing else existed. Every one of her senses wrapped around Aiden. The texture of his skin. The hardness of his muscles. The heat radiating from him. The scent of his cologne. She wiggled, trying to get closer.

If he didn't hurry up and make love to her soon, she'd—

The insistent, blaring ring of a cell phone penetrated the lust-induced haze wrapped around her brain. She dragged her lips from his, leaned back and gazed down at him with wide eyes.

He reclined against the tattered, stained seat. His heavy -lidded gaze hot enough to melt steel. His body language was that of an exotic sultan reclining on a pile of lush silk pillows. His expression, however, was all bare-chested, virile warrior riding hell-bent-for-redemption across the American plains, bearing down on his target with the intent to pillage and seduce.

And that hot gaze of his slid down, down, taking in the sight of her naked breast, and his hands where they still rested upon her. He licked his bottom lip, as if seeking the taste of her.

Her lips parted and she sucked in a shuddering breath.

Dear Lord, she'd never felt so…so vulnerable. So exposed. And not just her body. She'd never been so out of control, so lost to…to raw lust before.

She jerked back, scrambling to get off his lap. Control. It was all about control.

Sex with Alexander had been good, but always controlled. In a bed. And never during the middle of the day. Muffled sounds and civilized coupling. And she'd been fine with that. More than fine.

But look at her now. Here she was, in a dingy mechanic's shop, half-naked and crawling all over what amounted to be damned near a stranger in the middle of the afternoon. Wild. Wanton. Anything but civilized. She glanced over.

*My God, the side door was even standing open.*

Anyone could have walked in on them at any given moment. She never would have known. Wouldn't have cared.

At first, he resisted releasing her. His hands pinned her hips to his.

"Let me go," she demanded, her voice little more than a sob.

He frowned then, but did as she asked, his hands

falling from her.

She hurried across the shed and scooped up her T-shirt, her flannel, her bra. Trying to get them back on was damned near impossible with her hands shaking so badly. But she managed. Barely.

Before she could race out the door, however, Aiden latched on to her wrist, spinning her around. The phone had long since gone silent, but the damage had already been done.

"No, don't—"

"Harper," he grated, giving her a bit of a tug until she looked up at him.

His features were drawn tight. He'd donned his shirt, but the bulge in the front of his jeans was impossible to miss. "You can't run from this forever."

"I'm not running."

"Aren't you?" He looked skeptical. "What are you so afraid of? I'll battle your demons for you. I'll slay your dragons. Just talk to me. Point me in the right direction. Tell me how to fix this."

"You can't fix this, Aiden." She shook her head, backing up a step, but she couldn't go far as he still held her wrist. "You can't fix *me*."

"Damn it," he growled. "You aren't broken. Stop letting him do this to you, Harper. Stop letting him make you into a victim. Stop letting him control your life, control *you*, even after you left him. Don't let him ruin what we could be together."

He looked as if he wanted to say more, but his phone began ringing again.

"You better answer that."

His lips thinned. "This isn't over, Harper."

No, she had a feeling it wasn't. Not by a long shot. And that's what worried her.

Chapter Sixteen

Aiden took the first exit into Devil's Canyon. Leisure Lanes, the local bowling alley above which Decker resided, was three blocks down and half a block over. As he pulled his truck into the parking lot, he caught a flutter of movement at the side of the building, noted the Kramer County Sheriff Department Yukon.

Aiden got out of his truck and strode across the gravel lot, pushing Harper and what had almost happened between them to the back of his mind. The drive down the mountain hadn't gotten the job done. But the yellow police tape fluttering around the base of the stairs leading up to Decker's apartment sure did the trick. Jonah climbed out of the Yukon.

"Thanks for coming into town," Jonah greeted him, his expression grim as he hitched both thumbs in the front of his utility belt. It was on the chilly side, but the sheriff, in full khaki uniform, wore his department-issued, dark brown coat unzipped.

Aiden nodded, a concerned frown pulling his brow tight as Jonah motioned him to follow. "Before we head up, I wanna show you something."

Jonah opened the passenger door and leaned in. Aiden caught a glimpse of the front seat and figured it was a good thing the sheriff had a big back seat, because there was no way in hell anyone was riding up front with him. The Yukon appeared to be a rolling office on wheels. Aside from the dash cam, the radar detector and the standard law enforcement radio, the seat and floor were piled with citation books, stacks of papers and files, plastic bags and other miscellaneous clutter. A small laptop attached to a moveable arm was anchored to the dash. Jonah shuffled around in an opaque filing bin before pulling out a clear plastic bag.

Turning, he held the bag out to Aiden. "You recognize this?"

Accepting the bag, Aiden rolled it around in his hands. The evidence bag contained a short, thick, copper chain with a nameplate, the kind a man would wear around his wrist. Dried blood crusted the links, smeared the nameplate. Angling the flattened piece of copper for a better view, Aiden read the initials aloud, "JDD." He handed the bag back. "It's Decker's."

Jonah bounced the bag in one hand. "You sure?"

"Yep. He never took that off, at least, not that I know of."

"Forensics recovered it from where the bear had stashed the remains up in the woods. M.E. couldn't get any viable prints. But that," he pointed to the bag, "combined with dental records should provide a positive ID...not to mention the apartment."

Aiden's frown deepened. "The apartment?"

Jonah drew a deep breath and glanced toward the second floor of the building. Ran a hand over the back of his neck. "Yeah. Decker didn't answer yesterday, so we did a wellness check." He drew another deep breath, and then swiped his hand over the bottom half of his face.

"It's a mess up there."

"You think this was where he was killed?"

"I'd say probably not, considering the amount of

blood behind that cabin. But it's a damned good bet this was where he was taken. Whether he was dead before he got strung up in that tree, who can say?"

Aiden crossed his arms, rocked back on his heels. "Any idea when he was taken?"

"When was the last time you saw him?"

"Friday, end of his shift. Five thirty, six maybe?"

"Bobby Johnson saw him over at the Gas'n Go Saturday morning sometime between ten and eleven. Said Decker filled up, came inside and bought a half gallon of milk and a carton of Marlboros. '*Was his usual asshole self.*' Johnson's words, not mine. Nobody saw or heard from him since. Sunday paper was still stuck in his screen door." Jonah paused to wave a fly away from his face. "Saturday nights are busy at the bowling alley. Parking lot's usually packed. Last weekend was a tournament, so even busier than normal. Plus, there were lots of out-of-towners. Anybody could have come and gone without being noticed."

Aiden shook his head. "Nobody noticed someone carrying a body?"

Jonah shrugged. "Not much for light out here, especially around the outer perimeter. We're asking around, but the list is long. Gonna take some time."

Aiden shot him a level look. "So why am I here?"

"Look, I'm gonna level with you. I know your background, did some digging. I know you served two tours in Afghanistan. And I know the same IED that killed Mark and two other members of your team put you in the ICU for several months. What I also know is, a man comes back from war, comes back from an attack that claims one of his best friends, leaves himself seriously wounded, that kind of thing leaves scars. Scars on more than just a man's body. I also know you ain't been to see a therapist of any kind since you moved to the Bar L."

Aiden bristled at how much the sheriff *knew*, but he bit his tongue. All the same, his lips thinned, and his eyes narrowed.

"I would imagine," Jonah went on, crossing his arms as he studied Aiden, "a man comes back from war, from an attack like that, he'd have some raw nerves, some exposed buttons. I'd imagine a man like Decker would know just how to push those buttons."

Aiden tilted his head, calm and cool. "Buttons can only be pushed if you allow it. Which I don't. Seems like you're trying awful hard to push a few buttons yourself, sheriff."

Jonah smiled at him for the first time since that body had been found up in the woods. "Just might be." He leaned back against the Yukon, fixed a steady look on Aiden. "Now that we got that out of the way…tell me what you know about Decker."

"Am I at the top of your suspect list?"

"Didn't say that."

"Didn't *not* say it either."

Jonah grinned again. "You aren't at the top of my list. Not unless or until something drastically changes."

"Fair enough."

"Decker?"

"Was an asshole. But he did his job. Never gave me reason to confront him or even think about firing him until I found out he'd been bullying the staff."

Jonah eyed him for a moment.

"Come on. I want you to look around, give me your opinion." He tossed Aiden a pair of latex gloves and covers for his boots. "Forensics has been through, but it's still technically a crime scene."

Aiden put on the gloves and booties, and then followed the sheriff up the stairs. At the door, Jonah paused.

"It's a real mess," Jonah repeated as he turned his head to glance over his shoulder at Aiden. "It's bad, Aiden. And not a bachelor pad kind of mess, if you catch my drift. You got a fairly strong stomach?"

"Strong enough." Christ, what the hell was he heading into?

Jonah pushed the door open, and Aiden followed him inside. The first thing that hit him was the smell. Old blood. Lots of it. Kind of a rotted meat smell. And sour milk. The refrigerator door hung open. Shelves were askew, food spilling out onto the floor. Warm food that was meant to stay chilled. A milk carton lay on its side amid a pool of congealed white.

The next thing to register for Aiden was the buzzing drone of flies.

Busted up furniture, broken dishes, overturned tables and scattered clothing littered the floor. And blood. A hell of a lot of blood. Everywhere. Splattered and smeared on the walls, on the counter. But no great puddles of it, not like what had been left behind the cabin.

"A mess like this speaks to me, tells me whoever went after Decker was pissed. Guy's got real anger management issues, and a damned explosive temper," Jonah said from near the door.

Aiden wandered farther into the room, put his nose in his elbow to mute the smells. His eyes watered.

"Now Jeb Decker wasn't a small man," Jonah went

on. He'd stayed by the open door, breathing the fresh air, while Aiden's stomach pitched and rolled as he walked the scene. *Lucky bastard.* "Had a bit of a temper on him too, from what I've gathered. Whoever went after him had to have been pretty strong, with a hell of a temper himself. Anybody come to mind? Anybody you know might have tangled with Decker? Had a bone to pick?"

Aiden rolled it around in his mind a moment or two, but no one came readily to mind. As with most bullies, the people Decker tended to target were smaller than he was, weaker. "Only two that might have been big enough, or strong enough to take on Decker and win that come to mind would be Bruce Grafton or Todd Sweeney. Grafton was in Decker's back pocket. Had his nose shoved so far up Decker's ass it was a wonder he could see daylight. And Todd...well, Todd's...simple. Don't really know how else to put it. Not exactly slow, but...childlike. Sheltered, almost, you know? Dependable. Eager to please. A hard worker, but he wouldn't hurt a fly. Jim Potts might be strong enough, I guess, but Jim tended to give Decker a wide berth."

"I'd agree with your assessment, except for Jim."

"How so?"

"Were you aware Decker had a little too much to drink down at the bar a few weeks back, got up in Jim's face, threatened to get him fired?"

Aiden scowled. "No."

"Were you also aware Decker liked to kick back, take a bit of a breather whenever you went out on trail rides and campouts? Liked to tip the bottle and give his pet Grafton a paid day off now and again. Pushed his workload off on the rest of the crew, Sweeney and the other part-timers."

Aiden was seething now. But he kept his temper carefully in check. "No."

"Grafton confirmed it, said there's a bottle of Jack in the bottom right drawer of Decker's desk. Might want to check that out for yourself."

*That rotten bastard.* Aiden's temper flared. "I will."

"Seems Grafton took Decker's lead to heart, been throwing his weight around when you're gone, bullying and threatening some of the guys in the stables. Always careful-like, though. Never does it when witnesses are around."

"I was aware of Decker doing it. Which was why I had the come-to-Jesus discussion with him Friday. I knew him and Grafton were tight. But I didn't know Grafton was pulling the same stunt. Where'd you hear this?"

"Todd Sweeney, for one. Ritchie Christensen for another. A couple of guys that left employment at the Bar L a few months back. Sounds like Grafton and Decker both enjoyed physical intimidation. Getting up in people's faces, verbal abuse, throwing their weight around, shoving people. Told them if they said anything, it'd be their word against his. Told 'em if they went to you, they'd plant something, make 'em look guilty, get them fired."

"God damn it," Aiden burst out, unable to keep a leash on his temper any longer.

"Grafton got a problem with authority?"

"We butted heads once, when he first started. But then he buckled down. Followed Decker's directives willingly enough. Apparently a little too willingly. He never had much for dealings with Emmie or Kathryn, or I would have heard if there'd been trouble on that front."

"Suppose it's a possibility Decker and Grafton had a difference of opinion. Maybe Decker's pet turned on him?"

Aiden thought about it as he glanced around the room one more time. "I suppose anything's possible."

Jonah motioned Aiden to follow once more. Aiden was only to eager to get out of there. Once outside, he drew one deep breath after another as they went down the steps and headed toward the Yukon once more, desperate to get that smell out of his nose and out of his lungs.

Jonah seemed to be weighing his next words. A crisp autumn breeze whirled through the parking lot, ruffling his golden hair.

"Are you aware Jim Potts has a record, Aiden? Assault. Vandalism."

Aiden nodded. "He served his time. I've had no problems out of him. In fact, I've come to rely on him quite a bit. Was considering giving him Decker's job, as a matter of fact."

"Todd Sweeney hasn't held a permanent address for longer than six months since he was released from the foster care system five years ago." When Aiden shrugged, Jonah shifted his weight, crossed his ankles. "You know Berta Connolly has a drinking problem, and a record of petty theft?"

Aiden scowled. Jonah had made a little too free with his digging, in Aiden's opinion. "Berta's been sober for a little over two years now, attends AA meetings every week in the basement of the First Presbyterian Church. Emmie hired her to run the Ranch Café, and the books add up every month since she's been in charge."

Jonah popped his jaw, looking thoroughly vexed.

"Melanie Smith once went by the name of Trixie Love, and her arrest record covered everything from petty theft and drug possession and prostitution."

Again, Aiden shrugged. "Emmie collects wounded souls the way some people bring home stray pets. And, with the exception of Grafton and Decker, she's had a good eye for those that just need a break, those willing to turn their circumstances around given the opportunity."

Himself included. He'd been on a downward spiral, riddled with survivor's guilt, suffocating with PTSD until he'd come to the ranch. Emmie and Kathryn had given him a sense of purpose. And family to look after. And the ranch itself had given him back his sense of self again.

Oh, he wasn't cured. Might never be. And there were still things he couldn't shake. The inability to sit with his back to a door, or to sleep without his back to the wall. Insomnia plagued him sometimes. Loud noises still got him now and again. And the driving need to protect those around him, even if it meant sacrificing himself in some way. But he could breathe here. Working with the horses, repairing things, just being outside. The Bar L had turned out to be everything he'd needed, before he'd even realized he'd needed it.

Jonah harrumphed. "Anymore sightings of that bear?"

"Not that I've heard."

"Well, keep me posted."

"Will do." Aiden turned away and headed for his own truck.

Once back on the road, he replayed his conversation with Jonah, growing more and more troubled. The glaring truth was staring him right in the face. Somebody had killed Decker. Whether they'd bled him out before they'd strung him up on that tree, or whether they'd only incapacitated him and then strung him up there as bear bait. Either way, he was just as dead, and they were just as guilty.

And there was every possibility that the killer was someone they knew. Someone who either worked on the Bar L, or someone from Devil's Canyon.

Someone far too close to home.

The miles flew by as Aiden weighed the best way to keep Emmie, Kathryn, and Harper safe, not to mention the rest of his staff. And he was coming up woefully empty-handed. He couldn't be everywhere at once.

Kathryn, he didn't worry so much about. She seldom wandered far from the lodge or the immediate grounds. But Harper and Emmie were another story. Emmie went to town nearly every day, driving roads that were desolate, with dangerous curves and lots of places for a predator to lie in wait.

And Harper…

Out in the woods by herself, going in and out of vacant cabins, right smack dab in the middle of a man-eating bear's hunting ground, to say nothing of the killer that walked upright on two legs. The possibilities for tragedy were endless on that front. But he could only lay down so many restrictions before Harper and Emmie completely rebelled. Shy of gagging and hog tying them, what was a man to do?

Chapter Seventeen

Aiden leaned back in the squeaky chair and eyed the man sitting across the desk from him.

"Are we clear? I mean it. If anything like this ever happens again, I need you to come to me. Let me know right away. You're too good of an employee, too good of a person to be treated like that, and we don't want to lose you."

Jim ducked his head, color riding high on his cheeks. "I will, Aiden. I swear. I should have come to you straight away. I'm sorry I didn't. I guess I was just afraid. I know how good I have it here, and Decker said…well, he knew I'd been arrested for vandalism, said he'd trash the stables, blame it on me if I said anything. And Bruce would back him up."

Aiden held up a hand. "I understand. But now that the air is cleared, I expect you to remember this conversation…and conduct yourself as befitting a stable master at the Bar L."

Jim's head shot up, and he peered at Aiden with rounded eyes. "Stable master?"

Aiden nodded, somber. "That was Decker, up there behind Dear Meadow. I don't know how much I can get into it, since it's technically an ongoing investigation. But that was him. Doesn't matter though. The job should have been yours quite a while ago. All I'm doing is correcting a mistake. The job's yours now, if you want it."

At first, Jim looked like he might bounce out of his seat. But then his smile slowly died.

"If you're worried about Grafton, don't be. That will be your first order of business, helping me hire a replacement for him. Because he is next on *my* list."

You could all but see the tension roll from Jim's shoulders. "Then, yes, I want the job."

"Where is Grafton, by the way?"

"Gone for the day. It's after seven."

Aiden glanced to the clock. "So it is. Guess I lost track of time. I suppose Todd's gone too?"

"Yep."

Aiden frowned. "Why are you still here?"

"Well, you hadn't come back from town yet at six when everyone else was punching out. I didn't want to leave the stables unattended, so I figured I'd better wait till you got back. Make sure everything was okay."

"Yet another reason for your promotion. Your dedication and common sense."

Jim glowed beneath the praise. Then his brow knitted, and he hesitated. "I have to be honest with you, Aiden. I don't have any experience in management. I might not be the best man for the job."

"So you'll learn as you go. You have to start somewhere, right? And I'm pretty confident you'll do fine. You just have to remember, Jim, *you're* in charge now. You can't be afraid to stand up for yourself or those that work for you. And if you are having problems with someone, don't be afraid to come to me. That's what I'm here for. To back you up. Remember the kind of supervisor Decker was. Don't be like that. Let your employees know you care about them, that you support them and want to help them however possible. But don't let them walk all over you either. Be fair but firm."

With a wide grin splitting his face, Jim said, "Thank you, Aiden. I won't let you down."

"I'll let you go on home now, Jim. I'm sorry it took so long in town." Smiling over the man's excitement, Aiden watched his new stable master walk out the door with a spring in his step.

Remembering the leaky pipes in Coyote's Den, Aiden checked his to-do list, rose and went to gather the necessary parts and tools. Harper would be tied up with Emmie for several hours, so he ought to be able to knock off quite a few of these repairs before she was ready to return to her cabin for the night.

And there was no way he was going to go up to his cabin and wait for her to call. The stubborn woman might get it in her head to talk Emmie into letting her drive herself back and not call him at all. At least, with most of the repairs he planned on tackling, he'd be able to keep an eye on the lodge…and catch her if she decided to try to sneak off.

\*\*\*\*

The next morning, Harper was positive she'd thwarted Aiden. She'd been ready and waiting when he'd pulled up to her cabin to take her down to the lodge to work. She'd rushed out and was already opening the truck door before he could even get out of the truck.

No more stolen '*Good morning, beautiful*' kisses on *her* doorstep.

It had been all she could do to dodge the goodnight kiss he'd clearly been anticipating last night when he'd dropped her off just after ten. She wasn't risking anymore lip-locks with the man, not after what had happened in the repair shed.

Smug, she hopped up inside the truck and settled into place. After buckling her seatbelt, a self-satisfied smile plastered on her lips, she turned to chirp good morning.

And got a faceful of Aiden. Or rather a mouthful.

His lips fastened over hers, quick as lightning. She slipped under his spell with mindboggling ease. He tasted of mint toothpaste. Smelled like sunshine and cedar and fresh air. And she was responding before she knew what had happened.

When he pulled back, a lazy grin upon his handsome face, she was left warm and wanting.

"Good morning, gorgeous." His voice was low and husky. A product of the early hour, or the kiss he'd just stolen?

Either way, it melted the last of her defenses.

She could only imagine what waking up in the morning next to this man must be like. All mussed and flushed from sleep. Tousled from a night filled with caresses and kisses and mind-blowing orgasms.

Good morning, beautiful kisses on her doorstep. Good morning, gorgeous kisses in the truck. Countless other stolen kisses every chance he got. And kisses that had rocked her world yesterday afternoon out in the shed. How was she to resist a man like him? He touched her and kissed her every chance he could.

Her heart didn't stand a chance.

Wait, her heart?

No, her heart had absolutely nothing to do with it. This was lust. Nothing more, nothing less. Lust. That was all.

"You aren't supposed to be kissing me, Aiden," she

scolded, sharper than she'd intended. But her emotions were in an upheaval, and her body—strung out on that kiss—wasn't helping matters.

"Uh-huh." Grinning ear to ear, completely unrepentant, he shifted his truck into reverse, laid his arm along the back of her seat and began backing down her lane.

Once they hit the main trail, he dropped his arm...and captured her hand in his, lacing their fingers together. Harper gave a half-hearted tug, but he held tight. Sighing, she let him have his way, and turned her attention to the wooded trail.

"Looks like it might rain today," she commented.

"Light showers early this afternoon, I think. Then it's supposed to clear off."

"Hmm," she murmured, taken back by how normal, how natural it felt to be with him like this, holding his hand, trusting her safety to him on these winding trails, making mundane conversation.

"Oh, I almost forgot," Aiden said. "I need to stop by Badger's Sett to check in on the new guest."

"I didn't think Emmie was going to rent out the cabins up here yet, not until they knew the bear was gone." She frowned, trying desperately not to notice how good his thumb felt rubbing along the ridges of her knuckles.

"She figured since we'd be close by it would be safe enough."

Harper nodded. A short while later, Aiden turned off the trails and angled back up into the woods. A tiny cabin came into view.

"I'll just be a minute," he said. He pressed a quick kiss to the back of her hand before releasing her and hopping down from the truck.

Flustered, Harper watched him bound up the three steps to the door. He knocked, and he waited. While he waited, Harper took in the details of the cabin. A single rustic rocker rested on the far end of the three season porch. The rough wood siding and shake shingles gave the cabin an ancient, settler's cabin look. The curls of smoke wafting from the chimney and the backdrop of pine made it homey.

Sheer white curtains twitched in the window, and then the door opened a crack. Harper tilted her head curiously, but all she could catch was a glimpse of camouflage pant leg, and an expensive-looking, black hiking boot.

Aiden spent a moment conversing with the guest, and then the door closed in his face. Aiden's head jerked back, just a bit, and he stood for a moment longer, his head tilted as though he couldn't believe the man had closed the door in his face.

After shaking his head and turning around, Aiden returned to the pickup with a strange expression.

"What's wrong?"

"I don't know." His mouth twisted to the side on a distasteful grimace. Starting the truck, he did a u-turn in the clearing and angled for the trail. His hand captured hers again. She didn't even think to protest as she studied his face.

"Aiden?"

"It's probably nothing. I just... I don't know. That guy was... There's something about him I don't like." He shot her a wary look and pressed another kiss to the back of her hand. "Just do me a favor? Make sure you wait till he's gone hunting before you clean his place? Or take one of the other girls with you. I don't want you up here alone with him."

Harper glanced over her shoulder, but the cabin was obscured by the trees now. Turning to face the road ahead, she shot a concerned glance his way. "Yeah, sure. I can do that."

"I mean it, Harper." He pinned her with a hard stare.

"I know, and I will. I promise."

Mollified, he peered at the trail again.

"Emmie said I should talk to you about scheduling riding lessons."

He glanced her way. "What's your schedule look like today?"

"I'm done at five-thirty."

"My last lesson is at five so that works perfectly. It's a date then."

Harper's head whipped around to fix him with a stern glare. "*Lesson*, Aiden. It's a lesson. It's not a date."

"Mm-hmm." He smiled innocently and planted another kiss on the back of her hand. And he just kept driving.

**** 

Aiden stood in the center of the stables, his feet planted, his arms and hands loose at his sides, ready. Bruce Grafton shuffled in front of him, like a bull pawing at the ground before it charged. Aiden knew a great deal of Grafton was bluster and show. But he also knew when a man felt cornered, a big man with a mean temper, he was liable to come out swinging.

"You ain't got no right to fire me," Grafton huffed.

"I've already explained the situation to you. And I found the bottle to confirm what I was told, spoke to other employees. You're finished here. Grab your things and leave."

Aiden had waited until the rest of the stables had emptied and sent Jim and Todd on up to the Lodge. Now he was rethinking his plan to keep the other two out of Grafton's line of fire. As brawny a man as Grafton was, and pissed off as he was just now, he might be more of a handful than Aiden had anticipated.

Red in the face, Grafton jabbed a finger in Aiden's direction. "I got the right to know who ratted me out."

"I've had complaints from multiple sources. And they've asked to remain anonymous for fear of reprisal. Given your temper, I'm liable to agree."

"That's bullshit. You got no right."

"As foreman of the Bar L, I have every right. Now I'm not going to tell you again. Grab your stuff and move on or I'll have to call Jonah." Thank God Grafton had chosen to live in town and only had a coat and a few personal effects right there in the stables. Aiden couldn't imagine trying to make this guy pack up an entire cabin.

"Fuck you, Aiden. You think that pansy-assed sheriff's gonna run me off? You think *you* got the balls to do it?"

Aiden narrowed his eyes, bracing himself. He'd caught the way Grafton's hand had clenched, the way he'd twisted his hip, planting his back foot just so, and the glint in his eyes.

When Grafton took a swing, it wasn't a huge surprise. Aiden ducked, and Grafton's beefy fist sailed over his head. When Aiden came up, he held both hands up, palms out.

"This is your last warning, Bruce. Take your things and walk."

But Grafton was beyond words, and well beyond

reason. He came at Aiden like a freight train, shoulder down, arms stretched to catch Aiden around the middle. The impact knocked the wind clean out of Aiden, even though he'd been ready. But Grafton wasn't done. He picked Aiden up, carried him three more steps, and slammed his back against the side of a stall. Jezebel whinnied in alarm, reared up and smashed her front hooves against the wood. Pinned against the stall as he was by Grafton's bulky weight, the reverberation hit Aiden like a shockwave.

Grafton, still bent slightly at the waist, pulled his arm back, his fist doubled to land a brutal blow to Aiden's ribs, but Aiden was faster. He clenched both fists together and dropped them like an anvil on Grafton's back. A split second later, he brought his knee up square into Grafton's chest. The bruiser fell back, wheezing.

Aiden sidestepped so his back was no longer to the wall. He stayed on the balls of his feet, arms at his sides, ready to pounce, ready to evade.

Grafton, his face a purplish red, roared and came at him, fists swinging. Aiden ducked another shot intended for his face and came up with a fist that caught Grafton in the middle, doubling him over.

Grafton staggered back a step, one arm around his middle. His breath sawed in and out, spittle dripping from the corner of his thick lips. He came at Aiden again, bearing down with dogged determination. Another fist flew, but Aiden, distracted by the small door at the front of the building opening, glanced away at the wrong moment. Grafton's punch hit him like a ton of bricks to the chin. Aiden's head snapped to the side, and for a hair's breadth of time, his vision twinkled and dimmed.

By God's own luck, he managed to evade the follow-up left jab to his ribs. Dancing away, he chanced a quick glance to see who had come in. Things happened almost too quickly to track at that point. He caught a glimpse of Harper, standing just inside the doorway, her eyes huge as saucers, her hands flying up to cover her mouth as she choked on a scream. And in that same moment, he registered the flash of silver in Grafton's hand.

Praying Harper would leave, maybe run for help, which would put her safely out of harm's way, Aiden turned his full focus on Grafton. And not a moment too soon.

Grafton lunged for him, swiping at Aiden's middle with a wicked looking switchblade. Aiden hunched his back like a cat and jumped nimbly out of reach. Ever aware of his surroundings, he snatched up a saddle blanket that was draped over a nearby railing. Made swift work of unfolding and then furling it till it resembled a rope. He was ready this time. Grafton charged again, his arm—and that glinting blade—slashing downward. Aiden whipped the blanket around Grafton's wrist, jerking down and away.

Off balance, Grafton stumbled forward. They tussled over the knife, slipping and wrestling on the hay-strewn ground. Sweat beaded Aiden's face. Grafton's arms were slick with it, and Aiden's grip slipped. He sucked in a sharp breath as the blade twisted, slicing through Aiden's shirt and digging into flesh. But he wasn't about to let go.

Getting a better grip, his opponent grunting and straining, Aiden managed to wrench the knife away. As he tossed the knife, his arm outstretched, Grafton took a cheap shot to Aiden's unprotected ribs, right where the blood was already flowing freely from his wound.

Aiden hunched sideways as pain ripped through his body. He brought his arm up to block the next blow, doubling his fist up to deliver one of his own.

But the blow never came. Grafton dropped to the ground at Aiden's feet, flat on his face, out cold. And behind the fallen mountain of a man stood Harper, chest heaving, face flushed, holding the handle of an upturned shovel like a Louisville Slugger.

Chapter Eighteen

"What the hell were you thinking?" Aiden stood in the doorway of the stables, holding a towel to his bleeding side, his attention torn between the woman beside him and the groggy man being shoved, none too gently, into the back of Jeff Darby's deputy sheriff's car.

"I was thinking you needed help," Harper snapped, her arms crossed, her spine ramrod stiff. "You know, since you were *bleeding* an all."

"Then why the hell didn't you get out of here and go and find someone?"

"Go and find someone? Like who? Jim? Todd? Why wasn't one of them here with you when you confronted Grafton in the first place? Go and find someone? I did just fine all on my own, thank you very much. Better than you were doing, dancing around with a blanket and your bare fists while the other guy tries to gut you. Go and find someone," her voice dropped scornfully. If looks could kill he'd be pushing up daisies any minute now. "If you think for one minute I'd just leave you alone in there with a crazy man with a knife, Aiden Whitebear, then you're a dumbass."

Aiden gritted his teeth and dragged in a steadying breath, partly to stave off the searing pain in his side, and partly to keep from losing his temper. He raised a hand to wave the deputy off before turning to latch on to Harper's elbow. His side burned like a mother, but he'd dealt with much worse in the past. Compared to a roadside IED, this was a minor shaving nick. All the same, his mood was in the toilet. Just thinking about what might have happened to Harper if Grafton had somehow incapacitated Aiden and gone after her next…

Well, it was more than he could deal with.

And the last thing he needed right now was a lecture in front of God and country. Especially not when he had his own lecture to deliver. He hauled her back inside the stables and slammed the door behind them.

"I had things under control," he began.

"In case you didn't notice, he had a knife in his hand and was trying his damnedest to carve you up like a Thanksgiving turkey. You had a blanket, Aiden. A blanket."

"Damn it, Harper, you could have been hurt. Grafton's a dangerous man. He could have—"

"Oh, just stuff it, would you? You and your sexist crap." She jerked her arm from his grip and stormed across the large bay at the front of the stables.

Pushing the towel tighter against his side, he stomped right after her. "What the hell's that supposed to mean?"

Harper whirled to face him, a storm raging her eyes. "You know exactly what that's supposed to mean. You think because I have boobs instead of balls I can't handle my business? That Emmie can't? We might break a damned nail, so we'd better just let the big important man handle things. God," she threw her arms up, her voice dripping disgust, "would you just get over yourself?"

His mouth fell open. No way had she just accused him of—

"Oh, yes, you do." She shook a finger at him. "So get that stupid, offended look off your face right now. So what if I don't know how to fix a leaky pipe. Or if Emmie doesn't know how. It's not like we can't learn. It isn't like we couldn't do just fine without you. You think I can't change a flat tire? Well, I can. Or...or shingle a damned roof? News flash, I helped my dad shingle our roof when I was sixteen years old. And Emmie helped too! We even helped rip off the old shingles to, for your information. Just because someone did this to me," she pointed at her face, at the faded bruises, "doesn't make me a weakling or incompetent."

Aiden opened his mouth to argue, to deny her claim that he doubted her ability, but she cut him off before he could utter a sound, waving a hand in his face. "Oh, shut up. I'm not done yet. I am more than capable of taking care of myself." She jabbed that finger at his chest, again and again, drilling it into him as she gave him hell, backing him up step for step until he either plopped down on the hay bale behind him, or went sprawling over it onto his ass on the other side. "Stop sheltering me like I'm this fragile little thing made of glass. Stop patting me on the head and treating me like the good little woman who shouldn't leave the kitchen. I'm not arm candy, damn it."

He blinked up at her, completely at a loss. Where was all this fury coming from?

*Arm candy?*

"What was I thinking, you ask? Well, what were *you* thinking? You ought to be in the back of an ambulance right now...or on your way to the hospital for stitches at the very least."

"I don't need stitches."

"What you need is a good, swift kick in the ass," she raged.

He gaped at her, couldn't believe she was speaking to him like this. She was way over the top. Irate. Pissed off beyond all reason. And here he thought he'd done a good job of pushing her buttons before. He never imagined she had it in her to come this unglued.

Color rode high on her cheeks. Her pretty blue eyes sparkled dangerously. Her hair was mussed, windblown and wild from her exertions with the shovel. Her chest heaved with the force of her outburst.

Damn but the woman was a sight to behold. Equal helpings of admiration and raw lust boiled through his veins.

If she even had an inkling of what he was thinking right now, how he'd like to tug her down onto his lap and give her temper another outlet…well, she'd probably deck him with the shovel too.

Still, as she continued to rail at him, it got him to thinking. Had her ex treated her this way, the way she was talking about? Like she was made of glass? Like she was incompetent? Or weak?

*Arm candy?*

Had Aiden been doing the same without even realizing it?

And then another thought hit him right between the eyes. Had she lost her temper like this with Grant? Was that when he'd beaten her? Because she'd…rebelled, for lack of a better term?

And, if that were the case, surely she must trust him not to do the same. Right? Not if she was going off on him like this. Surely, it was trust. Something warm and welcome swelled in his chest, squeezed his heart and went straight to his head faster than a bottle of whiskey.

Did she...*would* she realize the same thing?

He could only hope.

*Maybe once the temper wears off.*

"Did you ever stop to think, for just one minute," she went on, totally oblivious to the fact that he'd gotten lost in his own thoughts, "that the sheriff's department had yet to catch the killer who tied that poor man to a tree? Did it even occur to you that Grafton might be the one they were looking for? That *he* could be the killer? Or that, even if he wasn't, he has one hell of a mean temper? Oh, I've heard all about him from some of the other staff. And you were just plain stupid for not having someone in the stables with you when you fired him."

She dragged in a deep breath, planting one fist on her hip. Her finger, now an inch from his nose, shook. As did the rest of her hand. In fact, her entire body was all but vibrating. With anger? Or with fear? "So don't you even think about lecturing me on safety, when you go and do something that could have gotten you killed." Her voice cracked, there at the end.

Aiden took a good long look at her. She'd lost the rosy flush of battle now. In fact, her face was slowly losing its color. Her lips were pressed tight...when she wasn't lambasting him. And her eyes, those big, beautiful eyes, had become glassy with unshed tears.

She'd been scared for him, he realized in a rush.

She'd been frightened, and this royal ass-chewing was the result. Oh, she might believe he'd been coddling her, treating her like...yes, like glass. And, truth be told, he probably had been. It was how he'd been raised. But it had been the fear that had broken a dam somewhere deep inside her, spilling out emotion she'd been bottling up for a long time, by the sounds of it. And his safety—or lack thereof—had been the catalyst to this explosion.

That warm swell in his chest turned to a fiery need and it swept through him like a hurricane.

It was more than lust that simmered between them, flaring up to boil out of control now and again. There were genuine feelings involved. She cared about him. She might go out of her way not to show it. She might not even like it.

But she *cared*.

Aiden angled his head and met her scowl with a look of contrition. "You're right," he admitted quietly.

"Of course I'm right, you big jerk," she yelled.

Harper dashed the back of her wrist angrily across her eyes, then she dropped to the ground before him. He widened his knees and reached for her, thinking to draw her into the circle of his arms. To comfort her. But she only huffed in disgust, shoved his arms impatiently away and reached for the towel.

Cool air seared along the wound as she peeled first the bloodied towel away, and then the wet layers of his shirts. He tried to reach for her again, but she slapped at his hands, glowering at him this time.

"I need a first aid kit," she muttered, her voice husky and low.

"I'll get—"

The look she shot him was hot enough to flash boil ice.

"Ah, there's one in my office, just inside the door."

Using his knees for balance, she pushed herself up and strode away. He watched her go, bemused. What a contradictory creature she was. Contradictory, and utterly adorable.

Damn, he'd known from the first sight of her that he wanted her. And the more time he spent with her, the more that wanting had grown. But it was more than wanting now.

He'd gone and fallen for her. Hadn't even put up a fight.

But her outburst? Fearlessly standing up to him, in spite of her past. And yes, even calling him a dumbass. It had put the final nail in his casket. He was officially a gonner. She was meant for him. He couldn't even imaging wanting to try with anyone else.

Nope. As far as Harper Colby was concerned, Aiden hadn't stood a chance.

Now he just needed to show the stubborn minx that he was the man for her...show her without scaring her off first.

By the time she returned, Aiden had shed his flannel and wrestled his T-shirt over his head and off. Her steps faltered for a moment as she looked up from the white metal box in her hands. For one unguarded moment, her eyes raked down over him, over the hard muscles of his chest and abdomen, his shoulders and his arms.

Desire rushed through Aiden like wildfire in his veins, kindled by her dumbstruck expression, fueled by the danger he'd faced, fanned by the peril she'd willfully placed herself in. He eyed the first aid kit in her hands, fearing that if she so much as touched him just then, even a simple, innocent bit of contact, it might be the spark to set the whole thing ablaze.

She lifted her chin, pressed her lips together and charged forward. A battle-weary soldier looking for a fight.

Aiden braced himself. Not against the pain, though

there was sure to be plenty of that in store given the way his side was feeling and the glint in her eye.

He braced himself against the raw lust, her actions adding more fuel to a blaze that could consume them both.

Harper knelt on the ground between his knees once more. Without looking at him again, she balanced the white box near his hip on the hay bale. Popping the latches, she set to work picking out the supplies she would need. And all the while he watched her, her trembling hands, her stony face. Falling a little harder for her every second. He dug his fingers into prickly hay to keep from reaching for her.

She'd only slap them away again.

But this time he didn't know if it would be enough to stop him.

Just as she began cleaning the area around the wound at the bottom edge of his ribs, slowly working her way closer to the epicenter of the pain, the stable door burst open. Startled, Harper jerked her hand away and sat back on her heels. Emmie and Kathryn shot through the doorway, hesitated for a moment as they glanced around, and then both women rushed forward, fussing and talking over each other.

"Oh, my God, Aiden! Are you okay?" Emmie cried.

"We met the deputy's car in the lane. What happened?" Kathryn demanded.

"Everything's okay. I'm f—"

"You are most certainly *not* fine," Harper snapped, firing up all over again. "He's a big, arrogant...*dumbass*," she growled, going back to work on his side, her touch anything but gentle as she wiped away the blood. Pretty soon, he was going to take exception to her calling him a dumbass. But right now, he was still basking in the glow of knowing she cared.

"He decided to fire Grafton all by himself. Alone. Idiot," she muttered beneath her breath as she pressed a pad of gauze tightly to the wound. Aiden sucked in a pained breath. Then louder, she added, "Grafton pulled a knife on him, tried to slice him to ribbons, as you can see, while Aiden decided to dance around the stables like a freakin' ballerina."

He scowled, glancing down at her. "A ballerina? Aw now, come on. That's hardly fair."

"A blanket, Aiden. A damned blanket," she snarled, going back to work on his side with a vengeance.

Gritting his teeth against the searing pain in his side from where she ruthlessly, liberally applied antiseptic, he chose to withhold any further argument. At least until she was done brandishing the rubbing alcohol.

"Well, since we saw Bruce in the back of the deputy car, Aiden must have—" Emmie started to defend Aiden, but Harper quickly shut her down.

Glancing over her shoulder, she clipped out succinctly, "I hit Grafton on the back of the head with a shovel."

Emmie's face registered her surprise. Kathryn cupped a hand over her mouth, her eyes wide, as she choked back a startled laugh. Aiden's face went hot.

"Aiden should be getting looked at by a professional right now. But do you think he'd go to a damned doctor? No. He's got to be stubborn about it. Manly." She rolled her eyes. "Just like with everything else." Harper threw the soiled gauze pads aside and reached for a fresh one.

"Well, then. It looks like you have everything well in hand, Harper. Come on, Emmie."

"Oh, but—"

"We've got groceries in the car that need puttin' away, girl. Let's go." Kathryn grabbed hold of Emmie's elbow and gave her a tug and a meaningful glance. One that Aiden couldn't miss if he were a blind man. "Harper can take care of this. Come on."

Emmie hesitated a moment more. Then the light of understanding dawned in her eye. She glanced between Aiden and the back of Harper's bent head, and then she nodded, grinning ear to ear.

"Oh, ah, yes we do." Damn that girl was a piss poor actress. Which was part of the reason Aiden had come to adore her so much. She had no guile. None whatsoever.

Mother and daughter all but tripped over each other in their bid to beat a hasty exit, leaving as quickly as they'd arrived. Aiden would have laughed, if Harper wasn't presently dousing his wound in rubbing alcohol. Again. As it was, all he could do was gasp and wheeze, squeeze his eyes closed, and pray he wouldn't pass out.

Harper paused a moment, and Aiden caught the sniffle. Faint, but there, nonetheless. It was hard to see her face from this angle, but he could almost swear she was blinking furiously. And he began to wonder if she were deliberately bathing him in rubbing alcohol, or if it was only because her hands were visibly shaking.

And then something hit his jean-clad thigh. Something small and round and wet, leaving behind a damp smudged on the pale denim. And then another plop of moisture. He gently gripped her shoulders.

"Honey, don't cry. You're ripping my heart out here. I'm all right."

"Stop it," she growled, pushing his hands away belligerently.

Grim, she refocused on her task, pulling butterfly Band Aids out and placing them carefully over his wound. Ten of them in all. The slash had been longer than he'd realized. Long, but not deep, thankfully. Once she had the last one in place, she smeared the whole row with triple antibiotic ointment and fresh gauze, and then covered the edges with enough medical tape to anchor three times as many bandages. That was going to be a real bitch to remove later.

Harper gathered the stray supplies and dumped them back inside the box. But before she could rise, he gripped her shoulders. This time he would not be denied. Though she resisted, he drew her slowly, inexorable against his chest. And there he held her tight. Until she stopped fighting him. Until she slowly melted into him.

Until her arms crept around his waist and the tears came.

"Shhh. Shhh, now," he crooned, petting her hair, rubbing her back. "Let it go, angel. It's okay. Let it go."

Harper buried her face against the side of his neck, burrowed into him. And she sobbed as if her life depended on it, shredding his heart in the process. He lost track of time as he held her in his arms. But eventually, sniffling, she quieted.

He glanced around. With the only other option being his bloodied shirt, Aiden handed her a handful of clean gauze pads from the first aid pack. Harper, let out a short huff of a laugh, and accepted his offering. She daubed at her eyes and blew her nose before tossing the soiled gauze onto the pile with the rest.

"I'm sorry. I seem to be making a habit of bawling all over you." She made to untangle herself from his arms. But Aiden was having none of that. Harper glanced up, and his heart turned over. Her eyes were puffy, her face splotchy, her nose red. She looked so vulnerable, her emotions lay completely bare.

He cupped both cheeks and, slowly, inexorably, he pulled her closer. Aiden brushed his lips over hers, again and again. Soft, gentle, lazy kisses as if they had all the time in the world. Harper gripped his wrists, but she didn't try to stop him. And so, he deepened the kiss by slow degrees. But still, he kept the kiss right there, hovering in that warm, fuzzy zone where passion lurked just beneath the surface, but tender affection held reign.

Reluctantly, he ended the kiss, allowing her to sink back on her heels. He followed, leaning forward, until he rested his forehead against hers, and peered deep into her eyes.

"I'm sorry for frightening you," he said simply.

"Don't do it again, Aiden," she whispered.

He closed his eyes, pressed his lips together and nodded, bumping their noses together. There were so many things he wanted to press her about, so many questions he wanted to ask. But they'd only upset her more, and she'd been upset enough for one evening.

Clearing his throat, he stood, and held a hand out to her, helped her rise to her feet.

"Are you ready?"

"Ready?" She blinked up at him, clearly lost.

"You have a riding lesson."

"Are you kidding me?"

"Nope."

"A riding lesson? Now?" She shook her head and bent to gather up the first aid kit. "You're out of your mind."

"Why not?"

"Well, for one, you don't even have a shirt on," she pointed out. And, he was pleased to note, after a brief stolen glance at his chest, she was extra careful to keep her focus glued to his face. He was getting to her. "For another, you're hurt. Things could have ended so badly—"

"It's just a scratch, and you did a great job patching me up. I hardly feel it at all now." Which was a total, bald-faced lie. The damned thing throbbed like an abscessed tooth. "Wallowing in what happened, in what might have happened only gives Grafton more power over us. The best way to take control back is get on with our lives." He stared pointedly at her, waiting for her to make the connection.

"It's getting late. Everybody's gone for the day."

God, the woman was stubborn. But he'd known that going into this thing.

"I have a spare shirt in the office. And the fact that everyone else is gone is just one more reason to have the lesson now."

A frown crinkled her brow. "Why?"

His grin stretched wide. "No distractions."

Chapter Nineteen

No distractions was a bad thing. A very, very bad thing, Harper mused for what seemed the hundredth time in the past hour.

Since the sun had already gone down, and the temperature was rapidly dropping, Aiden decided to keep the outdoor portion of her first lesson short. They'd begun inside the stables by familiarizing Harper with the horses and the tack. While Aiden didn't let her actually saddle the horse herself, he'd taken her through the process, step by step, showing her every piece and explaining how and why it was used.

By the time he actually got her up on a horse, a docile creature named Flapjack, Harper felt pretty confident. And she understood why Aiden was such a popular riding instructor. Looks aside, the man was extremely thorough and had the patience of a saint.

"You're doing great," he encouraged over his shoulder as he led the gelding from the stables out into the exercise ring. Once outside, he stopped to flip on the switch for two of the huge yard lights that spotlighted the ring, then he stepped up to her side to adjust the stirrups. When he was through, he rested a hand on her thigh. His palm was warm, even through her jeans, his caress lingering. For a moment, she lost herself in his eyes.

"We'll take this nice and slow," he said, but the look on his face, the gravity of his tone said he was talking about much more than the lesson.

Or was he? Was she reading more into this than she should?

All she knew was that her heart had yet to settle, even all this time later. The sight of Aiden dodging swipe after swipe of that wicked blade…and the horror when he'd finally been struck, would stay with her until the day she died. Just remembering caused her chest tightened and a lump swelled in her throat.

She tried—desperately, she tried—to put it aside. To tell herself she'd feel this way about anyone who'd been in that situation.

And yet she couldn't shake the unsettling realization that she wouldn't, not really. Not to this extent. She was developing real, serious feelings for the frustrating man.

But that was just silly, wasn't it? It was much too soon. She hardly knew him. And she'd only broken her engagement to Alexander such a short time ago.

And yet…

And yet the feelings were still there.

Harper worried her lower lip, filled with doubts. But she nodded at him, as he seemed to be expecting some kind of response.

He smiled then, reassuring. Confident.

Confident enough for the both of them? Was that the message he was trying to send? She just didn't know, couldn't tell. Thanks to Alexander, she doubted every last one of her instincts when it came to men.

Turning away, Aiden lead the horse farther into the ring, put the animal through its paces, controlling every step at first. But then, when it became obvious Harper had a knack for riding, he gradually let her take over. Propping a booted heel on the bottom rung of the fence, he crossed his arms, leaned back and observed. Occasionally, he'd call out a suggestion, always helpful and never bossy or demanding. But he didn't interfere again, instead letting her learn her limits on her own.

About the tenth time around the ring, Harper tossed her head back and laughed aloud. Feeling the big, powerful horse flex beneath her, pliable to her commands, was…freeing. Invigorating.

The shadows crept in around the edges of the gated enclosure, but Harper didn't mind. She was in control. Fearless. Nothing could touch her right now.

The shush and tumble of fallen leaves rustled all around, punctuated by the steady drum of the horse's hooves on the hard-packed ground, the creak of the saddle as her weight shifted, and the occasional equine snicker. The scent of leather and horse and crisp fall air with just the hint of pine was a heady relaxant. So much so that she barely felt the bite of the wind on her bare face. Snug and warm inside Aiden's coat, Harper would have been content to keep on riding indefinitely.

Aiden approached, his hand held up for the horse. Trained to the command, Flapjack slowed and returned to Aiden, pushing his muzzle against Aiden's palm. Aiden ran a hand along the horse's neck, patting, crooning praise for the animal straight into its ear. And then he turned to Harper, and he smiled up at her once more, stopping her heart. There was pride in his eyes, unmistakable pride, and so much more. More than she dared analyze.

"You, Harper Colby, are a natural. You sure you've never been on a horse before?"

Heat rushed to Harper's cheeks as she allowed Aiden to help her dismount. The feel of his strong hands spanning her waist sent nerves winging through her belly.

Once both feet were firmly planted on the ground, she turned to him, tilted her head back to compliment him on his teaching technique. But the words got all tangled up in her throat. The look on his face…

The look on his face took her breath away.

Slow enough that she had ample time to evade should she want to, he lowered his head, his intention clear. But she didn't give evading a second thought.

She went up on her tiptoes and met his lips halfway. Aiden, keeping one hand steady on the horse's bridle, swept an arm around Harper's waist and dragged her up tight against him. And he sank into the kiss like a dying man who'd found the light at the end of the tunnel. She slid her hands up his chest and over his broad shoulders until she could wind her arms around his neck. Shoulder to knee, she pressed against him, and she reveled in sensation as the long hard length of him bent over her, wrapped around her. Made her feel sheltered, protected…and desired beyond reason.

All else faded away. The ranch around them, the chilly air, the circumstances that had brought her here. She was lost to sight and sound, focused solely on the man and the kiss.

A massive equine chest bumped impatiently into them, nearly tumbling them to the ground. Laughing, they broke apart. Aiden, patting the horse's neck reassuringly, said, "Ok, Flapjack. You did good too. Let's get you inside and rubbed down. How about an extra treat for being so nice to the lady?"

As if he'd understood every word, Flapjack tossed his head and let out a long whinny.

Harper laughed again and followed them inside.

But the lesson wasn't over yet. Aiden unsaddled the horse, and then took her into Flapjack's stall. There he briefly touched on how to care for the horse, explaining the feeding and exercise schedule, and grooming. He was a patient man, answering each and every question she asked, even if they were probably silly to him.

Then he handed her a large rectangular brush. He maneuvered her alongside the horse and, standing behind her with one hand anchored on her hip, he placed his free hand over hers on the brush to guide her through the motions of grooming the animal.

The strokes were leisurely, repetitive, and soothing. His large body so close behind her, the heat of him surrounding her, his breath softly fanning the hair at her temple was anything but. The combination of Aiden's proximity and the motions of brushing the horse in the tiny, enclosed space propelled her into an unfamiliar place. All her senses seemed heightened. Her skin was just a little more sensitive, the scents surrounding her—the sweet hay, the horse, leather, and Aiden—slid through her veins like a drug. The light overhead made everything appear golden.

Enchanted.

No candlelit ambiance with fine champagne, decadent chocolate-covered strawberries, and romantic music could top this.

He'd been steadily, determinedly laying siege to her defenses from the moment they'd first kissed. Every day since, he'd gentled her to his touch, accustomed her to his voice and his scent. Addicted her to his kisses.

She hadn't realized it until it was too late.

Now? Now, she just didn't care anymore. She

wanted him too badly.

"That's it." Aiden's husky whisper at her ear sent a shiver down her spine. "Just like that."

She'd pulled her hair up into a ponytail earlier to keep it from blowing into her eyes while she was riding and had yet to take it down. Now her skin was bare, vulnerable to his lips and his breath. He released her hand and feathered the backs of his fingers along the side of her neck, slow and sure, timing each caress to the strokes of the brush against the horse's hide.

He eased closer, until his chest pressed against her shoulders, the undeniable ridge of his arousal against her backside. Harper's eyelids slid closed and she shuddered.

And then his lips replaced his fingers against her skin, and she moaned, deep in her throat. The hand at her hip crept forward, coming to rest, splayed, across her lower abdomen, holding her caged against his hard, hot frame. Sparks of awareness and desire ignited deep in her belly, dancing there. Her knees went to jelly.

Harper parted her lips and dragged in a shuddering breath. But her chest was oddly tight, and the air was exceptionally thin inside that stall. A faint thud just to her right barely registered. Her hand, now free of the brush, lifted. Her fingers tangled in the warm silk of his hair as she cradled the back of his head.

His hand dropped from her neck, slipped around her side. And then her breast was nestled in the searing heat of his strong palm. Harper's head fell back on his shoulder with a tiny whimper. His lips worked their magic up and down the column of her throat. Nipping. Slowly. Nibbling. Languidly. Tasting. Savoring.

Through the layers of cotton and flannel, he rolled

her nipple between thumb and forefinger. At the same moment, he found the sensitive spot, just behind her earlobe.

"Aiden." His name was torn from her on a ragged moan.

The stall suddenly spun as he whirled her around in his arms. With a hungry growl, he scooped an arm under her bottom, hoisting her up against him. Harper, oblivious to her surroundings, sealed her mouth over his, swept her tongue inside his mouth, wrapped her legs around his waist. She sank the fingers of her right hand deep in his hair, fisting it. Her other arm, she anchored along the back of his shoulders, bracing herself. She reveled in the bulging ripple and sinuous flex of his muscles. A the raw power beneath her fingertips.

Her back slammed into the rough wood wall, and Aiden followed, leaning all his weight into her, squeezing what little breath she'd managed to recover from her lungs. His erection thrust against the juncture of her thighs, over and over. Harper tilted her hips, eager and tormented, as he commandeered control of the kiss, devouring her. More. She wanted more. Needed more. This wasn't enough.

His hand was on her bottom, squeezing. His other hand slid up her shirt, his calloused fingers splayed, skimming her belly, up, up, settling over her breast. With nothing but a thin layer of satin and lace to separate them, his heat scalded her flesh. Her nipples, already puckered, ached for him.

He tore his mouth from hers, aiming for the side of her throat. "You make me forget about going slow," he rasped. "Make me forget where we are."

What was he saying? She could barely make sense

of the words. Didn't care. As long as he kept doing what he was doing with his hands and mouth and hips.

"Oh my God." The words were wrung from her on a tortured gasp. "Aiden, don't stop."

Questing fingers left her breast and angled down over her belly once again. The button at her waist popped free, her zipper slid down. Those dexterous fingers slipped beyond denim, dipped beneath cotton.

The first touch was almost her undoing. The texture of his slightly rough skin, the unyielding authority with which he claimed her, sliding through her folds, caressing the tiny bundle of nerves at her center made her eyes roll back in her head. Her breath hitched. And then, on a long slow glide, he eased a finger into her. Delicious friction shuddered through her entire system. Over and over. A second finger joined the first, stretching her, melting her from the inside out. His thumb pressed along her clitoris, rubbed, as he stroked her deep inside, and stars burst behind her eyelids.

His mouth found hers again. Lips meshed, teeth bumped, tongues tangled. This kiss burst at the seams with tightly leashed, barely restrained, pure, raw, unbridled lust. And it pushed her over the edge. She clung to him as a mind shattering orgasm rolled through her, shaking her to her core. She cried out, screamed really, as wave after wave of ecstasy catapulted her to the heavens. His mouth captured her cries, muffled them, ate them up like the most decadent of confections.

Boneless, she drifted back to earth, back to Aiden's arms as he peppered her face and neck with little kisses. He eased back, just a tiny bit, and peered at her face, his expression strained, hard and hungry.

He held her trapped in his steady stare, and he slid

his fingers from inside her, slowly, carefully. The movement, the way he looked at her now, was every bit as intimate as the orgasm he'd given her. Maybe more so. He withdrew his hand from her pants.

And then he kissed her again.

But this kiss was different. Just as heated as before, just as sexually charged. But more. Somehow…more. She couldn't put her thumb on it, but something had changed, the lines she'd drawn between them had been obliterated.

His hungry lips moved over hers, never losing their intensity. It comforted her in some strange, inexplicable way. Wrapped her in a thick, buffering layer of reassurance, even as it amped up her desire once more.

His erection pressed against her, reminding her that while she'd found release, he was still deep in the throes of need.

"I have to make love to you, Harper," he said, his voice little more than a throaty growl. "God, I need you so much."

Just now, timelines didn't matter anymore. Alexander Grant didn't even exist. Harper peered into Aiden's eyes for a moment longer.

This man…

He'd gotten under her skin. She'd just experienced probably the best orgasm of her life, and he'd only just started with her. She'd actually screamed, for the love of God. Her. The silent one during sex. From an orgasm he'd gifted her with just his fingers, in the middle of a very public stable.

And she'd screamed.

She licked her lips, took another deep breath. And then she pulled his head down, meshing her lips to his.

She couldn't come right out and say the words, not yet. But she could show him what she felt. Show him what she wanted.

And right now, more than anything else in the world, she wanted Aiden Whitebear.

He froze for a split second, as if he couldn't believe what her body was trying to tell him. Then he wrapped his arms around her and squeezed her tight. The horse shifted nervously behind him. As if coming to his senses, Aiden lifted her away from the wall and began carrying her toward the stall door. Where he was taking her? She didn't know. Nor did she care. As long as he made love to her once he got there, he could take her anywhere.

"Aiden, are you still here?"

The male voice coming from somewhere at the far end of the stables brought Aiden to a halt. He tore his mouth from hers and whipped his head toward the sound. His breathing was labored, ragged with pent up desire.

A door banged somewhere. "Aiden?" Another door opened, closed.

"Damn it," Aiden hissed beneath his breath. He lowered her to the ground, reluctantly released her. "Stay here," he said quietly.

Nodding, feeling adrift, like a stranger in her own skin, Harper moved back into the corner, out of the line of the door as he opened it. Aiden stepped into the wide walkway that ran the length of the stables, and he closed the door behind him, disappearing from view.

"I'm right here, Todd," she heard Aiden say.

"Oh, hey. I saw the lights on, thought I better come check on things. I didn't expect anyone to be here anymore."

The sound of Todd's voice penetrated the desire-induced fog, bringing Harper to her senses. Frantically, she began tugging at her clothes, zipping up and re-buttoning her jeans.

"It's late. What are you still doing here?"

"Well, I, ah, I was helping. Up at the lodge." Todd paused for a moment. "I was getting ready to leave, and I saw the lights on in here," he repeated.

"Everything's fine, Todd. I'm just finishing up. You go on home now."

"Sure thing. See you tomorrow." A moment passed, and then she caught the sound of a door closing.

She didn't wait for Aiden to return. Instead, she pushed the stall door open and strode out into the walkway. He turned, his chin dipped, and his gaze ran down over her. The look he gave her rocked her back on her heels.

He started forward then. Determined.

Quickly, Harper threw her hand up, palm out to stop him. "Wait. Just wait."

Frowning, he drew up short. Waited.

"What just happened in there…" Harper trailed off, trying to figure out what to say. "We shouldn't have…"

He pressed his lips together, and his shoulders rose and fell on a resigned sigh. "I said we'd take this slow. And you're right. That wasn't slow."

"No. No, it wasn't." She eyed him, wary. "Are you upset?"

"Well, I'd be lying if I said I wasn't disappointed. But upset? No." He closed the distance between them, cupped her face between his palms. He kissed her forehead. "Slow, it is."

He walked past her, reached for the light switch, flipped it off.

"You ready to go?" he asked over her shoulder.

She stared after him, completely at a loss. Why wasn't he angry? How could he just...just...

She shook her head and followed as he finished locking up the stables, shutting off lights. And she followed him, silent and pensive, across the darkened yard on the way to the parking lot. He opened the door for her, stood back while she climbed up and in. Aiden closed the door behind her, then went around the truck to climb in behind the steering wheel. But he didn't start the truck yet. Instead, he stared at the big lodge looming nearby, silhouetted by a harvest moon.

"I want to be clear. This isn't over, Harper," he said, turning to look at her at last, "I want you. I do. More than anything. I'll wait till you're ready. But I'm not going to give up."

She swallowed, not knowing how to respond to his honesty.

He waited a heartbeat longer before turning over the ignition. Aiden didn't speak again until they were nearly to Eagle's Nest. He didn't reach for her hand either, as he'd been doing every time he'd given her a ride to or from her cabin. She was surprised how much it bothered her, how used to holding his hand she'd become in such a short amount of time.

Maybe he was angry after all. Maybe he just kept it buried down deep like Alexander had.

Frowning, she peered out the window. Everything felt off now. Wrong somehow. As if, by leaving things unfinished between them, she'd thrown the balance of things out of kilter. Out in the open, the moonlight had been bright, illuminating the landscape. Here on the trails, with the trees dense and so close to the trail, completely overshadowing it in some places, the shadows seemed almost sinister. Oppressive. Chilling.

As he slowed to round the turn into her driveway, Aiden broke the silence. "I'll plan on you coming down for another lesson tomorrow when you're done with your shift."

"I'm done at four tomorrow."

"I know."

She tilted her head, questioning him with her gaze.

"I looked at your schedule." He grinned, unrepentant. "And, just in case you're wondering, I'm available every night this week for lessons when you're done working."

Just like that, with an easy grin, he put them back on track. Much as she might hate to admit it, relief swelled in her chest, making it difficult to talk at first.

"I'll keep that in mind." She glanced over to him then, expecting him to lean in and try to kiss her as she'd grown accustomed to. Or try to walk her to her door.

Instead, his smile turned rueful. "I'm not going to kiss you goodnight, angel."

She blinked at him, astonished. Had she been so transparent. And then disappointment settled in. He was angry after all—

"I can see all the questions floating around in that overactive brain of yours. And before you go jumping to the wrong conclusion, and I see you're already starting...if I get my hands on you again, Harper, if I kiss you? There's a very real chance I'm not going to be able to convince myself to slow down again, let alone stop. A man's control can only be pushed so far."

Her breath left her in a rush. Just like that, as fast as you could snap your fingers, a swarm of butterflies took flight in the pit of her belly, and a warm ache began deep in her core.

"Go. Now, before I change my mind," he urged.

Giddy, heat flooding her cheeks, Harper bounced from the truck. She all but floated across the gravel and up the steps. But halfway to her door, she paused, frowning.

Tilting her head, she surveyed the front of her cabin. Aiden's headlights slanted brightly across the window, the siding...and the door.

The door that was slightly ajar.

Backing up a step, her frown deepened. Had she left it open this morning by accident? Had she been in such a hurry to thwart Aiden that she'd not closed it properly? Stranger things has happened. But that wasn't like her at all.

Anxiety crawled up her spine. Montana was a long way from Philly. And yet...

The sound of a truck door slamming behind her drew her attention.

"Harper, what wrong?" Aiden was by her side in a flash, taking her elbow.

She blinked up at him, nodded toward the cabin. "The door's open."

Aiden's grip tightened on her arm. "Go back and get in the truck," he ordered, his tone terse, brooking no argument.

But she was having none of it. That was her cabin. If someone had broken in, she had a right to know. "Don't pat me on the head, Aiden. We've already had this discussion."

He shot her an aggrieved look, pressed his lips together and tugged her behind him. Aiden eased across the porch and, with the toe of his boot, he pushed the door open, paused. Then, careful as a thief, he moved inside, always keeping himself between her and the room.

Harper reached over and flipped on the light switch, casting away the darkness and bathing the room in soft white light. The room was empty. Aiden crossed to check the bathroom, looked behind the door and in the shower. She felt like a little kid waiting while a parent checked under the bed for the boogie monster. When he finished his sweep of the small cabin, he turned his attention to the windows, testing the locks.

Everything was, apparently, okay because he returned to her side and said, "All's clear."

When she turned troubled eyes to the door, he ran a reassuring hand from her elbow to her shoulder and back again. He went to the door, crouched down, inspecting the lock, the door handle, and the frame around the latch.

"It doesn't look as if it's been tampered with." He stood and faced her as she approached.

"Maybe…maybe I just didn't get it latched this morning."

"Maybe." He frowned, glancing around. "Everything look all right in here? Anything missing?"

Harper made a circuit of the room. She paused by the chest of drawers. The top drawer was slightly ajar. Frowning, worrying her lower lip with her teeth, she pulled it open and sifted through the papers she'd carefully tucked away for safe keeping. Her passport, her bank book…it was all still there. But had it been moved at all? Shifted around? She didn't think so…but then again, hadn't her passport been turned the other way?

No. She was probably imagining things. "Nothing

seems to be out of place. I'm sorry I kept you."

"It's no trouble. Better safe than sorry." He took her by the hand and walked toward the door with her in tow. "Maybe you should come up to my cabin and stay with me. You know, just to be on the safe side."

Smiling, she gave him a little push out the door. "That wouldn't be going slow."

"I can be a gentleman, angel."

The moment the word "gentleman" left his mouth on a seductive purr, it was as if someone had sucker-punched her right in the gut.

"That's exactly what I'm afraid of," she muttered, all but shoving him the final steps out onto the porch. And then she whirled around, nearly slamming the door in his puzzled face.

Turning, bracing her back against the door, she dropped her head forward, shook it. He was probably going to think she was nuts. He should. Because she was. Look at her. Running hot and cold. Look how quickly she'd forgotten that trusting a man could be dangerous. Her instincts screamed that she could trust Aiden.

But look how wrong she'd been before.

After what felt like an eternity, the sound of Aiden's boots crossing her porch echoed on the other side of the door. His headlights slid sideways and disappeared down the lane. Shoulders drooping, Harper shed Aiden's jacket and dropped it onto the back of a chair.

She wandered over and plopped down on the bed, kicked off her shoes. Kissing him, nearly making love with him in the stables had seemed so natural. Easy. Right. But now, after giving her libido a chance to cool down, she just wasn't sure anymore.

Wasn't sure of herself.

Wasn't sure of Aiden.

Or of anything anymore.

*"Go slow,"* he'd said.

But he'd also said he wasn't going to give up.

Harper raked her fingers through her hair. Then, some of the other things he'd said tonight came back to her. Things she'd deliberately avoided thinking about earlier. Now she couldn't get them out of her head. How wallowing in worry or not doing the things she wanted to do gave Grafton power.

Was that what she was doing with Alexander? Letting him have power over her, letting him control her still? Letting him dictate her life, even from his padded leather throne high up in that glass and steel castle back in Philly?

She'd left him, left it all behind. Or so she'd thought. But had she? Had she really?

Flopping back, she threw a forearm over her eyes and groaned. Unbidden, the memory of Aiden came to her. Aiden smiling at her, joking with her...kissing her. How he looked on a horse. How he treated Emmie and Kathryn. How he treated those that worked for him. And every single memory urged her to do the one thing she feared most.

Trust him.

Trust *in* him.

*What am I going to do about that man?*

Chapter Twenty

Harper put the last of her cleaning supplies away and glanced at the clock on the wall above the door. She'd had all day to think about what she was going to do about Aiden. And she still had yet to decide. She was due to meet him in the stables in less than ten minutes, and she couldn't come up with one valid, believable excuse why she couldn't, or shouldn't, go.

Emmie and Kathryn had gone into town to meet with the principal of the local school to finalize the last touches for the elementary Halloween field trip to the Bar L. She couldn't even hang out with Melanie as the girl had refused to come back to the ranch until the bear had been caught.

Besides, she couldn't avoid Aiden forever.

He still insisted on driving her to and from her cabin…just in case. And so, dragging her feet as though she were off to the gallows, Harper made her way to the stables. The large double doors near the driveway were thrown wide open to the unseasonably warm October afternoon. As soon as she stepped inside the building, voices drifted to her and she turned to locate the source.

Jim, the new stable master, stood across the bay near the stalls with his back to her as he spoke to another man. When Harper moved closer, she realized he was talking with Todd Sweeney, one of the stable hands, and her steps faltered. She didn't want to interrupt.

"Thanks again," Jim was saying, "for coming in to cover Bruce's shift today. I really appreciate it. And for picking up some of his other shifts until we get someone to fill the position."

"It's no problem," Todd replied. Then he caught sight of Harper and turned a shy smile her way. "Hi, Miss Harper."

Jim turned. "Oh, hey! I'll go on back and let Aiden know you're here. He's in the office finishing up some calls. I'm sure he'll be out in a few minutes."

"Thanks," Harper called to Jim's retreating back. She turned to the eager young man wielding a pitchfork like it was his mission in life. "Good afternoon, Todd. How are you?"

"I'm good, Miss Harper. Real good. Beautiful day, isn't it? I didn't realize it was supposed to get quite this warm." He paused to swipe the back of his forearm across his damp brow before digging back into the pile of aromatic straw at his boots. She tried not to smile at the way his cheeks bloomed with color or how he couldn't meet her eyes. His shyness was kind of endearing.

"It is beautiful. My favorite time of year. It's awfully quiet in here today. Where is everyone?"

"Won't be quiet for much longer. There's a group coming in for a Guided Trail Ride in about," he paused to glance at his watch, "oh, about fifteen minutes. And Randy took the intermediates out about forty-five minutes ago; they should be back any time now."

"Oh. Maybe I misunderstood. I thought I was supposed to—"

"Mr. Potts...ah, Jim, he's taking the next one. I overheard Aiden tell Mr...Jim that he's taking you for a riding lesson." Another pitchfork full of soiled straw found its way into the wheelbarrow. The long, pointed tines stabbed back into the dwindling pile of used straw on the floor. "I'm sure he wouldn't want anyone else teaching you."

"I see." She shuffled her feet, not knowing how to respond.

Dare she ask what rumors were going around about her and Aiden? Did she even want to know? Todd sure seemed to be acting as though Aiden had every right to be proprietary where she was concerned.

She was saved from having to comment any further by the steady clop of shod horses' hooves on concrete. She glanced over. Aiden led two saddled horses down the long isle between the rows of stalls.

"Have a good time, Miss Harper," Todd said.

Harper cast him a friendly smile. "I will, Todd. Thanks. You have a good evening too, in case I don't see you later."

His grin widened, and the color in his cheeks deepened. "Oh, you bet. I sure will. Thanks!"

Harper met Aiden as he entered the open bay. "Hi."

"Hi yourself." His gaze, heated and unmistakably hungry swept over her before settling on her lips. As though he were contemplating stealing a kiss. She fought the urge to moisten her lower lip, and instead took a step back. His lips twitched on a wry smile. "You did so well last night, I thought we might try one of the beginner trails."

A genuine smile crept over her face as delight lit her up from the inside out. "Really?" But then she hesitated. "You're sure it's safe?"

"Yep. We had Vince Abernathy—he's our resident

bear expert—come up and scope out the trails and the surrounding area. If he can't find evidence of bears—and he didn't—then there aren't any bears around to find. He figures the one that…the one from behind Dear Meadow probably didn't like that its stash had been disturbed…ah, I'm mean where it stored…well," he rubbed the back of his neck uncomfortably. "Abernathy figures the bear moved on back up closer to its den. Besides, this time of year, they tend to stick to the higher elevations, and the beginner trails are all lower, closer to the ranch. We've never had any problems with bears this far down the mountain before. So we'll stick to the lower trails, and we'll be fine."

A frown crinkled Todd's forehead. But Aiden was handing Harper the reins and nudging her forward before she could ask if anything was wrong.

For a moment, she thought about pointing out that if the trails were safe enough for trail rides, then they should be safe enough for her to resume her daily commute to and from her cabin via ATV. Independence dictate that she make the trek on her own. But…wasn't it better to be safe than sorry? What harm was there in letting things stay status quo…for now, at least.

She firmly shushed the little voice in the back of her mind taunting her that it had far more to do with liking the time she got to spend with Aiden, one on one, and very little to do with the bear that had ravaged that poor man up behind Dear Meadow.

"I'm ready when you are." Then she spotted the soft-sided cooler tied to the pommel of one of the horses. "What's that?"

He shot a shameless grin over his shoulder as he turned to tie a blanket to the back of his saddle. "Part of the guided trail ride is a picnic. There's this really nice little clearing up past the creek."

A small sound drew her gaze to Todd. But the stable hand quickly ducked his head and studiously turned back to his chore.

One corner of Harper's lips quirked up as she turned back to Aiden, and she shook her head. "It is, is it?"

"Yep." Aiden avoided eye contact, but he couldn't hide the dimple in his cheek, or the way his lips twitched. "It is today." He glanced over at Todd. "You be sure to knock off early tonight."

"I will." Todd nodded, his head down as he shoveled faster.

Side by side with Aiden, Harper led Flapjack from the stables. Once clear of the building, Aiden helped her up on the tall horse. His hands lingered on her thigh a little longer than necessary before he checked her stirrups. Then he mounted his own horse and nudged it into motion. Harper watched him for a moment, her heart doing little summersaults at the virile sight of Aiden on a horse before she urged Flapjack to fall in line.

For the first little bit, as they rode companionably along, Aiden gave her the spiel she was sure was standard with every trail ride. A brief history of the area and the Bar L. A run down on some of the scenic features, a gloss over of some of the wildlife they might encounter. And, once again, Aiden impressed her with his knowledge and patience.

The foliage had made the final transition into fiery autumnal colors, and the path Aiden led them along was alive with wildlife. Chipmunks and squirrels scampered here and there, hoarding supplies for the coming winter. Birds chirped and sang, fluttering overhead. As they crossed a shallow mountain stream, Aiden pointed out a beaver dam at the edge of the adjoining lake. They paused for a bit, silently observing the busy creatures as they chewed industriously at a small tree near their humble abode.

A little farther on, they came to a modest, secluded glen. Aiden drew his horse to a stop and dismounted. He tied Juniper's reins to a low branch, and then turned to assist Harper down. His hands lingered at her waist a moment, his eyes on her lips. But then he pulled away to tie Flapjack near his own mount. Her disappointment caught her by surprise. She'd been expecting him to try to steal a kiss.

And why did it bother her so much when he hadn't?

Wasn't that what she'd been trying to tell him she didn't want? Him kissing her all the time?

"Here you go," he said, handing her the rolled up blanket. A blanket much like the one he'd used to fend Grafton off with.

Harper pushed that troubling thought aside and accepted the blanket. No bad thoughts today. Aiden had been right about that much at least. The more she allowed negative thoughts like those into her head, the more power she gave to the man who'd caused it.

She turned to spread the blanket out in the middle of the clearing as Aiden retrieved the cooler, and she focused on the lush beauty of late autumn all around. Fiery reds and oranges, flaming yellows speckled with lingering sage and deep greens. It was still pretty warm out, yet the air held the scents of fallen leaves and a hint of wood smoke.

Harper dropped down on the edge of the blanket. She leaned back on her outstretched arms and tipped her head back. Closing her eyes, she drew the fresh air in, savored the warm caress of the sun on her face. The sound of Aiden's boots shuffling through the fallen leaves drew her attention.

"Nice place you got here," she said, shielding her eyes to glance up at him.

"Why, thank you, ma'am." He dropped to his knees, opened the cooler and began rooting around.

"I bet you bring all the girls here," she commented flippantly.

He glanced up at that. His dark brown eyes narrowed, and he cocked his head. He was silent for a long moment, and then, his voice holding a deeper note, a somber one, he replied, "Only the important one."

And, just like that, the playfulness disappeared. Harper swallowed and pushed herself into a more upright position. She crossed her legs and reached for one of the containers he'd unpacked.

Harper cleared her suddenly dry throat and asked, "So…what do we have here?"

"Cold fried chicken sandwiches, potato salad, apple pie, and…" Aiden held up a big thermos. "Hot chocolate. Though as warm as it is, I'm thinking I should have brought sweet tea or something cold instead."

"Oh, no. It'll get cold soon enough. Hot chocolate is just fine. Hand it over, buddy."

"Never let it be said I stood between a woman and her chocolate…liquid or otherwise." He passed the thermos and a tin mug over to her.

Humor restored, they settled into their meal with lighthearted banter. As they wound down to the last crumbs of pie, a single container they shared between them with two forks, the conversation turned personal.

"Emmie said you came to the Bar L a few months after Mark died?"

Aiden glanced over at her, clearly surprised by the sudden shift in conversation. She was surprised a bit as well, not having intended to broach the subject as she didn't know if it would be painful for him or not.

"Yeah. Soon as I got out of the hospital."

"So you were with him when he…when he…"

"Died. Yeah."

"I'm sorry. I shouldn't have—"

"No, it's all right." He licked his fork and tossed it into the cooler. Aiden fell silent as he repacked the rest of their finished meal before setting the plastic tote aside. Then he settled onto the blanket, laying on his stomach beside her, their hips nearly touching. His gaze turned distant as he looked to the trees on the far side of the clearing. "Took a while," he finally said. "But I'm okay talking about it now."

Harper remained quiet. She'd opened the subject, but now she didn't know how to proceed.

"I'd known Mark for years. We'd met in basic, ended up in the same unit, battle buddies. During deployment, we watched each other's backs." He reached out, plucked a long strand of grass and twirled it between his fingers. Harper lay back and turned on her side to face him, propping her head on her raised hand to see his face better. "We were running security sweeps through a particularly hostile area. We were leading the unit. The IED took out our Humvee, damaged the one behind us. As soon as the bomb blew, insurgents came swarming out of the hillside like cockroaches.

"The IED killed Gutierrez in the passenger seat instantly. Mark was driving. He was…he took the brunt of the explosion. I was in the back. Took shrapnel in my hip and thigh, my right arm. Not nearly as bad as Mark though." His voice trailed off there at the end, and his expression turned haunted. He squeezed his eyes closed, shook his head.

He might have said he was okay talking about this, but she could tell it was a raw wound that might never heal. Harper forced down the lump in her throat, clamped down on the urge to reach for him. She wanted to tell him they didn't need to talk about it anymore, but it was already too late.

He drew a deep breath. "So there we were, Gutierrez was...well, there wasn't much left of Gutierrez. And Mark was bleeding out, fast. Bullets were raining down on us, pinning us down, the mangled Humvee on fire...and Mark making me promise to look after Emmie and the Bar L."

"How did you get out?" Harper asked, her voice hoarse with suppressed tears. The sheer terror he must have felt. And watching his friend die right before his eyes, knowing he was dying with no way to save him? And Aiden himself injured...

"The rear detail managed to lay down enough cover fire for an evac. They gathered up survivors, called in for an air assist." He paused a moment, as if lost in the memories. When he spoke again, she knew there was much more that had happened that he hadn't shared. Was it to spare her? Or himself? She didn't push. "Spent almost three months between a hospital bed and physical therapy. And here I am."

Harper was quiet for a long time, thinking about what he'd said. She could barely wrap her mind around what he must have suffered through. Aiden had known

Mark since basic training. That was well before Mark and Emmie had married.

"I don't remember seeing you at their wedding."

"I wasn't there. My grandfather had passed away that weekend. I was needed at home."

"And where is home?"

His lips pressed tight for a moment. Then he turned his face to the woods once more. It was almost as if this conversation were more difficult for him than talking about nearly dying. "The Pine Ridge Indian Reservation."

Harper angled her head, curious. "Where's that?"

"The southwest corner of South Dakota, on the Nebraska border."

His manner was stiff now, almost taciturn. *Why?*

Now she pushed. This was where he'd grown up. This was a portion of his past that had molded him into the man he was today. This she...she *needed* to know.

"Tell me about it?"

He turned to her, his expression as closed off as she'd ever seen it. Guarded.

Did he fear she'd judge him?

Or was it something else? Something more personal?

He dragged in another breath, and then, his gaze still resolutely turned away, he began to speak. "The government established Pine Ridge in 1889. It's the eighth largest reservation in the U.S. Stronghold Table in the Badlands National Park was the location of the last of the Ghost Dances. When the U.S. government attempted to stop the dances on December 29, 1890, it resulted in the Wounded Knee Massacre.

"Miniconjou Lakota and Hunkpapa Sioux, led by

Chief Spotted Elk, sought sanctuary at Pine Ridge after fleeing the Standing Rock Agency where Sitting Bull had been killed. A heavily armed detachment of the Seventh Cavalry attacked the families, killing women and children as well as warriors. And in 1973, during the Wounded Knee Incident, members of the Oglala Lakota, my grandfather among them, and their supporters occupied the town in an armed standoff that lasted seventy-one days."

"Spouting off random statistics and interesting trivia facts isn't going to make me forget my question, Aiden. I can Google that information. I want to know what *your* life was like there. How you grew up. I was hoping you'd tell me about the people that were important to you."

One cheek crinkled up on a half smile when he realized she wasn't about to let him off the hook. "My father's people are Oglala Lakota." There was a wealth of emotion in that statement. Not all of it good. And when he continued speaking, his tone was bleak. "We lived in poverty. I'm talking overcrowded homes with leaky roofs and no running water. An unemployment rate of eighty to ninety percent, with a suicide rate more than twice the national rate. Someone was always sick, and health care was...strained at best.

"My father couldn't take the shame of living that way. He was so caught up in the glory of the old days, when warriors lived off the land and provided for their families, when they defended the tribes against all threats. He wrapped himself in stories the elders told like a cocoon against the world. Stories my grandfather told." Aiden shook his head. Bitterness had crept into his voice, and his expression turned grim.

"The old ways. Lot of good those stories did my dad.

He got wasted one night, went up on Stronghold Table and shot himself. My mother fell into the bottom of a liquor bottle—any liquor bottle she could get her hands on—and never came back out. I was six. So my grandparents took us in. Me and my sister. She was three. Four of my cousins were already living with them.

"My grandparents tried to make the best of it for us. But it was tough. We could see it. And every day, I was always hearing about the old ways. But those days were gone and staying on the reservation…it would have been a death sentence for me. Don't get me wrong. I'm proud of my heritage. I didn't turn my back on my people or their beliefs. But in this world, you have to adapt to survive. Living in the past without looking to the future is no good. You have to be able to honor the past, uphold the traditions, and still keep an eye on tomorrow. My grandfather didn't understand that's all I was trying to do.

"So, I took the only way out I could come up with. The day I turned eighteen, I joined the Army. My grandfather said I couldn't honor the old ways if I willingly sold my freedom to the same government that had abused my people so badly. He took my enlisting as a betrayal, a betrayal of my people, and a betrayal against him. I'd joined the enemy. The day I told him, he said I was dead to him. He never spoke to me again."

"Oh, Aiden," she whispered, unable to resist reaching out to him any longer. Harper gently touched his shoulder, ran her hand along his arm. "I'm so sorry."

He turned to face her at last, his eyes guarded. But, as a tear slid from the corner of her eye, his features softened. He reached up and, with the pad of his thumb, he brushed the moisture away. "You're tears kill me, angel. Don't cry for me. Please."

She couldn't speak. Anguish for the boy he'd been, sorrow for the man he'd become through pain and suffering twisted her heart, piercing it like a knife.

"I mean it, don't cry for me. I'm happy now. I found where I belong."

"Did you?"

"I did. Emmie and Kathryn...they're family now. The Ranch is my home. I do what I love, taking care of the horses, taking care of the ranch."

*And taking care of the people that live here*, she silently added.

She could see the truth of his words in his eyes. He was content here.

"What about your sister? Your mom?"

"My mom died when I was twenty. Cirrhosis of the liver. My sister, she's married. Still living on the Res. Three kids and a dog. She works as a liaison between the community and government agencies to bring assistance to those in need."

Harper bit her lip. She wanted to offer sympathy for the loss of his mother. But the look on his face as he'd mentioned her fate had nipped that in the bud. There was still too much anger there for him to willingly accept condolences.

"Turn around is fair play. So tell me about you." Now he rolled onto his side to face her, mirroring her by propping his head on his upraised hand.

"I was an only child. Grew up in a middle-class household. Went to a good public school and graduated with Emmie. I lost my parents in an accident after graduation. I was already out on my own by then, so it wasn't quite as hard to navigate. But you're never really prepared to lose a parent, no matter how old you are. I attended a local college and ended up in Philly. I had a good job as a bank teller, got along well with my co-workers. Had some good friends. Had a great apartment."

"So what happened then?"

Harper dropped her gaze to the buttons on his open flannel shirt. Without thinking, she reached across the small space dividing them and began plucking at his third buttonhole, running the soft fabric back and forth between her fingers. "Alexander Grant happened."

Wow. And she'd thought *he'd* sounded bitter earlier. He had nothing on her.

He remained silent, waiting.

"A friend of a friend introduced us. Alexander was very good at sweeping people off their feet. Before I knew it, I was giving up my apartment, moving in with him. My friends slowly began disappearing. Pretty soon he was controlling nearly every aspect of my life. Where we ate dinner, the gym where I worked out. He paid for a high-priced personal trainer. He even gave my entire wardrobe a makeover."

The fabric slid between her fingers, soft and hypnotic, soothing. She reached the fourth open buttonhole, poked just the tip of her finger through the opening. "And then the final straw. He sent his hired henchman, a guy named Sloan, to the bank where I worked. You see, he didn't like the fact that I worked. Said it hurt his reputation. I can't prove anything, but shortly after his henchman left—I'm talking less than half an hour later—my boss called me into his office and more or less fired me. Offered lame reasons, alluding to discrepancies and misconduct. But I was good at my job.

Always honest. I never did anything wrong.

"When I went to Alexander's office to confront him, he hit me in the face, punched me in the ribs. Left me lying on the floor like…like a piece of trash. He called Sloan to come drag me out of his office and dump me in my car."

She kept playing with that red and black flannel, focusing on it as though it were a talisman, unable to meet his eyes for the shame that filled her.

"I went back to the penthouse. I was in shock, didn't know what else to do. My first reaction was to pack my bags and leave. I had the suitcase open and some stuff thrown in. But then I…I started second guessing myself, second guessing everything really. I'd been raised to believe that when you made a commitment, you didn't just bail when things got tough. So, I unpacked it all, and I stayed. Just long enough for him to come home so we could talk it all out.

She huffed out a mirthless laugh. "I had this stupid, naïve notion that it had been a mistake. All some giant misunderstanding. That when he came home he'd apologize or something and we'd work it out."

She shook her head, her brow tightening on a frown. But she kept her gaze fixed steadily on the white T-shirt stretched taut across his muscular chest, and the red and black fabric between her fingers. If she looked at him, she'd lose her nerve. She just knew it.

"So I waited for him. Like a fool, I waited. And when he came home…" Her voice trailed away as she fought down the bitter gall in her throat. "Well… needless to say, when I regained consciousness, I could hear him in the shower. I dragged myself up off the floor and crept through the penthouse, quickly tossed some stuff in a bag, and ran away with my tail tucked between my legs."

He'd held himself so still, so utterly silent the whole time, and she couldn't stand it any longer. What judgment would she see in his eyes? Disgust? Disappointment?

Finally, she risked glancing up.

Fury. Raw and startling.

He looked ready to kill something…or someone.

Shocked, she began easing back. But his hand shot out, caged her shoulder in a gentle, but inescapable grip. "He knocked you unconscious, and he left you on the floor?"

His voice shook with rage.

Harper blinked and nodded, unable to speak. She must look like an owl right now, her eyes felt so huge.

"I'll kill him," Aiden whispered, his voice dangerous and deadly soft.

"No!" She pressed her fingers to his lips. "No, Aiden. It's over. He's out of my life. He can't hurt me anymore."

His eyes narrowed. "Are you sure about that?"

She thought briefly of Sloan, how he'd been waiting for her outside her hotel room that morning. As livid as Aiden was right now, there was no way in hell she'd tell him about that.

"Yes."

"Really?"

Now he was talking about something all together different than her physical safety, and she knew it. He was talking about letting Alexander control her, and stopping him, the way they'd stopped Grafton from controlling them by going ahead with her riding lesson anyway.

Harper sucked in a sharp breath. She'd feared sharing her shame with anyone...well, anyone other than Emmie and, by extension Kathryn. But telling Aiden what had happened to her had been...cathartic. Like expelling poison from her system. Aiden made her feel safe, without threatening her peace of mind. Yes, he could be controlling, but not like Alexander. Not at all like Alexander.

Aiden held tight to people, looked out for them, did what he thought was best...because he cared. Because he'd lost what little he'd had, lost the people he'd loved.

And he was a better man for all that he'd lost. He hadn't let it twist him or turn him into a horrible person. Oh, he had bitterness in him still, resentment. And so much anger. He had issues he still needed to resolve. Some might never be put to rest. He wasn't perfect.

But he was...he was Aiden.

And she'd fallen for him.

"Yes," she whispered.

## Chapter Twenty-One

"Yes," she whispered one more time. But this time she wasn't thinking about Alexander. Alexander didn't matter anymore and never would again. She was taking back control, seizing the power. Right here. Right now.

She wouldn't let Alexander steal another moment's worry or fear or anxiety from her. And she wouldn't let Alexander steal another moment of happiness either...from her, or from the man she'd come to... Come to...

She wasn't ready to say the words, not even in the quiet of her own mind.

Harper searched his face. Some of the anger had faded, but he was still visibly upset. And yet his hold on her arm was so tender, so...comforting.

Just like last night in the stables, she realized. She's railed at him, got up in his face and yelled. She'd called him names, something she never imagined she'd ever do to someone, and she'd behaved like a harridan. And what had his reaction been?

He'd tried to comfort her.

Aiden would never hurt her. He might drive her crazy. Might irritate her and piss her off.

But he'd never hurt her. And that she'd stake her life on.

She scootched up, leaned over him, and sealed her lips to his. Startled, his eyes went wide. She watched with no small degree of satisfaction as his eyelids eventually slid closed. And she savored the moan she wrung from deep in his throat.

His hand slid around her waist, drawing her closer, pulling her down on top of him as he lay back. Harper followed willingly. She slid her thigh up and over his until she straddled him. Angling her head, she deepened the kiss. Time and place melted into nothingness. She sank her fingers into his hair and gave herself up to the kiss, gave herself up to him.

Aiden, his arms wrapped tight around her, suddenly sat up, taking her with him. He didn't break the kiss as he wrestled his arms from the flannel, flung it away from him. Then he pulled and tugged until her flannel outer shirt came off as well.

Lips meshed, tongues tangled. Hands explored. His body was so hot and hard against hers. She writhed in his arms, desperate to get closer, desperate to feel skin on skin.

Movements frantic, he rolled them over until he was on top. And he kept right on pulling and tugging and kissing and murmuring until they were both naked.

The air had begun to cool, but she barely noticed. His heat surrounded her now, his skin molten as he reared up over her, dominating the kiss. There was nothing cold or calculating about Aiden. He was all passion, all flame and out of control. He lavished kisses along the column of her throat. He closed his hand over her breast, his calloused hands gentle as he kneaded and caressed. Dexterous fingers plucked and thrummed her nipple, and she arched her back into his touch. Murmurs of delight rose up, and she did nothing to stifle them. Instead, it seemed, the more sounds she made, the wilder, the hungrier he grew. Driven to hear more.

He nudged a knee between her thighs and one hand trailed down over the curve of her waist and the flare of her hip. His erection, hot and long and oh-so-hard, lay heavy against her thigh. Her core ached for him. She lifted her hips in silent plea, dug her fingertips into his skin in greedy demand. She needed him inside her, now. Right now. It was the only thing she could focus on, the only thing she could think about.

But he, apparently, had other ideas. His lips left a trail of fire down over her collar bone and between her breasts. He paused for a moment, paying homage first to one, then the other, suckling and lapping ravenously at her inflamed nipples, nipping and nibbling at the sensitive skin on the underside of her breasts.

Then he slid farther down, peppering her stomach with nips, nibbles, and lingering kisses from breastbone to navel. Harper was helpless to do more than whimper and squirm. He captured her hips in his hands as he eased farther down, trapping her in place as he nudged her thighs wider with his broad shoulders.

"Aiden, I—oh!" Whatever she'd meant to say flew away at the first touch of his lips and tongue on her most sensitive flesh.

Hot, wet, rasping flicks of his tongue made her mouth fall open, made her head tilt back, made her chest arch. And when he closed his mouth over her, sucking and lapping…her legs shook, and her body trembled.

He was a voracious lover. Hungry. Demanding. And so completely *un*selfish. Showering her with attention. Drenching her in sensation.

She couldn't take anymore. Thought she'd go crazy if he continued another second. She reached down to push him away, gasping, all but sobbing. Ready to beg for him to take her.

Aiden ignored her movement, sinking farther into his current obsession instead. He slid his hands up under her thighs and around her hips, grasped her wrists, and tugged them to the ground at her sides. There he pinned them as he continued his quest to make her lose her mind.

"Oh God, Aiden, please," she sobbed.

He growled against her and stroked her quivering flesh with renewed vigor.

Harper came in a blinding flash. Her body erupted, flying into a million pieces. The sound of her own scream was startling. Wave after wave of bone-melting spasms rocked through her. And when, at last, she finally made the descent back to earth, Aiden was right there, peppering the insides of her thighs with dozens of butterfly kisses. Her heart stuttered and then pounded harder at this unexpected tenderness so fast on the heels of his ruthless sensual onslaught.

Harper forced a swallow, her mouth dry, her throat suddenly hoarse. Her whole body was quivering. One great big exposed nerve. She cracked her eyelids open in time to see him prowl up the length of her body. The muscles in his shoulders bunched and flexed. His swollen, pulsing shaft hanging heavy between his legs. His expression akin to that of a hungry wolf stalking, anticipating, ready to devour.

He lowered his large frame over her, settled between her thighs. His muscular arms braced on either side of her head, supporting his weight and caging her at the same time. This moment, as the broad head of his penis nudged her slick entrance, as his body surrounded her, as he stared deep into her eyes, was, hands down, the most intimate moment she'd ever experienced in her life. Even more so than the stolen moment in the stables. And she'd thought *that* one untouchable. This was a moment branded upon her very soul.

He waited.

What was he waiting for?

She moved restlessly beneath him and searched his strained expression.

Harper lifted her legs, wrapped them tight around his narrow waist. She slid her hands up over his ribs and around his back, anchoring them on his shoulders.

And still he waited.

Harper let a smile slowly slide into place. A wide, satisfied, brilliant smile.

As if that was all he'd been waiting for, he pushed inside her in one long, slow, steady, unstoppable flexing of his hips. He stopped once more when he was seated all the way to the hilt. And he searched her face, as if to reassure himself that she was doing all right.

And then he began to move.

He began to really *move*.

His hips rolled with each thrust, changing the angle ever so slightly. His muscles coiled and flexed beneath her hands and all around her. With every glide inside her, the hard six-pack of muscles on his abdomen crunched and released. His rock-hard pecks rubbed and pressed against her breasts providing just enough friction to drive her mad.

And deep inside, the fullness of him sliding in and out, stretching her, filling her, broke the last of her defenses. A fine sheen of sweat covered them both now. Aiden slid one hand down to her thigh, lifting her knee a little higher against his hip as his tempo began to pick up speed. This new angle brought him deeper inside her, and she gasped and moaned approval.

The coils of another orgasm were already tightening low in her belly. Harper shivered as Aiden turned his hot mouth to the side of her throat, kissing and licking upward until he sucked her earlobe between his teeth.

"Aiden," she panted, clutching at him. "Please, oh God! I need—"

He rolled his hips and thrust deeper, harder, sending her skyrocketing to the heavens once more. She screamed his name, her nails digging into his skin as she fought to hold on, fought to anchor herself. But it was no use.

The orgasm she'd had before beneath his mouth was nothing compared to this. This one crashed through her like a tsunami. Sweeping her away, drowning her in ecstasy.

Above her, as her inner muscles clenched and spasmed around his shaft, Aiden groaned and shuddered. Her name was ripped from him, a hoarse growl. A soul-deep exultation. And then he began pounding into her as though a dam had broken. Four hard thrust that shook the earth and shattered him, sending him careening over the edge after her. He buried his mouth in the curve of her shoulder and gave a guttural shout as deep inside her his shaft jerked and pulsed.

Limbs tangled together with hers, still buried deep within her, Aiden raised his head and sprinkled soft kisses along her jaw.

He lifted his head, peered down at her through slumberous eyes, and turned her world inside out. "Promise me you'll never leave me, Harper, and I *swear* to you I'll never give you reason to want to."

His dark eyes were so solemn, so deep. She reached up with a trembling hand and tenderly cupped the side of his face. "Oh, Aiden," she whispered.

And she kissed him. Pouring every ounce of emotion she could into the moment. Pouring every word she couldn't bring herself to speak into the kiss. As the kiss deepened, he grew hard inside her once more. A testing flex of his hips brought her legs up to lock around his waist again.

And then they were moving as one, the pace slower this time, languidly moving them toward that shining, earth-shattering, soul-fusing moment. Binding them together more deeply than any spoken vow could.

\*\*\*\*

Aiden was the first to reach for their clothing. As reluctant as he was to end this interlude, the sun was beginning to go down and if they didn't get moving soon, they'd be negotiating the trails in the dark. His original intention had been to woo her some more on this picnic, to soften her up. Not to seduce. Though, at this point, he wasn't quite sure who had seduced whom. Either way, it was all right with him.

She was his now. And he'd do everything in his power to make sure she wanted to keep it that way.

A shiver worked its way through his system. With the setting sun, the temps were beginning to fall. He didn't want Harper catching a chill, and he could already see the goose bumps on her bare arms.

He still couldn't believe things had gone from hashing out painful past experiences to full-on sex in zero-to-sixty. Not that he was complaining. He was a guy after all. He just didn't want her to have second thoughts…or regrets.

Aiden watched from the corner of his eye as she pulled her clothes on. The satisfied smile curling the edges of her kiss-swollen lips was a pretty strong argument against possible regrets. And, truth be told, the sight of it puffed his chest up just a little bit.

Okay, a lot.

"What are you thinking about?" he couldn't help but ask.

"That was the first time I've ever had sex outside of a bed."

He paused in zipping up his jeans to stare at her. "You serious?"

"Mm-hmm."

"Not even when you were a teenager? No backseats for you?"

"Not even then. Tommy Jensen's parents were out of town on a business trip and we had sex in his room on his bed that first time. The second time too, come to think of it. We broke up a few months later. I caught him in the back seat of his Nova with Sally Kindrick. I was devastated," she said with the air of a jaded adult remembering childhood angst as she buttoned her flannel shirt.

Grinning, he asked, "Shall I hunt him down and break his nose for you?"

"No, but I appreciate the offer." Laughing, she stepped closer to him, stepped into him, and went up on tiptoes to steal a quick kiss. But he was having none of that. His arms wrapped around her waist and he tugged her closer, deepening the kiss with the intent of curling her toes.

When he released her at last, albeit reluctantly, the dazed look on her face said he'd succeeded. His chest puffed a little more.

"Come on," he prompted, catching her hand and dragging her over to the horses. "We better get a move on. It's going to get dark fast now."

He helped her up onto Flapjack's saddle, then he quickly retrieved the remnants of their picnic. Soon they were on their way. Aiden eyed the angle of the rapidly setting sun and made a judgment call. Harper seemed pretty sure of herself in the saddle, and if they took the Otter Creek Trail instead of the Beginner Trail as they'd done coming up, they could shave at least twenty minutes off their ride back. Decision made, he angled the horses' descent through thicker bush and undergrowth until he found the switchback, and then he guided them onto the new trail.

The horses were fine until they cut back once again across the creek about a mile later. Juniper tossed his head and sidestepped, his eyes darting this way and that. A quick glance over his shoulder confirmed Harper was struggling to control the normally obedient Flapjack as well.

"What's that sound?" Harper asked, her worried gaze skimming the trees around them as she gripped the saddle horn with one white-knuckled grip and clenched the reins with the other.

He'd been wondering that himself. It sounded like a low hum. Or buzzing. A constant drone that grew louder the farther they went. Frustrated with the suddenly skittish horses, Aiden dismounted. He gathered Juniper's reins and took hold of Flapjack's halter, and then turned the animals away from the buzzing. He soothed the animals, controlling them from the ground.

"Are there a lot of bees around here? Like beehives

or something?"

"No. Not on the ranch. And definitely not this close to the trails."

"What was that sound then?"

"I'm not sure."

"Stop the horses a minute," she said, making to dismount. "Don't you want to find out?"

He drew the horses to a standstill so she could get down. He thought about telling her to stay up there, but, from the determined look on her face, he figured it would be pointless.

"I'll come back and check later."

"When, after it's dark?"

He pressed his lips together. He didn't want to have this argument now. He didn't know what was out there. Probably a deer carcass or something. It sounded like the drone of flies. A lot of flies. But he didn't want to mar their evening with the stench of a dead deer. Besides, on the off chance that the bear was still in the area, the smell might draw it. And he sure as hell didn't want her around *that*.

"Tomorrow. I'll come back tomorrow."

"Well, that's just silly. We're here now. We might as well go and see what it is."

He leveled her with a look that put most of his stable hands in line without a word. It didn't even phase her.

He rolled his eyes. "Fine."

He turned away to tie the reins loosely on a low nearby branch. But as he turned back around, instead of standing by the horses, she was right at his side. He dropped a kiss to her forehead, thinking that's what she'd been waiting for. "You stay here on the trail with the horses, I'll be right back."

"I'm going with you."

"Like hell you are. I have no idea what's out there."

"Yeah, well," she glanced around, displaying the first sign of nerves she'd shown yet. The shadows were beginning to lengthen, damn it. He didn't have time to argue with her. "Well, what if that bear does come back? I don't want to be out here alone."

Aiden gritted his teeth. "They usually steer clear of the ranch, and we aren't that far away now. For the most part, they like to avoid people."

"Really? 'Cuz the other day back at Deer Meadow, that bear didn't look like he minded people all that much. Especially while he was smacking his big beary lips and all but singing, 'mmm, mmm, tastes just like chicken.'"

Aiden peered at her, hard, his lips parting, his gaze disbelieving. At length, he drew in a deep breath, closed his eyes, and shook his head. Heaving a sigh, he cautioned, "Stay close. Stay quiet. And do exactly as I tell you. Even if I tell you to run. Understood?"

Harper nodded.

"Harper—"

"I promise."

Knowing it would do no good to try to argue with her anymore, he turned to creep into the woods. He reached back for her hand and was somewhat mollified when she immediately placed her palm against his, twining their fingers together.

Aiden cursed the folly of this. The light was fading now, the shadows far from the immediate vicinity all but indecipherable. This was stupid. They should go back.

But the buzzing was near deafening now. And that's when he caught his first whiff. The stench was—

Oh man. That smell…

He buried his nose in the crook of his elbow. A quick glance over his shoulder told him Harper had slapped her free hand over her mouth and nose. Her eyes were huge.

He'd smelled that stench before. Too many times before. Many, many times overseas. And once right here on the ranch.

And he knew what it meant.

But before he could do an about face, he spied something in the woods, just up ahead. The flash of stark yellow. A few more steps, and a closer look confirmed the worst. He made to turn, to shield Harper and bustle her away before she could see. But he was too late. She gave a muffled cry and thumped into his back, tucking her face between his shoulder blades.

Chapter Twenty-Two

For the second time since she'd arrived in Montana, Harper saw a dead body. This one was suspended by the ankles by bright yellow rope from a tree. The back of the man's wrists dragged on the ground, partially submerged in a pool of still dripping blood. She couldn't see his face as it was covered in too much...gore. And while his boots and his camouflage pants were relatively clean, the man had been...gutted, for lack of a better term. Cut from sternum to the waist of his pants...or vice versa. And everything inside had just sort of spilled out.

Squeezing her eyes closed, Harper pressed her face to Aiden's back.

*Oh, God, that poor man. Who could do such a thing?*

She fought down the bile rising in the back of her throat.

Aiden spun on his heel and clamped his hands on her shoulders. "Run!"

"What? We can't just leave him up—"

"Run, damn it." He pushed her around and propelled her in front of him.

"But, Aiden, he's—"

"He's dead. And us stickin' around isn't going to change that. Damn it, Harper, don't argue with me. A bear can smell a dead carcass upwind up to twenty miles. And right now, the wind is sweeping up the mountain like a dinner bell. If that bear isn't already on its way, it will be soon. I don't want either of us here when it arrives."

"But you said—"

She tripped over a root concealed under a patch of leaves. Aiden caught her under the armpits and hauled her to her feet before dragging her along in his wake. "I don't care what I said. Move!"

"Aiden—"

Tree branches slapped her in the face. The shadows were all around now, closing in on them from every direction. And, but for the unnaturally loud drone of the flies, the woods were silent. Too silent. Eerily so.

And the smell—though it was probably fading the farther they ran—seemed seared in her nostrils. She'd never forget that stench as long as she lived.

"He was still dripping, Harper," Aiden hissed.

*Still dripping?*

*What the hell is that supposed to mean?*

And then it hit her right between the eyes. *Still dripping.* As in a fresh kill. As in, the killer could still be out there, following them in the dark. And it was dark now. They'd never see him coming. If Aiden wasn't leading her, she'd be completely lost to the trail.

Now she kicked up speed, keeping pace with him, for once grateful for the brutal regimen that high-priced personal trainer had insisted on.

They were probably making too much noise trampling along in the fallen leaves, slapping branches aside. Heaven knew, someone—or some*thing*—could probably hear the breath sawing in and out of her burning lungs from a mile away. But there was nothing she could do about that right now. The only thing she could do was hang on to Aiden's hand like the lifeline it was and try her best not to trip again.

The soft whicker of the horses was the best sound she'd ever heard. But instead of Aiden helping her to mount Flapjack, he all but tossed her up on Juniper's back. He swiftly gathered the reins for both mounts, and then he vaulted into the saddle behind her, reminding her of those old timey movies with Native American Warriors stealing away with a captive. Wrapping one arm around her, pinning her back to his chest, he growled at her ear, "Hold tight."

*Hold tight to what?*

But she couldn't find her voice. Thumping his heels to the horse's sides, hunched protectively around her, Aiden urged the animals into a pace far faster than Harper would have been comfortable with in the dark…probably in the daylight too…provided there wasn't a dead body, a blood-thirsty killer, and potentially a hungry bear behind them.

Every shift in the shadows made Harper bite back a scream. She half expected the path to be blocked around every curve in the bend by a ghoulish knife-wielding fiend, or to hear the blood-curdling roar of a man-eating grizzly charging after them. It was the one you don't see coming that was always the most dangerous.

They reached the ranch not a moment too soon for Harper. Aiden took them straight to the stables first. He dismounted, then helped her down. He led the horses inside, left Harper holding the reins, and hurried to the phone in his office. When he came back from filling the sheriff in, he made short work of unsaddling the horses and getting them tucked into their stalls. He took one look at Harper's face, and then drew her into his arms.

"Are you okay?"

"No. I-I don't think I am." She clutched the back of his shirt in her fists as hysteria began to creep into her voice. "I'm about finished with finding dead bodies, Aiden. I don't think I can take it anymore."

He ran his hands up and down her back, gave her a squeeze. Drawing a deep breath, he pressed a kiss to her forehead. "Come on," he said, drawing back before capturing her hands. "Let's go to the Lodge. We need to talk to Emmie and Kathryn, let them know what's going on."

She nodded, distracted. She couldn't get the ghastly sight of that body hanging from the tree out of her head. What had ever made her think coming to Montana would be safer than staying in Philly?

Somewhere, Aiden had located his coat, the one he'd loaned her that first night, and helped her pull it on.

"I need to get my own coat," she said. The disjointed thought popped out of nowhere. She waited as he buttoned the front for her.

He brushed his hand down her hair before pinching her chin lightly between thumb and forefinger and lifting her face to his.

"No, you don't."

"You need your coat back, Aiden." Why she was suddenly so concerned about the coat, she didn't know. Probably a coping mechanism, deflecting her focus so she didn't think about… "First thing in the morning, I'll go—"

"Don't worry about it. I have another. Besides, I like seeing you wear it." With that, he took her by the hand and, flipping off the last of the lights on their way out, he led her from the stables.

The lodge was lit up like a beacon in the night. The

big, ornate windows gave off a warm golden glow against the dark autumn sky. But tonight, the scarecrow and cornstalk bundles cast malevolent shadows, unsettling her. The trees in the distance were inky with the night, harboring threats that no one could have anticipated.

They covered the short distance between the stables and the lodge in silence. Once inside, he took her straight to Emmie's rooms at the far end of the lodge. A quick rap brought Emmie to the door of her apartment.

"Well, I wasn't expecting you two." Emmie said with a smile as she pulled the door farther open. But then she tilted her head and frowned with concern when she caught sight of Aiden's expression and Harper's utter stillness. "What's wrong?"

"We need to talk," Aiden said without preamble, pushing past Emmie. He strode inside the room, dragging Harper with him. "Where's Kathryn?"

"I think she's at the café."

"Call her over. It's important."

Aiden pushed Harper down onto the sofa in Emmie's living room. Harper went without a fuss. She'd fallen into some strange fog where very little mattered just then, and she couldn't seem to shake it. She caught the way Emmie's eyes flared in alarm, but Harper couldn't sooth her friend, couldn't reassure her that everything would be all right. Not tonight. Not now.

Not with a dead man hanging in a tree.

The second dead body she'd seen in a week.

Emmie hurried across the room and picked up the phone. A few quiet words were exchanged, and then Emmie hung up the phone and dropped down beside Harper on the sofa. She turned a worried gaze to Aiden.

Aiden, in turn, had been pacing the length of the living room, running an agitated hand through his hair and across the back of his neck.

Harper watched it all in silence, wondering if this was what an out of body experience felt like. She knew she was here. Could feel the chill in her own skin against the warmth of Emmie's hands, the softness of Emmie's sofa, hear the words Emmie and Aiden were exchanging. But none of it seemed to matter, none of it computed.

"Aiden, what's going on? What happened to Harper? She hasn't spoken a word since you got here."

"I'd like to wait for Kathryn. I don't want to go through this any more than we have too." He sent a pointed look Harper's way.

*I'm still here, Aiden. And I saw that,* she wanted to say. But her vocal cords didn't seem to be functioning.

"Maybe you should give her some hot coffee or something. She's had a bad shock."

Great. Now Emmie really did look worried. Couldn't Aiden just spit out what had happened so Emmie wouldn't jump to conclusions?

Then again, how much worse could it get than a dead man dangling from a tree?

"Here," Emmie said.

Harper blinked and glanced down when hot ceramic met her chilled skin. Numbly, she clasped the coffee cup, wondering what she was supposed to do with it.

Aiden muttered a soft curse before crouching in front of her. He carefully took the mug from her and lifted it to her lips. "Drink, angel. Just a little. It'll help."

Harper obediently complied before Aiden set the cup aside. He took her hands in his and began chafing warmth into them. Emmie sat silently by, observing, visibly bemused. Just then, Kathryn came barging in, followed nip and tuck by Jonah and another deputy.

"What the hell's going on?" Kathryn demanded the moment she laid eyes on Aiden and Harper.

Harper felt like a voyeur, observing everything through a detached perspective. Jonah crossed the room, stopping beside Emmie. Hovering almost protectively over her. He cut a fine figure in his uniform, with his broad shoulders filling out his sage green coat, his shiny badge, and the loaded utility belt strapped around his lean waist. His neatly trimmed, golden blond hair was damp, the ends curling just a little over his collar.

He and Emmie would make a fine pair. Like Snow White and Prince Phillip. Wait…Prince Phillip belonged to Cinderella, didn't he? Then who was Snow White's prince?

Once the deputy had closed the door behind him, and everyone seemed to have taken up their stations around the room, Aiden dropped onto the sofa beside Harper. He slipped his arm around her waist and drew her closer.

"What's going on, Aiden?" Kathryn pressed once more.

Aiden's arm tightened almost imperceptibly around her. Did he think she was going to go running off? Where would she go? Into the woods?

An old rhyme came back to her then, and she nearly giggled.

*"If you go out in the woods today, you're sure of a big surprise. If you go out in the woods today, you'd better go in disguise."*

Lord love a duck, she was losing her mind.

She blinked and focused on Aiden. His warmth

along her side and the sips of coffee sitting warm in her stomach were starting to penetrate the bone deep cold that had settled over her system.

Aiden laced his fingers through hers. "There's another body up on the trails."

A split second of stunned silence fell over the room. Then all hell broke loose. *How could that much sound come from four people?*

"Okay, okay, settle down," Jonah said, taking control of the situation. Levelheaded, ever the voice of reason, he instructed, "Give me the rest, Aiden."

"Harper and I went for a trail ride. We were headed back to the ranch, coming down Otter Creek Trail to save time since we were losing daylight so fast. Just after the switchback," he glanced to Emmie, "right before you get to the big boulder with the tree growing out the side," she nodded, indicating she knew where he was talking about, "we heard this really loud buzzing sound. We dismounted, left the horses tied up, and we walked closer.

"There's a guy tied by his ankles to a branch about six feet up in an Elm tree. Yellow nylon rope, looked new. Worn hiking boots, camo pants. Camo jacket, open. Couldn't tell the color of the shirt underneath. Too much…" he glanced to Harper and finished with, "ah, blood. He'd been gutted. Waist to sternum. I'd say a hunter maybe, judging by the clothing. I didn't see tracks, horse or ATV, no sign of the killer, but it was getting pretty dark. He could have been standing twenty feet away, and it would have been hard to see him."

Jonah eyed him, expression grim. "What else?"

"He was still dripping." Aiden's voice was flat, emotionless.

There were those words again. *Still dripping.* God, she didn't want to ever hear those words again.

"I got Harper back to the horses, and we took off down the trail back to the ranch. And then I called you."

"Miss Colby, did you see anything?"

"Harper," she whispered. Then, finding her voice at last, she drew a deep breath. Harper stiffened her spine, met his kind blue eyes, and she spoke a little louder. "This is the second time you've questioned me about a dead man, sheriff. It's probably about time you called me by my first name."

His gaze roved over her face, dropped to the arm Aiden kept anchored around her. He nodded. "Harper. Did you see anything up there that Aiden might have missed?"

"No. It was just like he said. The noise from the flies was so loud. And his wrists…the backs of his hands were partially submerged in a pool of blood." She shuddered at the memory, refusing to let herself become physically ill.

Aiden's hand began rubbing up and down her spine, beneath the jacket. She watched as Jonah shot a glance over his shoulder at the deputy. The man looked familiar. That's right. He was the one who'd hauled Bruce Grafton off last night. Darby. Jeff Darby, Aiden had called him.

The deputy reached for the radio clipped to his collar as he moved toward the door. The sound of his voice requesting the M.E., additional deputies, and forensics equipment trailed him into the hallway until the door closed behind him.

"Any ID on the vic?" Jonah's voice drew her attention.

"Didn't get close enough to look. Saw all the fresh

blood, figured the killer couldn't be too far away. And with the wind blowing up the mountain like it is tonight, odds are good that bear's gonna make a return visit. Didn't want to stick around to greet him."

Jonah pressed his lips together, nodded. "Didn't recognize the vic?"

Aiden shook his head. "His face was…well, it was hard to see." He shot a glance to Emmie's white face, and Kathryn's. At her own. "Gravity had taken over."

At first, Jonah frowned. Then, as understanding dawned, he too shot a swift glance at Emmie and Kathryn. His troubled frown slid to Harper before returning to Aiden. "Maybe we should take this conversation someplace else.

"Why?" It was the first time Emmie had spoken up. She twisted in her seat to peer up at the lawman. "This is my ranch. I have every right to know what's going on here, don't I?"

Jonah shifted his stance, hooking his thumbs in the front of his utility belt. "Some thing's you probably don't need to hear, Emmaline. I just thought—"

"Really?" She pushed to her feet and faced him, her shoulders squared in defiance as she planted fists to hips. "There's a killer running around out there on the loose, stringing people up for bear bait on my land, and you're going to try to shield my delicate sensibilities? Lord, spare me from chauvinistic men."

Jonah's face turned red. "Now, Emmaline—"

She tossed a hand up between them, palm facing him. "Don't. Just don't."

The muscle in the sheriff's jaw began to twitch. Ignoring Emmie, he turned to Aiden. "I'm gonna need you to take me back up the trail, show us where the body…the location of the crime scene."

Harper stiffened. She grabbed Aiden's forearm. "You can't go back up there." She twisted to face Aiden. "It's dark out now. You won't be able to find anything anyway. And what if that bear—"

"It's okay. I'll be fine. I'll have Jonah and a whole fleet of armed deputies with me. I'll even take my own gun. But we have to go before too many animals disturb the evidence. It can't wait till morning."

Harper closed her mouth, knowing it would do no good to argue, much as she might want to. He was right. If they were going to catch this killer, they needed every advantage they could get.

Aiden tugged her around to face him. "You're going to stay here with Emmie and Kathryn till I get back." Harper opened her mouth, but Aiden cut her off. "No arguments."

"I'll assign a deputy to the lodge for the night," Jonah added. When Emmie opened her mouth, Jonah cut her off. "No arguments."

Emmie took a seat beside Harper and huffed out a breath. The look she shot Jonah should have seared all that golden hair clean off.

"I'll be back before you know it," Aiden said. He dropped a kiss to the side of Harper's forehead, and then he followed Jonah out the door.

"Damn chauvinistic, pigheaded men," Emmie muttered under her breath.

Harper couldn't agree more.

## Chapter Twenty-Three

Jonah waved Aiden over to where he crouched above the black body bag. "Do you recognize him?"

The area bustled with activity. Yellow police tape fluttered in the wind. Huge spotlights had been set up all around, and the crime scene was lit up like high noon. Two armed deputies stood sentinel, presumably keeping an eye out for predators. Human or otherwise.

Aiden bent over the corpse, studying the face. It was difficult to say, given the amount of blood coating it, given the amount of swelling...both from hanging upside down and from the vicious bruising around the nose and eyes, the split and swollen lip. Whether he'd put up a fight or not, Aiden couldn't say. But whoever this guy was, he'd taken one hell of a beating.

Clayton Jensen, the deputy who'd been conferring with the M.E., came over and handed something to Jonah. "Dobbs found this in the vic's back pocket.

Jonah turned what appeared to be a man's wallet over his gloved hands. He flipped the folded leather open and held an Idaho driver's license up to the light.

"Gavin Thompson. Boise, Idaho."

"Damn it," Aiden swore, rocking back on his heels the moment he heard the name.

"I take it you know this man?"

"Yeah." Aiden pushed to his feet and staggered back two full steps. Lifting his arms, he ran both hands through his hair. "Yeah."

Jonah stood. He handed the wallet back to the deputy, who deposited it inside a clear evidence bag.

"Thompson was at the Lodge the other night. He had reservations but we had to cancel, what with the bear attack and having to close some of the cabins. He got belligerent. Started hassling Emmie when she tried to make other arrangements for him." Aiden frowned. "He got into it with Todd before I got there, actually."

"Todd Sweeney?"

"Yeah. When I came in, Todd was up in his face demanding he apologize to Emmie. I was worried they were going to come to blows, so I stepped in the middle. Todd was defending Emmie, but…"

"But what?" Jonah pulled a small notepad from the chest pocket of his coat and began taking notes.

"Todd was… I've never seen him like that. He was irate. Nearly out of control. Not like himself at all."

"Were there threats made?"

"I don't know. Maybe." Aiden glanced from Jonah to the now-zipped body bag and back. "You don't think Todd had anything to do with this, do you?"

"Where does Mr. Sweeney live?"

"Um, out on Oak Ridge Road, I think. Just on the outskirts of town. In that apartment building Rick Haag owns."

Jonah nodded, jotting his notes.

"When's he scheduled to work again?"

"He's supposed to have tomorrow off. Works the next day…unless he picked up one of Grafton's shift. I'll have to check with Jim."

"When was the last time you saw Sweeney?"

"This afternoon," Aiden said. "Around four. He was

here when Harper and I left for our ride."

"So he was on premises at the time of the murder?"

"Yeah, I guess so. You don't really think Todd is capable of..." He motioned toward the body bag. "Of *that*?"

Jonah glanced up from his notes, but he didn't say anything. His look, however, spoke volumes. Aiden shook his head. He just couldn't believe it. Not Todd. Grafton, maybe. But Todd was just too...nice.

"Grafton's still in jail, isn't he?"

"He was released this morning on bail."

"So this could have been Grafton?"

"It's possible. Did Grafton ever meet Thompson that you're aware of?"

"No. I don't believe he knew Thompson. At least, not that I know of. That's not to say they didn't meet in town at the bar or something."

"Uh-huh." Jonah tucked the notepad into his pocket, zipped his coat back up. "Like I told Emmaline, I'm going to leave a deputy up here at the ranch tonight. I'll see what I can come up with for the foreseeable future."

Aiden's lips quirked up. "Emmie's gonna love that."

"Frankly, I don't care whether she likes it or not," Jonah said, his tone heated for the first time all evening. "Until we find the bastard that's doing this, she's not— no one up here is safe."

"Fair enough."

Aiden waited by the ATV's while Jonah and his deputies finished processing the scene. When they were through, he led them back to the lodge. In the parking lot, Jonah stopped to give instructions to Clayton Jensen, then he assigned Jeff Darby to stay at the lodge until his replacement came at six in the morning.

Aiden followed Jonah back to Emmie's apartment. He expected to find Harper passed out on Emmie's couch. But she was wide awake, pacing the floor. Emmie was the one passed out. She'd curled up on the end of the sofa, propping her head on her bent elbow. Harper must have covered her with the pale blue throw. Emmie's long dark hair streamed around her shoulders and spilled over the arm of the sofa. She looked so young.

"Oh, thank God," Harper breathed, more or less throwing herself into his arms the moment Aiden walked through the door. "You were gone so long. I thought maybe—"

Aiden caught her up in his arms, pressed her head against his chest. He dropped a kiss to the top of her head. "It's fine. Everything's fine."

He glanced over to Jonah and caught the unguarded look of longing the lawman sent the sleeping woman.

"Kathryn went to her own room. Should I call her?" Harper said, stepping back. But he didn't let her move too far away. After the day they'd shared, he couldn't bear to be parted from her any longer. Needed to touch her, just to make sure she was alive and well.

"No," Jonah answered for the both of them though he never took his eyes from Emmie. "Let 'em sleep. There'll be enough for them to deal with tomorrow. Where's her room?"

Aiden frowned, confused by the question. "Um, down the hall, first door on the right."

Then, to his utter surprise, Jonah bent and scooped Emmie up in his arms, blanket and all. With a soft sigh, Emmie snuggled against the sheriff's chest, nuzzling her face into the crook of his shoulder. Without a word, Jonah turned and strode down the hallway, disappearing into the door Aiden had indicated.

Aiden glanced down at Harper, who in turn was staring up at him, her face registering her shock. A moment later, Jonah returned.

"You two staying at the lodge tonight?"

"No," Aiden replied, catching the drift that Jonah wasn't about to explain why he'd carryied Emmie to bed. "Rooms are all booked up."

The sheriff glanced to Harper. "Emmie wouldn't want you staying by yourself up at your cabin. Not tonight. I'm sure she wouldn't mind if you crashed on her couch."

"She'll be staying with me," Aiden assured him.

"I will, will I?"

Aiden pinned her with a hard stare. "You *aren't* staying alone."

She crossed her arms. "Maybe I'll sleep right here on the couch."

"My bed's much more comfortable," he said, his voice dipping to a seductive murmur.

"And on that note, I'll be going. I'll let you two hash out sleeping arrangements on your own," Jonah said as he headed toward the door.

As Jonah pulled the door open, Aiden called out to him, "Hey, Jonah."

The lawman looked back, arching a brow.

"It's been three years, you know," Aiden said.

Jonah's brow wrinkled. Then his brow eased as his gaze slid to the doorway of Emmie's bedroom.

Aiden glanced down at Harper, then he met the sheriff's questioning stare.

"I've been informed that women don't like to be treated as if they're made of glass," Aiden advised.

Jonah grunted, cast one more speaking glance toward Emmie's bedroom, and then he slipped from the apartment, closing the door quietly behind him.

Aiden glanced down at Harper. She smiled up at him, a long, slow smile that inched across her lips and lit up her eyes. She had dark shadows beneath those beautiful eyes. Her hair straggled from a lopsided ponytail. Her clothing was rumpled, and her complexion was pale, to say the least.

And she was so beautiful his chest hurt just looking at her.

"The couch *is* a little lumpy," she said.

He grinned. "Come on, angel. I've got a cloud for you to sleep in."

He helped her put his jacket on, and then held her hand as he led her from Emmie's apartment, down the hall, and out of the lodge. Aiden helped her up into his truck.

"Do you want to stop at your cabin for a few things before we go on to my place?"

She gave in to a huge yawn. "Honestly? Not really. Could I borrow a T-shirt to sleep in? I just want a hot shower and a soft bed. It's been a really long day. Beside, Aiden, this is temporary. Just for tonight."

"You're welcome to my shirts anytime. But you don't have to wear one to bed on my account." He wouldn't press her on the rest. Much as he might want to. Not after the way Grant had handled things.

Harper gave him a long look when he completely avoided her last comment. Another yawn snuck up on her. "You're incorrigible."

The grin he sent her was completely shameless...and full of promise. "I do try."

\*\*\*\*

Fatigue weighed Harper's limbs down as she climbed from the shower and reached for a towel. Aiden's bathroom was twice the size of hers, but it still wasn't big enough for two people. She dried off, pulled Aiden's T-shirt over her head, and then made quick work of running a comb through her hair. The manly scent of his soap and shampoo covered her. It was strangely comforting.

As she padded back into the main living area, she caught the tempting aroma of warm cinnamon and apples. Aiden stood in the open kitchen in front of the microwave. The machine beeped, and he popped the door open.

As Harper approached the counter, Aiden pulled a bowl from the microwave, closed the door with his elbow, and then turned to deposit the bowl in front of her.

Harper's stomach growled. "Apple crisp?"

"I conned extra from Berta this morning."

"That looks really good."

"You know what would make it even better?" Aiden asked as he pulled the freezer door open. He scooped a large helping of vanilla ice cream from a container, plopped it on top of the steaming dessert and offered her a fork. "This. Now eat up. I'm going to go hop in the shower."

Harper slid her fork into the melting ice cream, through crunchy topping, and into gooey goodness. "There might not be any left when you get out."

"That's all right. I had some while you were in the shower." Grinning, he made his way toward the bathroom, stripping his shirt off along the way. But, before he got to the doorway, he paused.

Harper stood there, unable to look away, the loaded fork suspended midway to her open mouth as she watched him drop his jeans and boxers. Giving her a full view of his very nice back side.

She nearly choked on her own drool. She'd seen him naked earlier today. She'd seen the brutal scars that sliced into thigh muscle, the puckered tissue that covered his right hip. And the scars that ran from shoulder to elbow.

But the whole package took her breath away once again. He was utterly masculine…completely scrumptious. Packed with powerful, lean muscles.

"Sure you don't want to come back in with me? Shower's small, but I'm sure we could make due."

She could just imagine them in that one person stall. Bumping into each other. Soapy skin sliding. Slick hands slipping…

"I'm sure," she croaked. At this rate, she'd be *needing* another shower. An ice cold one.

Giving her a you-don't-know-what-your-missing shrug, he turned and sauntered through the bathroom doorway, with her eyes glued to his taut behind every step of the way.

*Holy Mother of God.*

Shaking herself, Harper forced her attention to the bowl of apple crisp. She made short work of it, and then wandered around his cabin as she waited for him to finish up in the shower. She thought briefly about picking his discarded clothes up, and then shot that thought down. She wasn't his maid, nor was she his mother. And she wasn't about to give him the idea that she'd make a habit of picking up after him like a…like a…

Well, that wasn't happening. *Temporary*, she reminded herself.

He had a nice place. Spartan. Clean. Functional. The kitchen, surprisingly tidy for a bachelor, opened up into the living room. The bathroom was just off the kitchen. And down a short hallway were two doors. One opened up to a small room housing a furnace, a water heater, and a washer and dryer. The other door opened to Aiden's bedroom.

Harper stood in the doorway, unsure about going any farther. True, they'd had sex this afternoon. Completely unplanned, mind-blowing sex. But that didn't mean she should be sleeping with him tonight. Slow seemed to have fallen by the wayside. Maybe she should insist on taking the sofa after all. But her eyes were drawn to the queen-sized bed that dominated the modest space.

The room smelled like Aiden. Woodsy, with the slight musk of man and cologne. A long, low cedar dresser with a mirror took up one wall. The surface littered with rolled up belts, a paperback book, a pair of work gloves, and a mason jar half filled with odd coins. A tall, matching armoire, also cedar, sat at an angle in the far corner. A dark blue comforter covered the bed, and a matching rug rested on the floor, just beside the bed.

"It's not much, but its home."

She jumped, spinning around, feeling unaccountably guilty, as if she'd been riffling through his drawers. She hadn't even heard the water shut off, let alone his approach. His dark tousled hair hung down to his shoulders. Crystal beads of moisture speckled his deep golden skin. He'd wrapped a towel around his waist, but the tuck was loose, and the thick green cotton dipped dangerously low on his lean hips.

"Maybe I should take the couch after all," she murmured, unable to tear her gaze from the lean slabs of defined muscle on display.

"Why would you want to do that?"

"Because it's late. And we should get some sleep." She glanced up, meeting his eyes finally. "Stop looking at me like that."

He angled his head. "Like what?"

"You know like what," she said, backing farther into the bedroom to attempt to put a little distance…and hopefully some perspective…between them.

She knew what had happened between them this afternoon had been mostly her responsibility. And she didn't regret it. But her feelings were fully engaged, and now she was beginning to wonder if she'd rushed into things too fast. She glanced around the room and then back to him. Honestly, they probably would have gotten to this point eventually. As in some point in the distant future. Was she really ready for this now? So soon?

It wasn't working.

"No, tell me. How am I looking at you?" His eyes narrowed and he dipped his chin. Stalking her. He was stalking her across the small room. A thrill shot through her. His voice was a rough purr that sent chills skating down her spine.

"Like you're imagining me naked."

Aiden's lips tilted up on a wicked grin. "I don't have to imagine, angel. I've already seen you naked." His gaze dipped down, skating over the soft light gray material of his shirt as if he were remembering even now. His smile grew wider.

She was suddenly conscious that beneath that T-shirt, she was completely naked. And that the shirt barely covered her to mid-thigh.

Harper had backpedaled as far as she could go, and the backs of her knees hit the side of the bed. "You're thinking about kissing me again," she whispered.

He was on her in a heartbeat, his body a mere sliver of space from her own. At her accusation, Aiden snaked an arm around her waist and dragged her up flush against his body. "It's all I've been able to think about since the last time I had you in my arms."

And then his mouth was on hers.

Dear God, the man could kiss. He used his entire body, not just his lips. His thighs pressed along hers as he bent his knees to align their bodies better. His erection was hard and long and unmistakable even beneath the thick layers of the cotton towel. He pushed the ridge of it against the juncture of her thighs, rubbing it there with a sinuous flex of his hips. His arms were steel bands around her. Trapping her, cradling her. The dampness from his chest seeped through the thin T-shirt, and the heat radiating from him was unbelievable. His strong hands left a trail of fire wherever they roamed. And roamed they did.

He kissed the living bejesus out of her. Till she couldn't remember her own name. And then, breathing hard, he released her and stepped back.

"Get in bed, Harper. Go to sleep. I promise I'll be a gentleman...for tonight, at least." He stepped away to turn the light off.

The room went dark, but for a stingy slice of moonlight filtering across the bed. The sound of dresser drawers opening and closing turned her head, but she could barely make him out in the shadows. Harper licked her lips.

"Aiden?"

"Yeah?" The muffled sound of a towel thumping into a laundry hamper followed his reply.

She drew a deep breath, feeling brave in the dark. Then again, maybe she was a coward for using him like this. She didn't want the last thing she thought of before going to sleep to be about that man out there hanging from a tree. She shifted from one foot to the other.

"I didn't ask you to be a gentleman."

The room was completely silent as Aiden went motionless.

And then strong arms swept her up against a solid chest. The bedcovers were tossed aside, and she was gently deposited upon sheets that smelled of Aiden. He swept his shirt over her head, and then warm skin covered her. Hard muscles bunched and flexed beneath her hands. His weight was delicious. The friction of his skin against hers divine.

The darkness enveloping them heightened all her other senses, turning the ragged sound of his breathing into an erotic soundtrack, making her flesh even more sensitive to every stroke of his lips and tongue and fingers.

She reached for him, not content to simply lie there and let him do all the work. He rolled to his back and accepted her attentions for a while. But as her kisses moved closer and closer to the thick, straining erection she'd been stroking, he suddenly reared up in the bed and flipped her over.

She gasped in surprise. He came down on top of her, urgent and needy. Driven, a man possessed. And then

Aiden roughly shoved her thighs wide open, pushing them higher with strong hands. He surged deep inside her with one deep, unrestrained thrust; the way already slick with her desire. Harper moaned and threw her head back. His mouth found her throat, suckling and nipping, as he shook the bed with every hard thrust.

As if he understood her need to forget—maybe he was a victim of the same need—he drove her relentlessly, ruthlessly toward a body-wrecking orgasm.

He didn't whisper words in her ear that she didn't need to hear. He didn't offer trite promises, didn't praise her efforts or spout dirty comments for effect. He let his body do all the talking for him. He simply took her with a savage, animalistic ferocity that staked a claim on her no other man had ever succeeded in doing. And it was perfect. Exactly what she'd needed.

The explosion of sensation shattered her, and she cried out. Aiden tightened his arms around her and captured her cries with his lips, drinking them up like the finest of nectars. His body tensed above hers, going hard as marble. And then he let out a hoarse shout, his body jerked, and he found his own release.

A long moment later, panting, Aiden rolled to his side. He dragged her limp body across the bed sheets, pressing her back flush against his front. He curled himself around her and pulled the blankets up over them.

With a contented sigh, Harper slipped into a dreamless sleep.

Chapter Twenty-Four

Todd pushed the Gas'n Go door open and stepped out into the night. He shivered and turned up the collar of his jacket. After shifting the gallon of milk and the plastic bag to his left hand, he buried his free hand in his pocket to jingle his keys. He glanced to his left as an old rusted-out Ford Bronco passed by.

"I like working for Jim," he said, resuming the conversation they'd been having before he'd gone inside the convenience store.

Danny kept pace with him as he walked east down Summit Avenue. "That promotion should have been yours, Scooter."

"No. No, Mr. Potts—Jim, Jim earned it. He did. Really. And it's nice working for him. He's a great guy. Really nice. A lot like Aiden."

"Whitebear's a self-righteous prick."

Todd swallowed. He didn't like that Danny talked about Aiden this way. But he didn't dare object. It would only set Danny off. And the last thing he wanted to do was make Danny jealous of Aiden.

"So…um, I overheard Miss Emmie talking to Miss Kathryn today. We're hosting a school field trip this weekend. It's going to be a Halloween Party. Doesn't that sound fun?"

"Some fun," Danny grumped. "Bunch of noisy brats running around, making a mess for you to clean up."

"No, it's not like that. It's going to be fun. Miss Emmie has all kinds of neat stuff planned. Bobbing for apples, a hayride…we're going to decorate the main room in the lodge like a haunted house. And we all get to dress up in Halloween costumes."

Danny didn't say anything. He wasn't big on holidays. Not like Todd was.

Todd paused at the corner and glanced both ways before crossing the street. He slowed his steps, waiting for Danny to catch up.

They walked the length of the next block in silence. Sometimes Todd didn't mind the quiet. Just having Danny near—near but not having to make conversation—was nice once in a while. But other times, the silence wasn't so comfortable. It usually meant Danny was upset about something. And when Danny was upset—

He rounded the corner, the plastic bag swinging at his side. The sight of three sheriff's cars parked in front of his apartment building brought him up short.

"They found the hunter," Danny said.

Why did he sound so smug? What he'd done was bad. Very bad. Even if the hunter had deserved it.

Todd ducked into a row of hedges. "But why are they *here*?"

"Early trick or treating?" The sarcasm lacing Danny's voice was heavy. "Think about it, Scooter. They know you went toe-to-toe with that bastard. You see? This is why it's best if you leave it to me to deal with people like that."

"I was just trying to—"

"Help. Yeah, yeah. Be quiet now. Let me think."

Todd watched as deputies filed from the apartment

building. The milk jug was getting heavy, so he set it on the ground near his feet, dropped the bag beside it. The uniformed men all climbed inside their vehicles and drove away. All but one. One of the deputies got inside an unmarked cruiser and pulled a little farther down the block, parked, and turned the lights off.

"They're staking the apartment out, waiting for us to go home."

"But...but he was a bad man, Danny. That's why you took care of him, right?"

"Yeah, but they won't understand that, Scooter. We need to go."

"Go where?"

"Away. It's time to move on."

Todd stiffened. "I don't *want* to move on. Not again. I like it here. I like working at the ranch."

"Well, unless you like the inside of a jail cell, you're just gonna have to learn to like it someplace else." When Todd didn't immediately agree, Danny's voice dropped. "We don't have any choice. I'm not going to jail, Scooter, and neither are you."

"I don't like leaving like this, Danny. Not even saying goodbye."

Danny was silent for a moment. And then, making Todd wish he'd kept his mouth closed, Danny said, "You know, Scooter, that's a good point. You can say goodbye...because I have some unfinished business up at the Bar L."

Chapter Twenty-Five

Another round of lovemaking—this one as tender
and sweet as the previous night had been wild and
unrestrained—a quick shower, and a fast breakfast saw
Harper and Aiden on their way. Aiden kept shooting her
sidelong glances and lifting their entwined hands to his
lips for butterfly kisses.

"Watch the road," she scolded with a smile. "You're
going to put us in a tree like this, goof."

He chuckled but turned his attention to the trail. It
didn't take long before he was steering the big black
truck around the turnoff into the driveway to Eagle's
Nest.

The moment they pulled up in front of the cabin,
however, Harper sat up straighter, resting her free hand
on the dash. The front door of her cabin stood wide open.

She'd closed it firmly yesterday, and she'd locked
it. She'd even tested it…twice.

Frowning, Aiden shifted the truck into park and
killed the motor. A quick glance in her direction, and he
asked, "I don't suppose it will do any good to tell you to
stay here?"

"Don't waste your breath." She was already
reaching for the door handle.

Aiden swore beneath his breath and hopped down
from the truck a spare second before her feet hit the
ground. He met her in front of the truck, and then,

ignoring her protest, he shoved her behind him, keeping a hand anchored firmly on her wrist to keep her there.

Harper followed Aiden up the steps, then stood by the door as he quickly swept the room.

"Whoever did this is gone."

This…being the utter destruction of her cabin. Dressers were toppled over, their contents spilled out and dragged across the room, shredded. The sofa and chair had been tipped over, smashed and slashed, the stuffing pulled out to litter the floor. The fridge door stood open, the sparse contents splattered across the kitchen rug, the shelves hanging awkwardly. The bed was shredded here and there, as if massive paws had used it for a scratching post. Leaves and debris had blown in and, even now, swirled around the cold room.

Everywhere she looked…complete devastation. She couldn't wrap her mind around this.

Aiden stepped over a chair leg and approached the bed. He kicked at the sofa stuffing with the toe of his boot. Leaning over the bed, careful not to touch anything, he examined the slashes on the mattress.

His lips pinched together. Stepping back, he caught Harper's arm and tugged her along behind him. "Come on."

"You think the bear will come back?"

"A bear didn't do this, Harper."

"But…" She glanced over her shoulder as he pulled her from the cabin. "The mess… And the mattress—"

"Trust me, Harper. This wasn't a bear. Anybody worth his salt can see that. Bears don't open refrigerators…they tip them over and smash them open. They crush cans in their teeth, they don't scratch at them and not puncture them. And where was the mud? The dirt? The paw prints? The stuffing from the couch and mattress should have been dirty. But the slash marks were all clean, and the stuffing is still white. Those cuts were put there with a knife." He shook his head, propelling her toward the truck. "And there was no scent marking the cabin."

"Scent?"

"Believe me. You'd know if you smell it."

"Who would do this? Why?" She shook her head, baffled. If she were still in Philly, she'd be laying the blame for this on Alexander...and Sloan. But here in Montana? She barely knew anyone.

*Why?*

"I don't know, angel." He paused to pull her into his arms in front of the truck. "We'll figure it out." He dropped a kiss to the crown of her head, and then he helped her up into the truck. "Come on. We need to call Jonah back, have him check your cabin for prints. Then, when he's done, you're going to sort through that mess, find what's salvageable and we'll bring it back to my cabin. You're not staying here alone anymore."

Harper opened her mouth to protest, but Aiden closed the door. She clamped her lips together, watching him round the front of the truck through narrowed eyes. She would not be railroaded. Not again.

This discussion wasn't over.

Not by a long shot.

\*\*\*\*

Aiden opened the door to Emmie's apartment and stepped back to admit Jonah. The sheriff stepped inside the apartment, then crossed to join the two women sitting at the dining room table while Aiden closed the door.

Emmie stood up and went to the counter, lifting the

carafe, her expression questioning. "Would you like a cup of coffee, Jonah?"

"I'd be obliged. Last night was a long night, and today's looking like it's gonna be even longer." With dark smudges under his eyes and a pale complexion, the man looked positively haggard. If Aiden were a betting man, he'd lay odds Jonah hadn't caught a decent night's sleep since the first body had been discovered.

Jonah dropped onto the chair across the table from Harper. Aiden took the chair beside her and drew her free hand into his. The sheriff leaned back and rubbed both hands over his face before briefly pinching the bridge of his nose.

Emmie slid a steaming cup of coffee before him. "Cream? Sugar?"

"No, thank you. This is fine." He lifted the brew to his lips like a dying man drinking from the fountain of youth.

Aiden waited till he set his now half-empty cup back on the table. "So what did you find?"

"Well, as you know, we brought Vince up with us. Had him scout the area, look the cabin over." He glanced at Aiden, his expression wry. "We keep having to bring him along every time we get a call up here, we're gonna have to put him on the payroll."

As far as a crack at humor went, the statement fell far short of the mark. Jonah's shoulders were already drooping, matching his expression.

"The official verdict? It wasn't a bear."

Aiden glanced over to Harper and arched an *I-told-you-so* brow.

Harper ignored him and focused on Jonah. "Were you able to get any prints, sheriff?"

The corner of the lawman's mouth curled up. "Considering how many times I've had to visit you in an official capacity, *Harper*, don't you think it's about time you called me Jonah?"

Harper sat back in her chair, and her lips twitched. "Touché. Were you able to get any prints, *Jonah*?"

"As a matter of fact, we did. We'll match them against the ones we took from you earlier, eliminate those, and see what we come up with." He took long drag of coffee, set the cup down. "Do you have any idea who might have done this? Any run-in's with anyone here at the Bar L or in town? Anyone with a grudge?"

"No." Harper shook her head.

"You're pretty new here. Where did you live before you moved here?"

"Philadelphia."

Jonah's gaze skimmed the almost indiscernible traces of the bruises left from Grant's fists that lingered around her eye. "Anyone that might have followed you here?"

Aiden's gut clenched. The thought had crossed his mind.

Harper hesitated. Beside her, Emmie made a small sound and turned concerned eyes Harper's way. Jonah pounced. Aiden gave her hand a small squeeze. "Tell him."

"Is there something you think I should know?"

Harper shifted in her seat. "Before I came here, I broke up with my fiancé. He'd…recently become abusive. But he'd been very controlling for quite some time." Harper licked her lips, her gaze sliding to the tabletop in front of her. She told Jonah about the events leading up to her impetuous trip to Montana.

Emmie, having already heard the story on the phone, and then again in greater detail shortly after Harper had arrived, slid her chair closer and slipped her arm around Harper, offering her support.

However, when Harper got to the part about Grant sending his hired thug to wait for her outside her hotel room door, Aiden saw red. She hadn't told him that part before. His nostrils flared, and he could feel his temper flare. But he clamped his teeth together. He'd talk to her about this later.

After he'd had a chance to cool down.

"Did you go to the police in Philadelphia? File a complaint?"

"No," Harper said quietly.

"This wasn't her fault," Aiden said heatedly, transferring his ire from Harper to the sheriff without intending to.

Jonah gave him a measuring stare. In a calm, reasonable tone, he stated, "Didn't say it was. I'm just trying to get all the facts." He turned back to Harper. "This Grant sounds like a real piece of work. He might not be too happy you slipped through his fingers. You sure there's no way he would have come after you? Decided to try to scare you into returning to him? Like he did by sending Sloan to wait outside your room? Maybe he decided the hired help wasn't doing a good enough job."

Harper immediately shook her head. "Alexander is city, through and through. His idea of roughing it is a three-star hotel. He would never come to a place like this. He'd probably go into anaphylactic shock from the fresh air and all the trees and wildlife around."

Jonah weighed her words in silence for a while.

Aiden ran his thumb along the ridge of her knuckles and over the soft, smooth skin on the back of her hand. He hated that she had to relive all this again. From her pinched expression, it couldn't be easy for her.

"What about this hired man you mentioned?"

"Sloan?" Once more, Harper shook her head. "I don't see that either. For one, Sloan strikes me as…well, he's as citified as Alexander. Though, don't get me wrong, he'd be from the opposite side of the tracks, if you get my meaning. He's ex-military though, I think, so he might be able to adapt. His official role isn't exactly specific. He falls somewhere between a personal assistant, a chauffer, and Alexander's bodyguard. But he's moved up in the world by working for Alexander. Would probably do anything Alexander told him to do. Not out of loyalty, I don't think. He's there for the money. He takes a lot of pride in the way he dresses, the car he drives."

Harper paused, chewing on the edge of her lip for a moment, as if trying to come up with the proper explanation.

"There are men…born to money. You know? You can tell…the way they wear their clothing, the way they speak, their mannerisms. And then there are men who dress the part. It's not second nature to them, but they want you to *think* it is." She huffed out a frustrated breath. "Am I making *any* sense at all?"

"Yes, you're doing just fine, Harper," Jonah assured her, his voice kind, his expression open and approachable. Aiden hadn't had much of a chance to see the lawman like this, like he was with a victim. Usually, Jonah seemed like an uptight, by-the-book uniform. But, right now, he was warm and caring.

He would have made a great doctor with that bedside manner.

Aiden stole a glance at Emmie.

Oh, she'd noticed as well. She wore a strange, bemused expression as she cocked her head to the side and studied Jonah as he handled her friend with kid gloves.

"Besides," Harper added, drawing Aiden's focus. "Sloan is Alexander's right hand man. Sloan might have shown up outside my hotel room, tried to intimidate me. But that was in Philly. I just don't see Alexander allowing him to stray so far away from home."

"I'll do some checking on that too, see what I can come up with."

"Speaking of checking," Aiden interrupted. "You didn't mention how things turned out when you went to see Todd last night.

"What about Todd?" Emmie asked, leaning forward, frowning.

"In light of the fact that Todd had had a run in with the hunter that was killed up on the trails, we went to his apartment last night to question him." Jonah glanced to Aiden, his expression grim. "No one was home."

Aiden frowned. It wasn't like he kept tabs on his employees. But it was, after all, a small community. Word got around if somebody frequented the bar a little too often, or if they were seeing someone special. Especially if that someone they were seeing had somebody else on the side.

To the best of his knowledge, Todd was a loner. He didn't visit the bar, at all. And he wasn't seeing anyone. He'd mentioned a brother…once, maybe twice in all the time he'd worked for Aiden. But he'd never talked about any other family.

"We checked around town. He was last spotted at Gas'n Go around nine thirty. We spoke to the landlord…Rick Haag," he added after referring to his little notebook. "Todd Sweeney signed the lease on the apartment, but when he rented the place, he said his brother Danny would be living with him. His twin brother. I've got a deputy working on it, but so far I've got nothing on Danny. No job anywhere in the area. No vehicle registration, no driver's license. Not a scrap of a paper trail that we've been able to come up with. Nothing. We've canvassed the neighbors, but no one's seen the brother at all."

"Maybe he was supposed to come live with Todd, and things fell through," Aiden offered. Why had Todd kept his brother such a secret? Especially a twin.

"Maybe." Jonah looked skeptical. "All I know is I've got a feeling that when we find Danny Sweeney, we'll start getting some answers."

Now Aiden wished he'd paid better attention the few times Todd had mentioned his brother. "Could this Danny be responsible for the murders? And, if so, could Todd be in danger?"

Jonah passed a wary hand over his eyes. "It's entirely possible. Hell, anything's possible at the moment. We don't have a single solid shred of evidence pointing at anyone yet. So, you all need to be extra cautious up here. Don't go anywhere unless you tell somebody else where you're going. Take extra safety precautions. Lock up at night. And don't be staying anywhere alone."

Aiden turned another pointed look Harper's way. She met that look with a sour one of her own. She hadn't liked hearing that from a second source. Especially not one in a position of authority. Well, she was just going to have to get over it. Her safety ranked far higher than some misguided attempt to prove herself independent.

Jonah drained the last of his coffee, declined Emmie's offer of more, and pushed to his feet. "I better hit the road. I need to relieve the deputy I've got staked out at Sweeney's apartment building, and I've got more than just this mountain to look after, believe it or not."

Emmie rose with him. "You're dead on your feet, Jonah. You need to go home and get some sleep."

Jonah's expression softened, as did his voice, when he spoke to Emmie. "I'll be fine, don't worry about me."

Emmie's lips compressed for a moment, and she crossed her arms. "I'll worry if I want to worry, Jonah Pedersen."

For a moment, the sheriff looked as if he was about to say something. But then, as if he'd thought better of it, he clamped his mouth closed, shook his head, and turned to leave the apartment. Aiden walked him to the door.

As he held the door, he leaned closer to Jonah and whispered, "Three years is a damned long time. How much longer are you gonna wait?"

Chapter Twenty-Six

Harper shifted the ATV into park in front of the cabin. She lifted her clipboard from the seat beside her and ran through her checklist.

Badger's Sett was the last one on the list for the day. She checked her watch. Damn it. Coyote's Den had taken longer to clean than normal. The place had looked more like it had been rented to a group of frat boys rather than middle-aged men, and now she was running late. She climbed from the ATV and went to Badger's Sett's door. After knocking twice and announcing herself with no response, Harper returned to her assigned work vehicle to gather her cleaning supplies.

And getting Aiden to approve ATV's going back up the trails, in and of itself, had been a battle and a half. But, since the bear hadn't been sighted in several days, not even after the discovery of the second body, he'd had little ground to stand on. Especially when it was nothing more than his protective instincts impeding the smooth operation of the ranch.

Harper had tried to put the incident at her own cabin this morning out of her head, but she hadn't been able to completely set it aside. She'd had to go back and picked through what precious little possessions she'd had.

Now, thanks to some asshole with a knife, she had even less.

But things could be replaced. She'd learned that the hard way. And whoever had trashed her cabin hadn't even taken anything...all her jewelry was still there, right where she'd left it. Her wallet, her cash, her credit cards, untouched. That is, they were all still in the same drawer, though the drawer itself had been overturned on the floor.

Heaving a sigh, she made her way up the porch steps and used her master key to open the door. She called out one last time before entering, just to be sure. But no reply was forthcoming, so she stepped inside and closed the door behind her.

Harper crossed to the kitchen and set the small tote down on the counter. She took out a pair of rubber gloves and was just about to put them on, when she caught a faint metallic click behind her. She spun around.

Harper froze, fear racing through her system like venom, paralyzing her, making her unable to speak.

"Well, well, well, what have we here?" Malcolm Sloan said as he stepped farther into the room. "What, no French maid costume? Or are you saving that for Whitebear?"

Harper forced a swallow and slowly eased back a step. Still, she couldn't find her voice, couldn't cry for help. It wouldn't matter anyway. Up here, there was no one to hear her.

He stretched his arm out to his side and dropped a plastic bag on the worn plaid sofa. A length of yellow nylon rope slithered like a snake from the opening. "You know, Mr. Grant was determined I come out here to this Godforsaken wilderness and do everything in my power…and then some…to convince you to go back where you belong." He ran the tip of his tongue over his uneven teeth. "But I don't think the boss is gonna be too happy to hear you've been puttin' out for some cowboy.

"In fact, I'm willing to bet he'd rather see you dead than with another man. And, since you won't been returning to the boss…" a malicious gleam entered his eyes as they trailed lewdly down her frame, "I've got an itch I've been dying to scratch."

Harper couldn't breathe. Sloan looked gleeful. She glanced to the rope again, quickly, before looking back to him. She didn't dare take her eyes from him any longer than necessary.

Was it possible? Had *he* been the one that had murdered those men? And, if so, why?

"You won't get away with it," she whispered, finding her voice at last.

"No? Because I think I will. There's a killer on the loose up here, you know. All the grisly details are being bandied around the local watering hole. I'm just some poor schmuck named John Smith from back east, picked an unfortunate week to come hunting, is all." He shook his head in mock pity. "And you? You'd be just another tragic victim."

He didn't admit it.

But he didn't deny it either.

Had he killed those men just to throw the authorities off? Make it look like she was just another unwitting victim so her death wouldn't point directly to him?

Harper eyed the wicked-looking hunting knife strapped to his belt. Her heart raced so fast, she feared she'd pass out. She darted a glance to the door. Not only was he blocking it, but she was pretty sure he'd locked it behind him. In the time that it took her to pause to unlock it, he'd be all over her.

Her mind raced. Her heart pounded triple-time. Terror clogged her throat.

With a cruel smile, Sloan slowly reached for the knife, metal slit against metal, and he began advancing on her.

And so Harper did the only thing she could do. She took four running steps to her left, twisted sideways as she leaped into the air, threw her arm up to protect her face, and she threw herself through the bay window.

Shocked by the impact of her body crashing through the big pane of glass, she gritted her teeth. The landing on the unforgiving wooden porch knocked the breath from her. Her momentum sent her rolling off the sharp edge and smashing onto pebbled ground. Harper gasped and lay still for a second, staring in disbelief up at the late afternoon sky. She blinked, stirring herself. The sound of a doorknob rattling and a man's furious swearing brought her up off the ground in a scrabbling crab walk. Shards of glass slashed her palms.

Pushing unsteadily to her feet, she shook pieces of glass from her hair and clothing and did her best to ignore the dozens of burning scratches and cuts that now peppered her hands and arms and face. A swift glance of longing toward the ATV was cut short when the cabin door flew open.

She'd never get to the machine and get it started in time. Harper bolted for the woods. Her only shot rested solely in getting lost in the trees and underbrush.

Uninhibited crashing echoed behind her as she ran full bore down the slope behind Badger's Sett. Tree branches whipped her in the face, ripped at her hair, flayed her cheek open. She ducked and dodged, batting them aside as she leaped over downed trees like an Olympic hurdler.

The sounds of the thrashing grew distant as she outpaced Sloan, and she caught her first adrenaline-laced shot of hope. She caught sight of a ravine to her left, and Harper changed her trajectory. She raced to the ravine and slid down the steep embankment, barely keeping herself upright. Something sharp caught her pant leg, ripping the denim and gouging into her calf. She didn't slow down. As soon as she landed on solid ground, she was off and running once more. But a short way down the gulley, the land angled up and around, and the ravine started to cut back. Right into, what she was *almost* certain, would be Sloan's path. Maybe. Everything had gotten twisted around, and she couldn't tell north from south, east from west anymore. The only thing she knew was to run downhill.

Her panting breaths heaved in and out, so loud he must surely be tracking her from the sound alone. Each stick that snapped beneath her weight sounded like the crack of a rifle. Everything seemed abnormally loud. In fact, the noise he was making seemed to be growing louder as well. Or was she just being paranoid?

She climbed up the opposite embankment, fingers digging deep into rocky, damp soil, and then she sprinted downhill once more. Was she running to the ranch? Or farther away? She couldn't tell anymore. Trees whipped by right and left. She risked a glance over her shoulder, trying to figure out where Sloan was.

Her foot caught on a partially exposed root, and she went tumbling down, down, arms flying, body cartwheeling, her balance completely gone.

Harper landed and then skidded on her shoulder and the side of her face. She flipped end over end, and then she began to roll and bounce. The grade of the hill grew sharply steeper. Down, down she tumbled, until the broad, prickly base of a white spruce stopped her with bone-jarring force. Pain exploded in her hip. But, driven by primal fear, she pushed to her feet once more and began a jogging, hobbling gait. Each step was a misery, but she pushed on. Better in pain than dead.

She couldn't hear him anymore. She stopped in her tracks. Her breath sawing in and out, her lungs on fire. Harper glanced all around her. Left. Right. Behind her. Trees. Mounds of fallen leaves. Fallen tree trunks. Boulders. And more trees. All a panicked blur in the fading sunlight. But no Sloan.

*Think, Harper. Think.*

She needed help. Harper reached for the radio

clipped to her belt. *Call Aiden. Get help.*

But the radio was gone. Lost in the fall and subsequent roll down the hill. Or maybe it had come off when she'd take the swan dive out through the cabin window. Either way, she was all turned around, lost in the woods, with no radio and no way to get help, completely at the mercy of the vindictive psychopath hot on her heels. In other words, royally screwed.

The sound of movement farther up the slope pricked her ears. Harper pressed her back to the bark of a wide maple tree and fought to control her breathing. She scrunched her eyes closed.

*Please, God, please help me. Anything. I'll do anything. Face anything. Just don't let Sloan find me.*

She didn't want to die like this.

"Peek-a-boo. I see you."

Harper's eyes flew open, and she whipped her head to the right. There he stood, not fifty yards away. The sharp edge of the long blade glinted in his hand. His expression was gleeful. As if the excitement of the chase has only amped up his fun.

Trembling, knees all but knocking together, bracing one hand on the rough tree bark to steady herself, Harper slowly turned her body to face him. He took a menacing step forward. "You can run, but you can't hide," Sloan taunted.

Harper lifted a hand to fend him off as she eased one foot back. Did she have it in her to run anymore? She glanced nervously down the slope to her left and slightly behind her.

She didn't have a choice. Not if she wanted to live.

She turned her attention back to Sloan and, in the blink of an eye, with a thunderous crashing and a bone chilling roar, a mountain of walnut brown fur plowed into Sloan from the side like a freight train, knocking him off his feet and bowling him over.

**\*\*\*\***

"Aiden, come in," Emmie's voice came over the radio. "Aiden, are you there?"

Aiden set the saddle he'd just taken off Jezebel and unclipped the radio from his belt. "Go ahead, Emmie."

"Is Harper with you?"

His heart stopped dead in his chest. "No."

Static clicked, and then Emmie said, "She radioed in after she finished at Coyote Den, but that was over two hours ago. She hasn't checked in since then, Aiden. I've been trying to get her on the radio and there's no response."

"What was her route?" He was already grabbing his coat and running for an ATV.

"She only had Beaver's Lodge and Badger's Sett left, last time she checked in."

"I'm headed up the trail right now. I'll hit Beaver's Lodge first, since it's closer, and then I'll head to Badger's Sett. I want you to radio Jim and Kendall. Pull them off the repair jobs they're on and have them waiting at the stables for further instructions, just in case."

"Will do. And, Aiden? Call me as soon as you find her."

"I will, Em."

He entered the side of the ATV at a running slide, still trying to clip the radio back onto his belt. With a twist of his wrist, he fired the machine up and slammed it into gear.

Dread squeezed his throat. It pressed down on his chest as if an elephant were sitting on him.

*Please, let her have just forgotten to call in. Let her have left her radio in the ATV where she couldn't hear it.*

Anything but the horrifying alternative. They still hadn't found Todd yet, or his elusive brother. And Grafton had been cleared of the murders. There was a killer, somewhere. On the loose. Possibly looking for another victim.

He braced one hand on the roof cage, the other clutched the steering wheel in a death grip as the ATV flew up the mountain trail behind the stables. He jerked the wheel to the right to avoid colliding with the big boulder marking the fork in the trail. Left took him to Beaver's Lodge…near where the second body had been discovered. Right, took him to Badger's Sett.

Aiden slammed on the brakes. Badger's Sett. He remembered telling Harper that he had a bad feeling about the occupant, how she shouldn't go there alone to clean while the guy was around. And, other than that one time, Aiden hadn't really checked up on the guy. Apprehension balled in his gut. He shouldn't have dropped that ball.

But on the other hand, Beaver's Lodge was closer. And wasn't it true that killers often returned to the scene of the crime? What if Harper had stumbled upon the killer up here, all alone?

Torn, he hesitated. Then, swearing, he cranked the wheel to the left and gunned the motor.

He could barely breathe as the cabin came into view. From the outside, everything appeared normal. Barely waiting for the machine to come to a halt, Aiden leaped off and raced up the porch. The door was locked.

"Harper," he yelled.

299

No response.

He jiggled the handle, and then frantically patted his waist. The spare set of master keys must still be in his desk drawer.

Without giving it a second thought, he lifted his boot, and kicked the door in. Aiden rushed inside, taking in his surroundings in one sweeping glance.

She'd already been here. The scent of lemon cleaner and disinfectant colored the air. The place was tidy as could be, the beds tucked tight enough to make a drill sergeant proud.

Swearing again, he raced from the cabin and rushed back to the ATV. Spinning the machine around, spraying a wide arc of gravel in his wake, he tore off back down the trail to Badger's Sett. His heart lodged in his throat.

The minute he came into view of the cabin, he knew something had happened. The big picture window on the front of the cabin was broken, shattered shards of it covered the porch and spilled down onto the ground. White curtains...white curtains with speckles of crimson...wafted in the breeze outside the casement. The door stood wide open. Harper's ATV sat in the parking space out front.

"Harper!" He jumped off the machine and raced to the cabin. "Harper!"

Her cleaning caddy sat on the counter. A pair of yellow rubber gloves lay on the floor. "Harper!"

And then he spotted the white plastic sack on the sofa...and the bright yellow nylon rope.

*Jesus, no!*

Spinning on his heel, he jerked the radio from his belt as he raced out onto the porch.

"Emmie," he radioed in. "Have Jim and Kendall

saddle horses, have them bring one for me too. Gather anyone down there, gather everyone. And call Jonah. Send everyone to Badger's Sett."

"What happened, Aiden?"

"I don't know, damn it. Just do it. Fast, Emmie." He looked to the blood sprinkled drapes fluttering nearby. "I think Harper might be hurt."

Trusting Emmie to do as he'd instructed, he left the porch and immediately began searching the ground for some trace of her. The good news was, he didn't see any bear tracks. The bad news was, just at the edge of the porch, he found a larger smear of blood. The gravel had been torn up and dislodged, as if someone or something had rolled around in one small spot.

And he found boot prints. Heavy on the toe, as if the wearer had been digging in for purchase while running.

Aiden's gaze followed the boot tracks into the woods on the east side of the cabin.

*Oh, my God. Harper.*

With another round of terse instructions into the radio, Aiden loped into the woods, his alert gaze seeking out the slightest disturbances.

*Please. Please, no.*

\*\*\*\*

Harper stopped breathing. She froze. Her mouth falling open on a silent scream. Her eyes wide as saucers.

The bear batted Sloan with a massive paw, playing with him, sending him careening and rolling over the ground. Sloan let out an ear-piercing, blood-curdling wail as the massive beast sank huge yellow fangs into the back of Sloan's thigh and shook him like a rag doll.

Harper ducked behind the tree once more, skittered around so she was concealed. She bit her lip hard enough to draw blood in an effort not to sob in fear. She held herself absolutely still as all sound of movement behind her suddenly stopped. All but Sloan's inarticulate mewling. Shaking like a leaf, Harper scrunched her eyes closed and she prayed as she'd never prayed before.

The bear's movements resumed. Snuffling. Grunting. Horrid snapping and ripping sounds. And Sloan's guttural moans.

Peering around the tree, Harper scooted back. The bear was focused solely on Sloan, its big shaggy back to Harper. It was toying with him now. Harper tiptoed carefully away, angling for a gulch some distance away. When she could no longer see the busy animal, she continued to tiptoe, just in case. But, eventually, she couldn't take it anymore. And she broke into an uneven jog. The only thing important to her now was putting as much distance as possible between her and that bear.

Chapter Twenty-Seven

Aiden had dismounted and now led Juniper by the reins. Searching from horseback had proven more difficult than he'd anticipated.

"Here," he tossed Juniper's reins to Jim. "Hang on, I think I see something."

He squatted near a rotted log. Damp leaves had been stirred up, and amidst those leaves something glinted. Aiden reached out and brushed debris aside. He picked up the object that had caught his eye.

His stomach dropped as he held Harper's two-way radio up so the others could see. The antenna had been broken, and the speaker was cracked. He stood, looking franticly around them. A wide strip of disturbed leaves led straight down the hill.

Without waiting for the others, Aiden took off. He followed the trail until it stopped at the base of a white spruce. Aiden lurched to the side, squinting at the ground, looking for some indication of what had happened, or which direction she might have gone from there.

But he could find nothing. They were in a cluster of pine now, and the telltale leaves were few and far between.

"Spread out," he instructed the four men with him. "But stay within shouting distance. Keep your eyes open but try not to make any noise if you can help it. We don't want to alert whoever's out here with her. Kendall, you stay behind with the horses."

Aiden picked his way down along a ridge toward a ravine. There, he caught sight of a piece of torn, blood-stained denim. Scrabbling down into the ravine, Aiden snatched up the ripped fabric. He glanced left, then right, trying to figure out which way she'd gone. Instinct said she'd keep heading down the mountain, so he turned right and kept jogging. But when the ravine wound back around, he thought he might have made a mistake.

Until he found claw marks in the dirt and roots. As if someone had used this place to pull themselves up and out.

Just over the embankment, a glint of silver peeked from the thick grass. A broken silver necklace was tangled around a root.

Breadcrumbs. She'd unwittingly left a trail of breadcrumbs for him to follow.

But if he could follow them, then so could the killer. And the killer had a head start. Swearing, Aiden rushed on. But then he heard something. A shout somewhere to the east of him.

"Here! Over here!"

*Harper.* He took off running.

As he rounded a huge boulder, he drew up short. Dewy Johnson, one of the men Jim had brought with him, crouched over a bloodied mass of…of meat. Blood soaked the tattered clothing covering the lump of torn flesh, making it impossible to identify. What was left was so mangled, so torn apart…half buried in leaves and dirt. Massive pools of blood. Deep gouges raked into the earth by massive claws.

"No!" Aiden shouted as he lurched forward.

Jim was suddenly there, leaping into his path, catching him across the chest. Aiden fought him, desperate. Devastated.

"Aiden," Jim panted, straining to hold him at bay. "Aiden, stop. It's not her. Aiden, it's not her. It's a man. Do you hear me? It's not her."

Finally, Jim's words penetrated the fog of grief. He stilled. His knees went out from under him, and he sagged to the ground. Relief swamped him, even as fear took hold once more.

Jim helped him to his feet. He staggered over to the disemboweled remains. Dewy used a stick to clear the leaves and dirt from the face.

Aiden frowned. Familiar. The face was familiar. But it wasn't Todd Sweeney as he'd been expecting. This was...

This was John Smith, the client renting Badger's Sett.

*What the hell?*

Aiden stepped back. He turned in a wide circle, searching for some sign of Harper. Hopeless, helpless fear rode him.

"We'll find her, Aiden," Jim said, coming up behind him.

"Alive?"

Jim didn't respond. He squeezed Aiden's shoulder and pulled the radio from his own belt. Aiden heard him instructing Kendall to bring the horses around.

As they waited for their fourth man Chris, Kendal, and their rides to arrive, they searched the area. Just when Aiden began to fear the breadcrumbs had run out, Jim spotted something and waved him over.

"Aiden, check this out."

Aiden bent down. A black ballpoint pen lay on the ground near the base of a tree some fifty yards from the corpse. He bent and picked it up. It wasn't much to go on, but it was all he had.

The moment Kendall arrived with the horses, Aiden mounted Juniper and began angling down the hill once more, using the location of the pen as a starting point. "Fan out," he said again.

Mounted now, the five men including Aiden began zigzagging their animals back and forth as they made a wide, sweeping arc down the side of the mountain.

A million things were running through Aiden's head at that point. Who the hell was John Smith? Was he the killer? And if he was, then what had happened to Todd Sweeney and his brother Danny? Had they become a victim of Smith? Or was Smith the Sweeney's victim? And where the hell was Sweeney? How did Danny Sweeney factor into all this? And above all the other questions, first and foremost, where was Harper?

They were beginning to lose the light. Aiden's chest tightened. He couldn't stand the thought of Harper up here in the dark alone, possibly hurt, possibly hunted by a man-eating grizzly. Damn it, had she witnessed what had happened to the bear's latest victim? She must be out of her mind with fear.

A lump of blue plaid caught his attention. His eyes flared. He gave a shout and spurred Juniper on. As he drew alongside the unmoving body, he leaped to the ground. Heart in his throat, dying a little inside, he dropped to his knees beside the woman lying face down in the dirt and damp leaves.

Long brown hair, tangled with leaves and small twigs, matted with blood, covered her face. Her clothing was ripped and torn, smeared with blood and mud.

"Harper," he whispered at first, nearly unable to speak. He reached for her, his hands shaking violently. Louder, he called, "Harper, angel, can you hear me?"

Was she breathing? He couldn't tell. Carefully, so carefully, he rolled her over, oblivious to the men who'd come to stand in a circle around them. As he moved her, she moaned, the sound music to his ears. She was alive. She was breathing.

His gaze swept her from head to toe. Blood covered the side of her face. A nasty gash sliced along the edge of her forehead. He looked over to the small, partially concealed rock nearby. Blood coated it. He couldn't find any slashes from big paws, no bites marks. And no knife wounds, thank God.

"Harper," he tried again.

Her eyelids fluttered for a moment, and then she was out cold once more. Cursing, he drew her into his arms and struggled to his feet. He passed her to Jim's waiting arms, and then he mounted Juniper. Jim lifted her up and Aiden tucked her into the protective shelter of his arms.

He didn't wait for the others to mount and follow. He took off down the mountain, his only concern getting her to safety.

"Woman," he whispered against her brow. "I swear to God, you are a magnet for trouble."

She moaned softly, turning her head into the warmth of his neck. Aiden scootched her higher against his chest, held her just a bit tighter, mindful that she could have injuries he didn't know about yet.

"Hold on, Harper. Do you hear me? You hold on, damn it. Don't leave me now. I just found you. I'm not going to lose you all ready."

\*\*\*\*

Harper sat up on the sofa and dropped her feet to the floor as the doctor moved away. The room spun a little, but she didn't want to be horizontal any longer. It reminded her a little too much of all the time she'd spent on the ground already today. Aiden stopped pacing the moment the doctor drew the stethoscope from around his neck and stood up.

"I'm fine," Harper assured the room at large.

Unfortunately, no one seemed to be listening.

Aiden, Emmie, and Kathryn all turned to Doc Erickson. The elderly man ran a hand through his sparse, salt and pepper hair.

"Well," Aiden prompted.

The doctor had butterfly stitched the wound on her head which, once all the blood had been cleaned up, hadn't been nearly as bad as everyone had assumed. The retired doctor had given her a thorough exam, grumbling about Aiden's presence the entire time. But Aiden had flat out refused to leave the room, swearing he wasn't about to let her out of his sight for a second.

Every time he did, he claimed, she ran headlong into trouble.

Before she'd come to Montana, she might have argued. Now? Not so much.

"She'll be all right with lots of rest. She has some minor cuts and scrapes, and she'll probably be covered head-to-toe in bruises come morning. She's got a minor concussion that needs to be closely monitored for a while…but nothing's broken, and she doesn't need stitches. Far as I can tell, there's no internal bleeding, but if she develops any of the symptoms I mentioned before, you need to call an ambulance and get her to the hospital right away." Dr. Erickson dropped his tools into the old-fashioned black doctor's bag on the coffee table and snapped the leather closed.

"Thank you so much," Kathryn said, stepping forward to clasp the doctor's hand. "I'm so sorry to pull you out of retirement like this, but you were the closest doctor around, and I remembered you used to make house calls. We were just too worried to make her wait for the drive all the way over to Albertsville to the hospital."

"Oh, now, don't you worry about it. Does me good to feel needed again. To be honest, I missed this more than I thought I would. Getting out, seeing patients. Some days I feel like I'm gonna grow mold if I don't get out and *do* something."

The doctor picked up his bag and Kathryn walked him to the door, promising to have one of Berta's lemon meringue pies delivered to his house within the week.

Aiden eased down on the sofa beside Harper, careful not to jostle her too much. Without waiting for permission, he gathered her close, tucking her against his body, and he drew a long, steadying breath.

Harper caught the knowing look Kathryn and Emmie shared, and her cheeks warmed. Thankfully, they refrained from making comment.

Emmie sat down on the coffee table, facing them. "Okay. What happened?"

She'd known this was coming. But she'd wanted to wait until Jonah came down, so she'd only have to tell it once. However, Jonah was tied up with processing the cabin and recovering Sloan's body from the woods. And Aiden, Emmie, and Kathryn weren't willing to wait any longer.

"I went to clean Coyote Den, but the place was trashed...I was going to tell you about it when I got back. The cabin was a disaster. Anyway, it took longer than I thought it would, and by the time I got to Badger's Sett...well, I lost track of time. I'm sorry I didn't call in."

"It's probably a good thing you didn't. Otherwise, it might have been much later before I sent Aiden looking for you."

She remembered slipping away while the bear had been occupied with Sloan. She remembered racing down the hill. But she didn't remember falling. Didn't remember how she'd gotten to the lodge. The doctor assured her that was normal. There was no telling how long she'd lain on the cold ground, unconscious. But thank heaven he'd come along when he had. If that bear had found her instead of Aiden...

Harper shivered. Aiden reached behind them and drew a throw from the back of the sofa and tucked it around her.

"Well, I knocked on the door a couple times like I usually do. There was no answer, so I went inside to clean. But once I got inside, I heard the lock engage, and turned around. Sloan was there."

"Wait a minute," Aiden said, twisting to peer down at her. "Sloan? As in Alexander's thug?"

"Yeah."

"When did *he* get here?"

"He registered under the name John Smith."

"I came face-to-face with that bastard." Aiden's voice dripped with self disgust.

Emmie gasped. "Oh, my God, Harper. He's been here for days. I'm so sorry!"

"This isn't your fault, Emmie," Harper said, leaning

forward to squeeze Emmie's hands. She turned to Aiden, slipped her hand in his. "Or yours, Aiden. There was no way for either of you to know. If I know Alexander, he probably had a full set of forged papers for Sloan anyway. Even doing an extensive background check probably wouldn't have made a difference."

She snuggled back into Aiden's arms and continued with her story. She told them that Alexander had sent Sloan. And that Sloan planned to kill her.

"I don't think Alexander has any idea what Sloan planned. And no, I'm not trying to defend him. It's just the way Sloan acted," she shook her head, "some of the things he said."

"Did he say anything else?" Aiden pressed. "I saw the bag with the nylon rope like what was used to hang Thompson from the tree. Did Sloan admit to killing Decker and Thompson?"

Harper shrugged. "Not really. I mean, he didn't admit it, but he didn't deny it either."

Emmie glanced to Aiden. "Has anyone found Todd yet?"

Aiden shook his head. "Not that I know of. I feel bad about that. I keep asking myself where he is. What happened to him, you know?" Aiden admitted. "With everything Jonah pointed out earlier, I actually started to think maybe he might have been responsible. Hard as it was to believe. But now, with Sloan factored into the mix… Maybe I rushed to judge Todd unfairly."

Harper ran her hand up and down Aiden's chest. "Don't. Let's just pray it's all over now."

"The bear is obviously still a threat," Kathryn spoke up from the rocker where she'd sat down after walking the doctor out. "Do we shut down the cabins farther up the mountain again? Do we cancel the Halloween Event? I mean, I know it's short notice, but I'm sure the school would understand, given the circumstances. We could push the event back to next week."

"Oh," Emmie said, frowning. "The kids will be so disappointed. And all that planning gone to waste."

"Emmie's right. We should go ahead with the event." Aiden said, conviction heavy in his voice. Harper glanced up at him. His expression was grim…and determined. "First thing in the morning, I'm taking Vince Abernathy and a group of hunters up the mountain to get rid of that damned bear once and for all."

## Chapter Twenty-Eight

Early Saturday morning, Harper woke snuggled in Aiden's arms. She was stiff and sore...everywhere. Just rolling over hurt. She carefully untangled herself from his arms, shushed him when he stirred. Aiden murmured in his sleep, reached for her pillow, and rolled onto his stomach.

She paused in front of the mirror over Aiden's dresser and peered at her face in the dim, early-morning light. Lifting the T-shirt she'd slept in, she surveyed her back, turned to view her ribs. Her hip was nearly black from where she'd smashed into the tree. Her ribs, arms and thighs were peppered with angry purple blotches. Doc Erickson had been right. She was pretty much one big bruise, head to toe. And here she'd just started getting rid of the marks Alexander had given her.

Harper crept to the bathroom. A long hot shower eased some of the stiffness. Three ibuprofen and a cup of strong coffee gave her a good head start on the rest. By then, Aiden had started moving around in the bedroom. He stopped in the kitchen long enough to drop a groggy kiss on the crown of her head, and then he made his way to the bathroom. Soon, the sound of the shower filtered through the cabin's wall. Harper brought her second cup of coffee to her lips, closed her eyes as she leaned against the counter—she was too sore to sit for long, and she let the bitter-sweet brew revive her spirits.

He joined her soon after, dressed in his customary jeans and soft T-shirt, this one a faded turquoise. His skin was shower-soft, his jaw freshly shaven, and his hair was still damp. He smelled of soap and cedar and aftershave. She just wanted to curl into him and hibernate for the winter.

Harper handed him a bowl and a spoon as he got a cereal box down from on top of the fridge. "So what's the plan for the day?"

"I'll be taking a group up the mountain to try to track the bear and kill it. The sooner we get started, the better, so I'll take you down to the lodge first thing, get the boys organized, then I'll head out."

Apprehension settled like a ball of lead in her stomach. "I wish you wouldn't."

She'd seen firsthand the damage that beast could do. It worried her that Aiden would possibly be within striking distance of the animal. Some of her fear must have shown because Aiden turned on the barstool to face her and pulled her close, settling her between his thighs. He rubbed his hand up and down her back.

"We'll be careful, I promise."

"I don't like it, Aiden." She played with the hem of his shirt as she rested her head against the hollow of his shoulder. "You didn't see—"

He nudged her head up and pressed a finger to her lips. "I saw what was left." Pinching her chin between his thumb and forefinger, he angled her head so he could see her face clearly and stare deep into her eyes. "Trust me. Everything will be all right."

He pressed a lingering kiss to her lips. But just as she began to melt into him, he pulled back.

"You need to take it easy right now, Harper. And

you keep kissin' on me like that, I'm liable to forget that. Go on, finish your bagel so we can head down to the lodge," he instructed. "Once we get there, I want you to hang out with Emmie for the day. You can help her with the final touches for the Halloween party tonight, but I don't want you to push too hard, okay?"

Her lips compressed. She drew a deep breath and let it slowly leak back out, knowing it would do no good to argue with him. Instead, she nodded and took a bite of blueberry bagel. If he could go out and do what he pleased, regardless of how she felt, then she'd do as she pleased as well.

****

Harper set the punchbowl on the decorated table. Frozen, plastic eyeballs and gnarled, green fingers floated in the chilled red fruity drink. She glanced around the room as she stretched the aching muscles in her back. Her ribs protested, and she stifled a wince. It was bad enough that she'd already started favoring her hip and begun limping slightly. If Emmie or Kathryn caught her cringing and groaning like some decrepit invalid, they'd shuffle her off to bed faster than she could blink. Dealing with Aiden had been bad enough. Emmie and Kathryn as a united front, well…combined, they were a force of nature against which she didn't stand a chance.

Orange and black streamers hung from the ceiling, forming a canopy in the Banquet Hall. The room was absolutely perfect for an elementary Halloween party, right down to the wispy ghosts and creepy scarecrows propped here and there and the scary masks stuck to the outsides of random windowpanes.

"I think that should about do it," Emmie said, coming up behind her.

Emmie slid a platter of little cakes and cookies decorated with plastic bugs and other creepy ornaments onto the table beside the punchbowl. Harper turned and laughed. Emmie looked like a shepherdess circa 1700, complete with shepherd's crook and a tiny stuffed lamb she currently held tucked beneath one arm.

"Yeah? Laugh it up. Wait till you see your costume."

Harper shook her head. "Who said I was dressing up?"

"You come to the party, you dress up. Ranch rules."

"Okay, okay."

"The school buses should be arriving any moment. You better go get your costume on…unless you hurt too much." Her anxious gaze skimmed Harper's face. "You are hurting aren't you? I knew you were pushing too hard. Now Aiden's going to kill me."

"I'm fine, just a little sore. Stop worrying." Harper glanced to the dark windows. The sun had set long ago. "Is he back yet?"

"No, but he radioed down a little while ago. They're on their way."

"Did they find the bear?"

"It didn't sound like it."

Harper didn't know whether to be happy about that or not. "They were up there all day."

Emmie grimaced. "I know. He wasn't very happy."

*But he's alive and unharmed, and that's all that counts.*

Someone called to Emmie, and she started away to help dump apples into a trough of water. As she walked away, she called over her shoulder, "I left your costume on the bed in my apartment. Go get dressed."

Harper rolled her eyes and moved out of the way as Berta and Kathryn carried the centerpiece over to the banquet table along the back wall. A huge, gruesome cake suitable for a Halloween bake-off on the Cooking Channel.

A short while later, clad in a Red Riding Hood cape and costume, Harper stepped out into the hall. The sounds of merriment echoed throughout the lodge. Giggling and shrieking children raced here and there, chasing each other with rubber snakes, fake spiders the size of dinner plates and plastic molded rats.

She stopped just outside the door to one of the conference rooms—aka the haunted house—and she grinned at the shouts and squeals punctuated the spooky music coming from the darkened recesses. Harper smiled as the wisps of low-lying smoke rolling along the floor. Emmie had gone all out.

Then she went to the Banquet Hall and she glanced around. Ghosts and goblins, vampires and witches, superheroes and villains milled all around. Everyone was in costume, adults and children alike. But she didn't see Little Bo Peep.

Frowning, Harper dodged to the side as a child carrying a candied apple came running by. She slipped from the room out into the darkened hallway and bumped into Batman's nemesis Two-Face.

"Oh! I'm so sorry," she gasped.

Two-Face didn't speak. Instead, grinning maniacally, he tapped his fingers to his painted brow and executed a regal bow. Smiling, Harper curtsied and then moved down the hallway toward the main room.

From the corner of her eye, she thought she saw a flash of pale, ruffled skirts identical to those Emmie was wearing dart into the kitchen in the opposite hallway. Curious, she followed. Maybe Emmie needed help carrying something.

But the kitchen was empty. Frowning, Harper went to the back door and peeped her head out. Another flash of white ruffles and dark ringlets disappeared around the corner. Frowning, Harper propped the door open just a bit so they wouldn't be locked out, and she slipped outside after Emmie. Where was that girl going? She shouldn't be out here in the dark.

Nerves skittered along Harper's spine, but concern for her friend pushed her onward. Swallowing the fear back, she eased around the corner of the building. For a moment, Harper was afraid she'd lost Emmie in the dark yard. She paused by the parking lot, craning her neck, going up on tiptoe to see over cars. Where had that girl gone?

Then she caught movement over by the stables. Harper hurried over, thinking it might be Aiden and his group returning. Instead, there was that skirt again, slipping in through the side door.

Frowning, pulling the thin red cape closer around her to fend off the worst of the chill, Harper followed.

What is Emmie doing?

Harper reached the door Emmie had gone through, but as she eased the door open, she hesitated. All the lights were still off. The fine hairs on the back of her neck stood straight on end, and her chest tightened uneasily. Something about this felt...wrong. She hesitated in the doorway. Licking her lips, catching the lower one between her teeth, she crept inside and closed the door quietly behind her.

A loud crash echoed down the hallway, horse's

hooves striking wood. A loud, distressed whinny. A stall door slammed closed. A muffled curse. Another door opened, closed.

Movement from one of the stalls, closer now, had her pressing back into the shadows on the far side of the bay. She hastily tugged the cape closer, lifting it to her chin to conceal the white of her shirt. From her hidden vantage point, she had a clear view of the hallway that ran between the stalls the length of the stables. A door swung open, and a tall, brawny figure led a horse out. She knew that horse. That was Flapjack. The figure was dressed in a swash-buckling pirate costume. And, draped across the horse's back was a woman.

A motionless, silent Little Bo Peep.

Harper's eyes went wide and her heart lodged in her throat.

The dark figure drew closer and, when Harper finally got a good look at the man's face, her breath froze in her lungs.

*Todd. Todd Sweeney.*

Harper stood rooted to the spot, terrified of giving her position away.

As Todd led the horse toward the wide door leading out to the lane, Harper caught a glimpse of the side of Emmie's face. Her eyes were closed, her mouth slack. Her hands were bound behind her back with some kind of pale material. She couldn't see Todd anymore, as he was on the opposite side of the horse. Her hand crept to her waist, reaching for her two-way radio out of habit. When her fingers brushed the decorative satin belt, she silently cursed. Her radio was still up in Aiden's cabin. They hadn't figured she'd be needing it since she was, technically, supposed to be having a "resting-only" day.

Then the horse stopped walking, and Todd stepped around the animal. He strode toward the corner where Harper was hiding. Harper's mind raced. Her blood pounded so furiously, she actually felt woozy. She'd been discovered.

But he stopped halfway to her and kicked at a pile of straw with the toe of his boot, uncovering a white plastic bag. He squatted down and dug inside the bag, as if checking to make sure everything was there, inadvertently revealing to Harper a length of yellow rope, several thick black zip ties, and a wicked-looking hunting knife.

Shoving everything back inside the bag, he stood and returned to Emmie and the horse. He tied the bag to the pommel, and then unlocked the wide, double doors and slid one to the side far enough that a horse and rider could easily slip through. And the whole time, his face was set in harsh lines, his movements jerky and uncoordinated. As he returned to the horse's side, he paused.

"We shouldn't do this," he said aloud, and Harper started. Who was he talking to? Without turning her head, afraid even the slightest motion might give her away either to Todd, or to whoever it was he was talking to, Harper scanned the stables. But she couldn't see anyone else. She watched as Todd paused in the middle of mounting the horse behind Emmie. Was his accomplice waiting somewhere for him? Communicating with him through one of those little blue tooth things in his ear? It was too dark, and she couldn't see well, so it was entirely possible.

"It isn't Miss Emmaline's fault. We shouldn't use her this way." He shook his head, released the saddle and backed up a step. "No, *please*. He's always been so nice to me. I don't want to—"

Todd paused, shaking his head slowly side-to-side. He wrung his hands together, obviously hearing something that upset him greatly. He cringed and ducked as if taking a verbal lashing. Whoever was on the other end of the line must have been giving him hell. "You're right. And you do. But—" Another pause. "I'm sure he didn't mean to—" Another pause. "Okay. But couldn't we just go away again. I won't argue anymore. I promise. I'll do what you say. Let's just go away, and forget about him, okay?" Todd asked, his voice a whiney plea. Todd's head suddenly dropped, his shoulders drooped submissively. "I know. I'm sorry."

Then, motions choppy, he led the horse from the stables, leaving the big door open behind him.

Harper panicked. Oh, lord, what was she to do? If Todd managed to ride off with Emmie, there was no telling where he might take her. Harper ran to the doorway and peered outside. She caught sight of Todd, now mounted behind Emmie, angling the horse toward the trails leading up into the mountains.

She spun around, her mind racing. She needed to get help. But if she didn't do something *right now* to keep Todd within her sights, they might lose Emmie forever. She ran to Aiden's office. She'd noticed several extra walkies on chargers when she'd been in there the other day getting new batteries for her own. Snatching one up, she scrambled from the office and darted back out into the hallway.

An ATV would be faster. But that would certainly clue Todd in that he was being followed. Apprehensive, she hurried to the last occupied stall. Every horse had his or her own designated stall, complete with golden nameplate. This one read Jezebel. The hunting party that had gone after the bear late this morning had been large, and they'd taken a vast majority of the ATV's, and nearly every horse.

Frantic, Harper gushed heartfelt gratitude and praise to the skittish creature. The animal reluctantly allowed Harper to put a bridle on her and lead her from her stall. Harper eyed a saddle for all of half a second before deciding against it.

Did she need one? Probably, yes. Could she lift it? Possibly. Lift it high enough to actually get it on the horse, let alone get all the straps laced and tightened correctly before Todd disappeared with Emmie on one of the gazillion mountain trails up there, never to be seen again? Not a snowballs chance in hell.

So, equipped with nothing but a saddle blanket and a harness, Harper led Jezebel out into the bay area where she'd noticed a couple empty five-gallon buckets.

As she hurried over to the buckets, she called Aiden on the radio. In as few words as possible, she rushed to explain the situation.

"Damn it, Harper. I'm less than ten minutes away. You stay put."

"He could be gone by the time you get here, Aiden," she argued.

"Harper, listen to me. Don't you go after her. It's starting to rain up here and the trails are getting slippery. You go back to the lodge. Jonah's with me, but you call the sheriff's department anyway, tell them to bring back up. Damn it, just wait. I'm on my way."

"We don't have time for this, Aiden. Emmie was unconscious. I don't know what he did to her, but the last time I saw her, she was face down on Flapjack's saddle. I'm not waiting. You'll have to catch up. He turned off onto that trail we came back on. The one behind the stables that leads up to Badger's Sett. I'm taking Jezebel and I'm going after them."

"Jezebel?" Aiden's voice exploded over the radio. "Do *not* get on that horse, Harper! Don't do it. She's not—"

Cursing, Harper spun the knob and silenced Aiden's voice. She didn't have time to argue. She'd lost too much time as it was. Harper flipped a bucket over, guided the horse closer, and then, using the bucket as a step, she climbed up on the shifting horse.

Crooning praise, she settled herself on the animal's broad, strong back. Gathering the reins, gripping Jezebel's sides tight with her thighs, Harper gave her a coaxing nudge. "Come on, sweetie. Please."

The horse, as if sensing her urgency, set out at a brisk trot. They cleared the open door with no trouble. Feeling a bit like a kernel of popcorn on a hot skillet, Harper held on for dear life and she gently tugged the reins, leading the horse up the trail behind the stables.

Chapter Twenty-Nine

Harper pushed the horse as fast as she dare go, which wasn't fast at all given she could barely see ten feet in front of her. But the animal was holding steady and, thankfully, Harper hadn't slid off into the bushes. Yet. So, all in all, she thought she was doing pretty well.

"I'm coming, Emmie," she whispered. "Just hold on."

The full moon had peeped in and out of clouds earlier. But it was completely gone now, concealed by a storm front that was slowly creeping its way down the mountainside, and Harper was set on a collision course with it.

Her nerves a jumbled mess, Harper pushed steadily onward. She reached a huge boulder dividing the trail. One she vaguely remembered from her and Aiden's mad dash down the mountain the night they'd discovered that poor hunter's body. It may as well have been a brick wall she'd run headlong into. What was she to do now? Which way had they gone? She'd been a fool to ever think she'd be able to find Emmie and Todd up here on this crazy maze of trails, much less do it in the dark. She didn't even have a damned flashlight, for heaven's sake.

Somewhere in the distance, the sky lit up. A few moments later, thunder came rumbling down the slopes, an avalanche of sound that made the nervous horse sidestep and cry out. Adrenaline shot through her already overloaded system as she nearly lost her seat.

"Shh, shh, Jezebel. It's okay," she crooned, leaning forward, all but laying along the animal's sleek neck to pet and stroke Jezebel's quivering hide.

And that's when she saw it. In the flash of another lightning strike, this one much too close for comfort, Harper spied one black Mary Jane sandal resting atop a clump of fallen leaves in the middle of the trail heading toward Badger's Sett.

Tugging Jezebel's reins, Harper urged the horse toward the cabin, pushing her harder, relying on the horse's sight more than her own not to run them into a tree or off the side of a drop off. She crouched low, hugging the horse's neck, as much to keep her perch as to avoid getting slapped in the face by branches she couldn't see until it was too late.

Very carefully, Harper pulled the radio from her satin belt with a death grip and turned the device on, careful to keep the volume low. "Aiden? Can you hear me?"

"Harper? I'm here. Where are you?" His voice, out of breath and frantic, crackled over the line.

"I followed them up the path. It looks like we're headed toward Badger's Sett."

"Goddamnit, Harper go back—" She hastily spun the knob to turn the radio off and tucked it back into her belt. She didn't have time to argue with him.

Harper slowed as she approached the cabin from the rear, looking for traces of man or horse. She wouldn't even consider the other four-legged creature that could be prowling around up here with them. If she did, she'd completely lose her nerve. Praying another lightning strike wouldn't reveal her, she coaxed the horse to slowly walk around the side of the building.

But the cabin appeared empty. No lights were on, the front window boarded over, and there wasn't any sign of a horse. Cutting through the driveway, Harper angled for the main trail. This trail she was slightly more accustomed to, having traversed it every day. She glanced to where the path angled downward, weighed her options, then resolutely turned left and urged the horse up the incline.

Big fat drops of rain began to fall. Slow and sporadic at first, then faster and steadier. Soon it was coming down in torrential sheets. The ground beneath the horse's hooves soon churned to a slippery quagmire bogging down every step until the animal struggle to trudge along.

Harper nudged the horse closer to the trees along the edge of the trail, which helped its footing some, but progress was still slow going. They paused to check Eagle's Nest, but, once again, there was no sign of horse or man.

Once more, gritting her teeth because she knew Aiden was probably foaming at the mouth by now, she pulled the radio from her belt. "Aiden, stop yelling at me because I'm not turning back." She was careful to keep her thumb depressing the button that allowed her to control the airwaves. "I think we're headed to Cougar's Den. Do you hear me? We are headed toward your cabin."

Holding her breath, she finally let off the button.

She didn't have long to wait. Aiden's voice came from the speaker, loud and clear...and very, *very* pissed off. "Copy."

Inwardly groaning, she turned the radio off once

more and clipped it to the strip of satin around her waist. If she survived this, he was going to kill her. Soaked to the skin, Harper tugged the drenched cape closer around her, desperate for even the meanest bit of protection. Chilled to the bone, teeth chattering, she hugged closer to the animal beneath her, grateful for the horse's body heat as they covered the last quarter mile, not stopping until they reached the turn off to Aiden's cabin.

She guided Jezebel to an impenetrable outcropping of vegetation near the lane. Then, carefully, she eased the animal forward until she could just barely peep around the edge. Flapjack, his head down, stood huddled against the rain, tied to one of the railing of Aiden's deck. The light in the cabin was on.

"Good girl," Harper crooned as she carefully slid from Jezebel's back. It didn't occur to her until it was too late that without stirrups and a saddle and having no step like the convenient overturned bucket back at the stables, she'd have no way to mount the horse again. With any luck, Aiden would be there soon and it wouldn't matter anymore. She rubbed Jezebel's neck one last time. "Good girl."

Gathering the reins, she started to creep closer to the mouth of the lane as she tried to figure out the best way to sneak into the clearing without being seen. But a blinding slash of lightning arced across the sky almost directly overhead. Jezebel reared up on her hind legs, pawing at the air. The reins were torn from Harper's hands. Jezebel's eyes wheeled wildly, and she let out a terrified shriek. Harper struggled to snatch the flying reins back, but it was no use. The spooked animal bolted.

But Harper wasn't out of harm's way yet. Another angry slash of lightning came hard on the first. The thundering sound of more hooves was the only warning she got a split second before the deafening crack of thunder. Harper wheeled around, throwing her arms up to protect her head and face.

A massive chest clipped her, sending her sprawling into the mud as Flapjack thundered by, hot on Jezebel's heels.

Harper scrambled on hands and knees patting the ground, frantically searching in the dark for the radio. Just as she was about to despair of ever finding it back, her fingertips brushed something hard and rectangular.

Snatching the radio up, she turned it on...or tried to. But twisting the knobs, thumbing the talk button, and thumping it against her palm did no good. Rain or mud or both had crept inside the two-way, or the batteries had died, either way it was dead as a doornail.

Closing her eyes, kneeling in the mud, Harper gritted her teeth to fight back the tears. She pressed the radio to her forehead for a moment, bit back a sob before casting the useless device aside.

Dragging herself up, she slipped into the tree line and did her best to blend in with the foliage, not easy with a bright crimson cape advertising her location like a neon sign. Harper crept closer to the cabin. But even going up on tiptoe she wasn't tall enough to see in the side window. Left with no other choice, she eased up on the deck. Crouching, feeling like one of those cartoon shadow spies, she crept closer to the big bay window, and she carefully peered inside.

Emmie was awake. She was tied to one of Aiden's kitchen barstools, bedraggled, gagged and helpless. Her wide, fearful eyes followed every move the man pacing in front of her made.

Todd moved across the length of the living room, back and forth, back and forth. His expression was, by turns, tormented and angry, afraid and threatening. He ran a crazed hand through his hair every so often. And he appeared to be talking to someone. Whether it was Emmie, or whether there was someone else in the cabin, Harper couldn't tell. She couldn't get a good enough view of the far end of the sofa or the corner of the room to say for sure.

Whoever he was talking to, Todd was highly agitated and, by the looks of things, only growing more and more upset.

Harper craned her neck, trying to see the rest of the room. Just then, another bright bolt of lightning shot across the sky. The moment her gaze connected with pea-soup green eyes, Harper froze, a deer in the headlights.

Todd burst into motion, and so did she. She was down the steps in a flash and running for the trees, slipping and sliding in the muck, but she was on her feet and determined to make it.

A man-sized missile came flying off the deck right at her. It hit her from behind. Beefy arms wrapped around her and they impacted the wet ground before cartwheeling through the mud and soggy leaves. Every last ounce of air was squished from her lungs as they came to rest with her face on the ground and a brute of a man plastered to her back.

Strong hands clamped around her shoulders, dragging her up. But those hands were gentle too. Even when she resisted, fighting to get away, instead of brutal fingers digging into already bruised flesh, or a meaty fist finding its way to her jaw, Todd simply hoisted her up and over his shoulder, like a sack of feed. He carted her inside as though her twisting and thrashing were of no consequence.

Before Harper knew it, she found herself sitting on a matching barstool beside Emmie with her hand's zip tied in her lap. Todd carefully, thoughtfully began mopping the mud from her face and hair with a damp wash cloth.

"Miss Harper, you shouldn't have followed us," Todd gently scolded.

Harper ran a confused gaze around the room, looking for Todd's accomplice. Where had his brother gone? Assuming it had been Danny that had been aiding him. Had Danny slipped out of the house while Todd had had her pinned down? Was he, even now, lying in wait to ambush Aiden?

Anxiety began to swell in her chest, making it difficult to breathe.

Todd dropped the rag on the counter, then he crossed the room to close the door. On his way back, he snagged the blanket from the back of the sofa and draped it over Harper's shoulders, tucking it snug around her.

"You shouldn't have come out in the storm like that, Miss Harper. You'll catch your death."

His face suddenly changed, right there before her eyes. Like a switch had been flipped. In fact, everything about him seemed to change. He stood taller, his shoulders pulled back. His head tilted to the side as he regarded her with eyes suddenly hallow and...eerie. And he laughed, a dark, ugly sound.

"Catch her death. That's funny, Scooter. Good one."

"Oh, not Miss Harper. She didn't do nothing wrong," Todd said, his demeanor changing once more.

His shoulders hunched as he turned slightly to the side. He ran both hands through his hair, and he paced away.

"You know I'm right. It has to be this way," he hissed beneath his breath, his voice sounding odd to Harper's ears as he did a pretty impressive Gollum imitation.

He suddenly spun back around, and his shoulders went back. His chest puffed out. And that hard look was back in his eyes. "Didn't do nothin' wrong, Scooter? Why, she was window peepin'." Todd eased closer to Harper, reached out and ran his fingers down the side of her hair. He lifted a wet, muddy, tangled strand and rubbed the ends between his fingers. "Now, I'm not saying window peepin's a hanging offense. But we gotta do *somethin'* to teach the lady a lesson." His leering gaze roved down over her bedraggled costume and Harper's blood turned to a river of ice in her veins. "Little Red Riding Hood. Now ain't that appropriate?"

Frowning, Harper peered up at him, then her gaze shot to Emmie. Emmie frantically shook her head, a warning if ever Harper had seen one. Her friend mumbled a frantic garbled speech into her gag as she nodded her head toward Todd and then shook her head once more.

"Now, now, Emmaline. It's not nice to interrupt. You'll get your turn." Todd turned back to Harper. He eased the blanket aside, running the back of one lecherous finger down the curve of her damp breast in the process. "Right now I'm talkin' to our Little Red here."

He hunkered down before her, placing his hands on her thighs beneath her short skirts as he peered hungrily up at her. Did she dare kick him? From this angle would she knock him out, or only make him angry? Well, angrier?

His voice dipped, becoming mockingly wolfish. "You know, it is Halloween. I'm not much of one for holidays, but maybe, just this once, it might be fun to play along. What do you say we set Little Red here loose in the woods?" His grin sent waves of fear crashing over Harper. "I'll be the Big Bad Wolf, just for you. What'dya say, sugar? Don't that sound like fun? I'll give you a head start, and then I'll track you down and gobble you up?"

What the hell was going on? Todd had never spoken to her like this before. He'd always been unfailingly polite. Helpful. Friendly. Shy even. Had it all been an act? "What are you doing, Todd?"

In the blink of an eye, the leering interest on his face was replaced by hard disdain. He rose to his feet, towering over her. And he sneered. "Todd's not here anymore."

Frowning, Harper went very still. Very carefully, she asked, "What do you mean?"

"It means little brother went bye-bye," he mocked her. "For now, at least. See, Todd doesn't have the stomach for these things."

"But you do?" She had to keep him talking, buy herself and Emmie as much time as she could. Aiden was coming. She was putting all her faith in him.

One cheek crinkled up, and Todd offered her a lopsided grin. "You could say that."

Harper licked her lips. "Who are you?"

"I'm Danny. You'll have to excuse Todd for not introducing us earlier. He does tend to worry so. And you're a mighty pretty little thing."

Unbidden, Harper's gaze slid to Emmie's. Her friend's eyes were glued to Todd/Danny, wide and filled with terror. Harper turned back to Danny. "Why did you make Todd go away?"

"Make Todd go away? No, no. I don't do that." He paused. Then, as if reconsidering, he added, "Okay, well maybe I do. But only when I need to."

"When you want to protect him?"

"Ah, see, now there," he slapped his hands together and then cocked his finger like a gun at her. "There it is. I knew you were a smart one. Sharp as a tack." He dragged another barstool in front of Harper and took a seat, as if settling in for a nice long, interesting discussion.

Creepy as that was, she pounced on it, willing to do whatever it took to keep his mind occupied until Aiden could get there. Desperate to keep his focus off Emmie.

"How long have you been…looking out for Todd?"

"Oh, ever since we were little." He crossed his legs and draped his laced fingers over his top knee. He shook his head, eyeing her like she was a novelty. "Now, isn't this fascinating?"

"Isn't what fascinating, Danny?"

"*You*. Usually, once I get to meet somebody, they're all," he flapped his hands in the air and adopted a whiney falsetto, "'*why are you doing this to* me?' '*I have a family that needs* me.' And '*please just let* me *go, I swear I won't tell anyone*.' It's really rather selfish the way they go on and on."

"Nobody ever asks about you?" Would he notice if she pulled at her wrists to test the strength of the zip tie? Probably. Having her hands bound in front of her was both blessing and curse.

"Nope. By the time they're done with their little '*me, me, me*' routine, well," he shot her a conspiratorial wink and grin, "that's when the screaming usually starts."

Harper forced a swallow. "I could see how that might get…ah, tiring." Damn it, where was Aiden? How much longer could she keep this guy talking?

She didn't think this was an act. The speech patterns were markedly different. The way he carried himself. The facial expressions. It was like talking to a whole different person.

"Why did you kill that hunter?"

"He was a bully. Todd tried to stand up for her," he shot an irritated chin in Emmie's direction. "He never should have done that. Never would have even tried it before her. But he's soft on that one. Until her, he always left that kind of thing up to me."

"Because you take care of him?" Get the focus off Emmie. *Please, Aiden, hurry!*

"That's what big brother's do." He leaned closer to Harper, touched her hair again. Then he slid the back of his fingers down her cheek and along the side of her throat. "You know, I *like* you Red. You get me."

It took every last ounce of her selfcontrol not to cringe away from his touch. Not to let the revulsion show on her face. She smiled at him. She blinked calmly at him. And she prayed with every last ounce of strength she had that Aiden would hurry before this monster decided to turn her into the *Bride of Chucky*.

\*\*\*\*

Aiden and Jonah, too anxious to wait while the rest of the group assembled, rode ahead. They brought their horses to a halt far enough away from the driveway that they wouldn't be seen by anyone in the cabin. The two men slid from their mounts and tied them to the trees. Then, on foot, he and Jonah crept closer to his cabin. Light from the living room window spilled across the deck.

Aiden glanced over as Jonah pulled his gun from its holster. Together, they eased up the step and stole a quick peek through the window. Jonah eased back to the side of the deck, motioning Aiden to follow.

Jonah leaned close and spoke in low tones. "Is there a back door? A window one of us could crawl through without Sweeney noticing?"

"The window in the bedroom maybe."

"Ok. You go around and get inside. I distract him, draw him out here. As soon as—"

"No," Aiden interrupted, shaking his head. "Todd's going to expect to see me. Soon as he comes out and sees you and doesn't see me, he's going to know what we're up to and he'll double back."

Jonah gritted his teeth. His worried gaze skated to the door of the cabin. "We can't go bursting in through the front door. We don't know what kind of weapons he has. He might hurt one of them before we could get to him."

"*You* go in through the window," Aiden suggested. "I'll stand out here, holler for him. Even if he doesn't come all the way out, it should be enough to draw him to the doorway, or even to the window to look. That should buy you enough time to get between him and Harper and Em."

"And if he opens the door shooting?"

Aiden took a deep breath. "Then let's hope he misses. The window is on the north side. Come on."

Aiden led Jonah to the window in question. Holding

his breath, he slipped a pocketknife from his pocket and wedged it between the old wooden-framed screen and the sill. Aiden cringed as the wood gave a little squeal before releasing. Both men froze, waiting to see if they'd been discovered. After a moment or two of nothing but wind and rain, Aiden leaned the screen against the side of the cabin, then he jimmied the blade between the windowpanes. After a few seconds of prying, the lock slid to the side, and he eased the window slowly up.

"We start having a rash of B&E's around here, you know I'm looking at you first, right?"

Aiden snorted.

"You learn that in the Army?"

"Nope."

Jonah shot him a look. "Do I even want to know?"

"Nope." Aiden cupped his hands and bent down a little, offering Jonah a step up. "Bedroom door squeaks a little."

With a little effort—Jonah wasn't exactly a small man—the sheriff was up and through the window. Aiden doubled back around the cabin. He paced about twenty-five feet back from the porch, figuring that was about far enough to draw Todd outside the cabin, hopefully, but not far enough to look suspicious. He waited a minute longer—a minute that felt like an eternity with Harper and Em trapped inside that cabin with a crazed killer.

Praying he'd given Jonah enough time to get into position, he cupped his hands around his mouth and yelled to be heard over the howling wind, "Todd! Todd! It's Aiden. Come on out here, Todd, so we can talk."

A moment passed. Then another. An unwelcome thought crossed his mind. Had Todd found Jonah? Had something happened to Harper or Em already?

He slid the back of his forearm across his drenched face, swiping rain from his eyes. At least it wasn't coming down in sheets anymore. But the steady downpour wasn't helping anything. Neither were those occasional flashes of lightning.

They could help. Could hurt too.

Aiden cupped his hands to his mouth again, preparing to shout once more, but the front door eased open.

His heart lodged in his throat. It wasn't Todd doing the opening. It was Harper. Todd stood directly behind her. And he had a wicked looking blade pressed tight to her throat.

So much for Jonah being able to get between Todd and both women. Hell, as long as Todd held Harper like that, Jonah wouldn't even be able to get off a shot, not without risking that knife slitting Harper's throat, or the bullet going right through him and into her.

Aiden took an involuntary step forward. A sudden wave of helplessness swept over him.

"That's far enough, Whitebear."

Aiden stopped. He lifted his hands up, palms out to show he didn't have a weapon. And he kept his eyes trained on Todd. If he caught another glimpse of Harper's pale face, or the stark fear in her eyes…

His teeth clenched, and his gut churned.

"I'm unarmed. Why don't you put the knife down, Todd? Let's talk about what's going on."

"Talk?" From his position behind Harper, Todd sneered. Aiden could barely see half his face. "I ain't naïve like my brother. I know you probably got half a dozen or more guys out there hidin' in the trees, just waiting for a clear shot."

"There's nobody out here but me, Todd. I give you my word."

"Todd might take you at your word. But like I said, I ain't my brother."

Aiden frowned. What the hell was he talking about? Then a thought occurred to him. Were Todd and Danny identical twins? They'd been able to find precious little about the mysterious Danny, so it was entirely possible.

Harper called out, "Aiden, he thinks—"

"Shut up, Red." Her sudden burst of speech was cut short when Todd jerked her back and dug the edge of the blade farther into her throat. Even in the dim backlighting, Aiden caught the ribbon of scarlet that burst from her pale skin and streamed down the side of her throat beneath the blade. His heart raced.

He waved his hands in a conciliatory manner and called out, "Wait, Todd…ah, Danny. Wait, okay. Everything's okay. Let's calm down, okay? Let's just all calm down."

*Where the hell is Jonah?* Aiden moved his gaze to Harper's face, desperately trying to convey with a look that she not do anything to upset Sweeney…whichever one this was.

He took a gamble. "Are you Danny?"

Harper got a peculiar expression on her face. Like she desperately wanted to say something. But, thank God, she kept her mouth shut.

"Yeah, I'm Danny."

"Is Emmie all right?"

"She's fine. You'll have to forgive her for not joining us. She's a bit…tied up at the moment."

"How about you let one of the women go, Danny?" Aiden tried reasoning with him. Jesus, what was Jonah doing in there, taking a frickin' nap?

"Well, now, I don't think so. See, I'd originally brought Emmie up here, thinking she'd be good bait. It's you that I want, after all. But then Little Red here had to come along and go window peepin'. And, well, see, it turns out I've takin' a shine to Red." He changed the angle of the blade and slid it along Harper's cheek like the caress of a lover. Safer than her throat, but dangerous nonetheless. "Me and her are gonna do a little role playing later…after I deal with you."

*Role playing? Christ Almighty.* The guy was deranged.

It made his skin crawl to listen to Danny talk about Harper that way. So he said the first thing that came to mind to turn the focus away from her. "Well, I'm here, Danny. What do you want to talk to me about?"

"Talk? I don't want to talk to you, you stupid shit. First I wanna watch you dance from the end of a rope, and then I'm gonna gut you."

"Why? I've never met you before, Danny. Why would you—"

"Oh, you've met me before. You just didn't know it." Smug satisfaction dripped from every word. "You're a nosy bastard, Whitebear. And you stepped into somebody else's business one too many times."

What the hell was this guy talking about? "How so?"

"Every damned time I turn around, you're there, schmoozing up to Todd. He's…simple. Easily influenced. And you think you gotta come riding in like some damned hero. Well, it ain't your place. You hear me?" With each word, Danny grew more distressed. Harper flinched as the tip of the blade pressed into her cheek mere inches from her eye. Once again, a rivulet of crimson marred her skin. Aiden silently cursed. He was going to kill Jonah for taking his own sweet time. Danny turned the tip of the blade toward Aiden, pointing it like a damning accusation as he extended his arm and shouted, "He don't need you to be his goddamned hero. I'm—"

Whatever Danny had been about to say was abruptly cut off as he was suddenly tackled from behind. Three bodies were ejected from the doorway and came hurdling across the porch, tumbling down the stairs. For a split second, Aiden thought the worst as Harper rolled ahead of the grappling men, tangled up in flailing arms and legs. Aiden rushed forward, wading into the fray. Unmindful of the slashing blade or the two men fighting for it, Aiden snatched Harper from the tussle and jerked her back.

The mud made his footing treacherous, and he struggled to stay upright and still hold on to the shivering woman in his arms. Loud thuds and muffled grunts ensued. Aiden looked around, expecting Todd to rush to his brother's defense at any moment. But Todd was nowhere to be seen.

Aiden pushed Harper back farther still when Danny managed to struggle to his feet. He staggered into an upright position, weaving on his feet, as Jonah crawled to his hands and knees.

Danny pulled his foot back and aimed it squarely at Jonah's stomach. The sheriff's hands and knees left the ground upon impact. Jonah's breath left him on an audible whoosh, and he crumpled onto his side. Danny turned to Aiden, knife gripped firmly in his hand, and he advanced, his face set in determined lines.

The crack of a handgun echoed in the small clearing.

Danny paused mid step. His expression slid into a confused frown. He opened his mouth, and blood bubbled out. Slowly, he slid to his knees. And then, with a final blink, he tumbled forward. A red splotch blossomed on his back. His arms still spread wide to shield Harper, Aiden glanced up. Jonah weaved on his feet. One arm was wrapped around his middle. Mud slicked his entire body, head to toe. His service revolver was clutched in his extended hand.

Jonah staggered the few steps to Danny's fallen body and bent down. Using his free hand, he pressed two fingers to Danny's neck. And when he straightened, his face was lax with relief.

Aiden let out the breath he'd been holding. He glanced up to the doorway of the cabin and let the final bit of tension slide from his body. Emmie stood clutching the doorframe, a gag hanging loose around her throat.

The sudden change in her expression, the shrill scream she let out…and the deafening roar from directly behind Aiden and Harper was the only warning he got. Aiden swung around, catching Harper around the waist as he turned.

Directly before them, not thirty feet away, stood a behemoth mountain of matted fur, lethal fangs and razor-sharp claws. The bear stood on its hind legs, towering at least nine and a half feet tall. It opened his maw once more and let out another blood-curdling roar, its lips rippling with the sound.

Aiden tried to spin once more, tried to push Harper ahead of him toward the safety of the cabin. But the ground beneath his feet betrayed him. Ahead of him, Harper slipped and went down. With his arm around her as it was, Aiden followed her down. At that point, the only thing he could think to do was cover as much of her as he could and pray she managed to get away when the bear got a hold of him.

A rapid succession of shots filled the night. Three, four, five. He lost count. The bear snarled and roared. Angry, hurt, Aiden couldn't tell. Another shot. And another. And then there was a massive crash. Trees branches cracked, a small tree snapped. Aiden, his body still covering Harper, one arm curled around the top of her head, glanced up. Directly into the black, sightless eyes of the fallen bear. Or rather eye, as one of Jonah's bullets had taken the other. The dead animal lay not three feet from Aiden.

Shuddering, Aiden scrambled up, dragging Harper with him. He half tugged, half carried her across the clearing until they stood well behind Jonah and his gun.

Closing his eyes, he wrapped both arms around Harper and dropped his cheek to the top of her head. Rain pounded down on them, washing the mud and the blood from them. In the distance, another bolt of lightning slashed the sky, illuminating the horror all around them. The dead bear. The dead man.

Aiden turned from the gruesome spectacle to thank Jonah. But instead of speaking, he simply smiled. There stood the sheriff, a gun in one hand, his arms full of Emmie, and his lips plastered to hers.

*About damned time.*

Aiden let out a long, ragged breath. Over. It was finally over.

He nudged Harper's head back. Using both hands, he swept her drenched hair from her face, and tilted her lips up for a brief, relief-filled kiss. "I swear to God, woman, you're going to be the death of me."

She blinked up at him as the rain streamed down over her face. "Oh, no. I'm only taking responsibility for Sloan. Todd and the bear are on you."

"Where is Todd?" Jonah demanded. The couple had come to stand nearby, but Jonah had yet to let Emmie out of his arms.

Emmie pointed to the dead man. "There."

Aiden frowned. "But he said—"

Harper shook her head. "He was both. When he was talking to me in the cabin, it was like…like a split personality or something. Or hallucinations. I don't know. But you could clearly see where one personality would…push the other aside. Everything about him changed. The way he talked, the way he carried himself. He was just…different."

Aiden fell silent and he looked to Todd Sweeney's body as he mulled that over. Then he turned to glance down at the woman in his arms. "How do you figure the rest is on me?"

"Bears? Psycho stable boys…I had nothing to do with all that. They don't have either of those where I come from. That's all on you."

Aiden dropped his forehead to hers. "No more, woman. Do you hear me? No more rushing headlong into danger. My heart can't take it."

Harper nodded, bumping her nose against his. Then a radiant smile lit her face. "You saved me. Again."

Ignoring their avid audience, Aiden cupped her face in his hands. "I will always do everything in my power to keep you safe, Harper."

Harper searched his face for a moment, her expression tender. "I love you too, Aiden."

"I love you." Aiden sealed his lips over hers. He

swept his tongue inside her mouth, tangled it with hers. Slowly, he slid an arm around her waist and dragged her up flush against his body and channeled every last ounce of what he was feeling into the kiss. Until his body shook with desire. Until she leaned weakly against him and wound her arms around his neck.

A throat cleared…loudly.

Reluctantly breaking the kiss, Aiden leaned his head back, but he couldn't stop staring into misty blue eyes. God, she was perfect for him.

"Hey, you two. Not to break up this lovefest, but the way your luck's been running, you're going to end up getting struck by lightning."

Grinning, Aiden grabbed Harper's hand and together they followed Emmie and Jonah inside the cabin.

Epilogue

Aiden sat down on the big rawhide sofa in front of the massive fireplace in the lodge. He tugged Harper down beside him, pulled her close and looped his arms around her. Contentment overflowed his soul as she snuggled her head into the curve of his shoulder and wrapped her arms around his waist, cuddling close. A cheerful blaze crackled in the grate, and outside the snow had begun to pile up.

November was rapidly giving way to December. The wait till Christmas…and the diamond ring nestled in his sock drawer…was all but killing him. He'd almost pulled it out twice now. But he was determined to give Harper the best Christmas she'd ever had.

"Here you go," Emmie said as she eased around the sofa and slid a tray loaded with cups of hot chocolate onto the coffee table. Picking one up for herself, she sat in the adjoining chair and tucked her feet up under her.

A spare moment later, Kathryn came out carrying a tray of cookies. Harper's head popped up. "Do I smell gingerbread?"

"You do. And chocolate chip as well, but don't you go ruining your supper," Kathryn admonished with a smile.

As the trio leaned for the cookie platter, the door swept open and a cold wave of air crept inside. Turning, Aiden raised his cup of cocoa in salute. "Hey, Jonah.

You're just in time."

From the corner of his eye, Aiden caught the way Emmie stiffened up. He also caught the way Jonah's eyes slid first to Emmie before taking in the rest of the room.

"Afternoon, folks."

"Afternoon, sheriff," Emmie replied, her tone prim, her expression guarded. She'd been put out with Jonah ever since the night Todd/Danny had dragged her up the mountain. Jonah had hugged her, kissed her, and then nothing. Not so much as an official house call...until now.

"Well hello, Jonah. What brings you by?" Kathryn asked.

Aiden leaned back in his seat, tucked Harper against his side, and settled in to watch the fireworks.

Jonah came to stand between the sofa and the chair where Emmie sat. He settled his stance and tucked his thumbs into his utility belt. "Just came up to let you know we finally got all the information back on Sweeney."

"Really? Wow, you wouldn't think it would take so long to follow up on—or follow through with— something so important, now would you?" This came from Emmie. She shot Jonah a gimlet stare over the rim of her mug of cocoa.

Jonah's nostrils flared. His lips compressed for a split second. But other than that, he gave no clue that Emmie's poke had gotten to him.

"We tracked him back to a placement facility in Texas. Seems Sweeney was diagnosed as an adolescent with Dissociative Identity Disorder. When he hit eighteen, he fell through the cracks in the system. There's a cold case reopening in Colorado and another in Idaho, same MO, and Sweeney was present in both places at the time of the murders."

Kathryn leaned back in her seat, her hand going to her throat. "So this wasn't the first time that he...that he'd killed?"

"No, ma'am. Seems like, given the way things unfolded here, he's good for both cases."

"So we were extremely fortunate things didn't turn out worse." Emmie placed her mug on the coffee table and leaned back in her seat.

"Fortunate?" Jonah turned to her, fire snapping in his eyes. "Damned lucky, if you ask me."

Emmie glanced up at him, her mouth hanging open, clearly taken aback by the ferocity in his words. "What's that supposed to mean?"

"It means, given the kind of people you hire up here, you're damned lucky something like this hasn't happened long before now."

"The people I hire?"

"You heard me. Criminals. Theft, prostitution, drug charges, assault and battery, PTSD..." At the last, he turned to Aiden and muttered, "No offense."

"None taken...I think," Aiden remarked, one eyebrow arched.

Turning back to Emmie, Jonah went on, apparently warming to his subject, "You're lucky you haven't been robbed blind or murdered in your sleep by now."

Emmie gasped. "How dare you?"

"I dare because *somebody* has to talk some sense into you." Although he wasn't exactly yelling, a vein had begun to bulge at the side of Jonah's forehead, and his face had turned a nice healthy shade of deep red. "You can't keep going around collecting wounded souls like this, Emmaline. You can't offer a job and a place to live to every sad, unfortunate soul you cross paths with."

Emmie shot to her feet. "The hell I can't. I can offer a job to whoever I want. I can do any damned thing I please, sheriff. This is *my* land now. *My* business. And you have no right to come in here and tell me what to do."

Jonah turned so he was squarely in her path, his nose scant inches from hers. Emmie propped her hands on her hips and scowled right back.

Aiden turned to gauge Kathryn's reaction to this spectacle. Kathryn sat back in her seat, hands clasped serenely on her lap. The woman had a speculative gleam in her eye, and one corner of her mouth tilted up, just the tiniest bit.

Aiden glanced down to Harper, saw that she'd been looking back and forth between Jonah and Emmie and Kathryn as well.

Looking back to Emmie and the sheriff as they argued toe-to-toe, Aiden broke into a wide grin. Yes sir. It was going to be damned entertaining watching these two get together. Damned interesting indeed.

## A word about the author...

Brenda Huber lives in Iowa with her husband, her two children, and her very spoiled dog Sam. You can learn more by visiting her on her website (brendahuber.webs.com), or following her on Facebook (http://on.fb.me/1F4VsNc.)

www.brendahuber.webs.com

Thank you for purchasing
this publication of The Wild Rose Press, Inc.

For questions or more information
contact us at
info@thewildrosepress.com.

The Wild Rose Press, Inc.
www.thewildrosepress.com

www.ingramcontent.com/pod-product-compliance
Lightning Source LLC
Chambersburg PA
CBHW051133030726
47504CB00004B/841